WET MY MOUTH WITH HONEY

SWEET, SWEET FARE FOR THESE TROUBLED TIMES

ELEANOR B. TAYLOR

6-6-13
To Mable,
You are a treasure,
Love & Peace,
Eleanor

This is a work of fiction. The events and characters described herein are imaginary and are not intended to refer to specific places or living persons. The opinions expressed in this manuscript are solely the opinions of the author and do not represent the opinions or thoughts of the publisher. The author has represented and warranted full ownership and/or legal right to publish all the materials in this book.

Wet My Mouth With Honey
Sweet, Sweet Fare For These Troubled Times

v2.0

Outskirts Press, Inc.
http://www.outskirtspress.com

ISBN: 978-1-4787-1401-9

Outskirts Press and the "OP" logo are trademarks belonging to Outskirts Press, Inc.

PRINTED IN THE UNITED STATES OF AMERICA

WET MY MOUTH WITH HONEY

Roses lay strewn by riverbeds
where water never ran,
and trees marched away,
longs floating in oceans now.
And mountains sank, like my heart.

God, wet my mouth with honey
sweet, sweet fare
for these troubled times.

Hold my hands in your thoughts today,
warm my fingertips, immerse
your hands in dawn's golden fire
to caress my soul's voice, echoing
I love you through jailhouse hallways.

My love, wet my mouth with honey,
sweet, sweet fare
for these troubled times.

I saw you yesterday, standing
with tears in your eyes.
Believe my love is strong
enough to melt iron bars
and end our separation.

Wet my mouth with honey,
sweet, sweet fare
for these troubles times.

Introduction

This story happened a long time ago. I cannot brush aside the significance of those years, the Vietnam War and social upheaval. A time when I had the heart to attempt to bring good change to a troubled world. Yet, I must acknowledge the obvious. I never made it to the cutting edge of change. I didn't come close. I thought consciousness-raising drugs would catapult the world into an aware and compassionate state of being. That didn't happen, but my experiences did flow into the evolving consciousness which ushered in a shift in the nation's attitude toward war, corrupt government, and the environment.

Woven through these pages are political idealism, passionate love, and a spirit in search of truth.

It is my story, and I invite you in.

Chapter 1

A Fork in the Road

Lights too bright. My eyes closed. Buzzing voices formed a coherent word here and there.

"Can you stitch this?"

"No. Wait for the plastic surgeon."

I rested in darkness. Fuzzy thoughts visited and asked what happened. A mist formed in the shape of my body against a man I loved. It dissolved into black nothingness then returned. His lips melted into mine, a familiar taste. The mist became an airplane rising above a mountain. Or was it a hawk? Then I saw myself in a car alone. My body ached.

Intense light. I needed to throw up. Cold. Words again emerged from the buzzing. "News anchor? He'll have to wait until we sew her up."

I swam in a pool, salty, like tears.

"Sylvi, open your eyes. It's Bob. If you can hear me, squeeze my hand."

I squeezed, opened my eyes enough to recognize my first husband. White radiance surrounded him before my eyelids slammed shut. With great effort, I asked, "Where am I?"

"The emergency room. You wrecked your car. I was in the Channel Two news van when we found the ambulance guys loading you onto a stretcher around midnight."

"My kids?"

"You were alone. I'm going to let go of your hand, Sylvi, and go call my sister. Judy will be glad to check on your kids. You rest." His deep voice absorbed my struggle for a moment. Then panic set in. *Where are my little girls?*

Calming myself, I thanked God Judy had come back to El Paso from L.A. Friends since we were both fourteen, I trusted her to find my daughters. Again, I drifted in black space.

Voices roused me to consciousness. "Sylvi, it's Judy." Her fingertips touched my hand. "I checked with your housekeeper. Kristi and Katrina are at home with her. What else can I do for you?"

Battling a strong desire to sleep and struggling to speak coherently, I answered. "Ask Estelle if she can stay with the girls until I get home? Call my boss. Please do not call my parents."

I awoke to summer sun blazing outside the window of my hospital room and began taking mental inventory of the last twenty-four hours. The emergency room being my most recent recollection, I labored to remember how I'd wrecked my car.

Recurring pain impeded clarity, but I forced myself to persevere. *Danny left last night on a plane, the end of our year-long affair. He was to finish his military service in Germany. Yes, better than Vietnam. Said he'd come back to me. My heart knows he won't—can't think about it.*

The nurse appeared at my bedside and gave me pills. "For the swelling and infection," she said.

"My arm?" The words slurred. Pain shot through my jaw.

She began applying fresh ice packs around my splinted arm. "The orthopedist is downstairs now. He will cast this." She noticed me looking at the bandages stretching from both wrists to my elbows. "They cleaned the asphalt out of the skin on your face and forearms in the emergency room. Don't touch the stitches on your head or your knees. A dental surgeon will wire your broken jaw this afternoon.

Too much to take in, but she bustled from the room before I could ask more questions. I waited for the orthopedist. *Waiting, like I'd waited with Danny for the plane to come and take him across the ocean. I'd kissed him for the last time, a long kiss. His plane had boarded and he'd had to run. I fled from the terminal to my car in the parking lot, collapsed against the steering wheel, and reached for the bottle of scotch under the seat. A swallow would steady me.*

The memory was too much. I lost consciousness.

Judy called in the late afternoon to say my children were fine and my housekeeper could stay as long as I needed her. *Bless Estelle.*

In the evening, Judy entered my room with a pretty, dark-haired woman. Awake and halfway conscious, I greeted them.

"Pat gave me a ride to the hospital." Judy motioned the other woman to my bedside. "I don't think you two have met. Sylvi, this is your first husband's second wife, Pat."

Curiosity coaxed my brain out of its fog into awareness. Bob, my first husband, had married Pat several months after we'd divorced. I concentrated on pronouncing words. "True we haven't met."

Pat took my good hand and held it between hers. "Sorry we're meeting under these circumstances, Sylvi, but I am happy to know you at last." Her smile and touch warmed me.

"Glad to know you, too." I did a calculation in my head. "Nine years?"

"Sounds about right," she said. "Have to admit I didn't want to meet you for a long time after Bob and I married. But time seems to have dissolved my petty jealousy. How are you?"

"Not too good." I smiled so they could see my wired teeth.

"I took Estelle and your kids to the store earlier," Judy said. "Your girls send you kisses. When will you go home?"

"Maybe Friday."

Pat stroked my hand. "Is there anything you need?"

"A good, strong drink."

After they left, I recalled Pat's warmth, a good person. I'd been relieved when she and Bob had married. He deserved better than me. Just before Judy and I graduated from high school, Bob and I began dating. We both loved to write and were mutually drawn to the philosophies of the "beat generation" that questioned the social norm of the late fifties. Even so, we had a grand Catholic wedding, him of the faith and me a Baptist. He'd been a newspaper reporter during our wedded life, and we drank and partied with gusto. I respected his literary prowess, but his harsh criticism of my writing crushed my spirit. I looked for approval elsewhere and began an affair with the man who worked in the news room with Bob. I excused the failure of my first marriage by telling myself I was too immature, marrying at eighteen and divorcing at twenty.

What excuse could I use to rationalize failing at my second marriage? Carl. Bad judgment of character. The only good things to come from our loveless five years together were our two little girls. If Carl and I screwed up everything else, at least I wound up with custody of them.

I wished the nurse would come with another pain shot and stop my mind. Stuck in a hospital bed, I focused on the dark side of my life. I'd partied for the three years since Carl and I split. It kept me from examining my failures. I drank too much, involved myself with too many men. But my life, as I had been living it, came to a halt once my body hit the pavement. Physically and emotionally broken, I could run from nothing. I had to look at the ugly images parading through my head. True, I'd never wanted a conventional life, the "norm," where I married properly, had proper children, attended the proper church. On the other hand, I'd never intended for my liberated lifestyle to land me in my present, broken condition.

My accident took place in the wee-hours of a Sunday morning in July of 1967. Judy drove me home the following Friday.

Although she said she'd warned my daughters, Kristi and Katrina's faces registered horror as I entered the kitchen door. Unable to gather them into my arms, I tried to reassure them. "It's okay, sweeties, Mommy is going to be all right."

They peered at me from behind Estelle's legs.

"Why can't you open your mouth good, Mommy?" Kristi asked.

"When your mommy's car wrecked," Judy said, stepping from behind me, "she got hurt." She helped me sit down and showed them my injuries, explaining them one by one. Gradually sympathy replaced their initial shock.

Once the girls understood I'd mend, they asked to go outside and play. Estelle went with them. That's when Judy told me she'd called my parents before she'd picked me up from the hospital.

My voice trembled. "Why? I can't see them right now."

She helped me into bed then sat on the chair at my dressing table. "Your mom and dad were going to find out soon enough. They'd feel bad if they didn't have the chance to help you."

"Get serious. They'd be relieved not to have to be involved in any of their errant daughter's mishaps. They're good people, Judy, but I don't fit in their perfect world, never have, not even as a child."

"The truth is you don't want them in your imperfect world."

"I always disappoint them. We're from two different universes. I'm sure I was adopted."

Judy laughed. "You know you weren't."

Hearing a car in the driveway, we exchanged glances. Judy ran to the front door.

I heard my dad's voice first. "We left as soon as you called this morning, Judy. Broke the speed limit, but it still took almost two hours to cover the eighty-five miles between Alamogordo and here."

My mother, full of questions, "Is she asleep? How is she? How did it happen?"

Judy ran interference for me. "She's awake but not a pretty sight, Mrs. Smith. The doctors assured me she'll be good as new in a few months."

I braced myself. Mother gasped and stumbled when she saw me. Daddy caught her. Judy peeked at me from behind them.

"You look terrible," Mom said, smoothing her hair. "What on earth have you done?"

"It's hard for her to talk," Judy said. Rather than telling them I'd been stone-drunk and flipped my car, she gave them a more acceptable version, then went on to point out my injuries: twenty-four stitches across my forehead, wired jaw, asphalt burns, broken left arm, stitches in my knees and legs.

My dad stepped to the foot of the bed. "Sylvi, you can't take care of yourself, much less the girls. We'll take them home with us. Can your housekeeper stay with you?"

"I talked with her earlier," Judy said. "She can do the weekdays, and I can help on the weekends."

My mother frowned. "Then it's settled. We'll keep the girls as long as we have to, or until school starts."

"I'm sorry," I mumbled. "I didn't mean to be any trouble."

"Trouble?" my mother said once Dad and Judy left the room. "You've been nothing but trouble. Marriages, divorces, children you can't take care of. We raised you to be a decent person, Sylvi, but you chose to go wild. What happened to you? Look at you now." She shook her head.

"I know, Mom." *God knows, they'd raised me better than to live in sin and drink to excess.* Still, I defended myself, "I love my kids, they're not neglected."

She turned her back to me. "All I ever wanted was for you to be happy. But, no, you don't want to be happy like the rest of us."

"Like the rest of who?" I blurted from between wired teeth, struggling to quell my anger. "I've lain up there in that hospital bed for five days trying to figure out where to go with my life, how to make it better. My mistakes are glaring, Mom, they haunt me, but I have to find my own answers. Your answers don't work for me."

"There you go. Life, mistakes, my answers, your answers. You talk in riddles. I could never understand you." She stalked out of the room.

Later, I related the argument with Mother to Judy and sucked soup through a straw.

"Maybe I shouldn't have called them, Sylvi, but they took Kristi and Katrina home. That's one less worry. You need to focus on healing."

"Yeah, healing and turning my life around."

She carried our empty soup bowls to the sink. "Let's get you back in bed."

Bracing one crutch under my good right arm, I hobbled behind her through the hallway to the bedroom and grimaced at my reflection in the mirror on my dressing table. "Mrs. Frankenstein." I touched the scabs and stitches on my face and drew a long, tired breath. "The insurance company says my car's totaled. My life is totaled, too."

"You're not in this alone, Sylvi. We'll figure it out."

I settled into bed against the pillows. "Thank you, Judy. Who knew, when we met at fourteen, we'd be going through this now?" Tears rolled down my face. "Life was so simple then, like plucking petals from a daisy—he loves me, he loves me not. When did it begin changing?"

"It's called growing up, Sylvi. It's life."

"All I wanted was 'freedom' for us all, a life of dancing in the streets. How did it get so fucked up? Now my latest lover is gone. My body hurts, and I'm so exhausted."

"You need to sleep. I'll see you in the morning." She gave my hand a squeeze.

I heard her drive away. My head throbbed, pain coursed through me. I questioned if my wild curiosity about life would nourish or destroy me. The latter seemed more likely. Sleep brought a vision of the wrecked car. I saw it as a symbol of my life.

Six weeks later, my cast came off. The orthopedist brushed the flaky skin off my shriveled arm. "Don't worry," he said, "It will be normal in a few weeks. Remember where it's healed will be the strongest part. It will never break there again."

"Is that a metaphor for life?"

He laughed. "Could be."

One week later, I sat in the chair while the dentist, wielding tiny pliers, pulled the wires from around my teeth.

"Don't tell me," I said. "Where my jaw was broken is the strongest part now, and it will never break there again."

He gave me a quizzical glance. "That is the nature of bones."

"Is it the nature of hearts?"

He did not answer.

During the next few months of my recovery, I received letters from Danny, pages full of concern about my injuries and saying he never understood why I wouldn't marry him before he left. I explained as best I could. After my first two marriages, I never wanted to marry again. I needed to change my life, noting that my exterior injuries were only symbolic of the wounds I carried internally. I mailed the letter and wondered if he would make sense of it. I swam in oceans of confusion. Steeped in failure, I wallowed in my inadequacy as a human being.

Many of my friends, though supportive, believed the troubles of the world could be solved with another drink, another night of boozing and philosophizing. We numbed our ability for authentic feelings and intellectually bantered about pseudo-solutions to love and war. Danny had been sent to Germany, but another friend, Pete, absent from our group for six months, had gone to Vietnam. Was he alive or dead? What was real and what was illusion?

In late November, I was asked if I would like to attend a teach-in about the Vietnam War being presented by a political science professor from a university in New Mexico. No question about it, I wanted to learn, to find answers, something I could recognize as real.

Judy and I arrived at the rented hall, both open to what a long-haired, red-bearded professor would tell us and the other twenty-five people there. "No war," he said, "has ever been fought for noble causes. Wars are always fought to gain control of another country's resources. President Johnson would have the American people believe we are there to stop the spread of communism in Southeast Asia. A total lie! This is an unconstitutional war. The Vietnamese have not aggressed against us. We entered it without a Congressional vote. We have no right to be there." He showed slides of our troops massacring villagers and burning their homes. We saw areas our army had defoliated by using a deadly chemical to destroy the jungle.

At the close of the teach-in, I had a clear picture of the inhumanity our government would inflict to ensure their place in the power structure of the world. His message shocked me, informed me, and jarred me to my core. I knew in my heart what he'd said was true.

A few hours later, Judy and I occupied a table in the back corner of a smoke-filled coffee house to reflect on what we'd heard.

I sat forward, a new awareness coursing through me. "Judy, this afternoon was almost too much to take in. I remember being concerned when Pete left for Vietnam six months ago. At the time, I understood little about the war except it was different from anything we'd studied in our history books."

"I remember Pete," she said and scooted to the edge of her chair. "He was going to keep in touch. Did you ever hear from him?"

"No. He's probably dead. It's too painful to think about. The war's in our face every day—TV news, newspapers, magazines, yet I've not been able to come to grips with it until now."

"The professor really brought it home today," she said. The whispered, rotten underbelly we didn't want to see."

The white vapor from our hot cups rose in the air between us like smoke from a battlefield.

"When are we going to get it?" I asked. "Don't we learn anything from history? Like the professor pointed out: one war begets another, one injustice begets another." My heart thumped hard in my throat. I couldn't swallow. My mind conjured grim scenes of massacred victims, tattered shreds of humanity. Tears rolled off my chin unchecked. "Are we so steeped in cruelty, so incapable of mercy that we honestly believe butchering our fellow human beings is okay? What in God's name is wrong with us?" The sobs I'd tried to choke back burst forth. Across the table, I saw Judy weeping with me.

I struggled to regain what composure I could. "So much more to life than my petty complaints—so much more to do in this life, Judy, than just play at it."

Our discussion lasted until midnight. As I drove home, the slaughtering of innocents, our taxes paying for the production of horrific war machinery, bombs, and chemicals reverberated in my head and my heart. It wasn't just about stopping this war. The bigger mission I saw, for the first time, was to bring peace to this wreck of a world. Overwhelmed, I pulled to the side of the road. The world and me in bad need of redemption.

In early December, I pulled a letter from Danny out of the mailbox, tore it open. He'd found someone else. I cried, somehow relieved. I didn't want him to be alone.

Rob phoned that same day. I hadn't heard from him in the year since we'd worked together. He'd quit and taken his guitar to Greenwich Village to pursue his jazz dreams.

"I hitched from the Village," he said, "wanted to come back to El Paso for the holidays, see my parents. After New Years, I'll go on to San Francisco."

"Come on over so we can catch up. Lots has happened since you left."

"No wheels."

"Estelle is here to take care of my kids. I'll pick you up in an hour."

He answered my knock, and we threw our arms around each other. "Sylvi. Man, let me look at you." He stepped back. "Yep, you haven't changed a bit, same poofy blonde hair, just like I remember. Maybe your mini-skirt's a little shorter." He laughed and enclosed me in another hug. "As beautiful and outrageous as ever."

"Such a liar," I said. "Look at you. Sure lost your old Ivy League look." His long brown hair fell below the collar of his Nehru shirt.

Beads hung around his neck, and moccasins stuck out from beneath his belled jeans. "Let's get going," I said, handing him the keys.

"Are you still writing poetry?" he asked, pulling out of the driveway.

"No. Been in too much chaos." I opened my heart and told him about Danny, the wreck, and the letter I'd just received. "I'm drinking way too much and experiencing black-outs. As bad as all that is, there's hope." I related the significance of the teach-in and how I wanted to be part of the movement to bring the war to a close. "But I don't know where to start."

He stopped on a dirt road in the foothills, a mile behind my house, and pulled a plastic baggy from his jacket pocket. "Smoking a joint might give you some new insight. I scored some pretty potent weed before I left the Village."

"You tried to turn me on to that stuff once before, Rob, and it didn't do a thing for me, but I'll give it another go."

"Cool, just a hit or two. Sounds to me like the booze has you down, weed will get you up." He cradled a rolling paper with the fingers of one hand. With the other hand, he placed a pinch of the marijuana in a straight line then rolled it up tight. "Go ahead," he urged. "Talk to me."

I stared at the precise way he licked the sticky end of the cigarette paper and smoothed it with his thumb.

"You're right about the booze getting me down, Rob. Danny's leaving derailed me, the car wreck stopped me in my tracks, but the teach-in is the big thing. I can't locate the guy that invited me, and I don't know anyone else connected. I'm champing at the bit to go further, to make a difference."

He struck a match and lit the joint as he sucked the smoke in and held it in his lungs before handing it to me. Exhaling, his words tumbled out. "What kind of difference?"

I hesitated, took a quick drag and handed it back to him. "Help get the peace message out and stop the war."

Rob inhaled and again held the smoke in for a moment while studying my face. "Tell me more."

"There is life to live and poetry to write and something to be done about this war, but I'm still a mixed-up mess. I do miss Danny. Hell, I miss being in a relationship. It seems trite to even say shit like that when the world is an explosion away from extinction."

He offered me the joint. I took it and tried to imitate the way he held in the smoke. "You're the poet," he said. "You know about the ebb and flow of life. Things are going to fall into place. Trust me. Just leave the booze alone."

Surrounded by cold, black night, we passed the joint back and forth in silence. I stared through the VW window at the sky. "Look at the lights on the airplane. Aren't the colors great?"

"Not an airplane. It's a star," Rob said.

"Is not." I watched a while longer. "It's blinking on and off. It's an airplane."

"Star," he insisted.

A few minutes passed. "It hasn't moved, Rob. Maybe you're right."

He laughed. "Get out and look at the whole sky. You're fucking stoned and don't know it." We got out and looked in awe at the heavens sparkling in colors.

A memory stirred deep inside me. "I was four years old when my dad went overseas in World War II. Before the War, I remember the stars being brilliant blues and greens, yellows, purples and reds. After the War, they only twinkled white and ordinary. All the killing and hating must have drained heaven of its colors. We have to bring peace, we just have to."

"I can dig it," he said.

We walked along the dirt road gazing up at the stars, quiet for a while. I sat down on a rock. "I watched a news broadcast a couple months back, Rob, covering a big demonstration at the Pentagon. Did you hear about it?"

He sat next to me. "Some friends and I were there," he said. "It was a love-in at the Pentagon. Word on the street had it Abbie Hoffman was going to perform an exorcism on the Pentagon and levitate it."

"Did he do it?" I asked, remembering I hadn't seen it being lifted off the ground in the TV report.

"Naw, but I swear there was a presence. A spiritual peace swept over the whole scene."

"Peace? The news showed violence. Kids dragged and beaten. What's the real story?"

"At first, it was peaceful, but when a few thousand of us moved to the parking lot in front of the steps, the troops blocked our way, formed a line and advanced to move the crowd back. Other guys, federal marshals, we found out later, came through the military line. The marshals grabbed people, clubbed them and hauled some off to jail."

"What happened to you and your friends?"

"We stayed. The marshals left. We could smell tear gas, but not close enough to get to us. The soldiers held their line, and we sat on our side. Some of our people talked over a bullhorn, telling the army dudes the war had to stop, not only our soldiers but innocent Vietnamese were being killed." He took hold of my hands, emphasizing his point. "Violence is wrong, drafting people to perpetuate war is wrong. We can live together in peace." He let out a long sigh. "It's just love, man. It's all about love."

"Did the soldiers get the message?"

"They heard. I felt the vibe like a mystical bond between us."

"I've got chill bumps. What did you do afterwards?"

"We left the Pentagon, got together at this one dude's pad, lit candles and shared our dreams for better tomorrows. Peace doesn't come in a day. Change happens in our spirits first, and then ripples outward." He stood and stretched. "I guess there are things that could make it happen faster, like smoking weed to slow things down so you can see more clearly, get in sync with the universe."

"Man, am I ever in sync." Our laughter, as we walked back to the car, echoed in my head like wind chimes.

We drove to my house. Estelle and the kids were asleep in their bedrooms. I plopped down on the long brown couch, and Rob slid onto the piano bench, letting his fingers meander over the keys, mellow, like he'd never left. Like the afternoons after work when he used to stop by the house, play jazz riffs and talk. Seven years younger than me, we were never a romantic item, but good friends.

"Think you'll get over Danny?"

"Yeah, thanks for asking. It really wasn't meant to be."

"Things draw people together and other things pull them apart." His fingers paused on the keys. "You're the one turned me on to Gibran, so you know from "The Prophet" both our joy and sorrow are drawn from the same well. Take time to heal before you love again—like a cycle, a rhythm in the universe. Dig?"

"I think so."

"From what you've told me, you have bigger things to do before you jump into another love affair, Sylvi. If you can locate someone from the teach-in, I'd like to meet them. Maybe we could get something going."

"I'd love that."

I rose from the couch, took sheets and a blanket from the hall closet and handed them to him. "The couch is all yours, Rob. Thanks for coming back to town. You're right, weed is much better than booze."

Monday came, a work-as-usual morning in the garment industry. Arriving at the office, I busied myself composing copy for our spring catalog of little boys' jeans. Rob called and asked if it was okay if he built an altar in the corner of my den with stones from the mountain. We could burn incense on it and meditate.

"What an enchanting idea. I can't wait to see it." When we said goodbye and hung up, it was hard to return to my task, but my boss and I had a meeting with the artist in another hour.

After supper, Estelle cleaned up the kitchen while I tucked Kristi and Katrina into bed. Rob showed me the altar of rocks he'd stacked three feet high in a corner of the den. He lit a cone of incense and placed it on the top. "Sandalwood," he said and pushed the door closed. We sat on the floor and smoked a joint.

"Very peaceful, Rob. I love your altar. Tell me how you meditate."

He passed the joint. "I never studied with a guru. For me, meditation is a way to empty my mind of clutter. Some people use a mantra, others scripture. I stay quiet, conscious of my breath entering and leaving my body, let music fill my head and spill into my spirit. It inspires and energizes me."

"I could use some inspiration. I've struggled to write just a poem or two these last few months. My job is sucking the life out of me. Remember when I used to get into it, Rob, when it seemed somewhat fulfilling?" I took a long drag and handed the joint back to him.

"You were pretty gung-ho when we worked together," he said. "You've been dealing with too much since you wrecked your car, huh?"

"Maybe I've become part of the millions who make a buck and play the game. I hate falling into compromise. I'm searching for more in life."

We finished the joint and sat for some moments before I said, "I quit going to church ten years ago. My religion professor in college said, 'To find God, one must first lose Him.' So I lost my image of the huge old man with a beard who sat on a throne in the sky and was angry with us. He breathed fire and brimstone and guilt."

"Pretty harsh image."

"In fact," I said, "I've drank, partied, screwed around and held down a job all these years without giving a thought to the spiritual part of me until lately."

"So what are your recent thoughts?"

"There is a God, or a Creator, or a Source, and there's order in His or Her universe. Promise you won't laugh, but pyramids come to mind. I think reincarnation is valid to one degree or another."

"Hey, man, I'm not laughing. I see it the same. I know a lot of people in New York who are hip to it. Like I said, it's all about pure love."

"Rob, when you head to the Village again, could I go with you? I could wait tables, get into my poetry, and work with the anti-war people. God knows I've got to do something to bring meaning to my life."

He smiled. "Cool. Join the peaceful revolution."

Thus, my road forked in December of 1967. I chose to follow the path of peace without having the vaguest notion where it would take me.

Chapter 2

Of War and Peace

December 31, 1967, brought Rob and me to the Lorelei to celebrate with my old friend Jake. "You sure the decibel level is high enough?" Rob said as we walked across the porch and through the door of the 1930's red brick house a friend had recently converted to a bar and restaurant. The smell of beer and German food overpowered my Channel No. 5.

Jake waved to us from a table next to the dance floor. "Glad y'all got here. Sit, sit." He hugged me and shook Rob's hand. Jake, a local radio talk show host and I had been friends for over three years.

Sitting across from us, a young returnee from Vietnam, Kurt, reached across the table to shake hands. He introduced Rex, who had served with him in Nam but was now out of the military.

"We were discussing the war when you two came in," Jake said.

Rob leaned forward and grinned. "Oops, I don't do war," he said. "If you'll excuse me for a while, I'll run an errand."

"Sure." I handed him the car keys. He rose and headed for the door. Jake gave me a quizzical glance. "He is a true pacifist," I explained "to the point of not wanting to discuss war at all."

"I understand," Kurt said.

Jake laughed. "Discussion is my thing. Without it, I'd be out of a job. The war in Vietnam is a hot topic. And I, for one, say we have an obligation to be there."

"Not only do we not have an obligation, we have no right." I recalled the words of the professor.

"Look," he said, "if we don't stop the Communists in Southeast Asia now, we'll fight them in our own back yard."

"Back in November, Jake, I went to a teach-in about the war. Wish you'd been with me so you could understand it's not about Communism or capitalism—not a question of ideologies. It's about dirty politics, power and resources. Then there's the moral dilemma of lives being taken on both sides."

"Maybe I don't have it all together," Kurt said, "but I see the Vietnamese as good people wanting to work in their rice paddies, raise their families, and live simple, quiet lives. They've gone through enough hell with the French colonization, then the Japanese occupation during World War II, then the French again, and now us." His pale blue eyes radiated compassion as he defended them. "I confess I smoked a lot of dope over there trying to escape seeing what we're doing to them."

Rex interrupted, "Smoking weed has nothing to do with it. I smoked it, too, but I don't see it the way you do. Those are not peaceful people. They're deceitful and dangerous." His jaw tightened. His eyes darted around the table. He jumped to his feet, toppling his chair onto the dance floor. With his elbows tucked against his rib cage, his hands stuck out in front as if holding an invisible M-16 as he swiveled from left to right. "Kill 'em all," he shouted, "The only good gook's a dead gook. Fuckin' Commies. Kill 'em..." He made loud rat-a-tat sounds. His body jerked.

Faces around red and white checkered tablecloths went slack, hands holding drinks stopped in mid-air. Only the jukebox continued playing.

Kurt scrambled to his feet and grabbed hold of Rex. "Cool it, man. Pick up your chair and sit down. We're home celebrating New Years. Get it together."

The glaze left Rex's eyes, Kurt released his arms. I sensed a collective air of relief creep through the crowd as he picked up his chair and rejoined us at our table.

"You get my drift." He spit the words like venom. "I fought those bastards, and the only way you knew they weren't going to kill you was to kill them first."

I cringed.

Kurt cleared his throat and persisted with his own observations. "Like I said, I see them differently. They are beautiful people—peaceful." He frowned. "But each of us saw it in whatever way allowed him to survive. It got damned ugly."

Before Rex could refute Kurt's perception, two girls came through the door and over to our table. Kurt defused the situation by introducing Mary and Deb then asking Mary to dance.

Jake and I trailed behind them. Although a big man in both height and girth, he danced gracefully.

"The end of another year," I said. "What does the new one hold?"

He spun me around twice before saying, "I'd say there's change in the air." Foreboding tinged his voice.

"I think so, too, but I'm not sure I'm ready—still grappling with Danny leaving and the car wreck. . ."

"I noticed both events hit you pretty hard, Sylvi. But you haven't been around much since Rob hit town. Something going on there?"

"With Rob? Come on, he's twenty-one and I'm twenty-eight."

"So what, Sylvi? Danny was younger, too. Are you afraid of guys your own age?"

"I hadn't thought of it that way. Maybe you've hit on my deep, dark secret. You won't tell, will you?" I batted my eyelashes.

He teased back. "Not if you'll run away with me."

"How exciting, Jake. Where shall we run to?"

"Stay with me. I'll show you." He made a few sweeping turns off the dance floor, led me through the tables and out the front door to the porch. With the door closed behind us, we could still hear the music and continued dancing in the wintry air.

"Now tell me," he said, "is Rob the new man in your life?"

"No, he isn't. He's a close friend who happened by at a good time to help me through a bad time."

"A good friend with marijuana."

He caught me off guard. "What exactly is it you want to know? Am I smoking weed? Am I sleeping with Rob?" I stopped, took a step back and looked him in the eye.

"Sylvi, you know I don't give a damn who you sleep with as long as you're happy, but you can go to jail for grass. Hell, you can lose your kids, your house and everything. You can lose it all. It's illegal."

"Cut me some slack, will you, Jake? I wasn't able to protect myself from loving Danny. I fell apart after he left, wrecked my car. You know I'm struggling with making changes in my life, and, true, I haven't been around much. In December Rob blew in from the Village and started encouraging me to leave the booze alone. He's right. How many times did you have to pick up my pieces when I blacked out and kept on partying?"

"Plenty."

"Rob didn't just tell me to quit the booze, he talks about life, and God, and love. I see things in a different light now."

"You're shivering, Sylvi." Jake took off his jacket and draped it around my shoulders.

"Thanks. But let's keep the record straight. I'm not sleeping with Rob, not broadcasting I smoke weed, not trying to get thrown in jail. Besides, Rob thinks it will be legal soon."

Jake leaned against a pillar, listening.

I enclosed both his hands in mine. "I think the changes will be good. We'll end the war. Peace is on its way—time to understand the element of love in the universe."

"What a mouthful, Sylvi. Marijuana is going to make all this happen? I don't think so. What if you get busted in the process and lose everything?"

"Don't, Jake. I can't go through another man a year, like I've been doing, and drinking so much I can't remember parts of my life. I haven't known what it was like to go to work without a hangover for a long time, and I've been calling it normal. I've tried to impart right and wrong to my daughters while racing into the arms of self-destruction. Now I'm waking up, wanting to believe in something better than I've been able to live these past few years."

"I hear what you're saying. Still, I'm afraid for you, Sylvi. As much as you and I have been through together, I can't hang with you if I go into politics."

I slipped my arms around his neck. The music leaked into the night, and we began moving to it. "I respect your position, Jake. For now, let's celebrate the New Year. Hopefully, there won't be any more outbursts from Rex. Wow, what a mind-blower, huh?"

"Sure surprised the hell out of me," he said. "Rex is one scary guy."

"For being buddies, he and Kurt are very different."

"Who's different?" It was Rob's voice as he mounted the porch steps. "What are you doing out here in the cold?"

"Rex and Kurt are very different," I answered his first question. "After you left, the war discussion got pretty heated, so Jake and I came out here to have a private conversation."

"Cool, don't let me interrupt. I'll catch you inside."

I noticed a twinkle in his eye. "Hold on, we're right behind you."

The New Year's Eve celebration grew more frenzied. Close to midnight, Rex and Deb were on the dance floor, Mary in the ladies' room, and Jake at the bar getting a bottle of champagne. With only Rob, Kurt, and me left at our table, Rob motioned us in close. "I went to score weed, but they only had a little bit, and we smoked it. But dig this, man, I walk through their front door, and in the middle of the room there's this big pile of peyote. Blew my mind."

"Peyote?"

We leaned in closer.

Kurt asked, "What do we do with peyote?"

A smile danced on Rob's lips. "It's cactus. Apaches use it in a ceremony. You can drink it in tea, or eat it raw. Usually your stomach gets upset and you vomit. After that, you feel great, see colors, and hallucinate. It's like your hang-ups make you sick. But once you throw them up, you experience a beautiful clarity. The Indians use it for visions and wisdom. . ."

As I listened to Rob describe the peyote trip, my Cherokee ancestry kicked in. I saw myself standing atop a mountain in moccasined feet with discovery fluttering like leather fringe in a wind at sunrise. Life spread out clear and bright before me.

Rob patting my hand brought me back to the present, and I heard Kurt say, "Yeah, around noon would be good. I'll just come over to Sylvi's, and we'll do it."

"What are we doing at noon? I must have missed it."

"I noticed you kind of spaced there for a minute." Rob leaned close to my ear. "We're going to trip tomorrow. I volunteered your place. Is that okay?"

"Sure, as long as I'm included."

He laughed. "You're the first one I thought of when I saw that pile of peyote buttons on the floor. But it's just you, me and Kurt," he cautioned. "Best with only two or three."

Rob looked up. "Hey, it's the champagne man."

Jake filled our glasses. Almost midnight, and the crowd was building to a ringing-in-the-New crescendo. The waiter waltzed between the crowded tables playing raucous German drinking songs on his accordion. We linked arms around our table, swayed back and forth, and sang along.

My thoughts drifted. *With the holidays almost over, Kristi and Katrina will be coming home from their grandparents. Once again time for school, work and expected things—ordinary life. I feel the unexpected tugging at me, begging to be invited in.*

The countdown to the New Year began. Rob raised his glass. "Sixty-eight's going to be the year to change it all."

We downed our champagne and joined the voice of the crowd, ". . .three, two, one, happy New Year!" I threw my arms around Jake and Rob, kissing one and then the other. The accordionist squeezed out "Auld Lang Syne."

Rob hugged me. "Are we the only ones who know what promise this year holds?"

"Maybe we all know something—just not sure what it is—exactly."

The bedlam began to subside, and Deb proposed we move the party to her place.

"Sure, why not?" I responded out of habit.

Jake said to count him in and asked Rob, who declined with thanks. I suggested he crash at the house. "Take my car. I'll catch a ride home with Jake."

Within a couple of hours, Deb's party dwindled. Jake had passed out on the sofa. I sipped orange juice and listened to voices, first, from the bathroom where Mary and Kurt lounged in a bubble bath. Mary tells him how she loves him like she's never loved anybody else. He tells her he knows she's drunk and doesn't believe her for a second. Then coming from Deb's bedroom, I hear Rex telling her how much he wants her. She tells him she's sick of life, she's done it all, and getting it on with him wouldn't mean anything.

Panic crept into me as I listened. For the past several years,

I'd been trapped in similar scenes. But there in the wee hours of January 1, 1968, I had no desire to be a participant or an observer. I had to get out, to shed the hopelessness hanging in the air, threatening to suffocate me.

Jake snored on the couch. I scribbled a note saying I'd found another way home and tucked it between his belt buckle and his pants. He'd find it when he woke up to pee. Then grabbing my jacket and purse, I walked out the door in pursuit of the sunrise, a brand new day, a brand new life.

Fear caught in my chest. My high heels clicked against the pavement as I crossed the street in downtown El Paso. *Was it safe to walk home? Better my body to perish in the street than my soul to die in Deb's apartment. An hour's time, and the darkness will flee, I'll walk into a sunrise, into a promise of new life with nothing to fear.*

The air, cold against my face, energized me. I stuck my hands in my pockets and walked east into the predawn gray. Pale violet lined the horizon and spread translucent purple across it. Glancing over my shoulder at the black night behind me, I welcomed the hope in the light ahead.

Tall buildings gave way to houses—*everyone asleep but me.* I clicked along the sidewalk watching lavender melt into coral. Coral morphed into delicate peach and pink, streaked with wisps of brilliant gold clouds. Then the sun, a ball of yellow flame, rose above the Guadalupe Mountains, infusing me with life.

The breeze bathed my soul in peace as I turned north on the last leg home. The sun climbed, and I kept breathing it in until I stepped onto my front porch. Excitement propelled me through the door.

Startled, Rob put his guitar aside. "How did you get home? I didn't hear Jake's car."

"The sunrise brought me." I laughed. "I've just taken the most incredible, inspiring walk of my life."

"You walked ten miles dressed in that skimpy evening thing and high heeled shoes? It's freezing out there. Why the hell didn't you call?"

"I'm wearing my furry jacket, Rob. I wasn't cold."

"Maybe not, but you could probably stand something hot." He settled his guitar into its case. "I put coffee on a few minutes ago."

Stepping out of my shoes and dropping my jacket, I followed him. The kitchen wrapped me in its fresh-perked smell. He poured two cups, and when we settled back on the couch, said, "Swing your feet up here, Sylvi, and tell me about your walk home."

He rubbed my feet as I described the party and my journey.

"I believe you did breathe in the sunrise," he said, "to prepare your spirit for the peyote." We sat in quiet, absorbed in the present moment.

"Speaking of peyote," I said, "is it time to start brewing it, or whatever we're going to do?"

Rob rose and stretched. "Yeah, I'll get it from the car."

In my bedroom, I shed my dress and threw on jeans and a sweater then joined him in the kitchen. He handed me a dark sea-green peyote button. "I thought it was cactus," I said, "but it's like an oversized pin cushion without the pins." I ran my hand over its smooth surface. Holding it by its long, yellowish root, I pressed it against my face.

"It's magic." He gave a soft laugh. "All the magic and wisdom in the universe, Sylvi, and we're about to open to it the way a flower opens to butterflies and bees."

He ran water over the buttons in the sink. "Help me slice them up."

"Do we cook the button, root and all?"

"Sure. We'll put them in a pan with water, bring it to a boil and let it simmer."

"What's in peyote that makes you hallucinate?" I asked.

"Mescaline alters your state of consciousness," he said, scooping the slices into a pan.

"Alters? Explain." I added water and set it on the burner.

"Lot's of things can change your state of consciousness. Booze, which you're familiar with, may relax you. But it also blurs your awareness. Hallucinogens, specifically peyote, produce a dream-like state through which you are totally aware. Depending on where you're at in life, peyote will expand your inner as well as outer awareness."

He started to talk about LSD when the doorbell rang. I knew it was Kurt and called to him to come in.

"You're not looking so good. What's happening?" Rob asked.

"Mary's happening, and I'm fighting it," he said, collapsing into a chair at the table. "I met her before Christmas. I like being with her. She's bright, and complex, and draws me like a magnet. Last night I wanted to be a part of her. I know it's not real, not real at all."

"What do you mean?" Rob stirred the boiling peyote and turned down the fire.

"I don't understand it myself. A few years ago when I got my notice to report for duty, I freaked. No way was I going to Vietnam. Sure, I'd registered for the draft, but when it came down to it, I couldn't see going over there and getting blown away, or blowing someone else away. I didn't have it in me."

"What did you do?" I asked.

"I didn't tell my folks anything, just went out one evening and drove with a friend from Philly, where I lived, to the coast. I got on this guy's boat, and in a couple days we're on an island in the Caribbean. Safe. Never going back. I'd found paradise." He paused as if savoring the memory. "Right away I'm with this woman a couple years older than me. She's a brilliant, talented, free spirit who opens her house to me. Hell, she opened her entire being to me, and we became a part of each other."

"How'd you wind up in Vietnam, man? Why didn't you stay on the island?" Rob asked.

"One morning she goes to the marketplace. I go out for a swim. Come back, and reach into a drawer for a shirt, but my fingers grab an envelope. It's that damned notice to report for duty. I didn't remember bringing it with me, but there it was calling me back as though it had a voice. At that point, sanity deserted me. I walked out of her house down to some boats and found a man who would take me back to the States. I was gone before she returned from the market. How could I leave something so good? I don't fucking know. I loved her, and leaving her was like dying. The boat ride was hell. Once we docked, I caught a bus back to Philly. I swear, people looked straight through me, and when I looked in the mirror, I wasn't there." He dropped his head into his hands then looked up.

"I reported on time. I didn't know who the hell I was or what I was doing. When I got to Nam I began to feel again—things like fear, so I could stay alive. Guess I'm damned lucky to be here. Never thought I'd experience anything like I did on the island ever again. Now, with Mary, it's happening, and I'm scared."

"Maybe you'll understand more in the morning," Rob suggested.

Without curiosity, Kurt asked, "How so, man?"

"The peyote," Rob answered as he rose to check its progress. "I want to guide you through this trip so you can gain some insight into where you're at."

Rob lifted the lid, the acrid steam engulfed us.

"Smells bad." Kurt wrinkled his nose.

"Is it ready?" I asked.

"Yeah, hand me a potato masher, please, Sylvi, and some cups for the tea."

I complied. "What did you call the active ingredient?"

Rob mashed the stewed peyote. "Mescaline. It messes with your mind and creates a trance-like state, although you do remain awake and very much alert throughout the trip."

"Hold it," Kurt raised his hand. "What if I freak? The way I'm feeling right now, I'm not sure I'm ready."

"You're as ready as you'll ever be," Rob assured him, "and I'll get you through it. I'm not a mystic, but I know this will break you on through to a new place."

"You don't want to stay in this desperate dilemma about Mary now and the island a long time ago, do you?" I asked. "We can trust Rob. He's done this before."

Rob finished mashing the buttons and roots together and strained the yellow-brown liquid into our three cups.

"Is this going to taste as bad as it smells?" Kurt asked.

"Well, it's not going to taste good," Rob said. "But it only takes a few minutes to drink it. You'll survive."

I began feeling uneasy. "I'm hungry, Rob. Maybe we should eat something with this."

"No, Sylvi. It's a better trip if you fast."

"Okay." Nervous, I lifted my cup. "Down the hatch. Kurt, Rob, let the visions come."

"Sip slowly at first," Rob cautioned. "Remember I'm here like a guide. I'll be telling you what I know from having tripped before. If you begin experiencing things that disturb you, tell me. I can guide you through it."

Kurt and I promised. We sipped the tea, looking at each other above the rims of our cups, wide-eyed.

I drained mine, and reached for the pan in the middle of the table. "There's more. May I fill yours up again?" I asked.

"Are you crazy?" Kurt shook his head.

"Mmm, but it's so yummy. Tops the gourmet list." I teased and poured more into my cup.

We finished the tea and retired to the living room where Rob played jazz tunes on the piano. I stretched out on the couch facing the Christmas tree, which, by tradition, I would be dismantling on

New Year's Day—but not New Year's Day 1968. Mid-afternoon left the room in shadow. Kurt plugged in the Christmas tree lights before sinking into a chair.

I closed my eyes and listened to Rob's music drift through the room. Behind my eyelids, I saw a muddy lake red-brown in color but transparent. Familiar, angry faces lay in the mud at the bottom. One by one, each floated upward, rippled the surface with a smile and evaporated into the air. With my eyes closed and the faces floating upwards, I described it to Rob.

"Cool," he said. "Anger is not always ugly. Sometimes it's simply a transition to a more loving state. Don't be afraid to see what the peyote will show you."

"Okay." I felt reassured.

"Look at the colors coming from the tree, you guys. They're phenomenal," Kurt said.

"I don't want to open my eyes." I moaned. "I'm not feeling so hot."

"Take some slow, deep breaths," Rob advised. "But if you reach a point where you really need to upchuck, get to the bathroom and let 'er rip."

"Try to open your eyes, Sylvi," Kurt urged. "You've got to see this."

I opened one eye. Ribbons of color radiated from every bulb. Then the other eye flew open. "Clear the way—got to get to the bathroom." I was there by the time I finished my sentence, slammed the door, raised the toilet lid, and hurled.

Rob called from the hallway, "Are you okay?"

"Yeah," I answered between heaves.

Done, I flushed, moved to the sink, turned on the water, and rinsed my mouth. Looking into the mirror, I recognized my eyes, but they looked back at me from a face of ancient, wrinkled parchment. Startled, I stared for who knows how long, finally deciding it had to be the age of my soul. Rob and I had discussed our journey through eternity. How many lives? How many deaths? But always one spirit spiraling upwards toward the Creator, the Source of life.

The reflection was drawing me into another dimension when Rob's voice at the door pulled me back—back into my bathroom, back into this life where the water ran in the sink. I turned it off and grabbed a towel. Glancing in the mirror, I noted my familiar face had returned. I drew in a long, deep breath and opened the door.

Rob stood in the hallway. "Feel better?"

"Excellent." I took another breath and added, "Very clear and open to whatever. Where's Kurt?"

"Backyard. I'll check on him. Relax for a minute, I'll be right back."

I wandered into the den, and flipped on the light—not prepared for the lightshow. Every color of the rainbow emanated from the bulb in the center of the ceiling, pulsating and filling the room like another sunrise. I breathed in the yellow and felt even more alive. The blues and purples rippled sadness through me. I could not grasp what was happening, so I simply let it.

The backdoor opened and closed. Footsteps clattered down the long hallway past the bedrooms. Kurt and Rob walked into the swirls of color where I stood.

"What did you do to the light, Sylvi?" Kurt asked.

"Turned it on, man." I began laughing. Rob joined me, and we became a duet. When Kurt chimed in, we became a trio. Our laughter took on color—swirling, rising, falling. We clasped hands and danced in a circle.

Children playing.

In a bit, Kurt settled cross-legged on the floor beside the stone altar and lit a cone of sandalwood incense. Rob and I paused in the doorway.

"We'll be in the kitchen, man. You doing okay?" Rob asked

"I'm great." Kurt grinned.

The night shone black through the window above the sink. Rob and I washed up the cups, utensils and the peyote pan. Scooping bubbles with my fingertips, I blew them upward into the light where they became magical, shimmering spheres before they popped.

"This is so beautiful. What's it like for you, Rob? You've tripped a lot. Do your experiences become mundane after a while?"

"No, not really. I think I get more peaceful," he said. "I can choose to lose myself in the trip, or I can choose to be the guide when one is needed, like tonight. But in every case, I understand more, see more, although I'm not as surprised at the difference between normal life and life when I'm high."

"Why?"

He let the water drain from the sink then filled the coffee pot. "The insights I attain when I'm high become more integrated into my daily living."

"Will that happen to me?"

"Each person is different. It depends on what you're looking for, what you're willing to leave open to discovery."

"Right now, I feel trembly inside, excited, like waking up and seeing with new eyes. I want to laugh for no apparent reason." I laughed and Rob did, too. When I could stop, I said, "Do you see the walls breathing and feel things in slow motion?"

"Sure. It's an increased awareness of everything being alive. It's a good thing, no cause for alarm."

"Do you think Kurt's all right in the den?"

"I'll take a look," Rob said.

"Let me know if he's okay," I called after him. Then I opened a cupboard door to choose a coffee mug. A lime green one looked appealing, but the turquoise one next to it drew my attention. *Turquoise, like my birthstone. How appropriate to celebrate a new birth.* I poured the dark liquid into it and felt the warmth against the palms of my hands. I pressed the cup to my cheek, not sure if the heat came from the mug or if I transmitted it.

From the couch, I watched lights on the Christmas tree send streamers of electric color into the room. *What a different world I've entered. The angry faces from the lake might teach me to stop being fearful of confrontation.* Laughter came up from my belly and out my mouth as natural as breathing.

"Are you all right?" Rob asked.

I emerged from something akin to a lazy dream.

He sat down beside me. "When you laugh, it sounds like low, mellow wind chimes." He rested his head against the back of the couch.

"I hear it that way, too."

Kurt appeared in the hallway door, slowly crossed the room and sat down on the floor a few feet in front of us.

"What's happening?" I asked.

"I encountered a great, green dragon." A smile spread across his face.

"You look happy about it," I said.

"I'm feeling pretty good now, but it was touch and go for a while."

"Tell me," I said.

"I was sitting in the dark next to the altar when the walls of your den began to expand. A giant foggy, fiery, green dragon materialized. It lunged for me. I dodged. His tail whipped back and forth, and his eyes glowed like hot orange coals. His mouth drooled and smoked. He came at me again."

"Were you afraid?"

"Hell, yes, scared to death. Thank God, Rob came in just in time."

"Yeah," Rob interrupted, "when I went in the den, I didn't see anything. No Kurt, no nothing. I freaked for a moment—never had anybody disappear on me before."

"Where were you, Kurt?" I asked.

"In the closet. The next thing I know, Rob opens the closet door, and sees me."

"He's standing in the middle of some coats," Rob said. "I ask him what's going on? He warns me about the dragon. I tell him I don't see his dragon. He tells me to either come in or get out, but to close the damned door. I get in the closet with him and close the door. It's pitch black. I ask him what's going on with the dragon?"

"I tell him I'm not sure," Kurt said. "I had been sitting by the altar thinking about our conversation before we drank the peyote, and the wind, or something, made the door swing shut. Then it looked like smoke seeping around and under it, and the dragon materialized. It was clearly after me. There wasn't any place to get away from it except in the closet. Man, was I scared. Then Rob shows up. He tells me to breathe slow, take deeper breaths and blow the air all the way out."

"Go on." I said.

"After I slowed my breathing, Rob starts talking about past hurts taking on the form of a beast that will destroy me if I don't turn and confront it. He tells me it takes time to work it all out, but confrontation is the beginning. I tell him I'm afraid. He tells me he'll open the closet door and stand with me while I instruct the dragon to leave."

I leaned forward. "And?"

"Rob opens the closet door wide. We step out together. I saw the beast and hesitated. Rob nudged me. I borrowed courage from him and commanded the dragon to leave. The fog disappeared under and around the door, the way it came in."

"Far-fucking-out, man. How do you feel?"

"Pretty good. Not as afraid as I was."

We drank more coffee, talked, and intermittently fell silent. On occasion, one or the other of us would wander into another room or out to the backyard.

In the middle of the night, Rob suggested we drive up Scenic

Drive, a two-lane road etched into the southern tip of the Franklin Mountains high above El Paso's downtown lights.

"Can you drive, Rob?" I asked.

"Sure. I have to maintain a frame of mind that allows me to concentrate."

"I don't know, Rob." Kurt looked doubtful.

"It will be okay," I said. "We can always park the car and walk home if it gets scary."

"Yeah, Sylvi's the walking queen today," Rob said. "Did you tell Kurt how you got home from the party this morning?"

"How?"

"I'll tell you as we drive." I pulled on my jacket, handed Kurt his, and we piled into my VW.

On the way up the mountain, I related my story about walking home from downtown and into the sunrise. By the time I finished, Rob pulled to the side of the road at the top of Scenic Drive. We stepped from the car into a million stars.

"Is this a gas, or what?" Rob hugged Kurt and me together. We huddled against the icy breeze. Once we grew accustomed to the cold, we began to inch down from the parking area to the large boulders embedded in the side of the mountain. Our descent was not terribly steep. We stopped and blew frosty breath at each other and laughed as we identified main streets below us.

"They look like arteries pumping life into the body of light and shadow down there, don't they?" I asked. We stood still, in awe. "Church bells," I whispered. "Can you hear them?"

"I hear them from inside me," Kurt breathed a soft reply.

"They're a blanket wrapped around us," Rob spoke aloud. "We're breathing them in, although they're inside already."

"Ordinarily I think I'd find that confusing, but tonight I totally relate. And the train whistle is off in the distance, too, but it's coming from here."

"Yeah, here." Kurt pressed his hands against his belly.

"Exactly. Rob, what's going on with this?" I asked.

"Be still for a while, listen and stay open." Rob settled himself onto a large rock.

Kurt and I wandered several feet apart from where Rob sat. The night grew softer, yet brighter, around me. I recalled the night before in the Lorelei when Rob had described tripping on peyote, and I'd seen myself on the mountain top with life spread out before me. *Here I am on this mountain looking down at the city where I've grown from a child to a woman and now I feel like I'm moving into another dimension.* My heart beat in a gentle, calming rhythm. The cold air around me made my face warm, while far-away city sounds rumbled within me. I was part of everything and at peace with it. No thought remained in my head. Empty and full.

I don't know how long we stayed quiet in those early morning hours content among the rocks, boulders, greasewood and cactus. I loved this high desert mountain, rugged, treeless. I turned to look skyward and saw the shadow of a hawk soaring up into thousands of electric, confetti stars.

Rob broke the silence. "How are you two doing?"

"I see a hawk way up there."

"A spirit. What does a hawk mean to you?" Rob asked.

"I saw one flying above a mountain when I was semi-conscious in the emergency room after wrecking my car."

"The hawk has a message for you."

"I'm not hearing it."

He led the way to the car. "Someday you'll be in a space to hear, Sylvi."

At home, Rob lit a candle and we sat around it. "Meditate on the flame." His voice sounded far away. "Don't work at it. Let it happen. Close your eyes first and empty out your mind. Then open up to the candlelight. Let your spirit go where the light takes you."

After some time passed, I left Rob and Kurt. In my bedroom, I found a pen and note pad.

Air is music all around me.
The scent of jasmine and honeysuckle
awaken catacombs behind eyes
closed from too many burials.

Light rolls in.
My thirsty spirit splashes in it,
dances in it
swallows great gulps.

Love rises from inside out.
And outside in.

I wrote it at sunrise. The wreck, the teach-in, the peyote, the hawk. That first night Rob blew in from New York, turned me on to weed, and told me about facing the soldiers at the Pentagon, he'd said, "Love. It's all about love."

"Yes," I whispered to the Universe. In that moment I understood my connection to all sentient beings. "I'm experiencing that kind of love, now. We're all One, and I love you."

Chapter 3

Ending the Trip and Beginning the Journey

I had fallen asleep after jotting down the poem at sunrise. Two things woke me. The sun's extraordinary brilliance and the thought that the second of January was a work day. I threw myself together, blew kisses to Rob and Kurt, who were crashed in the den, dashed through the house, and burst through the kitchen door into the cold shimmering air. The air hung like crystal sheets all the way to the horizon. I stood in amazement.

To tear myself away from such beauty seemed impossible until some tiny spark of practicality reminded me my work was necessary to support the girls and me. But necessity notwithstanding, the one thing I knew for sure: after the peyote trip, my life could never be the same.

Judy and I met for lunch. Over tacos, I told her about my peyote experience. She told me about Pat's brother, Ted, getting out of the army. She noted he'd been in Germany and not Vietnam.

"He's starting at the university this semester. He is a really cool dude."

"You sound interested. Are you?"

Nodding, she smiled. "We smoked a pipe of hashish last night and sat up all night talking. I'm pretty sure we're both interested."

After lunch I received two phone calls. First, Rob let me know that he was driving to Las Cruces with Kurt. The second call, a half hour later, came from my housekeeper saying she was at the house and starting dinner.

To my delight the afternoon sped by. My parents would be bringing Kristi and Katrina home after their weeklong, holiday visit. I looked forward to seeing them again and had barely greeted Estelle when I heard car doors slam and children's laughter.

My daughters raced through the door holding their new baby dolls for me to see. I dropped to my knees, gathered the girls in my arms and knew they were the most important things in my life.

My mother, tall and smiling, trailed behind them.

"Where's Dad?" I asked.

"Getting the girls' suitcases from the trunk."

I gave her a brief hug and ran to the car. "Happy New Year. Can I help?"

"Grab those boxes, Sylvi, and we've got everything."

I set the boxes on the floor by the Christmas tree and invited Mom and Dad to stay for supper. My mother answered, without hesitation, "No, thank you. We're on our way to your sister's house."

I hadn't expected they would stay. Since my car wreck in the summer, Mother and I had never resolved our differences—not that I hadn't tried, but she always cut me short with, "That's all past, we never have to speak of it again." Truth is she spoke to me as little as possible no matter the subject.

The girls had been asleep for an hour, and Estelle had retired to her room when I heard the door open. Rob called, "Just me, Sylvi. Kurt dropped me by."

"Hey, what was happening in Las Cruces today?" I put my book aside to greet him with a hug.

He sat down beside me on the couch. "We never quite got there—mostly hung out along the river and talked. The peyote proved to be disturbing for him, but I think we broke through some issues today."

"Like what?"

"For one, he'll be out of the army in a few days. He recognized the great, green dragon from last night as a composite of his many fears about his future. At the end of the day, he decided to enroll at the university, continue his relationship with Mary, and take a part time job at a floral shop."

"So, I assume he's off to tell Mary the good news."

"You would be right. How are you doing? You sounded like you were handling work all right when I called earlier."

"It was like reentry into a vaguely familiar world from a multi-dimensional 'other' world. Like, the trip yesterday opened so many doors to places within me—peaceful, loving places where I would like to be all the time. Walking through the office this morning, I loved every person I work with in a new, connected way, but I couldn't express it to them. They would have thought me quite mad. I looked at the work on my desk, correspondence from retail outlets nationwide, catalog copy and artwork, fabric and color swatches for our next line of boys' jeans. I contemplated how complex the way we live is—how a simple breach cloth would suffice as clothing. How pointless all the complications are. It took some time, but I arrived at a conclusion."

"And that would be?"

"Acceptance of a sort. Having to function in our 'real' and 'practical' world does not negate the truth I experienced in the 'other' world. I can do what I have to do and still hold within me all the insights the peyote gave me yesterday."

"A wise conclusion, Sylvi."

A month of new beginnings, January ushered a variety of kindred spirits through my door. Some would call it a crash pad, I thought of us as family.

Old friends brought new friends. Kurt having finished his Army gig, registered at the university where he met Aiden and brought him to meet me.

"You're the Sylvi Kurt's been telling me about." He stuck out his hand and gave mine a hearty shake.

"That provokes slight paranoia." I winked at Kurt. "What's he been telling you?"

"You're a far-out chick, and I should meet you." He ducked his head and grinned.

"How old are you, Aiden?"

"I always get that question. Twenty-one."

Stepping back, I took in his shoulder-length blonde curls and baby face and looked at Kurt for confirmation.

"Honest, Sylvi, he'll graduate in June."

"I believe you. Interrogation's over."

"I'm used to it." He pulled a joint from his jacket pocket, lit it and offered it to me. "It's not a peace pipe, but it'll do."

As the evening progressed, he mentioned a rock concert he'd helped a friend promote, something he wanted to devote all his time to once he finished school.

By mid-January, Irish and Syd joined us. Old buddies of Kurt's, they still had several months left in the military. Irish, his head barely clearing the top of my front door casing and sporting as much of an afro as the Army allowed, strode in with a pipe in hand. His generous mouth curved into a smile against teeth glowing white in his face of midnight black. He bent, encircling me in his arms while introducing himself.

Once I recovered my breath, I welcomed him and asked who his friend was, the shorter man with wild red hair, stroking his mustache, and leaning against the door, gazing at us through inscrutable, blue eyes.

Irish stepped to one side. "Sylvi, I'd like you to meet my good friend from Long Beach, California, Mr. Sydney Olafsen, bass guitarist formerly with the Public Porpoises, now an unwilling servant in the United States Army." His voice boomed, matching his commanding presence.

"Just call me Syd." Mr. Sydney Olafsen spoke as soft as Irish was loud and, with some effort, detached himself from the door casing to extend his hand in greeting.

"Delighted, Syd." I took both their hands and led them into the den to meet Rob who sat on the floor with Judy, Ted (her new interest), Bob (her brother), and Pat (his wife). Kurt and Aiden preceded us and sat down. Looking round the circle at my old and new friends, I asked each one to introduce themselves to Syd and Irish.

Judy began then looked toward the man to her left.

"Ted, Pat's brother," he pointed across the circle at Pat. "Just got back from Germany with some hashish. We'll do a bowl later, if no one objects." Laughter rippled through the smoke in the room.

"I'm Kurt, and I know everybody."

"I'm Aiden, and I'll just add that I love y'all."

"Thanks, Aiden—didn't know you cared." Bob chuckled, then revealed his name and that his wife sat to his left.

"Pat." She gave a little laugh and looked up at me. "Actually, I'm his second wife. Sylvi was his first."

"You're kidding," Kurt said. "I didn't know that."

"I think all parties are happy with the present arrangement. Oh, and I have news. I'm going to have a baby in about seven months—wanted you all to be among the first to know. I'll just skip the hash, if nobody minds."

"Baby?" Bob bestowed an incredulous look at Pat. "Why didn't you tell me?"

She punched his arm. "I told you, you big goof."

They joked back and forth as Irish, Syd, and I settled in the circle on the floor.

Ted pulled out his pipe and placed a sticky ball of hash into it. "Let me light that up for you, brother." Irish flicked his lighter.

The military draft soon became the subject of conversation. No one defended it, but most had an opinion or personal story. Kurt declined to tell his, but Rob offered that he, personally, didn't have an address. Therefore, he planned to ignore the war mongering government of the U. S. of A.

Later, among much laughter, we suggested names for Bob and Pat's baby. "Did you know," she asked "that Dr. Spock, yes the one who wrote the book on raising babies and children, has been arrested for opposing and picketing draft offices? His civil disobedience inspires me to read his book."

Toward the end of the month, Pablo came to the door with Syd and Irish. He'd received a package in the mail that day. I followed them into the den. "A buddy in Nam sent it," Pablo explained. "It's dynamite grass." He rolled a joint and handed it to me.

I lit it and passed it to Irish. "Where are you from?" I asked Pablo.

"San Diego."

"You're all three from California."

"Yeah, but Syd and I are short-timers. Pablo's volunteered to go to Vietnam," Irish said.

"You volunteered? Why?" I asked.

"I want to experience the weed first hand."

"You're crazy." I couldn't believe what he'd said.

"Maybe, but I surfed back in San Diego. You can't get the rush from sitting on the beach. You've got to get on your board and get out there before you can look up and see those cathedral-ceiling waves arched above you."

"My God, man, Nam is not a surf board and the mother of all waves," Irish said. "We've tried to tell him not to go, Sylvi."

Pablo defended himself. "For me, it's the total experience or nothing."

I especially liked this man who possessed a curiosity about life. But from my peyote experience I'd gleaned the wisdom of not entering another relationship for a long while.

The last of January, several of us gathered at Bob and Pat's for the a new comedy TV show, *The Laugh-In*. We brought whatever weed we had and plenty of munchies. The show reinforced our hope for change to come soon. If Rowan and Martin could joke about marijuana, and bring a stoned show to national TV, anything was possible

At the very end of January, the Tet offensive chipped away some of that promise. Vietnam exploded as the North hit the South with everything they had, focusing on Khe Sanh, Saigon, and Hue. Television news thrust it into my den, and we talked of nothing else for days.

One evening in February, Ted, Judy, Rob and I sat in the den sharing a bag of Sweet Tarts when Irish showed up with his California buddies. "Can you believe that fucking Johnson?" he boomed. "He keeps pouring on more bombs, more agent orange, more of everything. He's on some murderous rampage, I swear."

I offered him a Sweet Tart. He took it, drew a joint from his shirt pocket and offered it to me. "Trade ya."

"The body count is high and getting higher by the minute." Syd shook his head and said to Pablo, "There's no way you can go over there, man."

"The die is cast," Pablo said as Ted passed him the joint.

"We'll tie you up and go AWOL," Irish's big hands tied an invisible knot in the air.

"If our lunatic President will come to his senses and get us the hell out of there, you won't have to go." Ted closed his eyes.

"You're lucky, Ted. You're out of the Army now," Rob said and got to his feet. "War should not exist. God's creatures and His earth should never be subjected to brutality. I'm going for a walk. Anybody want to go?"

"Me." I extended my hand, and Rob helped me up.

In the darkness, we trudged up the sidewalk toward the mountain. "Bummer, huh?" I commented.

"More than that, what will it take to stop it? I know peace doesn't come in a day, but don't we ever learn anything?"

"It's the politicians on their fucking power trips. What blows my mind, Rob, is how they close their eyes to human suffering as though it doesn't exist."

"Blows my mind, too," he said.

I shivered. "It's cold. Let's go back."

"I've been thinking," he said. "I'm going to take off for San Francisco this month."

"Seems like you just got here. Are you ready to go again?"

"I was ready a month ago, but I wanted to be sure you were okay before I left. Are you?" he asked.

"I am, thanks to you, my guide extraordinaire. Think we could trip one more time before you go?"

Rob did score more peyote, and after my kids left to visit their grandparents over the weekend, we dropped it. I didn't get as sick as the first time.Once more, we wound up on Scenic Drive early in the morning. Rob and I stood among the boulders as the eastern horizon came alive with color. The sun, large, flaming, lifted an inch at a time above the Guadalupes, revealing the face of God. Rob's hand clasped mine. We held tight, connected to life—to Source.

I experienced a stirring in my spirit, further opening my world to the nurturing love in the universe. I saw sparkling, crystal light glancing off the wings of my mystical hawk.

In the face of what I was learning, war remained a puzzle. How could the dark, bloody death of war prevail over love, enlightenment, and peace?

The end of February saw Rob on his way to San Francisco. Newspapers told us the Tet offensive was over. Who could believe anything released to the media by those people in Washington who turned on the faucets to the bloodbath?

Around the same time, Eric Burdon and the Animals were in concert at the County Coliseum. Several of us passed a joint around as we drove to the event. We parked, joined hands, and ran, laughing, across four lanes of traffic. We ran forever before reaching the opposite side. Then it took another forever to get to the box office. Weed did slow things down, like Rob told me that first night we smoked together.

Inside, we made our way through the crowd. The air hung heavy with marijuana smoke.

The music soared as the light show intensified. "House of the Rising Sun." Pablo squeezed my hand. Every note resonated in my soul as the strobe lights jerked the musicians on stage this way and that.

They played "Sky Pilot" for their last number. The lights pulsed as scenes from Nam flashed behind the band. Sounds of bomb bursts filled the building. Smoke swirled around the stage. Eric belted out judgment on the chaplains who condoned the war. As it ended, we jumped to our feet screaming, crying, applauding. The music twisted my insides in knots and at the same time, gave me wings to fly.

When I arrived home from work the next day, Syd and Irish were on my doorstep. "Come in," I said. "Where's Pablo?"

They steered me to the couch in the living room.

"He left this morning for Nam."

"No." I looked from Syd to Irish. "You're putting me on. We were all together last night, he would have told me."

Irish put an arm around my shoulders. "He didn't want you to know."

The air went out of me. "What the hell happened? You guys said you'd kidnap him, get him to go AWOL. You said you wouldn't let him go. How can you tell me he left? How can you?"

"Damn, Sylvi, he's a grown man. He was determined to do what he wanted, and he wanted to go to Vietnam," Irish said.

"Honest," Syd added, "we tried our best to talk him out of it."

I stared into space. "Such a gentle soul, they'll eat him alive over there."

They both gave me hugs. "We're really sorry to drop this on you and run, but we've got duty back at the base."

I followed them onto the porch, watched them drive away, and contemplated the total insanity driving this country.

Kurt pulled up. "You look spooked, Sylvi. What's happening?"

"Syd and Irish came by a few minutes ago. They told me Pablo left this morning for Nam. Did you know, too, Kurt?"

"Nobody told me anything. I swear." He draped and arm over my shoulders and walked me back in the house. "Why don't we drive out to the river and watch the sunset?" he asked.

"Estelle has dinner ready. I shouldn't."

He insisted.

In the kitchen, I told Estelle to call the kids and eat without me. I'd be home to tuck them in.

We drove in silence until we parked on the levee road at the Rio Grande in the upper valley.

"How long do you think he'll last, Kurt? You've been there and made it back. Do you think he'll make it, too?"

We got out, piercing the quiet evening with our slamming car doors.

We sat on the edge of the embankment, and Kurt answered my question. "Maybe he'll find the beauty in the middle of the horror like I did. He'll find the courage, or the smarts, or whatever it takes to survive."

"You're just saying that to appease me, aren't you?"

"I mean it. He'll find whatever it takes to survive."

"That is if they don't blow him away first. I hate this fucking war."

The sun sat stubbornly on the horizon, watching us from the edge of the world. Below us, wintry trees graced the meandering river. Above us, telephone wires ran from pole to pole. Kurt and I glanced up at the wires. Birds called to one another.

"Do you see that?" I asked, pointing skyward.

"I see the clouds have formed a giant hand."

"And it's positioned right on those wires like they're guitar strings."

"Yeah, God's music." He put a finger to his lips. "Listen." And so we did until the birds settled for the evening, the sun disappeared, the clouds spread rose and coral brush strokes across the sand dunes, and the hand on the guitar strings faded into the heavens.

"We just received a gift," he said.

"I need a gift. A gift of promise. Like the sun will rise again tomorrow, Pablo will come back, too."

Great, March winds blew in springtime. I became aware of the Spring Equinox because Ted moved in with Judy, and they loaned me his book on astrology. It went beyond the daily horoscope bullshit to explain the twelve houses and all the planetary influences at the time of a person's birth. I was delighted to have peoples' differences explained. Weed, peyote, and now astrology. New doors continued opening to illuminate the road I'd begun to travel.

One night in March when Judy and Ted came over. He asked if he could turn on TV.

"Sure," I said. "Anything special?"

He flipped through a few channels and stopped on one discussing the primary in New Hampshire. "I want to find out who's winning," he said.

Politics never had held any fascination for me. "Who's winning what?"

Ted patiently explained that whoever won the New Hampshire primary election was likely to win the presidential nomination at the Democratic Party's convention in August.

"Johnson's a Democrat, isn't he running for his second term?" I asked.

Ted fooled around with the rabbit ears trying to get better reception. "Most likely, but the Democrats are pushing for an antiwar candidate."

"We've got to get someone in there who will end the war," Judy said.

Ted pointed out that some of the Democrats wanted Bobby

Kennedy to run, but others weren't sure where he stood on ending the war.

Eugene McCarthy, the antiwar candidate, received forty-two percent of the New Hampshire vote, while Johnson got forty-nine percent. Close. We were encouraged. Three days later, Bobby Kennedy declared his candidacy.

"Politics?" I said to Judy in the kitchen. "I guess I have to pay attention."

"It's a burden, but a necessary one right now."

I still checked in at the Lorelei from time to time and kept in touch with Jake. He was astounded at McCarthy's showing in New Hampshire. He guaranteed it wouldn't happen in Texas. But when the end of March came, Lyndon Johnson announced to a nationwide TV audience, "I shall not seek, and I will not accept, the nomination of my party for another term as your President." Jake sat in stunned silence, while the rest of us cheered.

The phone call I received on April 4, tipped the scale from joy to despair. Judy's voice came over the line in a whisper. "Sylvi, did you hear? It's all over the news."

"I can barely hear you. What are you talking about?"

"King. Martin Luther King, Jr. He's been shot in Memphis. He's dead." Her voice broke.

"No. He can't be dead."

"Who?" Kurt asked.

"Hang on, Judy. Martin Luther King has been shot and killed in Memphis," I said to Kurt and Aiden.

"No way." Kurt turned on the television.

"Are you okay, Judy? Is Ted with you?"

"Yes." Her voice faltered. "I just wanted to let you know."

In shock, I returned the receiver to its cradle. We stared blankly at the screen as the report unfolded. King had been in Memphis to support the garbage workers' strike. Someone shot him on the balcony of his motel.

"This is really fucked up," Aiden muttered.

Reports of rioting filled the following days. Black and white communities across the nation expressed their outrage. Every evening my den filled with friends. Blown away by the madness, we clung together for support.

The TV screen rippled and flashed from the flames of one city to another as neighborhoods burned from the East Coast to the West.

"King is—was—the conscience of the Movement. What now?" someone asked.

No one answered.

Had the revolt at Columbia University not exploded on April 23, April would have dissolved into May licking its wounds. Irish thundered into the house yelling for somebody to turn on the TV.

"My little brother is in his second year at Columbia and there's some heavy shit going down."

"Wait a minute, Irish. He's a California boy like you. What's he doing at a New York university?" I asked.

"My dad's a lawyer in L.A. He does all right and told my brother he could go to school anywhere he wanted. Now me, I went to U.C. Berkeley and made it through pre-law before the Army nabbed me, but my little brother gets it in his head he wants to live in Harlem and go to Columbia. Half an hour ago the cat on duty in my barracks calls me to the phone, says it's an emergency. My brother's on the other end of the line. He runs down what's happening there."

Ted had turned on television, and the evening news took us

to New York where the students were confronting Columbia University's Administration.

Irish's brother was in the thick of the protest and had told Irish the catalyst was the piece of land separating Harlem from Morning Side Heights, a park where the University wanted to build a gymnasium. It would displace several thousand blacks in Harlem. His brother said there were a couple of other hot issues, too, one being that the students and faculty had no voice in how the school was run, and the other that many of the students and faculty opposed Columbia's participation in weapons research for the U.S. Department of Defense.

"You'd think prestigious universities would be above doing research for the Defense Department. Bastard warmongers," Ted said.

According to the news report, after the confrontation in the park, the students marched back to campus, took over Hamilton Hall, and held a dean hostage.

By April 24, Irish lost touch with his brother, and we had to depend solely on the news. It reported the students had released the dean. Several of us gathered each night to support Irish and send good vibes to the strikers. What drew us to their cause, other than Irish's brother, was our own desire to see changes come at whatever levels would help dismantle the existing system. Why shouldn't students and faculty be given a significant voice in how their school is run? Why should the Department of Defense manipulate a school financially by funding weaponry research? An institution of higher learning researching how to kill people disgusted me.

By April 26, the students occupied five buildings, formed a Student Strike Committee, and the faculty involved themselves as mediators.

In the dark morning hours of April 30, the police began to assemble on campus and by late in the night, the cops broke through, kicking and clubbing the students who sat nonviolently behind the barricades. They carried them to the waiting paddy wagons. The evening news reported there were over seven hundred arrests. Irish heard the same number from his dad who had flown to New York to bail his brother out of jail.

As rebellion continued into May, other schools across the nation observed a one-day strike in solidarity with the Columbia students. We cheered them on. In the end, the Administration met only enough demands to placate the students and faculty. The rest of what they asked for got lost in the shuffle, and the university continued its research for the Defense Department.

During the ordeal, in our private conversations, Judy and I tried to reconcile the concept of nonviolence, as taught by Gandhi, with what was transpiring at Columbia in New York.

"I admire what they're doing," I said. "But it seems a bit marred because they held the dean hostage."

"They let him go within twenty-four hours," she pointed out.

I insisted hostage taking was a violent action. "We have so much to learn to bring peace to this earth."

There was more to learn.

Those gathering in my den spoke seriously of events, of how we had to personally be ready to face the upcoming challenges although we couldn't guess what those might be. We huddled together in expectation, co-conspirators preparing for nonviolent revolution.

However, as May progressed, I found the challenge I faced quite different from anything I had anticipated.

Chapter 4

McKenzie

How could I know when the day began, what its end would bring?

Aiden and Syd pulled into my driveway that warm Saturday morning in mid-May and crossed the front yard, avoiding the water sprinkler where the girls and I played.

I joined them on the porch. "You guys are up early, what's happening?"

"I think the town has dried up, Sylvi. We can't find weed anywhere." Aiden leaned against the porch railing.

"And believe me, we've looked," Syd added.

"Tell me about it. Judy doesn't have any either," I said. "Got any ideas?"

"We were thinking of driving over to Juarez to see if we could score. You want to come along?" Syd cocked his head to one side and stroked one end of his mustache.

"Better not." I waved at Kristi and Katrina as they darted in and out of the water, hooting in delight. "I don't want to take the girls over there. But come on by when you get back."

They sauntered down the sidewalk to their car.

"Good luck." I said a silent prayer for their safety.

After lunch the phone rang.

"Sylvi, anything going on at your place?"

"Not a thing, Judy. The kids are up the street playing. I'm contemplating changing out of my bathing suit. I have the top of one suit on and the bottom of another. One of my more attractive looks." I laughed.

"What are you doing in a bathing suit?"

"The girls and I were running through the sprinkler earlier. Oh, yeah, how could I forget? Aiden and Syd were by. They've gone across the border to see what they can find."

"Those dudes are nuts. What if they get busted going through Customs?"

"Send them positive vibes. I'll call you when they get back."

I hung up the phone in the den and started toward my bedroom to change clothes when I heard the front door open and bang against the wall.

"Sylvi, are you here?" I recognized Aiden's voice.

I looked into the living room and caught my breath. Sunbeams swirled through the open door painting a golden rectangle on the carpet. Three shadows walked through those dazzling particles of light. I watched Aiden and Syd's forms materialize.

The third figure came into focus carrying a duffel bag, which he dropped on the floor and extended his hand. "McKenzie Raintree."

I clasped it and looked up to meet his eyes—wide, green and set above high cheekbones. His gaze intense, his handshake strong.

"Sylver Smith." I said, unable to look away, unable to let go.

"You're putting me on." He smiled and held on to my hand.

I smiled back. "My dad has a sense of humor. Please, call me Sylvi."

Aiden's voice, like the snapping of fingers, released us from our hypnotic gaze. "Bring it in the den, Z. Set it down here, man." Aiden patted the couch.

The plaid wool shirt draped over McKenzie's arm had escaped my notice until that moment. He let it slide to the couch along with the two large, filled-to-bursting plastic bags it had concealed.

"Gold." Syd grinned. "Acapulco gold. Z said he'd lay some on us for getting him across the bridge."

"Wow. Tell me about it." I looked at Aiden.

"Z brought it from Acapulco. I knew we'd score. El Paso may be dried up, but I had a feeling about Juarez."

McKenzie retrieved his duffel from the living room floor. "Do you mind if I change clothes somewhere?"

He looked fine to me in his Levis, a white tee shirt and heavy work boots. "The bathroom's right through that door and straight ahead."

"Thanks."

"You should have been there, Sylvi." Syd stroked the ends of his mustache. "It was a trip. Z walks up and fucking asks if we want to buy some weed. I thought Aiden was going to soil his drawers. Z asks if there's some place we can smoke a joint. We get in Aiden's car, Z rolls up two fat joints, hands them to us. A couple of tokes, and we're so fucked up we hardly know where we're at."

"Then," Aiden said, "he tells us he'll give us some weed if we get him across the border. 'Hell yes,' I tell him. But first, he says he wants to get a haircut, get cleaned up because he's hitched up from Acapulco on a gasoline truck."

"You guys are too much." I laughed. "Then what happened?"

"We walked around Juarez stoned out of our minds, waiting for him," Syd took up the tale. "But we had no problem at the border. Customs Man says, 'Citizenship?' Cool as anything, we say, 'American.' Customs Man says, 'What do you have to declare?' We say, 'Nothing, sir.' Customs Man says 'Go ahead.' We drive on across that international bridge, and here we are."

"Do you have a scale so we can weigh this stuff?" Aiden asked.

My peripheral vision caught Z coming from the bathroom barefoot, tanned and wearing only a pair of white cut-off jeans.

"No, I don't have a scale, but I think Pat might have one. I can give her a call."

"What do we need a scale for?" Z asked, dropping his duffel beside the couch.

"Thought you'd want to weigh what you're giving us," Aiden said.

"Hell, I'm a generous man—we'll settle up in a while. Let's roll some joints." He picked up a newspaper from the end table. "Okay if I use this?"

"Sure," I said and turned to put the *Jefferson Airplane* album on the stereo.

Z placed a handful of golden leaves from one of the plastic bags onto the newspaper, lifted one end of the paper with his left hand, and scooped the dried weed to the elevated end with his right, letting the small round seeds fall to the bottom.

We watched him sort leaf from seed like he was performing a sacred ceremony. His brown, sun-streaked hair flopped over his forehead as he squatted pretzel-like on the floor with his armpits hooked over his knees. He drew rolling papers from their orange wrapper and rolled four big joints.

"I don't like passing it around. Hope nobody minds." He handed one to each of us.

I was dumbfounded. We always rolled thin joints, stretching what grass we'd managed to score as far as possible. *Does he have a never-ending supply? Is he trying to impress us? What is his trip exactly?* I felt a little uneasy and put the joint he'd given me down on the newspaper.

"I need to check on the kids. I'll be back in a few."

I went first to my room and changed out of my mismatched bathing suit into some jeans and a violet tee shirt. Glancing in the mirror, I wished there was time to do something with my hair. The sun and sprinklers had left it hanging against my shoulders without any curl. *Why should I care?*

Outside, I spotted the girls skipping down the sidewalk toward me. "Can we play longer?" they asked.

I knelt and hugged them both. "Yes, but check back with me in a little while." They promised and ran back toward their friend's house. "Love you," I called after them.

Back in the den, Z reached toward me, offering the joint I'd left behind. When I put it between my lips, he lit it. I glanced above the flame and was again aware of his eyes. *Is he penetrating my being or drawing me into his? Must be my imagination.*

"You came up from Acapulco?" I asked. He nodded. "How long were you there?"

"A few months. Guess it was the last of January when I hitched down there."

"From where?"

"Around San Francisco. I worked there."

"Did you just pull up stakes and leave?"

He hesitated. "I did acid a couple of times. Then I heard about the mushroom down in Oaxaca. I wanted to try it."

"So, did you?" My face felt a little tingly, and I wasn't sure my words were coming out the way I intended.

"Not yet," he said. "Got hung up in Acapulco smoking dope and listening to stories about Che." Quiet for a moment, he asked, "Would you mind if I painted on your walls?"

"Here in the den?"

"Yeah. I have paints in my bag."

"Rob left the stone altar in the corner. Why shouldn't you leave murals on the walls?" I'd taken a couple hits off the joint. "This is extraordinary weed."

"Watch your head when you get up." He laughed as he extracted paints from his duffel.

"Oops, I almost forgot. I have to call Judy."

"Who's Judy?" he asked.

"We've been best friends since high school. I was married to her brother once."

"Is he the father of your kids?"

"No. They belong to my second husband."

"How many times you been married?" He stopped painting and looked at me.

"Two times too many." I laughed. "I don't think marriage agrees with me. Anyway, I'd better give Judy a call." I started up from where I sat on the floor. "Whoa, I don't feel too steady here in the upper atmosphere."

"I told you to watch your head." Z returned to his painting.

I dialed her number and stretched the phone cord into the living room where I could hear above the music.

"Hope you all are up for a celebration," I said.

"Sure. What's going on?" she asked.

"The falcon has landed. We're having a party."

"Sounds like it. We'll bring pizza, be over in a little while."

By the time Ted and Judy arrived, Z had covered half of one wall with four different faces, three of which looked tormented. He pointed to the fourth one, identifying it as Che Guevara.

"He's the revolutionary who fought beside Fidel Castro in Cuba. Anybody heard of him?"

We all shook our heads except for Ted who pointed out Che was dead now.

"Killed last year," Z said, "in the revolution in Bolivia. I'm betting it's the CIA who took him out. They figured he was too committed to the cause."

"Why do you say that?" I asked.

"Because after he and Fidel liberated Cuba, he went on to the

Belgian Congo to organize guerilla operations. He thought oppressive governments everywhere should be the targets of change, and he wanted to be an instrument of that change. That's why he went on to Bolivia. There's a lot to tell, but I think we've lost Syd and Aiden."

"We're not lost. We're here," Syd said.

"Don't let the weed put you to sleep," Z warned. "Let it wake you up, open your head."

"I have to call the girls in for supper," I said.

Judy got up. "I'll go with you." Once outside, she added, "My God, I've only been here fifteen minutes, and it is way too intense in there. How long has Z been carrying on like this?"

"I don't know, maybe a few hours."

We followed the sidewalk toward the mountains, blue in late afternoon shadow. The heat of the day was dissolving into a cool evening breeze.

"Is he dealing out of your house, Sylvi?"

"Of course not. He promised Aiden a cut for driving him across the bridge, through Customs. That's all. He'll be gone in the morning."

"Are you sure? There seems to be something going on with you two."

"For somebody who's only been here fifteen minutes, how can you say that?"

"For starters, the dude closely resembles Michelangelo's statue of David, and the vibes between you two are so strong I'd have to be dead not to notice."

"Okay, mostly it's his eyes. They make me a little breathless. But he's in there promoting violent revolution, Judy. I'm not into that, for God's sake."

"Sure. I also know since you dropped peyote you think you're not going to involve yourself with another man. But I'm telling you, this is pushing my caution button big time."

"Trust me. It's not happening," I said as we reached the house where six or seven neighborhood kids played in the front yard.

"Katrina, Kristi, time to come home."

They begged to stay.

"No, come on, girls, it will be dark in a while. Time for a bath and supper." Relenting, they ambled to where Judy and I stood on the sidewalk, waved to their friends then ran ahead of us.

In their jammies, after their bath, I introduced them to Z. He offered them brushes and asked if they wanted to help with the mural.

"Not tonight," I said. "They need to eat supper, and then it's bedtime."

Back in the den, after tucking in the girls, I found Z encouraging everyone to paint something.

"I've got more brushes in here," I said.

Z handed his brushes and pallet to Syd and followed me into my bedroom where my easel set in one corner.

"Not bad," he said, looking at the canvas.

"I call her the Scarlet Woman, something I painted after wrecking my car. A self portrait you might say."

He studied the nude silhouette of the woman painted in shades of red who danced against a fiery background, her hair flying out toward her extended fingertips.

"But the word 'Scarlet,' is that because of the colors or like in the book *The Scarlet Letter*?" he asked.

"The latter. It's me. The accident followed a messy affair and a divorce."

"You don't have to explain anything to me."

"I know. But since the peyote trips, I see no reason not to be open about my life. The peyote also brought me to the point where I'm not letting any more men in my life until I get myself together."

It sounded stupid coming out of my mouth, but what if Judy was right? I wanted to be straight with him.

Our eyes met as I handed him the brushes.

I think I'm not going to ask what you mean by that." Before I could comment, he left the room.

In the den he'd distributed the brushes, and all present were painting. I lit a stick of incense, stuck it in the altar and began to dance to the music. Holding his brush in one hand, Z joined me. I felt caught in a ritual where we circled each other with a magnetic field between us that made it hard to breathe. I had to retreat.

"I need to see if the girls are asleep." I danced into the hallway, relieved he didn't follow.

In the doorway to their room, the intensity of the scene in the den eased. Katrina slept soundly, but Kristi sat up.

"Who is McKenzie, Mommy?"

I smoothed her covers and sat beside her. "He's a friend of Aiden and Syd's." I said it as though I really knew who he was.

"Is he staying with us?" Her brows came together in a frown.

"Maybe overnight. He lives in San Francisco, and he'll probably go home tomorrow." I kissed her forehead.

"Are you sure he's going home tomorrow?"

There was more to her question than she asked aloud. I was sure she wondered if he would stay with us for months like Danny and, before him, my German. I sensed she hoped he would not.

"My dear, Kristi. Don't worry. I'm sure he'll be leaving." I kissed her again. "You go to sleep now. I love you."

"Goodnight, Mommy. Love you, too."

"Sweet dreams," I whispered.

Avoiding the crowd in the den, I headed straight for the kitchen for a drink of water and found Z fumbling with the coffeepot at the sink.

"I think I put this together okay. Take a look."

There in the bright light of the kitchen, doing something common like making coffee, he seemed like a nice, ordinary guy. *No need to panic.*

"Looks good to me." I took it from him and plugged it in. "So you're from San Francisco. Is it the beautiful scene we hear it is? I mean, like Haight-Ashbury, love, peace and good vibes?"

"It's a mix of things, I guess. I used to score acid and weed on Haight Street. It was pretty wide open then. I don't know what it will be like when I get back. The cops probably will have it all fucked up."

"When are you going back?"

"Probably tomorrow. Don't want to wear out my welcome." He smiled and our eyes connected .

I prayed not to react, to block any vibe that might exist between McKenzie and me. *There will be nothing to end if I don't let it begin.*

"What will you do when you return to San Francisco?" I reached in the cupboard for cups.

"Turn a few people on to the gold and get front money to go back to Acapulco."

"What about family, job, that kind of stuff?"

"My dad's still in San Francisco with some of his family. We're not close. I broke off an engagement before I left. Nothing to go back for except the people I know who can front the money I need."

I poured coffee into our cups. "What's with your whole Che trip? You're the only person I know who talks about violent overthrow. What have you got against nonviolence?"

"It never stays nonviolent—always turns ugly. Look at the Civil Rights marches, they started out peaceful and wound up bloody.

The cops and the government don't let the old order die peacefully. They're so fucking threatened. All they know to do is lash out. If something opposes the status quo, kill it."

"Wow, according to you, there's no hope for a peaceful revolution." Placing both cups on the table, I sat down.

He straddled a chair, his arms hanging over the back, and his hands moving as he talked. "I know what you're saying. Gandhi won the salt war and all that. But it's not practical. Look what happened to Martin Luther King just last month. Then the Columbia revolt in New York City."

"How'd you hear about Columbia when you were in Acapulco?"

"They carry the *New York Times* on a newsstand down there. The students could have won."

"They came close," I countered.

"Not even, although the media played it up like they won, only a few of their demands were met. They sure weren't successful at kicking the Defense Department out."

"Yes, that's true."

"One big thing." He stressed the word "big." "The university administration's greedy. They want the money from the Defense people. Let's face it, it is a lot of money. It's not just universities that want those dollars, look at all the corporations with government contracts to make weapons of war."

"I see what you're saying, Z. But everything has to start somewhere, so, in a way, the uprising succeeded."

"Ah, shit, Sylvi, don't you see the administration made just enough concessions to appease the students? They didn't win a thing. The students should have picked up guns when they took over those buildings. Then someone would have taken them seriously." His hands came to rest around the coffee mug on the table. He raised it and took a drink. Peering above its rim, his eyes locked onto mine.

Two strong impulses pulled me in opposite directions. One was to run, and the other was to get as close to him as I could. Words failed me. I sipped my coffee and lost myself in his eyes, shades of green like the jungle at noonday.

Finding my voice, I said, "You're wrong. Peaceful demonstration is the better way. But I'm too tired to argue my point. You can grab some sheets from the hall closet, and crash on the couch whenever you want. Goodnight." I stood up.

"Wait, come in here." He caught my hand in his and led me to the long brown couch in the living room. "Lie down, and I'll massage your back."

Oh, my God, intentional personal contact. I stretched out on the couch and briefly wondered if I were surrendering, but once he pressed his hands against my back, it didn't matter. I closed my eyes. He sat astraddle my butt and kneaded my neck and the muscles on either side of my spinal cord, clear down to the top of my hip-hugger jeans. How can I describe electric relaxation? I fought back the immense desire to roll over, rip off his clothes and make mad, passionate love. Once that thought formed, with all its implications, I freaked.

"I really have to go to bed, Z. Let me up."

His hands lifted from my back. He stood and helped me to a sitting position. "What are you afraid of, Sylvi?"

"I'm not afraid. I'm exhausted. It's been an intense day, and I need sleep. Goodnight. Again."

I closed my bedroom door and feeling reasonably safe, fell onto my bed.

Where the hell are you when I need you, Rob? You and your candlelight, and meditation, and clarity of mind and purpose. I get somebody like McKenzie dropped into my space. What do I do?

Sleep mercifully overtook me.

"Sylvi." The voice reached me as if in a dream. "Sylvi." A hand on my shoulder rocked my body back and forth. My tee shirt was being pulled up and over my head.

"What's happening?" I opened my eyes as I felt his mouth on my breast.

"Pretty obvious." His fingers tugged at the button of my jeans.

My hands searched his nakedness.

His hands gripped my jeans and slipped them down my legs, and off my toes. I heard them plop on the floor at the end of the bed. He kissed my inner thighs and licked my bare belly before he sank against me, his tongue exploring every cranny of my mouth.

I do not remember how many ways or how many times we made love. I do remember waking entwined in his warmth. Morning sun painted Venetian blind slits on the floor. I stared at the lines of light for a moment, trying to remember what day it was. *Sunday. If I move my leg from where it's draped over his, the movement will break this enchanted spell.*

Panic seized me. *What have I done?* I struggled to quiet my thoughts. *After all, he will leave today. Still, his being in my bed violates my resolve not to involve myself with yet another man. Why, McKenzie? Why now? Tomorrow you won't be here, and everything will be like it was day before yesterday. I'll be back on course. This is merely a slight tangent, not months or years.*

I glanced at the clock on the bedside table. I had to get the girls to Sunday school.

"Where are you going?" he asked as I moved my leg off his. His arm caught me around my waist as I sat up.

"I have to get the girls dressed for Sunday school." I wanted to collapse back into his arms.

"Sunday school?" He yawned.

"You know, like church. Today's Sunday, and I take them every week."

"Yeah, I know what Sunday school is, but why do they have to go?" He sat up.

"They enjoy it. After I drop them, I hang out in the park until time to pick them up. Then we go back there and play."

"What do you do while you're waiting for them?"

"Write poetry."

"You're a poet and an artist?"

"Poetry's my passion. Painting is a hobby."

He kissed the back of my neck.

"I have to get up," I said, but my body turned and leaned into his. "I'm sorry, Z, this is what we do on Sunday mornings. It's a bit of stability in their lives, and they don't have a lot of that living with me."

"Sounds like you're selling yourself short."

"No, I'm not." I got to my feet.

"Do we have time for a shower?" he asked.

"Let me check on the girls first." I grabbed my robe from the closet and hurried to their room.

Both were awake. "Good morning," I said, entering their room. "Why don't you two get ready, and I'll meet you in the kitchen?" I said, pulling two dresses from their closet. "And here's matching socks. Catch." I tossed one pair to Kristi and one to Katrina. They laughed, jumped from their beds, and caught them.

Padding back through the hallway, I popped in my bedroom door, staying a safe distance from the bed. "Go ahead and take your shower, Z."

"Okay," he said and started toward me.

"Where are your clothes?"

"Right here." He stepped into his cut-offs that lay on the floor next to the bed and finished buttoning the fly just as he reached me. "Mm, I was looking forward to that shower," he said and kissed me.

"Well, it's not happening. I'm going to fix breakfast while you shower." I checked the clock again. "After that, I'm taking them to Sunday school. Do you want to ride along, or do you need to get on the road?"

"I'm not on a schedule, but like I said last night, I'm not into wearing out my welcome." Drawing me close, he waited for my answer.

Could he possibly make this more difficult?

"Okay, here's the plan. We'll eat breakfast. I'll take a quick shower, and we'll drop the girls by the church. Then you and I can hang out at the park, if you want to."

"Yeah, I want to," he said.

The park covered a square block. Great spreading elms and tall spires of cedar rose heavenward, sentinels uniformed in spring finery. Z and I sat in the playground swings.

The sun drenched us in rich May warmth as we drifted slowly back and forth, dragging our toes in the sand.

"You always take them to Sunday school then come to the park?" he asked. The church thing seemed to bother him.

"Almost always. Except for going to work, this is the only routine thing in my life right now. I've been working on living more deliberately since I turned on last December."

"Last December, huh?" he mused. I couldn't tell if he was squinting at the sun or scrutinizing me. "Why did you decide to turn on? Have you ever done acid?"

"It was more like it happened, rather than I decided," I answered his first question. Choosing my words, I related the story of Rob blowing in from the Village with some grass followed by peyote. "But, no," I answered his second question, "I haven't done acid. From what I understand, it's similar to peyote but somewhat unstable."

"Yeah, that's a good way to put it. But it was acid that made me take a good look at my life. Religion, for instance."

"What about it, Z?"

"When I was about fourteen I lived on a boys' ranch. A man and his wife ran it. They had a daughter about the same age as us boys, and the man fooled around with her. I'd grown up Catholic, you know, and it bothered me. I went to the local priest for help because it was a bad scene. He told me to do the best I could, said there was no way he could help. That's when I walked away from religion, and I've never looked back."

I twisted my swing sideways to look at him. "It's probably none of my business, but how come you were on a boys' ranch?"

He looked down for a moment, shuffled his bare feet in the sand as if weighing what to say and what to leave unsaid.

"My parents divorced. By the time I was twelve, I was giving my mom a hard time. My younger brother and I got into some scrapes, shoplifting and stuff like that. Once I ran away to Nevada. The cops called my mom to come get me. She didn't have a way and asked my dad to pick me up. He refused, figured I'd be a problem for his new marriage. Long story short, the court gave custody to the State of California."

As he told his story, he kept his eyes on the treetops. I thought the memory must be painful for him.

"That's pretty cold, Z. How could your old man let it happen?"

"Guess it all comes down to how either of them could do it. How could the priest turn his back? How could a man do that shit to his daughter? How come the whole world's so fucked up and nobody seems to be able to do anything? Is everybody helpless?"

His eyes nailed me with the question.

"I don't have an answer." I didn't know what to say. I'd never met a person who'd lived through his early teens in state-run foster care, never considered how they got there or the possibility of abuse.

Since Z's arrival, things churned inside me that didn't fit with the flowers and peace sign images common to the Flower Child scene. We sat in silence for a few minutes before I gathered courage to speak.

"You haven't had an ordinary life have you, Z?"

"Ordinary? You mean like Sunday school and playing in the park? My mom tried, but my old man made it too rough for her. Plus, I was born with a cleft palate. I went through a bunch of surgeries before I was ten."

"I feel like I've led a protected life compared to yours, although I've grazed the borders of the wild side. But it was my choice, you know what I mean? I chose to spit in the eye of convention, and it's made my life difficult. But you, you were born onto a hard road. Do you think of it like that?"

"Not exactly. It's what I make of it. I do think I was born pissed off."

"Are you still pissed off?"

"Sometimes I am, Sylvi. Right this minute I'm not." He pulled my swing toward his. "I feel pretty good right now."

"Me, too," I said. "But I've got to be honest with you."

"Honest? What do you mean?"

"About the peyote trip."

"You mentioned it before," he said, drawing a joint from his pocket. He lit it and handed it to me. "I remember last night you said something about not letting any more men in your life until you got yourself together."

I took a long hit and held it in while recalling waking up to him that morning and thinking I'd betrayed myself.

"You remember what I said last night, but you still came on to me?"

He nodded. "I had to. I really wanted you."

It seemed so simple for him. I kicked little bits of sand with my toes. "God damn you, Z. I don't know what to say. When Rob left..."

"Tell me about Rob."

I told him how Rob and I had worked together and had become friends, about Rob going to the Village, and Rob turning me on to grass and peyote when he came back to El Paso.

"That's all he was to you?"

"All?" I asked. "He's a very close friend."

"But you didn't sleep with him?"

"No, I didn't. Is that what matters to you? Who I have or haven't slept with? I don't have a clean and tidy past, Z. What's yours like?" He was beginning to piss me off.

"Simmer down. I didn't mean it that way. Like I said last night, you don't owe me any explanations."

"All right then, what happened on the peyote trip was a spiritual awakening. I realized, at some very deep level, that I couldn't get off on another man-tangent. I have to figure out stuff about myself, like where I'm going, how to really connect with the universe—with God, how to end wars and bring lasting peace." I searched for words to continue. "Then you walked through my door yesterday."

"Am I a problem?"

I nodded "Last night you asked me what I was afraid of. I think I just answered your question. But it seems insane to spend one night with you and think there's any real connection, anything to fear." I wanted to shut up, go back to Friday before he entered my life, and not be sitting in a swing at the park trying to explain something I couldn't understand.

"I'd like to help you figure it out, Sylvi, but what do I know? I blew into town, and I like being with you. Can't we just see how it turns out?" He stood in front of me.

I slid from my swing thinking he carried so much less baggage than I did. "Maybe," I stretched by body up against his. It felt good. "Maybe."

We sealed our nonbinding agreement with a kiss, gathered our shoes, and walked toward the car.

"I like the way you are with your kids," he said. "You put a lot into it."

"Not as much as I should. I'm a little preoccupied with the changes I'm going through. Things I've thought and believed all my life are being brought into question these past several months. It seems in trying to sort through it, I don't do enough for Kristi and Katrina. I grew up in my parents' peripheral vision. Not that I wasn't well provided for, I was, but I want my kids to know I'm focused on them, that I hear where they're at. It's hard to be preoccupied with my own crap and hear them, too."

"I wouldn't worry about it, Sylvi. Why not just let it happen?"

"Just let it happen." I echoed. It resonated with a bit of truth residing somewhere inside me. But somewhere else inside me an alarm sounded.

Chapter 5

The Second Sunrise

Sunday night I said prayers with the girls. As they snuggled under their covers and I kissed them goodnight, Kristi asked the inevitable question.

"You said McKenzie was leaving today, Mommy. Why is he still here?"

"He's not ready to leave for San Francisco yet, sweetie." It sounded like an answer that might suffice.

Katrina chimed in. "I like Z. We had fun at the park today."

"But Mommy kissed him."

"Yes, I did. People kiss each other. It's a pretty natural thing, not the end of the world." There was so much I couldn't explain to myself, much less my children. "How do you feel about it, Katrina?" I asked.

"It's okay." She shrugged. "Mommy kisses us, too, Kristi."

"We can talk more later—tomorrow, girls."

"Later" always bought time, and time seemed to be what I needed in Z's case.

As she did every Sunday evening during the school year, Estelle my housekeeper arrived, and I introduced her to McKenzie. She put her things away in her room. When she returned to the kitchen, she asked,"Will he stay long, Sylvi?" It seemed to be the question of the night.

"Maybe, for a while, Estelle. I don't know yet."

She considered that for a moment. "Like Danny and the German man?"

"I don't think so, maybe. I don't know," I stammered. Her command of English being somewhat limited and my Spanish being worse, I finally shook my head.

She smiled and patted her cheeks, indicating I was blushing. I laughed and gave her a quick hug then joined Aiden and Z in the den.

Aiden was saying, "Given a couple of weeks, we could get several hundred dollars front money together." He suggested to Z the two of them take his car.

Other friends dropped in as the evening progressed. I not so much participated in the conversations but observed how enthralled they were with Z's rhetoric as he rolled joints. He expounded about U. S. corporations using governments of third world countries to exploit their own indigenous populations. U. S. companies, Z said, got cheap labor, while certain of those governments' officials got rich, the people remained impoverished. With grandiose brush strokes, he painted more faces on the walls of my den and spun tales of violent revolution toppling corrupt governments in an attempt to replace them with new systems based on equality and justice.

Was it psychological manipulation, or simply contagious enthusiasm for a message long overdue? Whatever the case, my friends opened to Z like thirsty flowers, and he seemed to pour out something akin to holy water.

I, too, felt caught in his spell. Yet, when he looked in my eyes or touched me, I knew it was no act. I sensed the earnest cry of his heart. It matched my own heart's desire to bring equality and justice to our suffering world. We differed, however, in methods. Mine involved peaceful change while he advocated for violent revolution. *Could I—no, surely not—enter into a relationship with a man of violence?*

After the house emptied of guests, Z asked how I felt about him getting front money together in El Paso.

"I thought you were going to San Francisco to do that." I ignored expressing how I felt about anything.

"If I can raise the bread here, why do I need to go to California? This way, I can stay with you, unless you want me to go?"

I considered Judy's warning against letting him deal weed out of my house. Too, my own desire for self-discovery tugged for recognition rather than offering my heart to yet another man. I recalled his question in the park—why not just let it happen. Did I want him to stay? I needed peace and peace would not come.

"Sylvi?" He reached for my hand.

"I want you to go."

He raised my hand to his lips.

"I want to stay," he whispered.

How could I explain to him the volcano of indecision erupting inside of me? I struggled to define what drew me to him. *Many men have surrounded me since I dropped peyote, yet I've not involved myself with any of them—haven't even thought about it.*

I heard myself say, "Stay for now. Like we said in the park, we can just let it happen."

He kissed my fingertips. "Please know, Sylvi, I understand you're at a crossroad. I'll give you as much space as you need."

The week passed in a blur of activity. On Friday evening, I pulled into my driveway and recognized two cars parked at the curb. My house would be full of people and loud music. I stepped from my VW into the cool twilight, stretched and thought about escaping.

Instead, I checked the mailbox and headed straight for my room. From behind, Z planted his hands on my shoulders and rocked me gently back and forth to the music.

"Would you like to escape out to dinner and a movie?" I turned to see him dressed in jeans, shirt and shoes. He'd brushed his hair back, but the front spilled over his forehead.

I hugged him. "You must be reading my mind."

Pepe, a small, lively man from Spain, had transformed the first floor of an ancient downtown building into a breath of Spanish culture called The Bar España. The smell of fresh tortillas, chili salsas, and beer hung in the dim light. A lone figure seated on a chair at the back of the room played classical guitar. Z and I sipped wine and ate as though we were starving.

"Thanks." I looked at him across the red tablecloth laden with plates of food, "I really needed to get away."

"Yeah, intense week, huh?"

"How are things coming together for your trip?"

"Good. Aiden's getting new tires put on the car. I have almost all the money I need. Another week and we'll be ready to go."

"Sounds like you'll be leaving for Acapulco around the same time I'm leaving for Phoenix."

"What's with Phoenix? You haven't mentioned it before." He registered surprise.

"I haven't? The week has been busy. The girls' dad lives in Phoenix with his wife and her two kids. According to our custody agreement Kristi and Katrina spend their summer with him. They'll be out of school a week from today, and we'll do our little road trip to Arizona."

"How do you feel about them going?"

"I hate it. He drinks too much and is something of an unreasonable tyrant, but I have no choice."

"Aiden and I don't have to leave for Mexico until Monday or Tuesday. Would you mind if I went along?"

"Are you sure it won't throw you behind schedule?"

"It should work out all right."

"Great," I said. "You can drive, and I'll sleep. The end of the school year always leaves me exhausted."

We finished dinner, walked to the movie theatre a few blocks away and watched *The Graduate*.

Walking to the car after the movie, Z commented, "Good movie." Then reflecting on the end of it where the graduate interrupted the wedding and ran off with the bride, he asked, "What do you think of marriage?"

"Not much. I tried it twice, but never again."

"Never?"

"I'm no good at relationships."

"I don't have any complaints." He opened my car door and bent to kiss me as I settled into the passenger seat. A minute later, he slid behind the steering wheel and added, "No complaints at all."

"I'm talking about long term."

"Who can tell about long term anything?" he asked. "How long is long?"

"In my case, it would be anything from eight months to five years. But there are people like my parents who have been together thirty-five years."

"That must be a year or two shy of forever."

Midweek, Estelle, Kristi and I went to Katrina's kindergarten graduation. Friday noon, Kristi finished second grade. In the evening, the girls and I drove Estelle to the International Bridge in downtown El Paso. She would be spending the summer with her family in Durango, Mexico. She hugged both girls and wished them a happy vacation. After hugging me, she said she might not return in the fall.

"Please think about it, Estelle."

She said she would. I watched her walk across the bridge, knowing she would not come back to us, knowing she knew what marijuana was. I was in her debt for sticking with me since December.

Early Saturday morning Z loaded the suitcases, two sleeping bags, and blankets into the car. We were off for Phoenix. Irish and Syd promised to hang out at the house and take care of my cat, Daiquiri.

Driving the VW to the max, we arrived in Phoenix before 2:00 in the afternoon. As we pulled into their driveway, Carl and family stood on the porch. The kids ran to greet us and whisked the girls off to play.

Carl did not budge, but in an attempt at good relations, I introduced McKenzie who extended his hand. Carl ignored him and grunted, "H'llo." Jazelle smiled and nodded amiably but remained at Carl's side.

I helped Z unload suitcases then rounded up Kristi and Katrina for hugs and kisses. It was difficult to leave them, but they were excited to play and didn't want to tarry over goodbyes. I waved one last time as we backed out of the driveway.

A mile or so down the road, Z looked at me. "You look a bit teary. Should we go back and get them?"

"No. Thanks for asking. I need a little time. Carl came off surlier today than I've seen him in a while."

"I don't think he was happy I came with you."

"I'm sure he wasn't. I've driven the kids out by myself the last two years. Guess you took him by surprise."

On the road, Z suggested we drop south out of Tucson and go

through Bisbee and Douglas, Arizona. "There's a town called Agua Prieta in Mexico, right across the border from Douglas. We could hit there late afternoon and check it out."

He blew my mind. Never would I have strayed off the freeway had I been by myself. I began thinking our time together, no matter how brief, would broaden my horizons. I should relax, I told myself, and go with the flow.

I dozed for a while and awoke to see we traveled a two-lane highway. It wound through a rugged, rocky desert painted dusty-rose and dotted with dramatic green bushes and gold grasses. The great saguaro cacti stood erect with arms pointing heavenward.

"Wow, I really crashed. I bet I'm charming when my mouth drops open and I drool." I wiped a corner of my lower lip with the back of my hand.

Z laughed. "Your snoring was the best part."

"Now you know what I'm really like." I kidded back. "God, McKenzie, would you look at this country? I can feel the spirits in the air."

"Spirits?" He glanced at me, then out the window. "What kind of spirits do you think they are?"

"Apache. They belonged to this land before the white man screwed it all up digging big pits to mine copper. Geronimo and his band were the last to go. But it still belongs to them."

"Maybe we'll run into a few."

"Make fun. I know they're here."

"We're coming into Douglas," he said.

"Thank God. Let's find a gas station. I've really got to go."

Around 5:00, we found our way across the border into Agua Prieta, a small town with streets criss-crossing each other at irregular intervals. Z parked in front of a weathered adobe building with a wooden awning supported by four posts. A sagging screen door opened into the bar.

Inside a cool, shadowy room greeted us. We made our way around mismatched tables and chairs to sit at the bar where a young, dark haired woman asked, in Spanish, what we'd like to drink. We ordered *Tecaté*. She disappeared through a curtained opening behind the bar and returned with two red and gold cans. A man followed her carrying a bowl of sliced limes. He stood about my height. Graying hair framed his round, weathered face.

"You'd like limes?" His accent was slight.

"Yes, thank you," I said.

He smiled. Each of his eyes looked in a different direction.

"Sit down with us," Z invited. The man came from behind the bar and sat on a stool next to him. "You live here in Agua Prieta?"

"Oh, no, I live in Douglas with my wife. She's German. But I have two wives here. Well, you understand what I mean. They run my bars. It's a good life." He grinned and nodded at Z.

"Do you have children?" I asked.

"Only one little boy. The woman at the other bar is his mother."

"What brought you to this part of the country?" Z asked.

"Forgive me. I did not introduce myself. I am Captain Juan Griego. I was born here. In Arizona, I mean."

"I'm McKenzie, and this is my woman, Sylvi."

Captain Griego shook our hands.

"You're of Mexican descent?" I asked.

"I am Yaqui. Douglas is my home, although I've lived away much of the time. I served for twenty years in the United States Army." He said it proudly.

"You must have seen action in Korea." Z said.

"Yes, right after I joined up. It's been a good life, not the war, but the military. I met my wife when I was stationed in Germany."

"Your wife in Douglas?" I asked.

"Yes." He glanced my way and called to the woman behind the bar, asking her to bring another round. We listened to stories of his travels for a while. Then I asked him about the Chiricahua.

He leaned forward, resting his elbows on the bar. "They were gone long ago. Cochise surrendered first, and some years later, Geronimo—in the 1880's—a long time ago."

"What do you know about them?" I asked.

"They were very brave. They belonged here, but the soldiers hunted them like dogs, chased them, pushed them beyond endurance." He waved a hand toward the door open to the east. "Their spirits still live in those Coronado Mountains. So many fought and died. The rest were taken to reservations."

I cast an I-told-you-so look at Z, who called for another round. "What else do you know about them?" Z asked.

"They didn't take scalps—never took scalps. Did you know that?"

No, we didn't.

"A strong family people. Their men raided for supplies and horses and only killed in self defense."

Z glanced behind us out the open door where daylight was fast fading.

"It's late. We better get going, Sylvi. Good talking with you, Captain. We've still got some miles to cover tonight." Z pulled some bills from his pocket and left them on the bar.

"Thank you." The Captain shook McKenzie's hand and nodded at me. "You must come back this way again."

"Thank you," I said. "We will." I thought we probably never would, but I could no longer be sure of anything.

As we drove the few blocks to the border, the air grew cooler and the sun slipped from the western sky. We proceeded through customs into Arizona, while sunset colored the evening until quiet twilight ushered us out of Douglas. Our lights danced along the two-lane highway, threading its way east through desert silhouettes.

"He was so out-there with his women. I couldn't believe him

telling perfect strangers about his German wife in Douglas and his other wives in Agua Prieta. It was plain to see he only had them to run his bars and provide him with extra-curricular activities." I folded my arms across my chest and stared out the passenger window.

"I wondered why you've been so quiet."

"Now you know."

"They play by different rules in Mexico, Sylvi."

"No, they don't. It's the same everywhere. I've lived both sides of the unfaithful game, and I've progressed to the point where I see it only as destructive behavior."

"Destructive behavior? What kind of psycho-babble is that? It seemed to work for the Captain." Z laughed.

"Laugh, damn you, it doesn't work for anyone. It just diminishes them and makes it necessary to build walls to protect one's heart. I don't see it surviving in an enlightened society."

"God dammit, Sylvi, you're just so fucking far above the rest of us with your love and peace," he yelled. "Your peaceful revolution bullshit. Enlightened society? What the hell's the matter with you?"

His anger startled me. His eyes caught mine and wouldn't let go. "Is that what you really think of me?"

"Not exactly." He looked back at the road and fell silent.

Some time passed, and he turned off the highway onto a narrower road leading into the mountains. The brush grew thicker as we climbed, and pines stretched skyward in front of us. Cold, I hugged my knees to my chest.

He pulled off the road, stopped, got out, and retrieved the sleeping bags from the trunk without speaking. Walking several yards into the forest, he spread them on the ground.

"Are you going to sleep with me?" he called.

I opened my door. "I don't know." Stepping from the car, I caught my breath. The moonlight on the sheer cliffs across the road made them look wet. Their glistening, white walls jutted straight up into the full moon. Gradually I became aware of Z's warmth at my side.

"They look like they could fall over on us," I said, and pressed against him. His arms encircled me.

"Did you mean the things you said in the car?" I asked.

"Not all of them. But you're different from anyone I've ever known. Give me some time."

The wind sang through the pines, a cold treble song, swirling from time to time into a soft whistle, and the gurgling of a creek came from the forest darkness beyond where we could see. The moon draped the giant treetops in a pale glow, while the breeze trembled shadows against the soft earth.

"Are those shadows?" I whispered. "Or are there things moving out there?"

"I don't know, but it's cold." he whispered back. "I'll get more blankets."

He draped a blanket around my shoulders then wrapped one around himself, and we hurried to the bedroll Z had spread on the ground. Sitting close together, we pulled the other sleeping bag up to our chins. He struck a match and lit two joints.

"Where did these come from?" I asked as I took one from him.

"I rolled a few before we left El Paso."

Warm in our blankets, we smoked and listened to the distant calls of a bird, and the howling of a coyote. The light from the moon and stars intensified.

After stubbing out our joints, I whispered, "I hear crying."

"Probably the wind."

"No, it's women weeping."

I listened while the moon moved away from the cliffs in its journey across the sky.

The moonlight paled as the night grew later. "Do you still hear the crying?" he asked.

"Far away now, but close when I first heard them. They came

from inside me, broken and lamenting."

Z wiped the tears from my face with his fingertips. "I think you found your spirits," he said.

We lay down. He drew his blanket around mine, holding me close. I rested my head against his chest and fell asleep.

I opened my eyes to the gray of predawn and stared through the pine branches at the cliffs, remembering them by moonlight. Z slept beside me.

"Good morning trees. Good morning magnificent cliffs," I whispered into the cold air. "Good morning twisted up blankets. How do I get loose?" I tried without success to disentangle myself.

"I've never heard you wake up talking to yourself, baby." His eyes opened, he lifted both arms from beneath the covers and stretched.

"Didn't mean to wake you. I'm just trying to extract myself from this cocoon."

His face brightened. "It would be an honor to assist an emerging butterfly." Putting an arm across me, he tugged the outer blanket free. "Better?"

"M'hm."

Despite the cold mountain air, warmth rushed through me. My heart beat faster as he pulled me to him.

We made love. The sun rising above those amazing cliffs witnessed our melting together. Something greater than my yea or nay had brought us to this place.

Around noon, we began gathering ourselves to drive on to El Paso. We shook dried pine needles from the bedding, folded it, and tossed it in the trunk.

Z took my hand. "Before we take off, let's find that creek we heard last night. Must be close by."

We found the stream less than a quarter of a mile from the car. The light danced rainbows where the icy waters splashed over boulders upstream. We knelt on the graveled bank, scooped water in our hands, drank and washed our faces in it.

"Let's bathe before we hit the road."

"You've gone mad, Z. The water's freezing."

"Once you get in, it's only cold for a minute." He unbuttoned his jeans and tossed them across the branch of a nearby bush. Naked, he started into the creek.

I pulled my shirt over my head, stepped out of my shorts, and draped them over the same branch. "I must be crazy, but here I come." Wading in, I followed him downstream into a calm pool close to the bank. He steadied me in the deeper water.

"This is good." The water covered us up to our necks. He rubbed my shoulders, and I felt like a floating lily pad in the sun glinting off the water, dazzling my senses. His mouth tasted good.

Eventually, we found our way back to the creek bank and our clothes.

"Wish we'd packed some food. We could stay a bit longer," I said as we trudged back to the car. "It's magical here."

Z squinted into the light breaking through the dense pines. "Magic? I don't believe in it. If it's true, the spell will be broken once we leave."

"Maybe that's what I'm afraid of," I said as we reached the car.

His eyes grew serious. "There's nothing to be afraid of, Sylvi. The other night, you told me your feelings on marriage. But I still have to ask. Will you marry me?"

I pulled away from him and slid into the passenger seat. He closed the door, walked around and got in the driver's side.

"Will you?" His face close to mine.

I had refused to even think about that question for three years. Now, here it was. How could I answer him?

Z turned the car around and started down the road.

"I could marry you," I said slowly. "But not on paper. I've had marriages on paper, first in the presence of a priest, then a justice of the peace. They didn't last, Z. Only the living of two lives together proves a union. If we need a ceremony, it could have been this morning in the presence of the spirits, the sun on the cliffs, and the forest shadows. And further confirmed when we washed each other in the creek."

He said nothing. Desert winds blew through the car. Some miles had passed when he stopped beside the highway. Coming around to my side, he opened the door, took my hand, and I stepped out, wondering what was coming next.

"Let's agree that this morning was our ceremony," he said. "Let's agree when we get back in the car and start down the highway it symbolizes the beginning of our road together. No paper, Sylvi, just the road of life ahead of us."

I took a long, deep breath. "Wherever it takes us?"

"Wherever it takes us."

"Agreed."

Chapter 6
Summer Changes

I left work early on Monday to spend time with Z before he and Aiden took off for Acapulco. Walking into an empty house, the silence, like a comforting hand, led me to the den where I lit a stick of incense. Calming sandalwood filled the room, while I sat in the middle of the floor contemplating the walls and ceiling of vibrant color surrounding me. The images of peace signs, flowers, and grim faces painted into those murals illustrated the conflicted life Z and I had agreed, just the day before, to share.

Had yesterday really happened? The cliffs by moonlight, the sounds of the spirits in the mountains where we'd made love as the sun emerged? The moment we'd committed to traveling the road together crept through me, and the part of me wanting to love and be loved shook with both radiant expectation and stark fear. My reasoning mind asked me how I would reconcile my attachment to Gandhi with McKenzie's attachment to Che? My heart soothed me with the assurance that love conquers all.

A door opened and closed. "Pizza." Z called from the kitchen. "Jalapeno and anchovy, just like you like."

"What time will Aiden pick you up tonight?" I rose from my contemplations.

"Around eight." Meeting in the living room, we held each other for a moment before he continued. "I'm ready to go, got all my stuff packed and the bread together. Are you expecting anybody to drop in?"

"I'd be surprised if they didn't, wouldn't you?"

"Good point. Don't mention to any of them that we're splitting tonight. Call me paranoid, but I don't know all the people who hang out here. Even if I did, I wouldn't trust them."

"You do sound paranoid."

"A certain amount of it is healthy, believe me. You trust the whole world, Sylvi. I trust only you."

"I won't tell anyone."

"We should be back in a week, maybe two." He opened the pizza box and grabbed napkins. I poured grape juice.

"Let's have a picnic on your bed," he said and headed to the bedroom.

"Our bed," I called after him, stopping in the hallway to pull a tablecloth from the linen closet.

Once settled, I took a bite of pizza and caught a long string of cheese with my finger. "So what's it like, scoring weed in Acapulco?"

"First, you telephone and make an appointment with the weed dude then you meet him in a big, fancy hotel dining room. His people frisk you before you sit down. He whips out an order pad and..."

"Okay." I laughed. "Tell me what really happens."

"It's not a cut and dried transaction, baby."

"I know, but I need to have an idea of what you're doing. When I think of you, I want a picture of what's happening."

"Okay. Once in Acapulco, I have to locate Miguel. He decides when we go into the jungle to pick up the weed. There are variations on that theme, depending on how many people are involved, time frames, availability. The weed I've bought from him in the past hasn't been bricked. We package it in newspaper so I can get it back up to the States."

"A lot of risk, Z. Are you sure you want to do it?"

"If we're going to turn on the world, somebody's got to do it. Why not me?"

"I know, but we just found each other. . ." We sat cross-legged in the middle of the bed, the pizza between us on a pale blue tablecloth. Realizing my face mirrored the fear inside me, and not wanting him to take that image with him, I changed to my strong woman face. "Guess I sound silly and clingy. I'm not. This is new for me."

He scooped the box of half-eaten pizza up in the tablecloth and deposited it on the floor next to the bed. Leaning against the pillows, he pulled me to him. "I'll be back safe and sound."

It was dark when Aiden knocked on our bedroom door. "Hey, man, are you going to sleep the night away?"

"Be right there." Z jumped up. "Where the hell'd the time go?"

"I don't know." I switched on the lamp next to the bed. "It's eight-thirty."

"Everything's cool." He kissed me on the forehead. "Let's get dressed. Come out to the car with me."

Outside, Aiden, in the driver's seat with the motor running, called to us through the open window. "Can you hurry it up?"

Z led me to the passenger door where I stretched up against him. We shared a long kiss. "Don't forget to come back," I whispered.

"How could I? Now I have someone to come back to." He got in the car, and I stole one last kiss before they backed onto the street, leaving me alone. Where we'd stood smelled of marijuana and recently made love. I breathed it in and watched them turn at the intersection.

I took my time crossing the lawn to the porch then through the front door. Judy motioned me into the kitchen. "Sit and spill your guts," she said. "When did you get back from Phoenix?"

"Last night."

"What's going on with you and Z?"

"I'm not sure where to start. I know I told you nothing was going to happen. How do I tell you everything's happened?"

"Just tell me." The tea kettle whistled, and she poured water into our cups.

The scent of warm rose hips filled my head. I sorted through words and attempted to put them together.

"Look," she said, "I know you've slept with him, but you kept assuring me you were on your own trip, that Z was merely staying until he got it together to make another trip to Acapulco. You told me, more than once, you knew where your head was at, Sylvi. What's the truth?"

I sipped my tea, found my voice and told Judy about all the things Z and I had experienced from Phoenix to the Coronado National Forest.

"I'm sensing there's more to your story," she said.

I told her the rest of it.

"So this is Monday night," she said, "and you're telling me that yesterday you and Z pronounced yourselves some kind of union under God? This is too far out for even you. Are you crazy?" She poured us another cup of tea.

"What can I say?"

"Nothing. There's nothing left for you to say. You've jumped into this with both feet, and God knows where it will end. He's dealing weed, for godsake. What are you thinking?"

"Somebody has to sell it if we're going to smoke it. He's not into smack or speed. I don't think dealing weed is a bad thing."

"No, it's not, but the law says it is illegal. If he gets busted, you get busted right along with him. What would happen to your kids?"

"He's not going to get busted. Don't stir up bad karma." I picked up our cups and put them in the sink.

"You're not going to listen, are you, Sylvi? What happened to your resolve to stay on your own trip?"

"I'm free to pursue whatever I want. He respects my space."

"He spouts violent revolution."

"Yes, he does, but I've seen his softer heart. He cares about people and doesn't want them exploited. He wants justice in the world. I know he'll find the peaceful way."

"You believe he'll change?" She searched my face. "Do you know when he was born?"

"No, but he's Sagittarius."

"Oh, my God, so are you. This will never work."

"Although same signs are usually not compatible," I said, "Sagittarians are more likely to have a successful relationship than any of the others. That's what Ted's astrology book says."

"We can only hope it's true."

I said nothing about Z and Aiden leaving, and we rejoined the gathering in the den where political discussions turned to the Democratic primary being held the next day in California. Our loyalties were split between Eugene McCarthy and Robert Kennedy, except for Syd, who would not desert the Peace and Freedom Party.

"I say we elect somebody who smokes dope. Then they'll make it legal, and we'll all live happily ever after in this great United States of America." Ted passed a joint to Judy.

"Don't we all wish that would happen," she said.

"My brother in New York sent me an underground newspaper," Irish said. "One of the articles talked about Eugene McCarthy and Bobby Kennedy being too co-opted. Sure, they want to end the war, but they're not true radical pacifists—not like Philip Berrigan. He and a few others raided a couple draft boards, poured blood on their files and burned some. No one got hurt, and it made a big statement. He's part of the real resistance, not just some half-assed politician grand-standing for votes. All that notwithstanding, I am voting for Bobby." Irish took a long hit on the joint and closed his eyes.

"Just so we don't get Nixon," Ted muttered.

Since politics was not the first thing on my mind, I went to bed and fell asleep thinking about Z on the road to Acapulco.

The next afternoon, Judy and I met at Pat's house and sat around her oak table. She laid out a Tarot card spread. The reading revealed that, although Z's and my relationship was strong, his occupation would attract oppositional forces.

"We all know what opposes Z's occupation." Judy rolled her eyes.

"Stop it," I said. "I need a little support here."

"We support you," Pat tapped the last card with her fingers. "But the cards don't lie. Sylvi, you've only known him a little while, maybe you could," she paused, "reconsider?"

"Look, if you think I made a careless commitment, you're wrong. Maybe it's not the perfect situation, but what is?"

"Bob has a regular job."

"But you hate it, Pat," I countered. "Since he quit Channel 2 TV news to be the public relations person for one of the worst polluters in El Paso, you've pressured him to get another job."

"I know. But still, the position he's in now is not jeopardizing our family, nor would any position he might take in the future."

"Sure, Judy, and Ted's in school, so he can get a 'safe' job when he gets his degree. Listen to yourselves. We all smoke weed. How would we get it if somebody like Z didn't take the chances?"

"Of course," Judy said, "but you don't have to take the chances along with him. Get out now."

I picked up the cards one by one and stacked them on top of the deck. "You know I can't."

"No. The truth is, you won't. You never take the easy road," Judy lamented. "I know you didn't make a commitment to him lightly—we only wish you had. But no matter what, we'll always stand by you."

When I got home, there were no children and no McKenzie, but Daiquiri jumped in my lap to greet me as I sat down on the piano bench. She put her front paws around my neck and rubbed her whiskers against my ear. Her purring sounded like a small motor. I whispered sweet kitty nothings to her and stroked her long gray fur until she grew bored with affection, hopped from my lap, and wandered into the hallway.

I picked at a tune on the piano and recalled how Rob insisted revolution happens in each of our hearts—that's how peace and change will come. I fished in my purse for a pen and pad and wrote.

Peer through smiling candidate nausea
in search of just one with tears
    for these uncertain times.

Hear war beasts howl through halls
where politicians deal living souls
    from the bottom of the deck.

Here in the desert, my shriveled
spirit squats in cactus shade
    open-mouthed, waiting
    to taste the rains of change.

The doorbell startled me.

"Syd, Irish, come on in. What brings you out so late?"

"Have you heard the primary results?" Syd asked.

"No."

"Bobby won," Irish said, "so we thought we'd come by and celebrate."

"And we wanted to share the grass from Nam. It arrived today." Syd pulled a baggie from his pocket.

As he rolled a joint, Irish flipped on the TV.

"It's after midnight, channels are off the air," I said. "Try the radio."

Irish searched for the acid rock station. "Where's Z?"

"I don't know," I said. "It's not my turn to watch him today."

Syd took a toke on the joint and handed it to me.

"You think this is as good as Z's gold?" He waited as I exhaled.

"Yeah, dynamite." I passed it to Irish.

"Life's kinda freaky." Syd twisted one end of his mustache. "Just a few weeks ago, the city's dried up. Now we got it coming out of our ears." He turned to Irish. "You trying to bogart that thing or can I get a hit?"

The news came on, reporting Kennedy's victory in the primary.

"I know you're not happy with the results, Syd" Irish said, "but I am. I think Kennedy will win in November. He'll get us out of Vietnam."

Syd shrugged. "In November I'm going to vote absentee in California for all the Peace and Freedom Party's candidates. The Democratic Party can go screw itself."

The DJ's voice interrupted the Jefferson Airplanes as they belted out "Don't You Want Somebody To Love." "We just received this news bulletin from Los Angeles." His voice broke. "Bobby Kennedy's been shot at the Ambassador Hotel." After a long pause, he added, "He's reported in critical condition. I'll bring you details as they become available."

The music resumed as we sat in shock. Syd stubbed out the joint and buried his face in his hands.

Irish paced the floor and raged. "Mother fuckers. First they kill King, now Kennedy." He slammed his fist against the wall and yelled profanities.

"They said he was in critical condition, Irish. We don't know yet whether he'll live or die." I tried to comfort him in between my own sobs. Turning, he embraced me and cried.

In the morning, I heard the newspaper thump against the front door. I grabbed it off the porch. The headlines screamed ASSASSINATION.

Bobby Kennedy was dead. At work, people functioned in a state of shock. I wondered if Z had heard.

The weekend arrived. Ted and Judy stopped by. "What will happen to free elections when there are no candidates because they're all too fucking afraid to run?" Ted asked. "Then the guy with the biggest gun will rule?"

Judy put her finger against his lips. "Don't say that stuff."

"What should we say?" he asked. "It's okay? Just go on with life. His brother gets his head blown off five years ago. King gets it in Memphis in April. Now Bobby. Who's next?"

Although I was devastated and had as many questions as Ted, I turned off the TV. The funeral train rolling across the country made my soul ache.

Long, dark days followed the assassination. Throughout the next week and a half, we gathered and bolstered one another's spirits.

McKenzie did not return at the end of two weeks.

My endurance wore thin by Tuesday morning. I called Judy from my office. "Where could they be?" I blurted into the phone. "I'm going nuts this morning trying to work, and thinking about where they are, if they're okay. Are they alive?"

Judy had figured out that Z and Aiden were in Acapulco and confronted me with it a week earlier. "Try to get a grip," she advised. "Calm down before you blow your whole scene. Where's your boss?"

"Out of town, thank God, so I can have a breakdown without any interruption from him. I couldn't sleep last night because I kept listening for Z at the door."

"All I can say to make you feel better is, don't jump to conclusions."

"I'll try."

After struggling through the week and tired of sharing my despair with Judy and Pat, I used my lunch hour to buy Tarot cards and two books on how to interpret them. Since I'd been so crabby all week, no one showed up at my house on Friday night, which left me free to study my new books.

As I read, I found myself drawn into the mystery schools of ancient Egypt and the halls where initiates received the oral traditions of the Kabbalah. The excitement of discovering the origins of the Tarot and how it revealed our journey through life kept me from sleep until the wee hours.

Waking around noon, I continued my studies until the phone ringing intruded in the late afternoon.

"Sylvi, it's Aiden."

My heart burst from my breast. "Where are you? Where is Z?"

"Slow down. I'm okay. That's all I want to say right now."

"And Z?" I persisted. "Where is he?"

"I don't know, and I don't care. Can you pick me up at the Chevron truck stop east of town on I-10?"

"Give me twenty minutes," I said, certain they were playing a joke on me.

From my parking place in front, I could see Aiden through the window sitting in a booth alone. I raced inside.

"You look like hell. What's going on?"

"I'm really pissed," he said, his voice tight and low. "I'd like to kill that fucking Z. He let Miguel talk us into giving a couple of guys a ride to the border. They were into a counterfeit money order scam." He paused to sip his coffee as it began to sink in. Z was not with him. "Hope you have some money," he said, "because I don't have a dime."

"Order whatever you like."

"I told him not to do it. It held us up over a week. We had the grass but had to sit around waiting for these two guys to get their act together. I was getting super paranoid with the whole scene."

"So are you telling me Z is still down there? Where's your car?"

"My car's history." He stared at his reflection in his coffee and fiddled with the spoon. "We'd come up through Saltillo and were on Highway 40 heading for Monterey. I let one of those guys drive. Z and I were half crashed out in the back when that son-of-a-bitching driver says he thinks something's wrong with the engine. He pulls off the road and tells Z to get out and see if there's a wrench in the trunk. Z tells me to stay in the car but, hell, I wasn't about to sit there. I got out behind him, and they took off with the car, the weed, and everything we had."

"Where's Z now?"

"I don't know, don't care. I flagged down a ride and left him there."

Not what I wanted to hear. "Why did Miguel hook you all up with those people?" The waitress brought our food.

Aiden waited for her to leave before answering. "Miguel wheels and deals, facilitates whatever's happening. You know what I mean?"

"No, I don't. I thought he was the contact man into the jungle, the one who dealt direct with the farmer."

"Yeah, he's that and a million other things as well. It makes me dizzy thinking about it. He's like a connection between people who want something and other people who can get it for them. Not just grass, but counterfeit money orders, artifacts, stolen stuff, or anything else."

"Wow, my image of him was much different," I said.

"Mine, too, before."

"But your car. What are you going to do about your car?"

Instead of answering, he fixed his eyes on the door behind me. "I don't believe it," he growled. "Son-of-a-bitch."

McKenzie slid into the booth next to me. "Sorry, baby. I smell like a cattle truck."

I grabbed him and kissed him. "I don't care." When I was able to get it together, I said, "Aiden just filled me in on the trip up to the point where you two separated. What happened?"

"We split up outside Monterey. He got a ride on one truck. Another one picked me up a half hour later. I figured if I got out at the first truck stop once we hit El Paso, I'd call you to pick me up. Lucky for me I didn't have to call. It's been a hell of a trip." He kissed me, but I pulled away, uncomfortable with Aiden glaring at him from across the table.

"Why did you let Miguel talk you into that shit?" Aiden hissed.

"Look, man, we've been over this too many times." Z turned to me. "We caught separate rides because we were about to kill each other." Then addressing Aiden, "Look, I'm sorry about your car."

"I know we've been over it. I want to hear how you're going to explain it to Sylvi."

"It was my bad judgment, pure and simple," Z said. "Miguel was trying to work out a way all of us could get what we wanted. He got our weed for us and asked me if we could stick around to give these other dudes a lift to the border."

"Hell, you were just plain stupid," Aiden shot back. "We'd paid for the weed. We didn't owe him anything. Why didn't you tell him to fuck off?"

"It's a matter of give and take. Since I do business with him on a regular basis, I wanted to help him out this time. Next time it could be me asking the favor."

"Bullshit, what are you going to do about my car being stolen?"

"We both lost everything, but I promise we'll get it straightened out."

"Yeah, how?"

"You guys are exhausted," I said. "Let's figure it out tomorrow. For now, we'll get you home, Aiden."

We drove in silence to Aiden's, but on the way home Z began opening up. "This thing with Aiden bothers me, baby. He was so hipped up on going, tuned up his car, got new tires, and now the damned thing's gone."

"You lost everything, too."

"Yeah, but I can recover it. Aiden just got out of school, lives with his parents. What the hell does he know about life? This is too much for him. Maybe he's got insurance, but whatever, I'll have to split the loss with him." Z laughed without humor. "Sure as hell made a bad judgment call. Not about giving those dudes a lift. That was between Miguel and me, but I flat didn't pick up on the bad vibes they had to be giving off. Look what it cost us."

"People make mistakes."

"In this business, a mistake in judgment could cost you your life. I'm lucky this time. Now I've got to pull things back together."

"What's your plan?" I asked as we arrived home.

"I'm thinking now would be a good time for me to go to San Francisco. I've got a few clothes, books, and papers stashed at my uncle's warehouse. Plus, there's a couple of paychecks there that would help me get to Acapulco again. I could square accounts with people who fronted me money and with Aiden."

"When will you go?" I asked as I ran water in the tub and poured in bubble bath.

"I'll wait another week and make the trip over the Fourth of July weekend if you'll go with me."

"Of course, I'll go." I'd never been to San Francisco.

He lowered himself into the tub. "I'll make some calls, get things lined up."

I lathered shampoo into his hair and scrubbed his back.

"Feels good, baby." He rubbed soap all over his body then ducked his head under the water. "We can stay with my mom," he said, coming up for air. "You can meet her." He let the water run out of the tub.

"Cool, but I thought you and your mom weren't close."

"We're not, but I'm sure she'd be okay with us staying a night."

He turned the faucets on and began refilling the tub.

"Join me?"

Chapter 7
From Haight Street to Points Unknown

The ten days between Z's return and our leaving for San Francisco sped by. We had little time for conversation. But once on the road, McKenzie related that he and Aiden had settled their differences and had decided they would pursue replacing Aiden's car after our return.

"Z, did I tell you why I asked Irish and Syd to watch Daiquiri?"

"Your cat. No, why?"

"Because Judy and Ted left for the Sandia Mountains outside of Albuquerque."

"Why there?"

"One of Ted's friends lives in a commune and is getting married. They wanted to check out the scene—maybe move there later if it's a cool place."

"We're all going to have to head for the mountains soon. The assassinations of King and Kennedy are only the beginning, baby. Revolution is coming."

"Peaceful revolution, Z." I reminded him.

"Full-on, bloody revolution," he yelled, his anger and frustration exploded. "Wake up, Sylvi. Those rubber-stamp bureaucrats and corporate bastards won't know what hit them. The fix was in—Kennedy didn't stand a chance, just like his brother five years ago. But people are fed up. Guns, bombs, whatever it takes, baby. Violence is what those bastards understand. All they give is brutality. Brutality is what they deserve back, wouldn't you say?"

"Z, you know I don't think that way."

His intensity filled the car. I found it hard to breathe. Yet he raged on and off for the next thousand miles. I tried interjecting a reasonable argument for peace, but to no avail. Then I closed my mind and heart to his deafening onslaught—stopped hearing him.

Outside of San Francisco, he got out at his uncle's warehouse and retrieved his belongings, hit the freeway again, and calmed down enough to point out landmarks along the way into the city.

"This is Haight, baby, couple blocks more and it intersects with Ashbury, so you're in the middle of the action." Z pulled to the curb, turned the ignition off, and got out of the VW. "Go check out the scene while I score some weed. I'll meet you back here."

I watched him make his way along the sidewalk, weaving in and out of the crowds. The magic of the life surrounding me drew me from my shut-down cocoon state into full awareness. Photos I'd seen in magazines, newspapers, and bits of TV news coverage did not compare to what I was seeing with my own eyes. People dancing, people walking, people sitting in circles on the sidewalk, and others calling from open second story windows to people below. Short dresses, long dresses all in living color, hair hanging long. Mustaches and beards, bell bottomed jeans and shirts in electric rainbow hues. White turbans and Nehru shirts. Music from Ravi Shankar's sitar floated through the air along with Janis Joplin's blues. Black bodies, white bodies, and brown bodies dressed in vivid patterns and colors moved to the music.

The beauty coaxed me from the car, and I, in my fringed bell-bottoms and midriff top, entered into the dance, sharing their vibe of love, acceptance, celebration. I followed the seductive aroma of incense into a shop. It took a moment for my eyes to adjust to the dim interior. I'd never seen anything like it. Strings of beads hung from hooks in the wall above a table stacked with cotton-print cloth from India. Rolling papers filled a tall basket. Sticks of incense in bundles of sandalwood, patchouli, and frankincense lay on a counter. Above, neatly labeled pints of herbs lined the shelves. I wandered through the room touching everything. Volume laden bookshelves spanned one wall, and I ran my fingertips along the book backs, astrology to Kama Sutra. Turning to my right, I almost bumped into a table on which sat a large water pipe, a hookah. Tarot cards, I Ching sticks, and books on divination lay around it.

As I leafed through one of the Tarot books, a guy finished buying some rolling papers, stuffed them into the pocket of his fatigue jacket, and turned to me. Dark curls framed his bearded face. I looked up into his glazed brown eyes. He flashed a broad smile. "I haven't seen you in here before. You into the cards?" He nodded toward the book I held.

"Yeah. Mine are back home in El Paso."

"Texas?" he asked. "What brings you here?"

"My old man's from here. We just drove out to pick up his things."

"They call me John Brown," he said. "What's your name?"

"Sylvi. Do they call you John Brown after the...?"

"Yes, after that John Brown. I tend to fight impossible battles. Not physical battles, but ones in the spirit world."

"Far out," I said. "Are you a warlock?"

"You could call me that. Here let me show you." He pulled a deck of cards from his pocket, and laid seven, face down, in a straight line on the table.

"Are you going to be staying here very long?" he asked.

"No, we're on our way to Sausalito. I'm going to meet my old man's mom tonight. Tomorrow we head back to Texas."

"Turn over every other card starting with the first one." He pointed to it with a grimy index finger.

I turned them over, and he studied the four laying face up. "Be very cautious when confronted with conflict this evening. Don't get drawn into it. Maintain a peaceful heart." He picked up the three cards laying face down and put them in his pocket. "I'll keep these separate from the rest of the deck."

"What will you do with them?" I asked.

"Later tonight when problems arise for you, I'll look at them and help you."

"How will you know if anything's wrong?"

"I'll know. All things are directed by divine plan. Do you have a place to stay?"

"I think so," I said, still absorbing the things he'd just told me.

"If you should need a place, look for the biggest tree in the park down the street. I live under it. You and your old man are welcome to crash there."

"That's really cool. Thanks."

"I've got to go check on some friends. Stay peaceful." He hugged me and went out the door whistling.

I touched the table where the cards had lain and wondered what kind of conflict was coming. Picking up another of the Tarot books, I opened it and found illustrations, descriptions, astrological significances, and interpretations filling each page.

The girl behind the register looked up from the book she was reading and smiled at me. A red headband of coarsely woven cloth kept her long, dark hair from falling into her face. Strings of beads rested against her paisley blouse.

"Hi." She leaned against the counter. "You've chosen the best book I've ever read on the Tarot."

"I kind of vibed to it." She rang up two dollars and fifty cents and gave me change.

"Peace," she said, closing the register drawer.

"Peace." I floated out the door, smiling, met Z by the car, and gave him a long, delicious kiss.

"Let's get going." He seemed uptight. "I don't want to get caught in the July Fourth traffic. You look happy, what did you buy?"

I showed him the book, and as we headed to Sausalito, told him about the store and John Brown. He had little to say in response and squinted against the sun as it dropped into the ocean.

Once we hit the traffic jam, he yelled, "Son of a bitch," cut the engine, and got out of the car. Ignoring me, he perched on the trunk of the VW, his knees drawn up against his chest, his back resting against the windshield.

I got out. "Might as well relax if we're stuck here." I leaned against the front fender.

In the cool, damp evening, a whole July Fourth scene unfolded before us. Hundreds streamed toward the entrance of a park for a fireworks display. Families carrying babies, ice chests, and blankets threaded their way through the cars. Flower children in patched jeans, long skirts, and floppy hats happily inhabited the scene as we waited for the street to clear. McKenzie, coming down off amphetamines he'd dropped so he could drive through the night, was short-tempered. I, on the other hand, loved the swirl of life around us.

Passersby, noticing our Texas license plates and the mural of pyramids Z had painted on one side of the car, stopped and chatted. They wanted to know what was happening in Texas. I talked with them. Z sat rigid and silent.

"This is absolutely cool," I said to him.

"It would be a hell of a lot cooler if we could get on down the road."

I hoped for his sake we'd soon be moving. As for me, I didn't care if we stayed all night.

The light from the living room glinted off Elise's blonde hair as she stood in her open door with her arms around Z. The top of her head reached his chin. "It's so good to see you, son. Heavens, it's almost ten o'clock."

"This is Sylvi, Mom."

She smiled at me, radiating a calm sweetness.

"I'm happy to meet you, Mrs. Raintree," I said and shook her hand.

"Please call me Elise. Come in and sit down. You two must be exhausted. Would you like coffee? Have you eaten? You must have been caught in terrible traffic."

"Yeah, we sat for over an hour. Makes me glad I don't live here anymore," Z said.

"Where are you living now? Wait, don't tell me. Let me get things from the kitchen. I'll be back in a minute." She disappeared through an arched doorway. "Make yourselves comfortable. But please excuse the mess," she called. "I just moved in a few days ago."

"What mess?" I asked Z. "Looks pretty together to me."

"Not for her," he said. "See the one painting leaning against the wall waiting to be hung? To her that's a mess."

We sat on a white brocade sofa opposite a red brick fireplace. I noticed the intricately carved oak accent tables and two large pastoral watercolors in ornate frames hanging on opposite walls. Behind us, a tall window draped in elegant lavender fabric looked out at the city lights below the apartment. "This is quite a place," I said.

"I guess. When you're a rich man's mistress, you can make out pretty good."

His statement puzzled me, but Elise returned at that moment.

She set a tray of small sandwiches and coffee on the table in front of us. "Please, help yourselves," she said, sitting down in a French provencial chair upholstered in purple velvet.

"Thank you," I said. "You're very kind. These look really yummy."

She smiled. "So, McKenzie, back to my question. Where are you living now?"

"I'm living in El Paso with Sylvi. We came up here to pick up my things from my dear uncle's warehouse." He said dear uncle with sarcasm. "We'll be heading back tomorrow."

"What kind of work is there in El Paso?" Her voice pleasant, her eyes kind.

Z picked up the china coffee cup but ignored the sandwiches. He rose from the couch, moved across the room to the fireplace, and sat on his haunches on the hearth.

"I'm dealing marijuana, Mother," he said.

She drew in a quick breath and glanced at me. It surprised me he would deliberately challenge her. "What?" she asked. I'm sure she hoped she'd misunderstood.

"Marijuana, Mother. I buy it in Acapulco and sell it here in the States."

Her blue eyes widened. Her carefully done hair did not move as she shook her head. "You can't be serious, son."

"I'm not laughing, am I? You know how you always taught us to respect authority? I've come to realize there is no authority that deserves my respect."

"I can't believe what I'm hearing. Sylvi, do you understand him?"

Well aware his antagonism stemmed, for the most part, from the speed wearing off, I wanted to be supportive. "I do understand him, Elise." Keeping my voice soft, I attempted an explanation. "McKenzie and I have come to question many things. We can't continue feeding into a system that denies civil rights and sends men to die in an illegal war. How can we respect leaders who not only allow these atrocities but actually cause them?"

Before she could respond, Z asked, "What do you know about American business in foreign countries, Mother?"

"I know we have oil and agricultural interests," she said.

"But do you know how those interests intrude on other cultures and exploit the natives of those countries?"

"Oh, McKenzie, why do you have to be so negative? Don't you think we're helping them economically?"

"Helping," he spit the word from his crouched position on the hearth. "You think that working people to death and paying them a pittance of a wage is helping them? The ones who profit are their fat cat government officials we pay to do business. The people don't see the money. We're not helping anybody. We're continuing in the tradition of corruption, exploitation, and greed. Only we're brainwashed to call ourselves the good guys. Millions of upstanding citizens like you eat up the propaganda because it allows you to live in comfort without feeling bad about it."

"I think that's a rather distorted view." She ran her hands over the knees of her slacks as though smoothing her wrinkled dignity. "I read the papers, watch the news on TV. I've heard all the rhetoric. I've seen the riots and the flower children, but I think those are just kids who aren't willing to buckle down and work hard. You were doing so well after you came home from the army, McKenzie. I don't understand what's happened to you."

"You don't understand?" he thundered. "How can you not understand? Your generation tried to sell us out, tried to make us think we lived in some kind of perfect world. You know, look the other way, don't rock any boats. Did you think you could hide Dad's brutality?"

Her mouth fell open. She raised her hand, palm outward, to silence him, but he continued to rage. "You don't remember Dad kicking me around, kicking you around? Why am I all of a sudden angry? I've been angry all my life, but it's not acceptable, is it? Fuck acceptable. Do you realize there are a lot of people who are as fed up with the bullshit as I am?"

I glanced from her perplexed face to Z, snarling and poised on the hearth like a panther ready to pounce. His eyes flashed, and I silently prayed for God to get us out of there.

"McKenzie," Tears dampened her cheeks, "I tried."

"Tried what? Where were you when I was in all those fucked up foster places?"

"I came to see you, but most of the time you refused to see me. What was I supposed to do?" Mascara melted around her eyes. She dabbed at it with a napkin.

"I'm sorry, Elise," I said. "He's driven straight through, and he's tired. The traffic jam upset him." I turned to Z. "Can't you forgive each other?"

"My God, Sylvi, are you on her side? What the hell do you know about anything?" He rose slowly to his full height and glared at me. I'd never seen him like that and could only attribute it to coming down off speed.

"It's all right, dear." Elise said. "I do love you, McKenzie."

"Too late for that, Mom, not that it matters."

"Z, let it go." I crossed the room, grabbed his hand, and pulled him toward the door. He jerked it open and nudged me out.

"I'm sorry, Elise," I called as we descended the stairs to the car.

The tires squealed as he backed into the street. "I'm really impressed with the way you took her side," he snapped.

"I didn't take her side. I was trying to calm everybody down. You're so fucked up on speed I don't think you realize what you're saying."

"Speed or no speed I always know what I'm doing." We stopped at a light. Its red glow illuminated the anger distorting his face. "Is that the way it is, baby? You doubt me when things get heavy?"

I tried to reason with him, but he was beyond reason. "Where are we going to spend the night?"

"I don't give a fuck where we spend this or any other night," he said and drove through dark streets for a long time before coming to a stop on a cliff overlooking the ocean. He grabbed the sleeping bag and a blanket from the backseat, and got out of the car. I trailed him through the tall, cold grass until he halted, spread the sleeping bag out, and sprawled across it. I stretched out beside him, covered us both with the blanket, and watched him close his eyes. He fell asleep.

Sleep would not embrace me. Instead, I listened to the waves crashing below us, and the foghorns calling to each other in the dark—unfamiliar sounds to someone from the desert. The clanging of a bell echoed in the fog and blew away on the wind. The salt air bathed my senses. W*hat had happened at Elise's place? I can not reconcile it with the Mecca of love and peace I looked forward to visiting. What did I expect? Certainly not the raging bull I've encountered. I blame part of it on the speed, but it spewed from a deeply wounded place in him. A part I'm not sure I want to know.*

Restless and thrashing about in his sleep, he pulled the blanket off me. The damp ground and cold wind forced me back to the car where I curled up in the back seat. Remembering John Brown, I wished I could walk away from this cliff, find his tree, and sleep under it. He had cautioned me not to get caught in conflict, to stay peaceful and everything would come down according to divine plan. *Was he, even now, pulling out the last card and wrapping my heart carefully in a spell to ensure peace and hope for tomorrow? What will I do if Z is still raging when he wakes up?* I took slow, deep breaths, accepted the peaceful heart offered me by John Brown, and slept.

I woke to Z's voice and the sun filtering through the fog. "I owe you an apology, Sylvi." With the car door open, he sat sideways in the passenger seat looking at me curled up on the backseat. "I can't explain any of it," he said. His face gray, his eyes dull. "I'm sorry."

"There's a part of you I don't know, Z. It frightens me."

"Scares me, too, baby. I wanted to talk to my mother and tell her where my head's at. Then everything began exploding, and I couldn't stop."

He climbed into the backseat next to me and fell asleep. *Would his apology be an end to the storm?* I crept out of the car and picked my way through the tall grass to the edge of the cliff. Great waves broke on the rocks below. Foam flew against a foggy sky then settled back into the open sea.

An hour later, I stood outside the car brushing my hair. When I glanced in the window, I noticed Z stirring. He patted the blanket next to him, and his eyes flew open. "Sylvi, where are you?"

"Right here." I opened the door. "Where did you think I was?"

"I thought you'd left me." He climbed from the backseat and crushed me in his embrace. The breeze chilled our faces while the sun struggled to defeat the fog.

"I wish I could help you let go of all the hate and hurting. I'm afraid it will destroy what we've found together, and I love you so much." I kissed him.

His eyes, no longer dull, met mine and said things only my heart could hear. "I'm afraid of that, too, but I won't let it."

All the questions I longed to ask fell away. I knew I would always live in his embrace.

Noontime found us checking out the scene on Telegraph Avenue as we walked toward the U. C. Berkeley campus. Like Haight Street and the traffic jam, the atmosphere was loose and friendly. Arriving at Sproul Plaza on campus, we stood at the outer edge of a small gathering. About fifty people stood in a semi-circle around a black man. His hair formed a great dark halo around his mustached face.

Being at the back of the crowd made it hard to hear every word he said, but his voice increased in volume when he referred to Stop the Draft Week.

"Last fall," he said, "was only a beginning. Not only does the war machine have to be stopped, but its death grip on the community has to be severed. We don't want military recruiters on our campus. We don't want them in our city."

A murmur of agreement went through the crowd, and he continued. "The draft board in Oakland is still operating, but we can stop it. Any of you who want to know more, step forward so we can get organized."

A dozen people stepped toward him. Others hung back discussing what he'd said. "My brother got his notice," a girl next to us said. "I'll do anything to stop him from going to this horrible war." She moved toward the speaker.

I squeezed Z's hand. "Wow, I'm amazed I'm standing right here. This isn't a news clip from TV, this is real. You'd never see anything like it at the university back home."

"Berkeley's the most radical of the U. C. schools. They're way ahead on stopping the war, civil rights, free speech, you name it."

"This is too cool."

"It may be, Sylvi, but I'm hungry. I want to take you to a soul food place over in Oakland. My dad and I used to go there sometimes when I worked for him."

"Can't we hang out here for a little while longer? I wish I lived here and could be involved in all this."

"Maybe it's not all you think it is." He steered me away from the gathering.

"But it's better than doing nothing," I persisted as we left campus. "What was Stop the Draft Week about?"

"Anti-war groups came together last fall to demonstrate at the recruiting office in Oakland and shut it down. They made their point, but the recruiters are still operating. Judging by the meeting back there in Sproul Plaza, they're revving up to do it again."

The double doors of the Ribs Joint opened onto a street corner. Neatly kept but modest homes lined the block in either direction. Small children played in some of the yards, and a few people strolled along the sidewalk in the July heat. Three black men, all dressed in blue shirts and black pants, stood in front of the restaurant talking with passersby.

As we walked across the street, Z said, "Hey, I know those guys."

One of the three men stepped forward. "Z." He gave McKenzie's hand a hearty shake. "Man, I can't believe it's you. Your old man told me he didn't know where you were when I saw him a few weeks ago. What's happening?"

"I been out of town, brother. This is my woman, Sylvi. Sylvi, meet Luke." We shook hands, and he introduced me to the two with him. They had a dozen or so newspapers clasped under their arms.

"I tell you, Z, when your pop told me he hadn't seen you since January, I wondered if you were dead. What the hell you mean, you been out of town?"

"I hitched down to Acapulco, Luke. Quit working for my pop, my uncle, the fucking steel mill. Quit all of it. Got to where I ran in circles. Made no sense. You know what I mean."

"I hear what you're saying, brother. But you should stay. Things are happening here."

"Come in and eat with us. I wanted to bring Sylvi here, wanted her to taste real barbeque."

"Shit, you want real barbeque? You got to come to my house. Although the brother here does put out a good spread."

Luke came inside with us, but his two friends declined, saying they wanted to finish selling their papers. Z bought one.

A black man with closely cropped, graying hair greeted us. He remembered Z. "Your daddy was in here a couple weeks back. Good to see you, son. You all want ribs with all the fixings?"

"That's what we're here for. Only been in town for a day, but I had to bring my woman by to taste your ribs." He introduced me to the old man.

With a gracious sweep of his arm, he said, "You all just sit down here in this booth." He turned and disappeared into the kitchen.

The three of us scooted in. Z read aloud the newspaper's banner, "The Black Panther." I haven't seen one of these since Stop the Draft Week."

"The week the paper got rolling. After that things heated up when we started the Free Huey campaign. You know his trial starts in a little over a week. What do you think will happen, brother?" Luke asked.

I didn't know who Huey was or why he was on trial but thought if I listened, I'd find out.

"I've been gone too long. Don't have a feel for the word on the street. Can't say how it will go down," Z said. "A lot's happened this year. Heard something about a shoot-out between Eldridge and the cops. Eldridge Cleaver," Z said to me, "is the dude who wrote *Soul On Ice*. I've got the book. You'll have to read it when we get home."

"Where you call home now?" Luke asked.

"Somewhere between Acapulco, El Paso, and here, brother. You might say my job keeps me on the road."

"I can dig it. Only one commodity I know comes out of Acapulco."

The old man emerged from the kitchen carrying a big round tray. We stared through hungry eyes at the feast he set before us. Bowls of black-eyed peas and collard greens, an iron skillet of corn bread, a great platter of ribs.

"Think you folks can handle this?" he asked, and plopped a pile of napkins in the middle of the table.

"Thanks, we'll do our best," Z said then returned the conversation to Eldridge as we began filling our plates.

"It happened two days after Martin Luther King was assassinated in April. The whole country was rioting," Luke said, scooping up a piece of cornbread. "The Panthers were trying to keep order here. Then as luck would have it, the brothers needed to transport some weapons from one place to another. Once they came to a stop, the cops opened fire, and the brothers returned it and scattered. They hadn't figured on the whole fucking police force turning out. Tear gas, shooting went on for almost two hours."

"We never heard about it in Texas," I said.

Luke helped himself to more greens before resuming his story. "The cops' fire power was so heavy that the empty shed Eldridge and Little Bobby took cover in caught fire. They ran out into the street. The long and the short of it is, the pigs killed Little Bobby. Eldridge was shot up, and they sent him to the prison hospital in Vacaville. They were going to revoke his parole, but just last month a judge cut him loose pending trial."

"The Panther Party's got their share of troubles, my friend." Z loaded more ribs on his plate. "My hope is Huey gets a fair trial. You say it starts next week?"

"The fifteenth," Luke said. "We've got a good lawyer."

Through the conversation that continued over second and third helpings, I discovered Huey Newton was a young black student who carried a law book, the *Red Book of Chairman Mao*, and a gun. He inspired a following to do the same. Two or three of them would patrol the black neighborhoods of Oakland to observe the action of the police. If the pigs stopped a sister or brother on the street, the Panthers pulled alongside to make sure the bust went down legally and without brutality. They carried their weapons openly, declaring their right to defend themselves against racist pigs.

The other two brothers joined us, and the old man brought

coffee. They explained to me why Huey was on trial. "Huey and another brother were riding night patrol one night last fall. Two pigs stopped them. Huey defended himself. In the struggle, their guns went off. The officer died. Huey was gut shot. Some brothers got him to a hospital, didn't think he'd live. He was treated and arrested for murder. Since then, he's led the Party from jail."

"We recently started a free breakfast program for kids," Luke said. "We got free legal and medical programs in the making, and there's another chapter of the Party starting in L.A."

Z paid the bill, and we talked on until the late afternoon sun blazed through the restaurant windows.

"Now is the time to be alive." Luke drained his cup. "I'm telling you we're going to turn it all around, brother." He took note of the time. "We got to get back to headquarters."

"Sure was a stroke of luck to run into you," Z said. "We appreciate all the news."

"You two better get your asses back here if you want to help write this page in revolutionary history," Luke called after us.

Z opened my car door. I waved. "We'll see where life takes us. Good meeting you."

In the car, Z pulled two joints from his cigarette pack, handed one to me, and leaned across the emergency brake to light it. Our eyes met as I inhaled. "That was a lot more than barbeque." Smoke trailed my words.

"Yeah, it was." He lit his own, started the motor, and pulled out into the early Friday evening traffic.

Cars whizzed by, blurs of color in slow motion. The yards backing up to the freeway invited me in, into some safe gathering of friends where no one spoke of guns or revolution. I settled back in my seat and smoked without talking.

I wanted to tell Z I admired the Panthers for their community programs. I liked Luke and his friends, all good men. I mentally sorted through the good I could accept and the violence I couldn't. This journey to the Mecca of peace and love had blown me away. Who was I, and how did I fit into creating a better world? What about my own little world, the one I'd taken Z into and found myself loving him so completely? Stay peaceful, John Brown had said, but my spirit thrashed about in turmoil. "Could we go back to Haight Street?" I asked.

"We're headed out of town, baby. Going to Nevada where I was born. There's got to be someplace I belong. It's sure not here."

"I was just asking myself where I belonged, too," I said.

"What did you come up with?"

"I want to be part of everything. Plan, organize, march, you know, be out on the front lines making things happen. At the same time, I want to be still and listen to my spirit, learn from the Creator and creation. I want to chronicle it all, too. I want us to usher in the Age of Aquarius, dancing at the gates, inviting the enlightened in."

"Whoa, you're losing me. You're out there again, baby. The enlightened? Who the hell are they? Who the hell are we? It's a funny thing, baby, maybe the only place we belong is together. I don't know about you, but it sounds good to me."

"Mmm." I leaned my head against his shoulder.

Darkness blotched the golden hills then swallowed them as we drove into it, following our car lights along the black pavement.

We drove toward the Nevada border, and I talked about my trips on peyote. He talked about dropping acid in San Francisco and how crazy he'd been to do it in the middle of the city. Our conversation moved from past to present. We both agreed San Francisco had left us shaken. Z had not resolved his differences with his mother. Even after six months away from his family, dropping acid, smoking dope, and finding love, he could not leave his anger behind. He'd not even tried to contact his father when we were in the city. Their relationship, he explained, was more hopeless than the one with his mother.

"The single most significant event of our San Francisco trip for me was running into John Brown," I said. "He alone, out of everything else, shone a light along my path. The activists, be they students, Panthers, or others, call to me, and I truly want to be a part of a peaceful revolution. But my spirit can't respond to them completely."

We stayed the night in Nevada and were back on the road by midmorning. "I'd like to spend some time here," Z said, scanning the rough terrain surrounding us, "but we don't have time this trip."

"Since we're going through Phoenix, do we have time to stop there, just two hours or so? I want to see the girls."

"I can't deny you that."

We stopped at a service station on the outskirts of the city. I used the pay phone to call Carl. I asked him if we could come by and take the girls to a nearby park.

"We?" he asked. "Is that hippie guy with you? What's his name?"

"You mean McKenzie. Yes he is."

Carl dismissed my request. "This is not a good time. You should have called before you hit town."

"I'm sorry, poor planning on my part, Carl, but I'll never forgive myself if I don't see them. We're so close."

" Don't know if we'll be here, but you can come by." He hung up.

When we arrived, I found him irritable and uncooperative. "You can't see them." A mean smile twisted his mouth. "If you'd let me know earlier, maybe."

"I'm sorry. I don't mean to be inconsiderate, but just two hours. One hour, if you like," I persisted. The girls heard my voice and came running from the backyard. I knelt and wrapped one in each arm.

"Are we going home, Mommy?" Katrina shouted.

"Are we?" Kristi asked with less exuberance.

"You're not going anywhere," Carl growled.

"You're not going home right now," I said to the girls. "I've asked your dad if I could take you to the park and then get some ice cream."

"Can we, Daddy?" They chimed together. "Please, please?"

Above their heads, Carl glared down at me. I smiled. "I'll have them back in a couple hours. Promise." I hugged them both to me and looked up at Carl as though I were oblivious to his ugliness.

"All right," he grumped. "But if they're not back here in two hours, you can bet I'll call the sheriff."

I took their hands and hurried them to the car where Z waited.

"He must be drinking," I remarked, careful not to let the girls hear as they settled into the backseat.

Once at the park, we played in the summer heat until sweat ran from our faces and soaked our clothes. Then we found an air-conditioned ice cream parlor and stuffed ourselves on sundaes.

In exactly two hours, I kissed them goodbye at Carl's front door. They ran through the gate to the backyard. "You and what's-his-name get off my property, Sylvi. Now."

Z, noticing my tears as I got into the car, asked, "Are you going to be okay?"

"Sure." I sniffed. "But I don't like them being around him when he's drunk and disagreeable. The custody agreement says they spend the summer with him, and that's that. Guess I can take comfort knowing they'll be home in six weeks."

We drove straight on through to El Paso. A note tacked to the kitchen door greeted us. It read, "Where are you? Please call me as soon as you get home. It's important. I'm at Bob and Pat's. Love, Judy."

Z carried the suitcase, blankets and his things from the car. I dialed Pat's number.

"Hello." Came the sleepy answer.

"Judy?"

"Thank god, you're home. Where were you?"

"We went to San Francisco to pick up Z's clothes and stuff—just got back and found your note. What's going on?"

"It's complicated." Her voice broke. "Ted and I are not together anymore."

"Why, Judy? What happened?"

"Can I tell you tomorrow, Sylvi? I'm so bummed, not to mention too tired to tell the story again today."

"Sure, tomorrow. Are you all right?"

"I'm not going to shoot myself, if that's what you mean. Bob and Pat are here. Like I said, it's complicated."

"I'm so sorry, Judy. What can I do?"

"Just be there in the morning. I'll see you then." We hung up.

"What's up with Judy?" Z asked, shedding his clothes in the bedroom.

"She's coming by in the morning to fill me in. Remember how they went to those mountains outside Albuquerque for a wedding?"

"Yeah, I remember."

"She and Ted broke up. She's bummed and exhausted."

"Did she say why they split?"

"No. She'll tell me tomorrow." I shook my head. "This has been the strangest trip, Z. I went to San Francisco to find peace, and Judy went to the mountains to deepen her connection to Ted. Neither one of us found what we were looking for, did we?"

He put his arms around me. "After all I've put you through, I'm thankful we're still together."

We stretched out on the bed. I reached for his hand. "Do we ever know for sure what tomorrow holds?"

Chapter 8

Following the Road

Judy arrived the next morning in tears. "Ted's friend got married." She pulled herself together. "A beautiful wedding, we gathered in a meadow full of wild flowers. All of us sat in a circle around the couple. They promised to respect each other's space and care about each other's dreams. His best man played guitar and sang. The ceremony inspired Ted. He started mentioning marriage to me."

"Your reply?"

"I found it difficult to keep my feet on the ground what with the fragrant wind through the pines, but I managed to play it down. I know I'm not ready to marry anybody, Sylvi, but Ted is one of those special men who can love you just the way you are. He's made me see I'm an asset to humanity when I've felt like a liability.

"A few days after the wedding, we start hanging out with this tall brunette, a potter, who had lived in the community for a few months. I loved being around her, a very cool lady." Judy looked away.

"Let me guess, Ted loved being around her, too." I said.

"Sadly, yes. Two nights before we planned to come home, he tells me he's falling out of loving me deeply. He cherishes me, and the time we shared, and nothing will ever diminish it. Then he confesses he is entranced with this lovely potter person. She has a name, but I can't say it this morning." She pressed a tissue to her face. "Then he tells me he knows she will be the love of his life."

"No shit. What did you do?"

"I felt like I'd just been hit in the gut, but I managed automatic responses. I nodded, muttered um-hums, and said I understood. We ended the evening agreeing he should take his things to her house. After he left, I cried and packed my suitcase. I wanted to sleep. I wanted to be angry. I couldn't do either, so I got in the car and drove home."

"Without saying goodbye?"

"I wasn't coherent enough to say anything, but my head cleared on the way home. In the midst of heartbreak, I experienced intermittent bursts of exuberant freedom. After all, I didn't want to marry him. I just wanted to love him."

"I wish I had the words to make you feel better." I enclosed her in my arms.

"You know me, Sylvi, Scorpio that I am, I try hard not to be vengeful, but I usually am."

"Yes."

"This morning I don't feel a shred of vengeance in me. You know where I'm at right now?"

"Where?"

"Realizing he's the same great guy he was before. He's just changed lovers. I'll probably feel good about it once I'm able to get through the initial separation." Her lip trembled again. "Haven't I moved beyond this kind of painful detachment?"

"Matters of the heart are matters of the heart, Judy. I can imagine how awful I'd feel if Z decided to change lovers, as you so delicately put it."

After I saw Judy off and came back in the house, I heard Z in the shower. "Mind if I come in?"

I joined him and related what Judy had shared with me.

"Pretty rough. How's she taking it?"

We let warm water run down our backs. "It's tough for her, but she says they're still friends."

In the bedroom, he caught my hand. "I'd rather be friends and lovers."

"Me too."

The Tuesday night following our return from San Francisco, McKenzie stopped the VW in front of the bus station in Juarez. With the money from the paychecks he'd recovered from his uncle's warehouse, he was making a run to Acapulco.

"Are you sure you want to take the bus down?" I asked as he reached across the emergency brake and kissed me.

"I'm fine with it, baby. When I get back, I can square accounts with Aiden and the people who fronted me money before."

I gave him a long, positive kiss. "Call me the minute you get back. I'll come get you."

"You bet I will." He grabbed his duffel from the backseat. "See you in ten days. I love you, baby."

He disappeared inside the terminal. I pulled out into traffic. Of course, I'd known Z planned to go. But that knowledge did not equate with my being comfortable with it. He faced the risks. I faced the waiting.

To occupy my mind, I focused on my work and spent more time with Judy as she recreated her life without Ted. I stopped by her apartment one afternoon after work to find her at her easel, brush and pallet in hand.

She splashed a streak of bright yellow across the canvas and said, "Instead of feeling lonely, I'm becoming acquainted with someone I lost as a child."

"Who?"

"Me."

We considered who we'd been as children, both from hard-working, conservative families—conservative, not politically, but in the way we lived quiet, simple lives.

"We weren't abused," I said. "My mom and dad thought I was cute when I spent hours, and days performing fairy tales for the cow, calf, and piglets on my grandma's farm. They laughed and said I'd be an actress when I grew up."

And so the time passed. But when night fell on the eleventh day of Z's absence, I became anxious for his safety and decided to distract myself by holing up in my room where I dropped a black beauty with the intention of writing poetry all night. The speed walked up my spine like fingers, and gripped the back of my neck. My mind began to fly above life, viewing situations with a clarity only the drug could bring. An hour later, the phone rang.

"Pick me up, baby."

"I'll be there," I said, wondering how I would manage the bridge, high on speed.

Z waved as I stopped at the curb. He opened the passenger door and threw his duffels in the back. "I'll drive," he said.

Street urchins clamored around the car as I made my way through them to the passenger side. Z dug in his pockets and passed out coins to the small, outstretched hands. Once behind the wheel, he leaned across and kissed me. "Sure is good to see you, baby."

"You, too, I was beginning to worry."

He merged into traffic. "Worrying is not allowed."

"Okay, but I do have a question. How are we getting this weed across the river?"

He lit two joints and handed me one. "We're going to drive to the outskirts of town and pack all the gold under the back seat. Then we'll drive across the bridge. No problem."

One toke on the joint and the streetlights radiated colors. *How am I going to maintain with the combination of speed and grass in my system? No choice. I can do what has to be done.*

We left downtown Juarez behind and drove through an outlying area. Shacks dotted the roadside. Z stopped the car beyond a well-lit electrical substation. We got out.

"We're off the road here but have enough light. Keep a watch, baby." He jerked the backseat loose, laid it upside down on the ground and started stuffing the packages of marijuana from his duffel bags in between the springs.

The shadows cast by the substation lights made patterns of ever-changing colors. I struggled to determine reality from hallucination. Then I spotted the three Christmas trees moving toward us. *How can I tell him? Christmas trees?* I narrowed my eyes and watched them. As the trees came closer, they changed into a mother and two children walking alongside the road. *Harmless enough. Thank God.*

Z loaded the backseat into the car. "Push that end down, baby."

I pressed with all my strength until it snapped into place. I looked across at him. "No one will ever know."

"Hold that thought. Hop in."

"I wish we could become invisible, rise in the air and fly across the border." I started to sweat.

"Take a deep breath, and pretend we're your average couple who's been in Juarez for a few drinks. Or, you're married and I'm your lover, and we came over here to shack up or something."

"Oh, aren't you funny. Shack up. I think I'd rather not in Juarez."

"See, you're relaxing." He patted my knee. "That's key to getting across the bridge."

As we declared our citizenship, I wondered how the U.S. customs agent could hear our voices above the pounding of my heart. He grunted and waved us through.

The end of July found McKenzie and me in an *au revoir*-embrace on the tarmac at the El Paso International Airport. A suitcase designed to fit in the overhead racks rested between our feet. Another bag hung from his shoulder. He was flying to San Francisco to sell some of his Acapulco gold. We stood at the foot of the steps leading up to the door of the plane. The stewardess gently reminded us it was time for him to board.

Walking back through the terminal, the recollection of Danny's departure, like a vague dream, rushed through my heart. But now there were no tears and no bottle of scotch under the seat—nor was there a car wreck.

Safely at home, I wrote:

Dry hot summer wind
blows yesterday away.
No more tears or fears
Of giving and taking love.

Dry hot summer wind
blows adventures of Now
Of stars above a desert bed,
tangled wet grass atop a San Francisco cliff.
Of Tarot card revelations,
the waking of my spirit.
Of weed and incense, gentle faces,
talk of assassination-sorrow.
Of political philosophies
and the changing of the guard.

I embrace Now.
Now is real.
Taking and giving love.

No more tears and fears.
Yesterday is blown away
by dry hot summer wind.

July turned into August. Two familiar questions gnawed at my gut. How much longer could my spirit survive in a world where money and possessions dictated life? When could I let go and how?

A great, unseen hand tossed August like a late summer salad. While Z made another trip to Acapulco, Judy met Gary, a drummer in a band. She sat at a club one night, with friends, not expecting to meet anyone new. The band took a break and Gary sat down beside her. Something connected during their conversation, and he never made it to Juarez. He told her later that he'd been disillusioned with his life and had planned, after the band played its final set, to go across the river to a shooting gallery. He thought heroin might be the only thing left to try. Instead, he met her. She, and not smack, changed the course of his life. Soon after their meeting, they came by my house and she introduced him—a tall, large-eyed man with a keen sense of humor. Laughter rolled from under his broad, bushy mustache. Wild brown curls topped his moon face. I liked him instantly.

The Republican Convention took place the first part of August in Florida. At the time, it seemed harmless enough except, of course, for the nomination of Nixon for their presidential candidate. We knew he was not harmless.

Also in August, I heard that Kurt had married the daughter of an Episcopalian minister. He and I first experienced the peyote together, followed by the heavenly hand strumming the telephone wire guitar strings at the riverbank. I felt close to him. I never met his wife. He dropped out of sight after their wedding, chose a safer route than the rest of us.

Then in mid-August, Judy, Gary, Aiden, Irish, and Syd gathered in my den smoking. I read aloud the first letter I'd received from Pablo since he left for Vietnam in the spring.

> Dear Sylvi and all you people I love,
> I wanted to write sooner, but words would not
> come. It's a hot wet morning. I'd follow that
> with wish you were here, but I'm glad you're not.
> They've got weed here that's off the charts.
> Better than I ever imagined. But then reality
> sets in. If you get really fucked up on it,
> you could very likely get yourself killed.
> Or worse, get your buddies killed. The jungle
> is treacherous. I've been soaked in the blood
> of dying men, just trying to drag them to safety.
> You don't know where the mines are, and you
> can't see the enemy. At least, I'm told it's
> the enemy out there. I personally feel our
> enemy is our own government. And I hate writing
> this bummer of a letter, but I can't write it
> to my mom, God knows, and I've got to let
> someone know what's going on. The longing in
> my gut is for us all to live in peace, but the
> big wigs, whoever they are, have their own
> agendas. I'm just a pawn here with a lot of
> other pawns that are going to get blown away.
> I hang on to the hope that I'll see you all again.
> Think of me on my surfboard down in San Diego,
> not in this hellhole. And, Sylvi, if I never

> get a chance to tell you in person, I have to tell you this morning. I love you and carry you with me. Gotta go. The shelling is getting closer. Peace, friends. Pablo

"I feel like shit," Syd said to Irish. "We're looking at getting out of the Army in February, and Pablo may not even see February, or tomorrow, for that matter. Fuck, he may be in a body bag while we're reading his letter."

"Don't say that, Syd." I swallowed back my tears. "He said to think of him on his surfboard, and I'm trying. I remember him telling me how the waves arcing above him looked like the ceiling of a cathedral, water like stained glass, red, yellow, purple against the sun."

"It's not like we can do anything now. We should have kidnapped him and gone AWOL when we had the chance." Irish bowed his head.

"I didn't know the dude," Gary said. "But I can really feel for him.

"I knew him," Judy said. "Remember when we went to the Eric Burdon and the Animals concert at the Coliseum? A far-out night, then he shipped out the next morning."

Wanting to escape the heaviness, I withdrew to the kitchen, poured a cup of coffee, and gazed into the black liquid, wishing it was a crystal ball. *Thinking of him on a surfboard is bullshit. I know where he is and what he faces.*

The phone's ringing drew me back to the den. It was Rob calling from San Francisco. "Sylvi, I'll be quick. I'm at a pay phone with four friends. We're about to take off driving to Chicago for the Democratic Convention. You want to meet us there?"

I had to adjust from the sadness of Pablo's letter to the joy of hearing Rob's voice.

"God, it's good to hear from you, Rob. You're going to Chicago?

But you're not political. Has San Francisco changed you?"

"Not for a second, but these cats I'm with know Allen Ginsberg. He and his people are going to sit in meditation in the park. I want to be part of it."

The operator interrupted to tell Rob to deposit more coins. "Put the charges on my bill, operator," I said. "I can't believe you're going, Rob."

"I went to the Pentagon, didn't I? This isn't so different. Anyway, it's time to head back to the Village. Why not go by way of Chicago?"

"Your invitation sounds tempting, but I have to work, Rob. And it's almost time for Kristi and Katrina to come home from their dad's in Phoenix. And McKenzie's not here right now."

"Who is McKenzie?"

"It has been forever since we've talked. My whole world has spun around a few times since you left. We call him Z. He's my old man."

"You're putting me on. I thought you were done with men for a while. What happened?"

"I've fallen in love for good—honest. We were in San Francisco over the Fourth of July. If I'd had your address, you could have met him."

"I'm sorry for being out of touch. I've been playing a lot of music, and I let everything else go to pot. Pardon the pun." I heard voices in the background. "My friends are in a hurry to get started. I wish you'd come to Chicago, Sylvi, and maybe go on to the Village together like we talked about."

"No, I really can't. I'll be with you in spirit. Promise me one thing."

"Sure, anything."

"Call me collect from Chicago as often as you can. I want to know what's going on and to be sure you're okay."

"Promise," he said. "I love you."

"I love you, too." I held the phone to my ear until the dial tone confirmed we were no longer connected. Overcome by Pablo's letter and Rob's phone call, I sought solace in my room to write.

> Is there a calm in the middle of this storm?
> Torn and stumbling through the hard rain of war,
> a troubled wind blows the Democrats into Chicago.
>
> With my heart breaking, where is my voice?
> Weary blood-soaked soldier, you can't hear me above
> the din of pompous politicians spreading their lie,
> We will stand against Communism in Southeast Asia!
>
> Who is WE?
> You bloated bastards occupying government palaces,
> feasting in the face of eyes haunted by too
> many tiny bodies broken in battlefield mud.
>
> It's more than a light switch
> you have to turn off
> to sleep at night.
> God help us.
> God, where are you?

I fell into a fitful slumber and awoke to Z's touch. "I'm home, baby."

I pulled him into bed and wrapped my arms and legs around him.

His return called for a celebration with the friends we trusted. Pat brought enchiladas. She, Judy, and I stood at the kitchen sink washing and chopping vegetables for a salad. Pinto beans simmered on the stove.

Like three sisters, we confided the concerns of our hearts. Pat said Bob was reaching a breaking point with his public relations job. His biggest client was the smelter, and part of their ad campaign included improving their image in the community they polluted.

"How can he take that kind of pressure?" I asked.

"It's a huge problem." Pat dumped the chopped carrots into the salad bowl. "He's about to blow. The weed mellows him in the evenings, but the next morning he has to face it all again."

"I know my brother." Judy sliced radishes. "He's pretty adept at a soft shoe and snappy patter approach to his job. But I see it, too. He's really fed up."

"Do you think he'll quit?" I asked.

"Maybe," Pat said. "How long can you promote something you despise? A monster-polluter copper smelter, for God sakes. Just getting the ore out of the ground is a crime against mother earth."

"Makes me glad I'm with a drummer." Judy laughed. "Music is good for everybody."

"Wish I could say Z's profession is one I'm comfortable with." I reached into the fridge for salad dressing.

"I thought you'd adjusted pretty well."

"I wish I had. I'm always afraid he won't make it home. How will I find him if he's dead or in jail down there?"

Judy pulled the pan of enchiladas from the oven. "Come and get it," she called.

The phone rang, and I ran to answer it.

"Sylvi, talk loud because I'm using a pay phone at the park," Rob said.

"Okay. Is this loud enough?"

"Yeah. There's a line of brothers and sisters waiting to use this phone. It took me half an hour to get to it. I'll talk fast. We pulled in this afternoon and haven't found Ginsberg yet, but there's a lot of people in Lincoln Park. It's beautiful. The delegates arrive tomorrow."

"Where are you staying?"

"The plan is to camp in the park."

"What's it like?"

"Lots of trees. There are rumors of a curfew being enforced in which case we're supposed to leave the park. But maybe not. Anyway, we're all happy to have arrived. Believe me, Sylvi, it's a long trip from the Bay to Lake Michigan.

"It could turn weird, Sylvi. People here have been talking about a seventeen year old kid who was camped out in the park two days ago. He arrived early for the shindig. They're calling it the Festival of Life. The cops shot him. Killed him. Did it make the news in El Paso?"

"No, we haven't heard anything. Why did they kill him?"

"Word has it the cops were making an example of him. Kind of like telling the rest of us they won't tolerate any trouble."

"My God, Rob, are you sure you want to be there?"

"More than ever. The place needs our peaceful element."

"I'm afraid for you. It sounds a lot more dangerous than the Pentagon. Please promise you'll be careful."

"You know I will. Don't worry about me. Just stay cool. I'll call tomorrow or Monday. Got to free up this phone for the brother behind me."

I heard the click on the other end of the line and whispered a prayer. "God, take care of Rob."

Back in the kitchen, I found Z ladling beans onto our plates. "Who was on the phone?"

"Rob. He's in Chicago to protest the convention."

"Last time you mentioned him he was playing music in San Francisco, and you didn't know his address."

While we filled our plates, I brought Z up to date on Rob's journey to Chicago.

"Didn't think he was political," Z led the way to the den.

"He's not, but he and his friends are going to chant and meditate with Allen Ginsberg's group."

"Was it Rob?" Judy, with feet crossed, lowered herself to an empty spot on the carpet next to Gary. "What's happening in Chicago?"

"They arrived there this afternoon. He said two days ago a seventeen-year-old kid who had camped in the park was shot and killed by the cops. Did any of you hear about it?"

The faces around the room stopped shoveling food into their mouths, looked at me, and shook their heads.

"I haven't seen it on the news. Why would they do such a horrible thing?" Pat asked.

"Rob said to make an example of him."

"Sons of bitches," Z said. "Fucking Mayor Daley. He's likely to kill everybody before it's over."

"I don't know why they're bothering with a convention," Bob said. "You know Hubert Humphrey's got it sewed up, endorsed by LBJ. Eugene McCarthy doesn't have a prayer."

Syd added, "Yeah, everybody who got 'clean for Gene' might as well light a joint, drop some acid, and take to the streets. That's the only place you'll find the will of the people."

Z growled, "You're right, brother, those kids who gave up weed and acid, and cut their hair to become campaign staffers should get a clue. Guns are what they need. There's no such thing as a peaceful revolution."

"We're not talking revolution," Pat said. "We're talking the Democratic National Convention. Why can't change come there? What if the delegates do listen to the protestors outside? What if?"

I thought she had a point but doubted it would happen. "Sure, democracy is something all the people are supposed to participate in. My question is, if the delegates inside the hall are automatons performing a ritual of democracy, how can they hear the protest outside? They have no ears to hear."

"Maybe if they took off those funny hats, they could hear better," Gary said. The visualization amused him, and he broke out in laughter, infecting us all.

Z put his plate aside, slid the newspaper from under the couch, and began to roll a fresh supply of joints.

The next morning I sat down on the bed next to Z and watched him sleep. A line of light escaped from the edge of the window-blinds, forming a headband across his forehead, a half inch below his hairline. Perhaps it could bore through his thick, revolutionary skull and illuminate the dark, violent places in him. Bending forward, I kissed the band of sunlight.

Z opened his eyes. "Sylvi, I thought I was dreaming, but you really are here." He held me, and I relaxed into his sweetness. "How come you're up so early, baby?"

"I had to call Carl. He gets up at five every morning, and I didn't want to miss him." I ran my fingers across the stubble on Z's chin.

"It is the end of summer, huh? Time to bring your little girls home." He propped himself up on one elbow. "Did you talk to him?"

Recalling the conversation, I answered, "Yes, but it was odd. He said they were leaving on vacation this week because he'd not been able to get time off from work until now. He said to call him next Saturday."

"That's cutting it close, baby. School starts the Tuesday after Labor Day."

"Mm-hmm. Maybe I'm reading too much between the lines, but something is not right."

Chapter 9

Empty Road From Phoenix

An early morning dream startled me awake. I painted the vivid image in words before it faded into another hurried Monday.

> August heat rises from earth,
> gasps for cool breath.
> Playground see-saw,
> wooden board bleached by sun
> warped by rain.
>
> I sit on the up-end.
> A person on the down-end ripples
> in hot vapors, unrecognizable.
> Feet dangling, I wait.

It clearly portrayed my position with Carl. I did not like hanging in mid-air waiting to know when I could pick up my daughters.

This wasn't just any Monday, it was August 26, 1968, the beginning of the Democratic National Convention in Chicago. My intuition, on high alert, sent me messages of caution. Caution as I dealt with Carl, caution-vibes to send to Rob who could be in peril. He'd not called since Saturday night. Was he dead, in jail, playing music, or hanging with Ginsberg? News reports carried only sparse details of delegates arriving, and cops forcing protestors from Lincoln Park.

Before I left for the office, I bent to kiss Z who smiled up at me. "When are you going to quit your job?"

"I didn't know I had the option."

"Believe me, it is an option, baby. Just let me know when."

The reality of his words hit me as I drove past the park—the park in my dream and the park where Z and I had hung out with Kristi and Katrina the day after he'd entered my life. When was I going to quit my job? The question loomed large, but remained unanswerable as I parked behind the three-story brick structure where I worked.

Seven-twenty in the morning and the wholesalers' docks, parallel to the back of my building, crawled with men loading and unloading trucks. Their whistles followed me down the sidewalk. My skirts had remained short, although I'd let my hair grow long and wore little makeup compared to last December when Rob came on the scene with weed and peyote.

The whistles flattered me eight months ago, but not any more. I wanted to tell the whistlers they were invading my space. Who were they to presume I'd enjoy their attentions?

God, why am I so crabby? Z wants me to quit my job. Shouldn't I be happy? But the uncertainty surrounding the return of my children and Rob's safety in Chicago pushed out lighter thoughts.

I stuffed both issues somewhere deep inside me and ran up the stairs to my office.

That night the news coverage of the convention reported a disturbance among the delegates. Some wanted to draft Ted Kennedy, and discussion became quite animated. The Democratic

Party machine met behind closed doors to nominate Hubert Humphrey. Then a fistfight broke out between the liberal and conservative Georgia delegates. Dan Rather, a CBS reporter, rushed to the scene where a cop slugged him, knocking him to the floor. Walter Cronkite, the anchor for CBS, called the police "thugs" as he reported the day's proceedings to Americans coast to coast.

"If things are bad inside, I wonder what's happening outside?" Z asked from where he sat in the floor rolling joints. I stood in the doorway to the den holding my breath, awaiting more news. The cameras moved from Cronkite in the convention hall to a reporter on the scene at Lincoln Park.

Against a background of people running and yelling, he told about a violated curfew on Sunday night, how the cops had chased and clubbed crowds who were leaving the park voluntarily. There were some arrests. He ended the report with a question. "What will happen when the eleven o'clock curfew comes tonight?"

Z gave me an apprehensive glance. "Hope your friend is staying cool."

"Me too."

"I'm telling you, baby. They need weapons. Love and peace just ain't going to cut it."

I switched off the TV. "I'm going to bed."

The phone rang at three in the morning on Tuesday. I bolted from bed, ran to the den, and grabbed the receiver from the wall. "Yes, I'll accept charges," I yelled into the phone before the operator could ask.

"It is good to hear your voice, Sylvi." I could barely hear him. "These last two nights have been hell."

I took a deep breath to slow my heart. "Where are you, Rob? What's going on? Are you all right? Are you hurt?"

"Slow down, Sylvi. I'm not hurt, not badly anyway. I'm not in jail. The five of us who came out from the Bay are still together. We're staying at somebody's house a few miles from the park."

"You sound tired."

"I am. Sunday afternoon, things began to get bad. The cops refused to let the musicians drive a flatbed truck into the park to use as a stage. They had to set up on the grass, so when people crowded around to hear the music, the cops baited the situation. Fights broke out. We were sitting with Ginsberg chanting."

"Chanting what?" I asked

"Om. Sitting still, breathing and chanting Om. The Universe inside my body was beautiful. We chanted for hours."

"Were things peaceful around you?"

"It was chaotic outside our circle, but none of us were disturbed." His voice trailed off either from the recollection or exhaustion. "But when it was time for the curfew, we tried leading groups out of the park. Even though we were voluntarily leaving, the cops started pushing people around."

"What did you do?"

"Some ran to get out of the way when the cops began clubbing them. Others fought back. Helicopters flew above us, and bullhorns on the ground yelled to clear the streets."

"Where could you go?"

By this time, Z had come from bed into the den. He sat close to me on the couch.

"Our car was parked about a mile away, so we made it there and crashed. That was Sunday. On Monday I went to a class in the afternoon held by the marshals in the park."

"Marshals, like cops?" I asked.

"No, our people who were trying to keep things organized and safe. They showed us how to protect ourselves when cops started beating the shit out of us."

"How?"

"Basically, by rolling into a ball with your arms covering your head, and your knees covering your belly." The telephone line went silent. It frightened me until I detected his labored breathing.

"What happened?" I urged.

"I didn't really think I'd have to use the tactic, but it got me out of the park last night."

"How badly are you hurt?" I asked, fearing his reply.

"Only a little. It's a funny thing. You know how you don't think of things in the normal course of life? You don't think of how rage turns a person into a hideous monster, or how you'll react when those hateful eyes glare right into your own, or how all their anger explodes and becomes your pain. When that moment came for me, I dropped and rolled into a ball like the marshals taught us."

Tears ran down my face. Z's arm around my shoulders held me steady. "What happened then?"

"I rolled one way and then another to avoid the blows when I became aware of the cop's night stick whaling away on my hands. I wanted to stand up and tell him, hit me in the face, man. Faces don't matter, but I play music with my hands."

I sobbed into the phone.

"That thought gave me the strength to rock to my knees and scramble out of the way. When I could get to my feet, I stumbled around until I found my friends. They weren't in real good shape either, but we made it out. Don't cry, Sylvi, nothing's broken. I'm okay. Just a mind blower, a fucking mind blower."

I tried to control my tears. "What are you going to do now?"

"We'll rest up a bit. These are good people here at this house. They say we can stay 'til the convention is over."

"Thank God. Will you go back to the protests?"

"Yeah, it's over Thursday."

"Don't do it, Rob."

"Easy for you to say down there in Texas. But when you're here and a part of it all, it's difficult to walk away."

"Why? Isn't the violence a total turn-off?"

"More like a nightmare. My spirit screams not to go, but I'll bet Gandhi's followers weren't overjoyed at the prospect of meeting the British Army, either."

"Isn't that example a little extreme?"

"These are extreme times."

His quiet answer, like a spike still hot from the forge, drove a truth into my soul. Right then all the rhetoric took on life, a flame, sucking the breath from me.

"Are you okay?" Z whispered. I nodded.

"Are you there?" Rob asked.

"I'm here. What you said, Rob, extreme times, yes." The conversations, observations, realizations that had taken place under my roof had all been words until that moment. Rob was putting everything on the line and turning all our words into actions. "I'm blown away. I wish I were with you."

"I'm glad you're not, Sylvi. Listen, I have to let some other folks use this phone, but I'll call again soon."

"Call me every day. I need to know you're safe, Rob. Promise me."

He promised and hung up. I cradled the receiver on the phone. Then my face found a place of protection where Z's neck met his shoulder. His arms drew me close against him.

"What was he telling you?" he asked.

I repeated Rob's report.

"This should make you see where we're headed, baby. Nonviolence has outlived its usefulness. Only people willing to fight will see change come." His words, harsh in contrast with the tenderness of his touch, made me pull away.

"Rob and I won't be fighting in the streets, Z, nor will others like us. Are you saying we'll be among those who won't make it through the changes?"

"I'm just trying to get you to see how it is, baby. Che and Fidel didn't roll into Havana after a peaceful march through the mountains of Cuba chanting and meditating."

"So you will survive to see victory because you have a gun in your hand? Then what?"

"Once we win, we dispose of those who oppressed the people and set up the new system."

"The winners crushing the losers?" I shot back. "An exchange of power where the victors become worse than their predecessors? Violent overthrow can never wrap victory in love and pour out healing on the earth."

"You remain the gentle poet, Sylvi, and me an uncivilized bastard. If I were Rob right now, I'd be looking for a way to blow up the police stations all over Chicago. Don't you get it? Force is all this fucking government understands?"

It was four in the morning when we returned to bed. "It bothers me," I said, scooting closer to him. "You and I both want an end to the war and to live compatibly with the earth." He opened his eyes. "So many common causes bind us together. Yet, we're worlds apart." I traced the outline of his lips with my fingertips.

He brushed my hand away. "What about the poor devils all over the world who break their backs for the pittance the rich American companies throw at them? They're worth more than Vietnam or pollution. Are they part of your common cause, baby?"

"You know they are. Those of us who talk revolution are searching for solutions in different places. Some like you, others like me, and some are even trying to work in the existing political system."

"How delusional is that?" He laughed.

"The point I'm trying to make is that the end result is division. How can we win when we're divided?"

"I don't know, baby. I do know I would not roll into a ball and let somebody beat the shit out of me. I would fight back."

Early Wednesday morning Rob phoned. Black Panther, Bobby Seale, had spoken at the rally in Lincoln Park Tuesday evening. He encouraged people to carry arms and protect themselves against the police state. Later, sometime before midnight, Rob and his friends had gathered with a group of clergymen and protesters around a large cross—a prayer service. As they sang, a truck rolled by. Police in the back of the truck lobbed tear gas canisters into the crowd.

"It was like suffocating," he said. "Like your face is burning, like pepper stuffed into your eyes, nose, and mouth. Your lungs are on fire. It was hell, but we made it to the house where we're staying."

Wednesday evening my morning conversation with Rob was the topic of discussion as friends gathered in my den. The television, its volume turned low, brought additional news of the crucial proceedings from inside the convention hall. Irish turned up the volume.

They rejected the Vietnam peace plank. Protests erupted inside the hall. Humphrey won the presidential nomination. I turned off the TV.

"Did we truly think the system would respond?" Judy asked.

Syd sat slumped against the wall. "Just more of the same shit," he said.

I went to bed.

Early Thursday morning, the ringing of the phone woke me from a troubled sleep. Knowing it would be Rob, I stumbled into the den to answer. My eyes adjusted to the dark as I accepted the call. Syd lay crashed on the floor and Irish on the couch. I sank cross-legged to the carpet and listened to Rob's report. He talked about a rally he'd attended Wednesday afternoon at the Grant Park band shell.

"This kid I'd met earlier climbed the flagpole during the rally. He'd told us his plan was to hang the American flag upside down as a symbolic distress signal to the nation. But it turned bloody when police charged through the crowd and attacked with clubs and tear gas."

"You got away?"

"Yeah, but a half hour later thousands of cops returned, joined by Army troops and the National Guard. God, it was bizarre. They had bazookas, and flame-throwers, and something called the Daley dozers."

"What are Daley dozers?"

He described them as jeeps in steel, chain-link cages. "It was surreal, Sylvi, because the attack ended abruptly, like someone gave the command, and the troops stood in formation. Then Ginsberg spoke as if things were normal, even though we were surrounded by artillery and soldiers standing absolutely still. When the rally ended, someone at the mike told us to, either stay in the park, join the parade to the amphitheatre, or split up in small groups. A bunch of us headed for the Hilton where the delegates were staying."

Just before dark, Rob and a few hundred others reached the Hilton where they joined a crowd of protesters and onlookers. "The networks' TV cameras were rolling when all of a sudden cops charged into the crowd clubbing, kicking, and using mace on us. We all began to chant, 'the whole world is watching, the whole world is watching.' The cops were in some kind of frenzy when this huge plate glass window caved in because so many people were being shoved against it."

"Did you go through the window?"

"No, I was in the street. My spirit left my body for a second as I watched the police rush through the broken glass. The cops were hitting people and turning over tables inside the Hilton. After a few minutes, I regained my senses and tried to help."

Rob went on to say word spread to bring the injured to the fifteenth floor, the McCarthy headquarters, where his volunteers had set up a makeshift hospital. "I helped get a couple of injured guys up there. McCarthy's people were tearing up sheets to use as bandages. Then the cops showed up and ran us all out."

"Where did you go?"

"Back to the street. I saw McCarthy delegates returning to the hotel. They walked slow and held candles. They told me Humphrey got the nomination. Guess they were lighting candles and trying not to curse the darkness, you know, like the Quaker saying." He emitted a long sigh. "It's been a crushing week, and it's not over."

I echoed his sadness. "The peace plank defeated, the peace candidate defeated. Are you ready to hang it up?"

"Good question. I'll talk to my friends. Maybe we'll split. I don't have the heart for any more. I'm ready to hit the road to New York."

"Please go to the Village, Rob. You know I support the protest a hundred percent, but it's gone too far."

"Yeah, I'm not sure what's happened here." He formed his words with difficulty, clearly exhausted and spiritually drained. "I need to get away and figure it out."

"I doubt we'll ever understand." I tried to console him. "But I'm sure we'll see and hear a lot on the news tonight."

He agreed. "The way the reporters got kicked around, the American public is going to be made a hell of a lot more aware."

"Do you think anyone in the straight world is going to pay attention?" I asked.

"We can hope."

Rob and I said goodbye. Getting to my feet, I hung up the phone. Syd and Irish still snored on the floor and the couch. I returned to our room where McKenzie slept soundly.

An eerie hush settled over the house as I stood, barely breathing, in the center of the bedroom. The quiet cleared the turmoil from my mind, and it hit me. Carl had been lying about his vacation. I glanced at the clock. He always woke before the sunrise and swallowed down his usual two shots of whiskey.

I ran to the phone, dialed his number, stretched the cord into the kitchen, and nervously filled the coffee pot with water while waiting for him to answer.

"You were lying about being on vacation."

"Who is this?" he demanded.

"Carl, when can I pick up Kristi and Katrina?"

I waited.

"You're not getting them back, Sylvi," he said, confirming what I'd suspected, but hadn't dared to let myself think.

"Why?" was all I could say.

"I don't have to give you a reason." His voice, cold and precise.

"Yes, you do"

"I don't. This conversation is over."

I heard a click on the line, a second of silence, then the drone of the dial tone. As my body sagged against the counter, I plugged in the coffee. *I'd taken them to him in Phoenix against my better judgment. Now this? He is fucking crazy if he thinks I will let him get away with it.*

Taking a long breath, I marched to the den, slammed the phone on the hook and stormed into the bedroom, shouting, "The son of a bitch is not returning my daughters."

"What are you talking about?" Z rubbed his eyes.

"I just got off the phone with Carl, and I know he didn't take his family on vacation. He's been there all week letting me stew. Bastard."

Z sat up. "Start from the beginning, baby."

"My intuition finally kicked in and told me to call Carl. I did, and he said he was not sending the girls back to me. He told me he didn't have to tell me why. He said the conversation was over and hung up." Tears of anger ran down my face.

Z wiped them away and wrapped me in his arms and said, "We'll drive out and get them."

Z dropped me at work at seven-thirty sharp. In my office, I dialed Judy's work number. "I'll make this fast. I talked to Carl this morning. He's refusing to return Katrina and Kristi to me."

"He what? He can't do that. You have custody."

"I know, but he told me this morning on the phone, and refused to talk to me about it."

"What are you going to do?"

"Z and I are driving out tonight after work. We'll be in Phoenix before Carl's had his two shots of whiskey tomorrow morning."

"Do you think it's wise? Carl's kind of unstable."

"If I can't get answers over the phone, what choice do I have, Judy?"

"Good point. Gary and I will look after Daiquiri while you're gone. Just promise me you'll be very careful."

"I will. I hear Jason at the reception desk. I have to tell him I'm going to take tomorrow off. Talk to you later."

McKenzie drove through the night while I dreamed fitful dreams beside him. "Wake up, baby. We're in Phoenix."

"My God, Z, I think I died." Pulling myself up straight, I tossed the pillow in the backseat. "What time is it?"

"Hell if I know. You're the one who wears a watch." He kissed me on the cheek. "I'd say the sun will be rising within half an hour."

"We'll be there right on time. Are you okay, Z? You haven't slept.

"I'm doing real fine, thanks, dropped a black beauty this side of Tucson." He reached for my hand. "What do you think we're walking into?"

"For starters, he'll be pissed, but I'm praying he has the good sense not to freak in front of the girls."

As the sun rose, we wove our way through the Phoenix streets until we reached the area where Carl lived. We stopped at the end of his long gravel driveway as he slammed out his front screen door. Determined to maintain control, I stepped from the car. Z did, too, and leaned on his open door.

"What took you so long?"

"Since you wouldn't talk to me on the phone, I had no choice but to drive out." I took a step toward him. "Where are Kristi and Katrina?"

"Visiting friends." His eyes narrowed. His lips curved slightly into a cruel half-smile.

Renewed anger flashed through me. I'd envisioned the girls running through the front door, giving me big hugs, and Carl would relent. Then I'd help pack up their things, we'd get in the car, and happily drive home. *Am I stupid, or what?*

Z closed his car door, took a step forward, and broke the silence. "When will they be back?"

"They can stay gone as long as need be," Carl said, pleased with the way he toyed with us.

I cleared my throat. "The thing is, Carl, I have the custody papers with me. Our agreement is you return the kids at the end of the summer."

"Those papers aren't worth a damn in Arizona." He smirked.

Something inside me told me he was right. "Bastard."

"I think you two better get off my property, or I'll call the sheriff."

"I'd appreciate it if you'd do that, Carl," Z said quietly, walking around the car to stand at my side. "I'd personally like to know what our rights are. So why don't you go inside and make that call?"

"You think I won't?" Carl walked to the porch and disappeared inside the house.

"I have no patience for assholes," Z said. "But I don't want any trouble. We'll see what the sheriff can tell us."

The brilliant, end-of-August sun climbed a bit higher in the sky, promising a hot day. We waited.

Carl did not rejoin us until the sheriff's car stopped in front of the property. A deputy sheriff got out and walked down the driveway toward the three of us. "Which one of you is Carl Stevens?" he asked.

"I am. I'm the one who called. These people have refused to get off my property."

The officer turned to us. "And who are you two?"

We introduced ourselves. I explained I had custody of my daughters, but Carl refused to return them to me after their summer visit. I handed him the divorce papers.

"These are from Texas." He took a few steps back and checked our license plates.

"Does it make a difference?" I asked, glancing at Carl, who flashed me a look of contemptuous glee.

"Yes it does," the deputy said. "Child custody laws don't cross state lines. You have custody awarded in Texas, but you don't have custody in Arizona." He continued leafing through the papers.

"That doesn't make sense to me," I said.

"No, ma'am, it doesn't, but it's the law." He appeared sympathetic.

Z, sensing my frustration, asked, "What can we do to straighten this out?"

"Your only choice is to take Mr. Stevens to court in Arizona."

"They need to get off my property," Carl interrupted, obviously irritated by the officer discussing the matter with us.

"Yes, you do need to leave Mr. Stevens' property." He handed the documents back to me.

"Of course we're leaving," I said. Carl backed away and went inside.

"Since we're from out of town, do you know of any lawyers you could recommend?" Z asked.

The deputy thought a moment. "There are a couple." I found a pen and scrap of paper in my purse and handed them to him. "These fellas are located downtown." He wrote down two names. "You can get their numbers out of the book. The way most folks wind up getting their kids back is by kidnapping them. I can't advise it officially, but that's the way it is." Wishing us luck, he got in his car.

We traveled south at the end of our long, hot Friday in Phoenix. Wind swirled through the open windows. The hills and mountains in the distance turned shades of melancholy blue.

"We're halfway to Tucson, and you haven't said a word." Z massaged the back of my neck with one hand and drove with the other. "Are you going to be all right?"

"I can survive anything, but I'm having trouble swallowing the kidnapping thing. Even the Phoenix lawyer said it was our best shot. When we get back to El Paso, I'll call Don. He handled my divorce. How can child custody laws be so lacking?"

"Have you ever seen just one law that was adequate?" Z asked.

"No. I'm so bummed. I never thought I'd be fighting for my kids. They've always been with me, always been my world. I never saw this coming." I leaned my head on his shoulder. "Thanks for being here for me. I couldn't do it alone."

"You don't have to do it alone. What do you think about getting some groceries, baby? We can spend the night in those mountains the other side of Douglas."

"It would be nice, but we don't have anything to cook with."

"Sure we do," he said. "I threw a couple skillets and a coffee pot in with the bedrolls. Everything's in the trunk."

Tall, shaggy trees stood against a black sky dusted with a million stars. I didn't know what time it was and didn't care. Z slept warm against me. I gazed upward and breathed the cool pine air.

How have I come to be in this spot grappling with my breaking heart? Of course, all our yesterdays bring us to today. Carl had always been more than happy to send them home before. I should have seen this coming down. Why couldn't I see it in time to stop it? How could I have been so careless when two young lives depended on me? I'd not even thought of doing a Tarot reading.

Finally, I turned and kissed the back of Z's neck and shoulders until he sleepily returned my kisses. We made love, not the kind filled with intense passion, but an intimate sort of sharing each other's souls. Then we slept.

The sun woke me. A morning breeze played among branches and flowers. Three months before, we'd declared our union in these mountains. The most beautiful place on earth.

"Are you finally awake?" Z laughed and pulled the covers off me. He handed me a joint and pulled me up close to him. "Come warm by the fire."

The smell of bacon and coffee mingled in the air, sharpening my senses. "You've been busy." I smiled up at him.

"You'll have to cook the eggs, baby. I'm no good at it."

While he rummaged in the grocery bag, I shook out the blankets to find my jeans and shirt.

"Where do we go from here?" he asked between bites.

I gazed up at the treetops, pale green in the sun with clouds drifting above them in a sky so infinite, I knew God painted it fresh that morning. Z sipped his coffee and waited for my response.

I told him about my self-doubts as I lay looking at the stars the night before. He lit a joint and held it to my lips. I took a long, slow drag. Tossing my empty plate into the fire, I watched the sparks pop and sputter.

Z piled more wood on then sat back down beside me. "Don't even think about all the stuff you think you should have known or done. It's going to be okay, and we'll go from here to wherever tomorrow takes us. You can read the cards when we get home and see what they say."

"And I'll call Don on Monday morning to talk over the legal aspects."

"I planned on going down to Acapulco in another week or so, but I'll wait and see what's happening."

With my head on his shoulder and his arms around me, we watched the fire dance red and orange-gold. Thin ribbons of flame burst upwards and disappeared. Where the fire licked the blackened wood, I saw shadowy faces.

"Remember when we were here before how I heard the wailing of the Apache women. Spirits?" I asked

"Uh-huh, do you hear them now?"

"No, but I see them." I pointed to the campfire. "They've lost children, too. They're encouraging me to go on, find mine, and bring them home. Their eyes speak to me here." I pressed my hand against my heart.

We sat then, quiet until the embers died and the morning grew warm. "Should we head on home today?" He asked, emerging from our trance.

"I hate to leave. I love these mountains. But my practical side says to go home, do the laundry, and get ready for whatever comes. You know, back to the real world. Does that make this the illusion?"

"No, baby. <u>This</u> is real, laundry is an illusion."

Judy met us at the kitchen door. "Where's Katrina and Kristi?"

"You tell her about it, Sylvi. I'll unpack the car and put things away."

Judy and I sat on the living room couch. Daiquiri jumped into my lap. Purring, she stretched up to rub her face against my cheek. I stroked her soft gray fur and told Judy about Carl's reception, the deputy, and the lawyer.

"I'm not sure about kidnapping my own children. Hell, they don't need more traumas in their lives. I'm hoping Don will offer another suggestion when I see him on Monday."

"You know, Sylvi, that Carl has never been one of my favorite people, but I never thought he'd go this far."

"Let's do a Tarot spread." I moved Daiquiri from my lap. "I'll get my cards."

Judy followed me. "By the way, Rob called at two in the morning after you and Z left for Phoenix."

"Where was he?"

"On the road to New York, but he wanted to let you know he'd survived, said they didn't march to the Amphitheatre on Thursday. They were too disheartened. He wanted to get to the Village, play some music, and put it all behind him."

"I'm glad he called."

Z joined us. I opened the wooden box, withdrew my cards, unwrapped them from the lavender cotton cloth, and handed them to Judy. "Would you do the spread?"

"Sure." She shuffled them and placed the deck in front of me. "How do you want to ask the question?"

"I'm not sure." *Is kidnapping them my only choice? What are the risks? Will it be traumatic for the girls?* I wanted a simple question, answerable with a yes or no. "Should I kidnap Kristi and Katrina from Carl in Phoenix and bring them back here to El Paso?"

"Make that, should we kidnap them." Z took my hand.

Judy turned the top three cards face up. We studied them for a moment and agreed.

Yes.

Chapter 10

A Road to Here and There

Tuesday, the day after Labor Day, we sat down in Don's office. I thanked him for seeing us on short notice and introduced him to McKenzie.

"I have to get right to the point," I said. "Carl has refused to return Kristi and Katrina after their summer vacation with him in Phoenix."

"Maybe you'd better start at the beginning, Sylvi. I need to know the whole story." Don tilted his chair back and listened to my tale.

After I filled him in on the details, he asked, "Why won't he give them back to you? Think it's because McKenzie is in the picture now?"

"No. I'll be straight with you, Don. I think the girls have mentioned to their dad what's been happening at my house since last December."

"What would that be?"

"An old friend showed up and turned me on to marijuana." I said it fast before I lost my nerve.

Z registered surprise at my mention of weed and leaned forward. "Sylvi is a great mother. There's nothing wrong with marijuana, and it'll be legal soon."

"Unfortunately, folks, it's illegal right now. If the girls have said anything, and you press the issue, Sylvi, you're in for a battle. Did you tell the attorney in Phoenix about the weed?"

"Of course not, I don't know him like I know you. Please don't tell me the same thing the Phoenix lawyer told me on Friday."

"What did he tell you?"

"Kidnap them."

Don rested his hands on his desk. "I hate to tell you, but the lawyer was right. If you take it to court in Arizona, the marijuana issue will raise its ugly head, and you'll be in hot water. My best advice is to wait a few weeks until Carl lets his guard down, and then kidnap them."

Z and I left Don's. "That is not what I wanted to hear," I said as Z drove me to my office. "I've never kidnapped anyone, and I'm not sure I can."

"We can do it, baby. But, like Don said, we need to wait a few weeks. Why don't we take off for Colorado over the weekend?"

"Why Colorado?"

"Why not? It will keep your mind off Phoenix." He stopped the car in front of my building, opened my door, and took my hands. "Can you really walk in there like nothing's happened? You're in no shape to work this afternoon."

"I'll be okay."

Standing at the curb we embraced. "Go in there right now and quit," he said. "Then we can go home, talk, and make love all afternoon."

With every inch of his body against me, his voice soft against my ear, his hands pressing me closer, it took all my strength to sidestep his embrace. "As good as that sounds, I have to do this my way, Z"

The week passed in something of a blur. I took off work at noon Friday, and we hit Highway 54 heading north. The hot September wind blew through the car, while I thought about Kristi and Katrina, wiggled my toes in my sandals, and picked at the fringe on my cut-off jeans.

The road took us through Alamogordo, but we didn't stop to see my parents. The names of towns along the way sang a funny rhythm in my head. Alamogordo, Tularosa, Carrizozo, Corona, Vaughn. All afternoon we drove through ranchland, but three-quarters of the way to Santa Fe, the sun began painting the horizon and changing the high desert grasses into slender golden threads trembling in the late afternoon breeze. Mountain ranges loomed misty blue and purple silhouettes against the broad strokes of bright rose and coral streaking the western sky. "I wish we could drive right into the sunset," I said. "Like being over the rainbow, our troubles melting like lemon drops."

"Let's try to forget our troubles, baby, at least for this weekend."

"I'll try," I said, not sure I could.

Darkness overtook Santa Fe an hour before we arrived. Thankful for a shower and a comfortable bed, we crashed in a motel and would travel on to Colorado the next morning.

Traveling northward as the morning sun crested the eastern horizon, Z asked me to roll down my window. He slowed, pulled onto the shoulder, and leaned across me to ask the hitchhiker, "Where you headed?"

"Taos," he said without a smile or elaboration. His dark hair touched the neck of his brown wool poncho, and a week's growth of beard framed his face. He carried a bedroll slung across his back.

"Hop in," Z said. I got out, pushed my seat forward, and sensed the traveler's weariness as he climbed into the backseat.

"Stay on this road," the stranger offered. "Hit Highway 68. It will take you into Taos, but you can let me out this side of it. I appreciate the lift."

"I'm McKenzie and this is my woman, Sylvi." Z reached over the back of the seat to shake hands. "What name you go by, man?"

"Gray Wolf."

"Are you Native American?" I asked.

"Only part. But that's what they call me."

"Who's they?"

"The people I lived with up here."

"Are they still here?"

"No." Silence filled the car for a moment befor he continued. "When I was a kid, I used to come up here with my folks. They have a vacation place this side of Taos."

"Where do they live their normal lives?" I asked.

"I don't think they have a normal life. They're scientists at Los Alamos."

"Heavy trip," Z said. "Home of the atomic bomb."

"Right, but anyway, I was going to college in Albuquerque in '67, and my parents wanted me to come to Taos to spend spring break with them. When I came up, my dad told me some of my old friends were living about ten miles away in a commune."

"A real commune? Far out. Are you headed there now?" I asked.

"No, I'm going to see my mom, dad, and little brother. But we could stop by where the commune used to be—if you want to."

"Used to be?" Z asked.

"Yeah, I think the last remnant of people left early this year. I stayed from the spring of '67 until Thanksgiving. Some, I hear, made it halfway through the winter."

"What happened?"

"Lots of things. Twenty, thirty miles up the road, you'll see a big pile of rocks. Turn left there. I've got to close my eyes for a bit."

Z hung a left onto a dirt road, two parallel ruts separated by a mound of grass. Tall pines, scattered through the juniper, spread out on either side.

Gray Wolf woke up. "You found the road."

We bumped along for about a mile, rounded a bend, and came upon a clearing where the remains of five wood-frame buildings stood in a semicircle. We stopped and got out into the cool morning.

Gray Wolf moved forward along a path toward the structure in the center, we followed. I estimated the building to be about twenty-five feet across and twice as long. Berry bushes grew along each side. Gray Wolf bent, pulled a long stem of wild grass from its bladed sheath and chewed on it. The birds called, and wind breathed through the trees for a time before he spoke. "A dozen years ago this was a retreat ground for some local churches. After a dispute, they abandoned it. Some of us used to come here, hang out and smoke dope. The commune evolved from that. We never got the plumbing to work right, but we believed we could grow spiritually here in the High Lands, as we called it."

"Great," I said. "A land where getting high was the norm."

"But it didn't work," Z reminded me.

"Yeah, there were plenty of reasons it didn't," Gray Wolf said and motioned for us to follow. He led us through an open doorway. Light swirled in dusty sunbeams through holes in the roof. "This is the common area, or the long house. Watch your step." He picked his way through pieces of wood and tiles strewn across the rough wood floor.

The walls commanded my attention. Painted against a forest background were all twenty-two Major Arcana cards from the Tarot deck, each measuring roughly two by three feet. A great, round mandala adorned the back wall. Its vivid design drew my eyes to its center of white light. Looking back, I noticed a perfect Tao, symbolizing the balance within the Universe, hanging above the door through which we'd entered.

Despite the damage done by the elements, the room exuded tremendous power. "This is where we expressed our collective consciousness," Gray Wolf said.

As we gaped at the scene, he told us about a community of people who had dropped out of careers as college professors, business owners, corporate accountants, mechanics, and students like himself. The population averaged around fifty. They organized themselves into daily work details, except nothing was work. It was discovering new things everyday. They elevated the mundane to the spiritual, shared their knowledge and lived simply so there was time for creative thought and expression. Their sole purpose being, he said, "to free their spirits and intellect from the chains of modern American culture."

I stood in the center of the room, mesmerized. Then one of the mini-scenes from the forest mural jumped out at me, a depiction of an obvious sacrifice of a human on a bloody stone altar. "What is this about?"

Gray Wolf looked troubled. "I'll try to explain. In the Tao, there is a balance between all things, life-death, feminine-masculine, light-darkness and so on. Without one, we would not be able to perceive the other, nor could we discover the true path. Look more closely."

I saw ghouls peering from dark thickets. One clutched a limp fairy in its wicked fingers, about to devour her. Gray Wolf saw the revulsion in my face. "Simply stated, we lost our balance." He motioned us to follow him outside.

Z lingered, studying the paintings, while Gray Wolf and I went out. He showed me where the garden had been. The morning stood still as he told me more about what had happened to the commune.

In a short time, Z emerged from the long house and joined us. "We'd better be getting on the road. Thanks for bringing us here, man." He shook Gray Wolf's hand. "It's still got a hold on you, doesn't it?"

"There is something." Gray Wolf's voice faded as he trudged along the overgrown trail to the car.

Settled again in the back seat, he directed Z onto the highway. "Why did you leave?" Z asked.

"The scene got too heavy. Like I told Sylvi, we lost the balance. A lot worked, but things got too dark, if you know what I mean. I tried to steer us away from the edge. Then I gave up and left it behind."

"Where'd you go?" I asked.

"To Canada to visit friends in the dead of winter. What a trip. Came back through here in the summer and found it deserted. Then I hitched down to Oaxaca. I found the magic mushroom experience to be healing."

"How so?" I asked.

"It enabled me to better open to the Universe, and I gained more understanding about the commune and my life in general. Not easy to describe."

"I can dig it. Peyote helped me in a similar way. The cactus and the mushroom both possess similar hallucinogens I think."

"It's cool you made it to the mushroom, man," Z said. "Did you grow your own weed at the commune?"

"Sure. Good stuff, too. We had acid and peyote connections on the outside. We tried to weave it all into ceremonies and rituals rather than everybody just dropping and not being able to function. It could have been a good thing. Guess we all forgot we were mere humans," he said as we arrived at his parents' house.

His dad walked toward the car from where he'd been reading on the porch, his red hair bushed out from his head like a halo. His mother's dark braids bounced against her plaid shirt as she ran down the steps with a boy of five or six at her heels. He darted in front of her, his red curls bobbing as he charged toward us.

Gray Wolf's family embraced him. After introductions and a few minutes of conversation, they invited us to lunch. We thanked them but declined, explaining we needed to get to Colorado before nightfall.

September sunshine colored our afternoon in fading summer meadows. At their edges, stood forests of tall quaking aspen with silvery green leaves, yellow tinged, and spinning in the wind. Z down-shifted as we climbed higher into towering pines and cooler air.

"Gray Wolf never told us exactly what happened to the commune, did he?" Z asked.

"He did tell me more about it while he showed me where the garden had been. Remember when we went outside, and you stayed in the long house?"

"What did he say?"

"He told me the people began to divide into two groups, the majority into white magic, but a dozen or so into black magic."

"Did he elaborate on the difference between white and black?"

"Yes. I didn't think of it as having to be explained, but he definitely wanted me to understand. White involved working with herbs, astrology, Tarot, and numerology to pursue life's path. They also embraced Jungian psychology and Buddhism. Oh, and the Tao. All these things were used to heal each other physically and emotionally, for the common good."

"And black?"

"He said those who used the black magic employed the teachings and philosophies of the white, but not for the common good. They took it a step further into casting spells, using all their knowledge and power for selfish ends. He later heard talk of animal sacrifice."

"That's some heavy shit, baby."

We stopped at the first cafe we came to, after passing the 9,010-foot elevation sign and walked into the aroma of barbecue and fresh baked pies.

"The black magic was too much and Gray Wolf left. Makes sense," Z said as we scooted into a booth.

"He said he'd tried to steer them back to their original goal to be a source of healing, reminding them they'd gone there for unity, not division. Others had given up sooner and left before he did."

"See, pursuing spiritual growth at the community level fails," McKenzie said. "It's only through politics that a community can be in agreement. Social evolution can take place in a commune only when it's politically driven."

"Nonsense," I countered. "Must spirituality be denied in order for social change to take place?"

"No, our spirits are individual things, Sylvi. We can believe what we damned well please. All I'm saying is religion is not going to accomplish social change, but politics will."

"I'm not talking about religion," I protested. "I'm telling you what happened at Gray Wolf's commune. They were trying to attain a tribal way of life by drawing from various spiritual teachings."

"But I'm telling you, bottom line, they didn't fucking make it, did they? That's the problem I have with all these love and peace communes."

"Your problem is they didn't make it? Or what exactly is your problem?" Irritation flashed through me.

"This is the problem. As soon as they find out life is not made up of hearts and flowers, they fall apart. Grey Wolf said as much when he told us they forgot they were mere humans."

"That's your interpretation," I muttered as I rounded up the last bite of cherry pie and ice cream on my plate.

The food was good, but the conversation left me with a bad taste.

"Come on, baby, we've got to get up to Monarch Pass and find a place to camp before dark."

We followed a two-lane road winding through dense forest. The sun faded behind the trees as we pulled onto a rutted trail. It led us to a small clearing with a stream running through it. Z stopped the car a few yards away from the water. "We're here," he said, breaking the silence we'd observed since the cafe.

He grabbed his hatchet and a blanket from the trunk at the front of the car and headed toward the trees bordering the clearing. "Where are you going?" I called.

"To gather bedding," he shouted over his shoulder.

"I'll get the fire together."

I noticed him chopping small branches of pine needles from the trees as I dug a hole in the soft earth, gathered large stones from the edge of the stream, and piled them around the shallow pit. As I moved, stretched, and lifted, the stagnation from sitting in the car fell away. I breathed mountain air and wondered why Z and I had to be at opposite poles.

Dark was fast approaching when he returned and dropped the blanket full of pine twigs next to the car. By the time night surrounded us, Z had a roaring fire going.

"Help me make the bed, baby?" He spread out the blanket with the pine twigs on top of it. Then gathering the bedrolls from the car, he shook one out. I grabbed an end and helped him stretch it over the fragrant pine needles. We collapsed on it together.

"This is the softest, best smelling bed in the world." I sighed. "Thank you."

"I had to do something to get on your good side after you got pissed off at the truck stop."

"Why don't we just drop it?" At a loss as to how to resolve our differences, I wanted simply to roll into his arms, but he sat straight up.

"I'd like to drop it, but it happens all the time," he said.

"What happens all the time?"

"When we have differences of opinion. You get mad, and close me out."

"I don't think I do that every time."

"Seems like every damned time to me."

"Well, you're so loud and intense. I feel I'm being attacked."

"Attacked?" He laughed.

"Go ahead and laugh. Like what I'm saying isn't valid, like it doesn't matter because you're bigger and louder. If I don't close you out, you'll consume me."

"Damn, Sylvi, I don't want to consume you." He placed both hands on my shoulders. "Is that why you stop talking to me when we see things differently?"

"Yes."

"I had the impression you felt I didn't have a right to my own convictions. Like maybe your silence was a way to force me to come over to your side."

"No." I slipped my arms around him, and his hands traveled from my shoulders to my back. We pulled each other close. "I would never use silence as a weapon. I watched my mother do it as I grew up. No, silence is not a weapon for me, it's a defense. I'm unable to express myself in the heat of an argument."

"I've done it all my life, baby, arguing and fighting. That's all I've known. Maybe we can work out a balance, the masculine-feminine Tao thing."

"I'm willing," I said, pulling him backward into the softness of our bed.

The stars were disappearing from the pre-dawn sky when Z woke me. "I have a little surprise, baby." He reached into his shirt pocket. I rubbed my eyes and struggled to sit up. The cold made me want to burrow back under the blankets, but Z had kept the fire going through the night. Its crackling warmth enticed me to throw the blankets aside as Z handed me my shirt and jeans.

"What kind of a surprise?"

He opened his hand. "Acid. I traded it for a couple of dime bags Friday morning. Thought the mountains would be the best place to drop. What do you think?"

"I think it's a beautiful idea." I dressed in seconds.

"You want breakfast first?" he asked.

"No, it's a better trip on an empty stomach." I brought a jug of water from the car. We popped the tabs in our mouths and washed them down. Then dowsed the fire with water from the stream and closed up the car, so it wasn't a target for curious bears.

The sky turned from gray to streaks of pink and brilliant white as Z took the lead, finding stepping-stones across the creek and heading up the hill into the shadowy woods to the west.

A morning mist rose up around us, softening the blast of sunrise bursting above the trees behind us. We turned so the fiery ball warming our backs washed over our faces like a caring hand then sat down to watch it with our eyes closed. Opening my eyes a little, I saw the light in many-colored streamers shimmering in the morning wind. I took great gulps of it into my lungs. It swirled around my heart, warmed my belly, and tingled my fingertips. I rested on the forest's breath as it inhaled and exhaled. The bright red flowers next to me pulsed, their faces beamed. The dew clung to their petals and leaves like teardrops, each drop caught all the colors in ever changing hues. I melted into the now of it all, rooted like a flower. My legs and body felt like the leafy stem of a blossom.

I touched a rough-barked pine with my palm. "It must be a groove to live here." A low growl interrupted my dialogue with the tree. The growl quickly built to a roaring crescendo. Z stood a stones-throw behind me with fists raised to the sky, howling. The shimmering streamers of light left me, replaced by anxious confusion. I tore loose from my roots and ran toward him.

Beer bottles, plastic containers and tin cans lay scattered around his feet. "Bastards. No respect for the earth, probably call themselves hunters. Fucking up nature is what they do." He dropped to his knees and began scooping a hole in the ground with his hands. I watched for a moment then sank to the earth and helped him dig. We buried the debris. On our hands and knees, patting the dirt and pine needles in place, we looked at each other. His mouth twisted between his mustache and beard. His tears of green flames melted down his cheeks. I looked away, unable to bear what I saw.

"Best we split up, baby." He rose and stepped back.

Bird songs, like marionette strings, pulled me to my feet. I nodded and clung to the melodies offered by my feathered allies as they floated from tree to tree. After a time, I danced on the dappled forest floor, a counterpart to their aerial ballet and so regained my balance.

After dancing forever, I sat down with the flowers who called to me, a chorus of tiny bells, asking me to share their colors and textures, their breath and heartbeats. Sitting very still, I beheld the opening of a small purple blossom. Its petals reveled in the patch of sunshine it occupied. Both sturdy and delicate, it embodied the whole of my life. The flower and I shared a powerful connection, spirit to spirit with the Creative Source.

Hours passed. I wandered, communing with the forest, exchanging energy through touch, and voice, and breath until I stood on the creek bank. I looked across at our campsite. The shadows from the trees behind me stretched long across the meadow. Shivering a bit from the coolness of the approaching evening, I studied the stones rising above the fast running water to choose the ones on which to cross. A human shadow rippled in the creek next to mine. "Let's cook some dinner," Z said.

I stepped onto the first stone, and he followed. Safe on the other side, I turned and extended my hand. He took it. "If you'll get the fire started, I'll gather more wood before dark," I said.

Coming down from the acid, I recalled the day as I foraged for firewood. Love and understanding settled within me. I feared asking Z about his experience.

Famished, we pulled a log next to the fire, and sat down to eat our feast of pork and beans, Canadian bacon, and eggs. What was meant to be our breakfast, instead, became a tasty supper. "I hesitate to ask, but how did your day go?" I said, watching Z's face in the glow of the fire.

"Let's just say I'm still waiting for a good trip. I wanted this to be it, but it wasn't." He stared over the flames into the woods beyond. "I'm sorry if my raging brought you down, Sylvi. Someday I'll get beyond being so mad. I watched you for a while after you walked away from me this morning and wished my anger would fade. I wanted to trip with you and be part of your world."

My heart broke for him. "Where did you go?"

"To the top of the mountain."

I reached in the paper bag by my foot, pulled out two apples for dessert, and handed him one.

"What was it like at the top of the mountain?"

"Closer to the sky where I could get a better shot at God or whoever's up there. I yelled and ranted, but there was no response, no answers."

"Someday they'll come," I said, knowing it sounded hollow.

He stood and faced me with his back to the fire. "I don't believe there are answers. I believe there are only questions, only riddles. God is like a cat playing with mice. We're the mice, and he bats us around until we die."

"That's not true." I stood and tossed my apple core into the fire. I put my arms around Z, but let them fall to my sides when he did not respond. Neither of us spoke as we watched our shadows dance in the flickering light.

The glare of the sun through the VW window woke me. I straightened my body, turned my head from side to side to work the stiffness from my neck, and remembered we'd left Colorado in the dead of night. "I wish we were still on our bed of pine," I said.

He agreed. "Making love to you as I came down off acid was the best part of my trip."

"Mmm." Excitement shot through my body at the recollection. I kissed his ear and burrowed my face into his neck. "Are you tired? You've been driving all night."

"I'm okay. I dropped a black beauty this side of Santa Fe, after you crashed. We wouldn't have left last night except I thought you were going to have an anxiety attack when you realized this would be Monday morning. You could have called Jason and told him you weren't coming in, baby."

"I couldn't do it. I'd taken off early Friday, and I couldn't bring myself to take Monday off, too."

"If you'd quit the damned job, you wouldn't have to worry about it, but I'm not pushing. You do it your way."

"Thank you for almost understanding." I smiled. "Want me to drive?"

"I'm good. I'll get us there faster, probably in time for you to shower and get to work on time." He laughed. "While you're working, I'll crash and burn."

The office loomed surreal before me, a far cry from the Colorado woods and a tab of LSD. Even though I arrived fifteen minutes late, I still beat my boss.

I moved mechanically through a busy Monday morning. Mid-afternoon Z called to tell me he was going to visit some friends south of town tomorrow, which was our flimsy code for him making a run to Acapulco. Since our return from Phoenix, we were sure our phone was tapped. He surprised me by asking if I wanted to go.

"Sure. But I'll have to clear with Jason."

"Fuck Jason," he snapped. "Now is a good time to quit."

"Soon, Z, just give me the time I need."

"Sure, I'm sorry, baby. Hurry home and we'll talk about it."

I told Jason I was sick, needed to see the doctor, and left work around 3:00 in the afternoon. When I got home, there was little to discuss. Z had already lined up Irish and Syd to take care of Daiquiri. He'd done a couple loads of wash and hung them on the clothesline in the back yard.

I called Judy. "So how was Colorado, Sylvi?"

"Why don't you all come over after you get off work, and I'll catch you up? Too much is happening to talk about it on the phone." Judy knew about the phone tap and said they'd be by.

After supper, as I folded clothes, she and Gary knocked. Gary settled in the den with Z, Syd and Irish, while Judy stayed with me in the living room. I told her about Colorado. "And tomorrow Z and I are going to Acapulco."

"You're moving too fast for me, Sylvi. I know Z's trying to keep your mind off kidnapping Katrina and Kristi, but Mexico? Are you out of your mind?"

"I'm sure I need to hear that, Judy, but try to understand. He does this on a regular basis, and I want very much to be part of his world."

"I feared it would come to this." She shook her head. "You're in too deep, but I'll always be here for you." I began to cry. "Go ahead." She reached across the folded laundry and put her arms around me. "You're fighting for your kids, living in a heavy relationship, and working a job that's draining the life out of you. Crying is therapeutic."

I called the office at 7:30 Tuesday morning and left a message at the reception desk for Jason. I was seriously ill, highly contagious, and the doctor said not to return to work for several days.

Z's visa was in order, but it took most of the morning in Juarez to obtain mine. We grabbed lunch and hit Mexico's Highway 45. "We're on our way, baby. I'm glad you're with me."

"I'm glad I'm with you, too." I tied my hair back, Z pulled off his tee shirt, and we settled in for our fifteen-hundred-mile journey.

An hour after dinner in Chihuahua, I watched thunderheads gather against the evening sky ahead. Then, noticing the squat adobe houses scattered on either side of the road, I asked, "What town is this?"

"Meoqui. There's a lake out there somewhere." Z waved his hand toward the west. "We'll see it another time. This weather looks bad."

As we passed through Meoqui, the clouds grew darker, slammed together and spit fat raindrops against our windshield. Loud claps of thunder rolled across the empty desert. The night and pounding rain swallowed us.

"How can you see to drive?" I yelled above the water hammering the roof of the VW. Grabbing Z's shirt from the back seat, I wiped the fog from the inside of the front windows and glanced at him. His white cut-off jeans interrupted the deep tan running from his bare toes right up to his tousled brown hair. I watched him, fascinated by the way determination tightened every muscle in his long, lean frame. He slowed down and studied the situation.

"There's lights up ahead, Sylvi."

The wipers slapped uselessly back and forth. Through the rain-drenched windshield, I made out fuzzy headlights. Z leaned forward squinting past the halo of oncoming lights into the wet darkness. "Holy shit, taillights." He came to a full stop behind a line of cars. "The fucking bridge over the Rio Conchos is flooded," he shouted over the storm.

Our headlights illuminated the cars in front of us awaiting their turns to cross. After one made it over from the other side, we moved ahead a car length as each vehicle ahead of us proceeded across. Four moves forward and I could see a torrent of water roaring over the bridge.

The pickup truck in front of us started across. The current hit it hard, shoving it sideways, but the truck straightened and made it.

Swallowing the lump in my throat, I watched the next car from the other side start toward us. Would it make it to our side of the bridge? *Perhaps in some other lifetime, not tonight. Tonight can not be happening.* "Volkswagens are watertight, aren't they, Z?" He did not hear me. I kept talking anyway. "If this flood carries us to the abyss below, can we count on its being watertight? How about if we hang a 'U' and wait until morning?"

Z gripped the wheel, his jaw tight, his entire frame wired. His eyes gauged every possibility as the oncoming car washed ever so slightly toward the edge of the bridge. I couldn't see a guardrail but prayed there was one to prevent the car from plummeting into the river below. I wiped the fog from our windshield. The lights of the oncoming car shone right in our faces.

Our turn.

Z renewed his grip on the wheel and revved the engine. No turning back. I grabbed the chicken bar on the dashboard and hung on. *Please, dear God, let us make it.* The floodwaters crashed against my door. Rain pounded on top of us, rushed in front and behind. He gunned the motor, propelling us forward to escape the water's sideways shove as the car slid to the left.

An eternity passed, but Z did not flinch. His determination did not falter. Should the motor die, should the entire exterior of the car wash away, one thing became completely clear to me. The sheer force of McKenzie's will would move us across that bridge.

Lights from the line of cars opposite us snapped me from the slow motion of our crossing into the relief of arriving on the other side.

Safe.

"Guess we were meant to live and fight in the revolution, baby," he yelled.

The next morning dawned with the promise of reaching our destination. The sun burst above unnamed mountains in the distance as we continued along Highway 45 south of Parral.

"After we survived the bridge last night, Z, you said it meant we were to live and fight in the revolution. Do you think surviving the flood was a sign?"

"Yeah, I do."

"So you believe we're destined to fight in a violent revolution?"

"You're reading too much into it, Sylvi. We're alive, so we'll be part of changing the world."

Is our relationship too perilous a path? Will my own journey be destroyed by his? What will happen to my daughters if I die in the process?

Hours passed as we pressed on. My heavy thoughts wearied me, and I fell asleep.

Z shook me awake, and I glanced at my watch. Three hours had passed since we'd passed through Durango. Prickly pear cactus covered the hills. As we rounded a bend, Zacatecas began revealing itself. "Local stone," Z pointed out. "Everything here is built out of it."

And it was. Stone in shades of dark browns, light browns and shades of orange rust. "An enchanting place," I murmured.

Over our *carne, rellenos* and strawberry water. He, at last, opened the sore festering within me all day. "The bridge really got to you didn't it?" he said. "You've hardly spoken all day."

"Damned straight it got to me. You didn't even consider turning around, did you? You didn't ever think of who would raise my kids if we drowned. All you could see was some fucking challenge you had to meet." I fidgeted with my fork and pushed food around on my plate. I watched him chew and waited for his response.

"That's what you've been stewing about all day?" He gulped down his strawberry water.

"I've thought about a lot of things, but it boils down to the bridge. Yes."

"All right, Sylvi, let's talk about it. I looked at the situation, the force of the water impacting the cars crossing ahead of us. I calculated the risk and decided our chances were good enough to try it."

"And?" I pushed for more.

"And, no, I didn't think about who would raise your kids. In my gut, I knew we'd make it. You and me will raise your kids."

Calm settled within me. I knew what he said was real. Why had I wasted most of the day doubting?

"Don't close me out, baby. Talk to me, I'm not trying to consume you. Tell me what's on your mind."

"There's too many things to sort out, Z. Bottom line, I was bothered all day thinking you put our lives on the line to prove a point, to get a sign."

"I wish you wouldn't take the 'sign' business so seriously. We made it to the other side alive. I took it as a sign. We lived therefore our lives must have purpose. Whether it means the revolution or not, I can't be sure. I don't have a crystal ball."

I reached for his hand. "I'm sorry I got so upset. I trusted you while it was all happening, but today I was bedeviled with misgivings. I'll let it go."

"Good," he said. "Let's get on the road."

Outside the restaurant, he asked me to drive. As he directed me back to the highway, he pointed out government buildings and a church. "Those are the malignancies threatening us all," he said, "the institutions sucking the life from the people. Instead of making it possible for them to feed themselves, the government and the church feed off them, take everything they've got. Poor bastards."

"The poverty is so much more evident here than in the States," I observed. "Back home we're comfortable hiding it as much as possible."

"Deceived is what we are. In the U. S., we're lied to and made to feel like everything's okay." He pointed in the direction I should turn to get back on the 45. "Down here the people are told to accept poverty, and injustice, and shut up."

"You'd think after all the revolutions they've fought, things would be better," I said.

"You have to watch out for revolutionaries who only want power for themselves and not for the people."

"How are the poor and illiterate to know what's true and what's empty rhetoric?" I asked.

"How do middle class, brainwashed Americans know what's true and what's empty rhetoric?" He challenged. "You think about it, baby. I'm going to catch a nap. Stay on 45 and wake me up before we get into Queretaro. From there, I'll drive on to Mexico City."

He leaned his head back. Soon his breathing relaxed into a slow, regular pattern.

His question about middle class, brainwashed Americans stuck in my head as I drove. *Our station in life doesn't really matter when it comes to evaluating political rhetoric. We're daily bombarded with TV commercials, sit-coms and news media feeding our apathy, making us manipulated masses just like the Mexican population. The difference between us and the Mexicans is that we fancy ourselves quite literate, intelligent and free. O course, we're not.*

Z always makes me think. Always takes me beyond my level of comfort. "I love you so much," I whispered to him as he slept.

The hot afternoon wind blew through the car, and my head filled with scenes from the summer. I saw my house like a stage overrun with players exploring the outer limits. The marijuana smoke pushed cobwebs from our minds. Peyote and LSD exploded us through new doorways to discovery. The American dream had dissolved into quicksand. We watched war and consumerism sucking the nation under and wondered what part we would play in saving it.

The mellow sun hung above the horizon in front of us. The air took on a golden quality, and my mind continued churning.

Only a world filled with love and compassion can bring about the needed changes. How will it happen? Rob talked of weed and hallucinogens ushering in this loving, caring world. But it strikes me now that everybody is on their own trip. Not everyone who partakes of these things love their brothers and sisters, or the earth.

I glanced at Z, watched the wind tug at his hair, and wondered if he was dreaming of revolution.

The miles went by, and I longed for the spiritual path I'd begun with Rob. *How can I move political obstacles out of the way and get to the truth, quit battling in my soul about how change will come? I recognize changes within myself, and maybe that's all it is, one person at a time, heading for the light, life's journey. Is that too simple? But how do we deal with the present social injustice haunting McKenzie, me, and others like us?*

The sun sank as I passed a kilometer sign. "Z." I shook him. "We're getting close to Queretaro. Wake up."

After several tries, he responded. "I'm awake, baby, pull over. I'll drive."

The other side of Queretaro, night crept around us. The trees and bushes along the highway, transformed by pale moonlight, became misshapen ghosts ushering us into the interior of Mexico. We'd left the desert behind.

In Mexico City, we gassed up the car and ate dinner quickly at a small café. "We'll get to Acapulco late tonight," Z assured me.

Back on the road, he told me Miguel's story. The man was born in Guatemala and had no memory of his real father. What he did remember was his mother climbing on a horse behind a man Miguel supposed must have fathered the baby his mother held in her arms. The man tried to drown Miguel, but he'd survived. At the age of twelve, he made his way to the coast where he stowed away on a ship bound for New York City. In the city, he found a job in a restaurant. During the hours he wasn't at work, he went to school and learned English, eventually moved to Chicago, and got a job in an electrical appliance plant. He married a woman, and they had four children.

"How did he get to Acapulco?" I asked.

"It started with his decision to return to Guatemala. He packed up his wife and kids, drove down through Mexico, and took a job as a cop in Guatemala."

"A cop? You're putting me on." I laughed. "But his wife was from Chicago, what did she think of all this? Where are she and the kids now?"

"Hold on, Sylvi, one question at a time. First, it's true. Miguel took a job as a cop. In Guatemala things are a lot different than in the States. Corruption is right out in the open. He figured he wanted to know how the system worked. Being a cop was the quickest way."

"And his family?"

"His wife couldn't take it. Life was too hard. He sold their car just to live. He says if it had been him and his wife, they might have made it, but the kids created too much of a hassle. She freaked out, went to the U. S. Embassy and asked for assistance to get her and the kids back to the States. She got it and left."

"Does he know where she is now?" I asked.

"He thinks she went back to her family in Chicago, says he never heard from her after she split."

"Doesn't he miss them?"

"Maybe, but it happened years ago. Sometime later he moved on to Acapulco, and his life now, well, I can't say it would be good for a family."

Miguel's story unsettled me, and left me with too many questions I didn't feel comfortable asking. "Is that the end?"

"I guess so. He's been in Acapulco several years, doing what he's doing."

I ventured one more question. "Does the fact that he abandoned his family bother you?"

"It would bother me if he had, baby, but they left him. He was trying everything he could to make it work."

"But he didn't have to go to Guatemala."

"Who knows what makes a man do what he does?"

Z's question made me uneasy, and our conversation dwindled. I dozed. A couple hours later Z's voice brought me awake. "We're in Acapulco, and I've got us a room. Come on."

I took his hand.

Blinking I watched mid-morning sunlight slip between louvered wooden slats covering the east window of our room. The slivers of light broadened, spreading across our loose, rumpled sheets. Above our bed, the blades of a ceiling fan clicked as they circled. I remembered arriving in the wee hours of the morning.

"Z, are you awake?"

"Now I am."

We followed a flower-lined pathway through the hotel courtyard to a nearby café. We sipped strong Mexican coffee. I looked out the window over red, tiled rooftops to the ocean beyond, sparkling in deep indigo and turquoise. The houses descended a terraced hillside, ending at the beaches and harbor below. "It's beautiful, Z. So much more so than I'd imagined. I couldn't picture you here when you'd kiss me and tell me you'd see me when you got back from Acapulco."

"After this trip, you'll know all about it."

"Now that I see it, I wonder why you'd ever leave here."

"At first, I left it to sell my weed in the States. Now I leave it to come home to you."

A woman in a bright, print dress set plates of *huevos rancheros* in front of us. I smiled up at her. "*Gracias.*" One of the few Spanish words I knew. The eggs, hot salsa, and tortillas smelled good and burned going down—the way I liked them.

"After breakfast, we'll buy you a bikini. You can hang out at the beach while I find Miguel," Z said.

"You don't want me to go with you?"

"No, baby, people would get paranoid if I had someone with me they didn't know. Best to track him down by myself, but I'll meet you back at the hotel room when the sun's about three-quarters down the sky."

"Between four and five?"

"You're the one who wears the watch."

I spent several hours at the beach. I smoothed coconut oil all over me, splashed into the water and floated under a sky bright full of hundreds of tiny clouds. Finally, I trudged across the sand and stretched out in a hammock, one of several hanging in a row and shaded by a long, thatched roof. There I drifted and dreamed, while humid heat made me sweat, and the ocean breeze cooled me. Having stashed my watch in my bag, I let the sun be the timekeeper. On my way back to the hotel, I bought pineapple and orange slices from a street vendor. Flavors burst in my mouth as I wended my way past pink and purple bougainvillea-covered walls. Hibiscus, in bright reds and yellows grew in great, tall bushes. *This is paradise.*

In the hotel room, I showered and packed before Z came through the door. "Looks like you're ready to go, baby. Let's check out. Miguel's in the lobby."

"My day was a dream," I said as Z crossed the room and picked up the suitcase.

"I'm glad." He stepped around me and kissed the back of my neck. "Took me a while to find Miguel, but we're all set to go into the jungle tonight."

"It's okay for me to go along?"

"Sure, but you'll have to stay in the car while Miguel and I walk the suitcases into the farmer."

"I'm cool with that."

Miguel sat in a rattan chair by the two glass doors at the front of the lobby. The doors stood open, inviting the night in to cool things off. He did not rise but acknowledged me with a nod. His black, wavy hair neatly trimmed, and his clothing conservative, right down to his shiny brown shoes. I wondered if my belled Levis and loose, embroidered blouse were out of place. Z had suggested I dress like a tourist. "So, you're McKenzie's woman, a real hippie, no?"

Obviously, I failed the tourist look, felt uncomfortable, and uncertain how to reply. I smiled. "You could say yes on both counts. And you are Miguel, Z's intriguing friend who tells stories of Che Guevara and the revolution. You are a legend. It is good to meet you at last."

Much to my relief, his face brightened. We strolled behind him out the door. I'd imagined him a taller man.

Miguel suggested we go to the lagoon for dinner. "The lagoon?" I asked

"It's a place where we sit at a table under the trees and have cool drinks while fishermen go out and catch fish. Then they cook them for us over an open fire," Miguel explained.

"Right on." I laughed. "Does this happen all the time, or am I still in my perfect dream from the beach?"

"What are you telling her, mon, Acapulco's paradise? Don't let this place charm you," Miguel warned as he held the car seat forward for me to get in. "Take care to watch your back, Sylvi. Your old man knows. He can tell you stories."

Close to eleven, we began our journey into the jungle. The night crowded, pitch black, around us. Miguel drove about twenty miles along a narrow blacktop road before stopping. "Here, Sylvi, having trouble staying awake?" He pulled something from his shirt pocket and offered it to me. "Take this. You don't want to miss anything." I peered at the capsule he dropped into my palm, a black beauty—my speed of choice.

"Thanks, Miguel."

"Wait in the car, baby," Z instructed. "Miguel and I have to walk the suitcases in." He'd explained this to me before—they would deliver the cases to the farmer, agree on the price, and return to the car.

I don't know how long they were gone, but it was long enough for the speed to wake me up. I watched the late-rising moon, only half-full, climb above the top of the ragged jungle and cast a shadowy spell. The crunch of gravel behind the car made me jump.

Miguel and Z got in the front seat, and we were off again. "We'll drive to a clearing and wait until it's time to pick up the suitcases," Miguel said.

In another twenty minutes he pulled the car off the road. The three of us walked across a pasture and sat down on a grassy cliff overlooking the ocean. Cattle grazed under the thousands of stars filling the night sky. A hundred feet below, waves crashed against the rocks. Salt air kissed my face.

We talked of revolution and its inevitability. "Don't you get it, Sylvi?" Miguel asked. "Che knew the only thing a man can do is pick up a gun against tyranny, against imperialism."

"Come on, you guys, this is two against one. Even if it comes down to an armed struggle, I will never pick up arms against another human being."

"Sure, baby, Gandhi made it to the sea, won the salt war. But before that victory, his non-violent followers shed a lot of blood and more than a thousand died at the hands of the British. You think governments are going to listen and volunteer to dismantle their framework so the common man's needs are met? No, you have to take them down with real bullets."

Miguel ground his fist into the earth. "It's easy, Sylvi, you crush them."

Z didn't give me a chance to respond. "You're one of the few people I know, baby, who grew up with everything you needed and most of what you wanted. How can you understand life at the bottom of the barrel?"

"Maybe you're right, but I do understand in my heart. Inside me, I can relate to the misery of being a have-not."

"Bullshit, Sylvi." Miguel pointed a finger in my face. "I was twelve when I climbed out of the hole where I hid on the ship and put my feet on sidewalks in New York. Nobody wanted to know me. I hustled for every dime, every fucking dime. You want to tell me how you can relate to living out of garbage cans? He shifted his intense glare toward the ocean.

The waves battering the rocks below filled our silence with a natural violence, while the bright heaven above kept a peaceful vigil. Z lit a joint.

"You're right, Miguel. How could I presume to understand? Things are more of a theory with me, but I feel compassion toward others experiencing the hardships you're talking about. I need to be part of the struggle, the peaceful struggle, even if it means I die like Gandhi's followers."

He turned from the ocean to look at me. I took a hit off the joint and offered it to him. "Okay, Sylvi." He inhaled. "I'll give you the benefit of the doubt."

Enough time had passed, and we drove back to pick up the suitcases filled with weed. Miguel set one on the floor behind the driver's seat. Z stacked the other two on the backseat next to me, and I covered them with a blanket. We began the journey back to Acapulco.

The moon slid down the night sky. Our headlights pierced the darkness. I reflected on the stars, the tranquil cattle, the sea cliff, the angry ocean, and the revolution as the blackness evolved into translucent gray. Trembling threads of pink trailed across the sky above lacy ferns and broad-leafed banana trees. Dawn pierced the dense jungle with slender shards of light, and tinseled the varied shades of green foliage in fragile gold. The wind carried the fragrance of palms, flowering vines, and moist earth through the car windows.

The sun had fully risen when we came to a stop behind a bus. Women, in brightly patterned blouses and skirts balanced baskets full of vegetables and fruits on their heads. Men in loose white shirts and trousers carried chickens in wooden cages on their shoulders. Using a ladder at the back, the men climbed up and tied the cages to the rack atop the bus. Then, climbing down, boarded, along with the women. Neighborly chatter floated in the morning breeze as the remaining people gradually disappeared into the jungle. The bus groaned and wheezed, sagging under its load, as it resumed its journey to the marketplace.

I leaned forward, my face between Miguel's right shoulder and Z's left, fascinated by this world wholly different from anything I knew. Happening to glance at the gas gauge, I saw the tank was empty. "Is there a gas station close by?" I asked.

"Why didn't you fill the tank before I met you at the hotel, asshole?" Miguel was pissed.

"I spaced. Shit. Can we get gas around here?"

"There's a garage down the road. I don't like making a stop for gas with weed in the car. Where the hell's your head, mon? You come down here with your woman and leave your brains in the States."

"Okay, Miguel, I apologize. You can bet it won't happen again."

Miguel turned onto a rough dirt road and passed a few huts

before pulling in front of a square building on our right. He honked the horn and got out of the car. In a moment, two big, wooden doors at the front swung open, revealing a combination blacksmith shop and garage.

Miguel spoke in Spanish to the man who had pushed the doors open. The man scurried back inside as Miguel opened the trunk at the front of the car and removed the gas cap. The man emerged from the garage with a tall, slender metal pitcher and poured its contents into the gas tank. Children and women watched from across the road. After he poured two more pitchers into the tank, Miguel paid him. They talked as Miguel replaced the gas cap, closed the trunk, and slid behind the steering wheel.

"I've never seen anything like this before." I saw it as an adventure.

We turned onto the blacktop.

"You wouldn't have seen it now, except your old man forgot to put gas in the car last night."

"Look, I get it," Z said. "I know we'd be up shit creek if we ran out of gas here in the jungle. It will never happen again, believe me. Can we let it go?"

"Let it go?" Miguel frowned. "Let's just hope he bought my small talk about being a guide for these *loco touristas*. Otherwise, we'll be answering questions by the *federales*."

After a tense hour between the garage and Acapulco, we pulled into a motel. I had no idea where we were. It clearly wasn't downtown. Z and Miguel carried the three suitcases from the back seat along with several newspapers we'd picked up at a newsstand on the way into town.

I got out of the car, and Z called over his shoulder, "Would you bring our bag from the trunk, Sylvi?"

Once inside, Z opened our case and pulled his two duffel bags from it. He and Miguel spread newspapers on the floor, opened one of the suitcases and began bundling the weed in sheets of newspaper. They worked in silence while I sat by the window feeling uneasy.

We heard loud voices and car doors slamming outside. "*Federales*," Miguel spat the word at Z. "You fucking asshole."

"Why don't you split, Miguel? You got your bread." Z raised his voice.

I tilted a slat on the louvered window and looked out. "They're just people," I said. "Two men and two women going into the room next to this one."

"You don't know shit about what we're doing, do you, Sylvi?" Miguel snarled. "Just two men and two women," he mimicked. "They're cops, and they're here because your old man fucked up."

"I told you, man, get out. I'll finish here. You want to leave? Go ahead." Z stood, walked around the newspapers, grabbed Miguel's arm and jerked him to his feet.

"You can't whip my ass, mother-fucker. Don't even try it." Miguel's eyes flashed. He glanced at me. I froze.

Z dropped Miguel's arm and shoved him backward against the door. "You've lost it, Miguel. You're crazy. What kind of pills you been popping?"

"Pills don't matter, mon. I keep my head together. You want to wait around and get busted? Go ahead." He brushed bits of weed off the front of his shirt and pants. "Is anybody out front now, Sylvi?"

"No."

Miguel opened the door, glanced quickly to his left and to his right, and walked away. I closed the door behind him wondering if he was right about staying and being busted, but my trust remained in Z.

"He freaks sometimes," Z said. "Paranoid, but he'll be okay. Help me over here, baby." He showed me how to gather a bunch of weed and fold newspaper around it to make cylindrical packages about eight inches long and six inches in diameter. He offered no other explanation about Miguel, and I felt it best not to ask. We worked quickly and finished packing it all into the duffel bags in about a half hour, put clothes from our suitcase on top of the weed and tied the duffels' strings.

"I'll load the bags in the car, baby. Pick up the newspaper from the floor, flush any loose weed down the toilet, fold the papers, and put them on top of the clothes in our suitcase. I'll be right back and help you finish."

My hands shook, but I carried out his instructions.

We left everything in good order and dropped the three empty suitcases off at a newsstand on our way out of town. Z explained to me that Miguel would pick them up later.

"Isn't this the newsstand where we bought the papers we wrapped the pot in?" I asked.

"Very observant, baby."

"What's the connection?"

"Miguel owns several newsstands around town. It's his legitimate business."

"Oh." I tried to grasp the many things that must have escaped me. "Is this what it's normally like?" I asked.

"There is no normal in this business. This trip has been better than some and worse than others."

"Was I the problem?"

"I think you were a problem for Miguel, but not for me. I'm glad you're here."

"Me, too, but I was really scared back there."

"I know you were, baby, I'm sorry. I should have remembered to gas up the car. Maybe he wouldn't have freaked, but it's not a sure thing. Sometimes he doesn't need a reason."

"Miguel aside, I'm glad we're on our way home." I rested my head on Z's shoulder. "Miguel was right about one thing."

"What, baby?"

"Acapulco's not always paradise."

By nightfall we reached Mexico City. "You must be starving, baby."

"Yeah, we haven't eaten since dinner at the lagoon."

He laughed. "I forgot to tell you, regular meals are not a part of this job. Tell you what, let's eat, then get a hotel and catch some decent sleep. I want to drive straight through tomorrow."

"It's almost twelve hundred miles, Z. Are you trying to kill yourself?"

"I've done it before. You'll help keep me awake, and I've got a few Dexedrine. I'll be fine. Besides, I have to get you back to your precious job by Monday."

"I probably don't have a job." I laughed. "If I were my boss, I'd fire my ass."

"However it happens is okay with me, baby. There are better things you can do with your time."

We ate dinner on the tiled patio of a café where we could keep an eye on the car and its cargo. Afterwards, we checked in at a nearby hotel. Our room had polished wood floors and heavy burgundy draperies. I opened our suitcase and extracted toothbrushes and toothpaste while Z settled the duffels in a corner. "McKenzie, come see. A sunken tub, isn't this great?" I turned on the faucets, shook off my sandals and dropped my clothes on the floor.

"Are there bubbles?" he asked.

"Get the shampoo out of the suitcase, and we'll make some."

Morning came too soon. After a quick breakfast and lots of coffee, we were homeward bound. Skies in a hundred shades of blue and adrift with cloud animals saw us safely to the gold-tinged, blood-red sunset a hundred miles south of Torreon. Translucent twilight slipped into a dark velvet night that carried us through Chihuahua. We skirted Juarez, headed east into the sunrise and, in a short time, arrived on the other side of a little town called Zaragoza where McKenzie would wade across the river. He stopped the car at the edge of the Rio Grande. I got out and joined him as he pulled duffel bags from the trunk. He set the bags on the ground, and we wrapped our arms around each other. Feeling the artificial energy from the speed pulsing through his tired body, I reached both my hands up to massage the back of his neck. I had caught short naps and was nowhere as spent as him.

"This is it, baby." He cupped my face in his hands. "I'll meet you on the other side like we planned." His lips brushed mine as he stooped, picked up the duffels, and shouldered them. He walked quickly to the river, made his way down the bank, and into the water.

I took a deep breath, settled into the driver's seat, started the car, and turned it around. Looking back, I saw Z waist deep in muddy Rio Grande water. My heart pounded in my throat and ears as I recalled his instructions. "Drive to the Zaragoza Bridge, like a normal person on a Sunday afternoon. Stay on the road from the bridge until you hit Highway 80, turn east, and drive about a mile to a café on the right.

While I drove to the border crossing, I tried out my voice a few times, rehearsing a relaxed smile and saying, "American."

In ten minutes, I was there. A uniformed officer came to the door of a small U. S. Customs building. "Citizenship?" His eyes scanned the inside of the car without any real interest.

I smiled. "American."

He waved me through, and I followed the road through fields of cotton on the U. S. side of the border. *How many roads have we traveled since my phone call to Carl in late August? And he told me he wasn't sending the girls back, not now, not ever. Arrogant bastard. He doesn't treat them well when they're with him. The only reason he wants to keep them is to spite me. After all, I'd dared to divorce him. A few years have passed, but he must still despise me. Funny, I thought we were nearing a plateau of reasonableness in our post-divorce relationship. Am I wrong or what?*

I turned east on Highway 80. *What happens to our innocent dreams? The ones we begin building in early womanhood, the ones with the perfect husband, beautiful children, and all the rest. Nobody ever told me what to do when the dream begins to corrode, when the toxins begin to spill through the cracks, and we all run for our lives. Then it's never the same.* The thought snapped me back to the moment.

I'd been watching along the right side of the highway without seeing our rendezvous point. At least I thought I'd been watching. I drove on, concentrating on the immediate and not letting my mind rehearse old dilemmas. *Where the hell is the café? I must have gone too far and passed it.* Slowing down, I hung a "U." *My God, what if I've missed Z, and he's come to the notice of the local sheriff? What if he's been busted? It's all my fault. Where is my head?* I sped up and watched closely for the café. I felt my heart hammering in my head, in my chest, in my belly, in my legs. *God, please let me find the blasted café.*

There it is. I swung across the highway and into the graveled parking area. Shaking, I went inside. Before my eyes had time to adjust to the dim light, I felt Z's hand on my elbow.

"Good timing, baby, I got here a few minutes ago. I ordered two cups of coffee to go."

I paid the bill while he took the duffels to the car. Once in the car, I threw my arms around him. "I am so glad to see you. I passed this place before. I was afraid I'd missed you, that something terrible had happened to you."

"It took me a little longer than I expected to cross the river and walk the mile through the fields, but everything's turned out okay, baby. Let's go home and crash. Tomorrow we have to plan a kidnapping."

Chapter 11
The Road to Phoenix and Back

Hard to believe, but when I returned to work on Monday morning, Jason believed I'd been seriously ill. I wanted to apologize to him for lying. I'd come to abhor it over the years, recognizing that a lie is the ultimate form of disrespect for another human being. Nevertheless I had lied to him in my fear-ridden attempt to protect my job. McKenzie, my children, my beliefs all in a state of flux, I couldn't risk my livelihood, too.

McKenzie picked me up from work at the end of that demanding Monday. "Can you get a lift to work for a few days, Sylvi?"

"I suppose. What's on your mind?"

"Thought I'd take the car to the coast and deliver the weed. On my way back, I'll call you. You get on a plane. I'll meet you at the Phoenix airport, and we'll take the kids. What do you think?"

I drew in a sharp breath. Our eyes met as I tried to imagine the actual kidnapping.

"Well?" he asked.

"I'm thinking about walking on to the school yard, placing my hand in theirs, and leaving with them. What kind of problems might arise?"

"I have a few reservations myself. I know what the penalty for kidnapping is."

"I know, too, Z. I really can't ask you to be part of this."

"You didn't ask. I volunteered."

A week later, on a Monday night, Z left for California. Around one in the morning of the following Friday, a knock on my bedroom door woke me.

"Sylvi," Syd called from the hallway. "Your old man's on the phone."

I opened my door, and he handed me the receiver. "Thanks. Were you asleep?"

"Yeah, me, Irish and Aiden crashed in the den a little while after you turned in." He stretched and yawned. "Guess we'll head out."

"Wait a minute, Syd, until I talk to Z," I said, then spoke into the phone, "What's happening, babe?"

"I had a dream. The falcon landed." Our code for me to get on the plane.

"It's not a dream." My reply meant I'd see him at the Phoenix airport. "I love you."

"I love you, too."

I hung up and turned to Syd. "Can you guys drop me at the airport?"

"No problem. Let me rouse my companions."

"I'll be ready in a minute." I hurried to my closet, threw a turquoise and yellow knit mini-dress over my head, pulled on yellow fishnet hose, and stepped into turquoise heels. It was the best I could do for a conservative look.

"I'm ready." I rushed through the hallway.

Syd, Irish and Aiden followed me to their car.

"So this is it, huh, Sylvi?"

"Yup, the day I get my kids back. I've got the addresses of the schools. Z has a copy too. Kristi's in one school, and Katrina's in another."

"How did you get the info?" Irish asked. "I'm sure your ex didn't give it up."

"That bastard wouldn't give me the right time of day. My lawyer retained a private eye in Phoenix. I guess we'll get the bill."

We parked. All of them got out with me. "It's pretty lonely waiting for an airplane this time of night," Aiden said. "We'll stay with you."

My flight didn't leave for two hours, so we sat around a table in the coffee shop and ordered breakfast.

"It may not be the best time to bring this up," Syd said.

"Bring up what?" I asked.

"Aiden and I have wanted to pull you aside, Sylvi, and apologize for bringing Z to your house."

"Apologize?" I stopped spreading jelly on my biscuit. "Why?"

He studied the faces of the other two for a moment before answering. "Because we didn't realize what a heavy dude he was. We don't think you realize it either, Sylvi. You're a poet, a gentle soul, while he's splashing murals of Che Guevara, the revolution, and violent shit all over your walls. Dig?"

"I'm not sure I do. I see you guys listening to him like you're in a trance."

"He's got charisma," Aiden said. "Even after our disastrous trip to Mexico, I can say he is inspiring. But ultimately, we can walk away." He looked from Irish to Syd for assurance. "The three of us have talked about it. We see you can't walk away."

"He's heavy duty," Irish said. "Syd and Aiden think they've put you in danger. He's balls-out dealing from your house, has you going down to Mexico with him, and now this kidnapping thing."

An awkward silence ensued. We fidgeted with our food, dabbed our mouths with napkins, and avoided looking directly at each other.

"Wow, you guys blow me away. I had no idea how you felt about Z."

"Maybe we've said too much. But we are worried about you." Syd tugged at one end of his mustache.

"Z didn't put me up to kidnapping the kids. It was the best advice the lawyers had to offer. You have no responsibility to protect me, for God's sake. And yeah, you're right. I can't walk away from Z because I don't want to. I love him, and I'm up for the whole trip."

"Okay. We just wanted you to know where we're coming from. Maybe we're off the wall or whatever. But we're here for you," Aiden said. Syd and Irish nodded.

I heard the boarding call for my plane and scribbled my office phone number on a napkin. "Would one of you call my boss around 7:30 this morning? Please do not use the phone at the house. It's a lot to ask, I know, but tell him I got on a plane in the middle of the night and am kidnapping my kids. Maybe he'll understand."

Aiden surprised me with his instant response. "I'll do it."

"I'm eternally grateful. You know Judy and Gary went to Albuquerque. Will you all hang at the house and feed Daiquiri?

"We will," Irish said.

"I love you guys." I dashed from the coffee shop, across the tarmac, and up the stairs to the plane.

Darkness yawned ever wider between the ground and the airplane. City lights glittered then disappeared as we flew over the mountains and headed into the diamond-studded sky. Drawing my notebook and pen from my purse, I began a letter.

My dear Judy,

How very much I wish you were here instead of in the mountains (although I hope you and Gary are really grooving up there).

I need to talk to you. Aiden, Syd and Irish laid something on me before I got on this plane.

I penned the account of the conversation at the coffee shop then continued:

I couldn't bring myself to tell them that sometimes Z scares me, too. Sounds like betrayal, doesn't it? It's not. Even though something inside of me trembles at his impetuosity and his revolutionary rhetoric, I still trust him, love him so much. When you get back to El Paso, I want to tell you about our trip to Mexico, something I never would have done if it weren't for him. Sometimes I feel like my life is out of control, I'm betraying myself and going off on his trip (you know, the man-tangent I've tried to avoid). On the other hand, it's not a tangent. It is all consuming, and life with him and my girls is all I care about. They are my poetry and the sunshine lighting new paths, finding new doorways. Am I insane? Today we are kidnapping Kristi and Katrina. I can't say more right now except I'm terrified. Hope to see you soon. It's almost time for Pat to have their baby. Please come home. We can sit around her big oak table and talk and laugh. We can cry and tell all our secrets. We can do Tarot spreads and figure it all out. We're about to land in Phoenix. Z will be at the airport. I know if you knew this was happening today, you would be praying for all to go well. I pray the same for you—whatever your day holds.

Night yielded to day as we landed. I descended the steps from the plane into the muggy, Phoenix morning. Z emerged from the crowd milling on the tarmac. I flashed on the conversation in the coffee shop with Syd, Aiden, and Irish. I would not mention it to McKenzie, not ever.

"You always feel so damned good," he whispered, holding me close. The anxieties that plagued me on the plane slipped away.

"When did you get to Phoenix, Z?" We made our way through the terminal to the parking lot.

"An hour ago. Long enough to grab something to eat and check out the schools' locations."

In the car, Z said, "According to the info from your lawyer, the girls arrive at their schools by bus--Kristi first."

"Where is her school?" I asked.

"We're here." He placed his left index finger at the center of the steering wheel and drew invisible lines with his right index finger, explaining how the streets connected from Kristi's school to Katrina's. "Are you okay, baby? You look a little pale."

"I'm fine," I assured him. "I just need to get my bearings."

"We'll drive by both schools. Then we'll circle back to Kristi's. By then her bus will be there."

The day had brightened by the time we parked across and down the street from where the bus deposited the children.

"There she is, Z."

"Okay, baby, let's get out just like we belong here."

We walked across the street and onto the playground. Kristi stood looking around, probably for her friends.

"Kristi," I called softly when we were about ten feet from her.

Her mouth dropped open. "Mom, what are you doing here?"

I knelt beside her. "I came to take you home, sweetheart. You want to go home?"

"Oh, Mommy." She shuffled her feet in the dust. I put my arms around her. Z kept a lookout.

"Daddy and Jazelle told me to never go with you. I love you, Mommy, but they told me not to go." Her little face twisted, close to tears.

"It's okay, sweetie, we can call them when we get home and let them know you're safe."

"Looks like a teacher heading this way," Z warned.

"It's my teacher." She pulled away from me. "Hi," Kristi said to the plump woman, "this is my mom."

"How do you do." I stood and extended my hand.

Her teacher ignored my hand and instead took a firm hold on Kristi's. She looked sternly at Z, then at me before she smiled ever so slightly. "Why don't we all go into the classroom where we can talk?"

"That's fine," I said. "We'd be happy to."

"Better not, baby," Z whispered as I grabbed his hand and followed my daughter and her teacher.

"We don't want to cause a fuss, Z. Maybe I can explain things, and she'll come with us."

We had lagged a few feet behind the two of them. They crossed a narrow sidewalk, and went into a schoolroom door, one of a dozen or so opening onto the playground.

"I'm telling you, baby. There's going to be trouble. We're wasting precious time here."

"We have to give it a shot. Kristi is frightened. I can't run away."

We stepped through the door, to see the teacher, dragging Kristi by the hand, run to the front of the room. She pulled a long cord hanging from the public address system box, which hung on the wall above the blackboard.

"Help us. We're being attacked," she shouted, repeating it three or four times.

"I told you, baby. Let's split."

I started toward Kristi.

"We're not attacking anybody, sweetie, don't be afraid."

I was halfway to Kristi with Z right behind me when four or five men charged through the door, shouting for us to stop.

One of them yelled, "We know who you are. You two come with us right now."

They blocked our only exit, surrounded us, and pushed us outside toward the school's office.

"I'm Kristi's mother. I have custody papers right here." I rummaged in my purse as they shoved us along.

"I'm the principal, and I don't care what papers you have. We've been told about you."

"My daughter is terrified. What's the matter with you people?"

They pushed me into the school offices. Then all of them seemed to trip over themselves to get to a telephone, leaving us unguarded for a moment. Z gripped my arm. "Let's get out now." He pulled me outside. I saw Kristi in the classroom doorway for a split second. She was crying—so was I.

Z and I bolted across the playground, jumped in the car, and took off.

"This is all fucked up, baby. But we still have to make a try for Katrina. It's five minutes to her school.

I blotted my face with tissue and blew my nose. "Did you see her when we ran for the car? God, she must be totally traumatized. Those ignorant bastards call themselves educators. You tried to tell me, and I wouldn't listen."

"It's okay, Sylvi. Try to calm down."

The minutes between one school and the other seemed to take forever.

"There she is." I pointed. "See, close to the merry-go-round. They've cut her long curls short."

We got out and hurried in her direction.

"Mommy." She ran toward us.

I scooped her up. "My beautiful baby, would you like to come home with me and McKenzie?" I asked.

"Is Daiquiri there? I miss her."

"You bet she is. She's missed you, too."

"I'll get my doll and lunchbox."

"I've got them." Z said.

We walked from the playground, got in the car, and pulled into the morning traffic, threading our way through it as fast as we could.

Katrina sat cuddled on my lap.

We were almost out of Phoenix before she asked, "Is Kristi coming?"

"Not today, little angel," I said, "but maybe soon. I hope."

I enrolled Katrina in school in El Paso and employed a neighbor to see her to and from there safely. We had been home a week when Z rented a car and left for Mexico.

The following Saturday, Katrina and I visited Pat and Bob, who joined us for a drive to the upper valley to see friends. The serpentine boundaries separating Texas from New Mexico wound through the upper Rio Grande Valley on the west side of El Paso. Artists, Luther and Lilly lived in a rambling old adobe in the middle of cotton fields on the New Mexico side of the state line. Their closest neighbor lived half a mile away.

"Luther's in Mexico," Lilly told us as we sat round an old wooden table under a giant shade tree. Katrina ran off to play with their son who led the way to a big pile of sand cluttered with toys.

That last weekend of September hung suspended in pre-harvest sunshine and restored our souls. We talked of Rob's reports from the Democratic Convention in Chicago, the previous month, and the bleak political possibilities. We assured ourselves the ultimate victory would come on the wings of our collective spiritual awakening. Yet, we acknowledged we had become greater targets of the law.

Pat stretched her legs out in front of her, arched her back, giving the baby more room to move inside her great belly.

"Let's go inside." Lilly stood and, with long fingers, combed her brown hair up off her neck. "I'll make some tea, and cut up veggies to munch on."

"You and Luther have built a peaceful life here in the country," I said, standing in the kitchen with Lilly.

"I guess it is, generally speaking." She sliced a slender zucchini onto a plate. "But I'd be happier if Luther would stop dealing weed."

"Wow, do I ever hear that." I began to rinse carrots and a large bell pepper in the sink. "Z's in Mexico, too. I was there with him a couple of weeks ago. I can dig how it is to be caught up in the adventure. But the chances they take are too much."

"The scene's not cool right now. A friend of ours got busted about a month back," Lilly said. "I asked Luther not to go this time, but he said things were all set, said he knew it would be okay. I really have a hard time when he tells me that shit. Like, I'm supposed to simply hang loose and wait."

"I can dig it, Lilly. It bums me out, too, to be on the waiting end. You think they'll ever legalize pot?"

"With either Humphrey or Nixon on the horizon, probably not anytime soon."

Bob and Pat left the kitchen early in the conversation. We watched them, through the kitchen window, walk past the shade tree toward the kids on the sand pile. The window framed them against a background of cotton standing tall against distant, desert mountains and sun-drenched cloud puffs afloat in blue. The picture spoke peace to my heart. Lilly draped her arm across my shoulder. I tilted my head against hers, sisters in our uncertain world.

Kristi's eighth birthday on the second day of October caught me with my guard down. I had put a gift and card in the mail a week earlier, but I was unprepared for the emotional blow I suffered when

I telephoned. Carl refused to allow me to speak to her. Before he hung up, he could not help but gloat over the power he possessed to withhold my package from her.

My long, sad day ended with a report on the late news about students protesting the Olympic Games, which were scheduled to begin on October 12, in Mexico City. Hundreds of Mexican police emerged from Aztec ruins there and opened fire on the protesters. The living, who had not dispersed, and the dead, who had not been removed by sunset were carted away in military trucks. The Mexican authorities admitted to thirty-two dead, while others interviewed estimated three hundred.

"And Z's down there somewhere," I half muttered to myself.

Irish patted my hand. "He'll be okay, Sylvi. He always makes it back."

"Thanks for the encouragement. It's Kristi's birthday. Carl wouldn't let me talk to her. I don't even know if she was allowed to have the gift I sent. This day has been a bummer." I rose from the floor and stretched. "Ya'll turn off the TV whenever you want. I'm turning in."

The next afternoon, my heart still heavy, I pulled into my driveway behind an unfamiliar car. Katrina bounced out the kitchen door.

"You look cheerful, angel." I hugged her.

"Come see." She wiggled away, and ran through the kitchen and hallway.

I followed her to her room where Z grinned at me, a paintbrush in his hand.

"We're painting ballerinas and kitty cats on my walls, Mama. Isn't it beautiful?" She jumped up and down.

"Thank God, you're safe." I threw my arms around Z. The wet paintbrush didn't matter. Nothing mattered. "Please tell me you weren't in Mexico City yesterday."

"I was there in the morning—before all hell broke loose."

I kissed his face and his mouth. Although I couldn't do anything about Kristi, I could touch and love Katrina and McKenzie.

"Brought back some dynamite weed, baby." He lit a joint, handed it to me, and resumed painting the pink-skirted ballerina on the wall.

Pat's call surprised me the next day.

"Can you come over?" Her voice sounded strained.

"Is the baby coming?"

"No. I need moral support. Can't say more than that."

"I'll be right there."

I found Z in the backyard pushing Katrina in the swing and told him of the phone call.

"I can stay with Katrina," he assured me, "unless you want me to go. I'm expecting Aiden."

"Thanks. I'll be back as soon as I can." I hurried to the car.

"Luther was busted last night," Pat said. Tears streamed down her face.

"Oh, my God." I enfolded her in my arms. "Where's Bob?"

"He's driving Lilly to the jail to get Luther out."

"Where did he get busted?"

"A couple miles from his house. He was in his truck with the camper shell on it and a hundred keys of weed in the back. Stay with me until Bob gets back." We slumped to the couch with a box of tissues between us.

"Z returned from Mexico yesterday."

"You've got to tell him to stop, Sylvi. It's too dangerous."

"Like I'm going to tell him he can't go. He'll tell me, 'sure, baby, I'll fucking run out, get a nine-to-five job, and forget the revolution.'

And we'll live happily ever after. Z's not going to listen to me any more than Luther listened to Lilly. This is simply the way it is. What else can I say?"

"Nothing, I guess." Pat pressed the tissue against her face and swallowed a sob. "But things are heavier now. People are getting busted. I never thought I'd see it happening to any of us."

"Lilly was worried. The Saturday we visited, she talked about how she hadn't wanted Luther to go."

"I know."

"Is getting busted inevitable, Pat? Am I willing to go through it? Is it the price I'm likely to pay for this life I'm choosing?"

"I hope not. But I have to stop and ask myself today, why did we choose to turn on?"

"For me, it was Rob coming to town after Danny left, after the car wreck, and my life was shit. We smoked his weed, and it lifted my spirits. A few weeks later, we dropped peyote, and it changed my life forever."

"For us," Pat said, "it was Ted getting out of the Army, bringing hashish, and his message about the illegal war in Vietnam."

"It seems to me it's the turned-on people who pay more attention to what's happening. They're the ones putting word out about the chemical companies wreaking havoc on the environment and the CIA's involvement throughout the world."

"True. Remember, I'm the daughter of an Air Force colonel, and it blew me away to find out we had ulterior motives for 'helping' other countries. You're right, Sylvi. It is we who smoke dope who pass along the information. We sure as hell weren't taught it in school."

"I wonder if we hadn't turned on, would we have been open to hearing this stuff?" I asked.

"Probably not. I think weed, acid, and peyote has really opened a door to make us aware of what's going on in the world. The downside is that people we love are getting busted." Pat glanced through the front window. "Bob's here."

Bob had Luther and Lilly in tow. Lilly shared her distress with Pat and me. Bob lent moral support as Luther phoned his attorney's office for an appointment. Then the four of them prepared to head to Lilly and Luther's place in the valley.

I hugged Lilly and Pat, fled to my car and managed to drive a half mile before falling apart.

"Where's Katrina?" I kicked off my sandals and collapsed on the couch.

"She's playing with the neighbor kids." Z sat down, and I put my feet in his lap. "What is it, baby? You've been crying."

"Luther got busted." I blurted out the story, trying to stay composed.

"I feel for him. A hundred kilos in the back of a truck is asking for trouble. I hope he has a good lawyer."

Avoiding Z's eyes, I looked out the window.

"You're way too upset about this, baby." He turned my face toward him. "Maybe we'd better talk about it."

"If I asked you to stop dealing, Z, would you?"

Instead of answering, he embraced me. "Sylvi, baby, please don't cry and stir up bad vibes. I don't intend dealing forever, but while I am, I need your positive energy."

Z was in California the night the Olympics opened in Mexico City. None of the reporting on TV even referred to the protests and the deaths, which had occurred ten days earlier, just the razz-ma-tazz of the opening ceremony from Aztec Stadium.

Later in the week several of us sat passing a joint and watching as an official of the Olympics presented Tommie Smith and John Carlos with gold medals. The Star Spangled Banner blared over the loud speakers. Once the medals hung around their necks, they each raised a black-gloved fist until the anthem was over. The announcer expressed shock at the gesture.

"Right on." Irish raised his fist. "Those brothers know where it's at, man."

"Are they expressing solidarity with the Panthers or Malcolm X?" I asked.

"Could be either." Irish said. "Or they could be making a statement for Black Power in general. In any case, they've got balls. The white establishment pretty much rules the Olympics."

During the Games, Bob and Pat's baby came into the world. They named her Merry Cloud. Judy, who had returned from Albuquerque with Gary, called me to tell me the news. Katrina and I met them at the hospital. In adoration, we stood together to behold the awesome child sleeping in the arms of her mother who also slept. We tiptoed out.

In the hospital lobby, Judy asked us to drop by and see their new apartment. Katrina and I followed them to a place they called The Ghost Town. Judy related how a few enterprising people had thrown in on the purchase of an abandoned set of ten storefronts, five on each side of 'Main Street.' It had been part of a movie set for several westerns. They'd converted each storefront into an apartment with few creature comforts but a lot of atmosphere.

Gary went to jam with musician friends a few doors down leaving Judy, Katrina, and I alone. She related their Albuquerque adventure. They'd encountered an abundance of speed, which impaired their relationship, so, in an effort to preserve it, they got themselves together and left the mountains.

"So far, so good here in Ghost Town," she said.

Our conversation turned to the letter I'd written to her on the plane to Phoenix. "I'm so sorry you didn't get Kristi."

"Makes me sad to think about it," I said. "Knowing she'll come home when the time is right keeps me going."

"Interesting how Syd and those guys told you they were sorry to have introduced you to Z. I confess I worry about you, too, Sylvi. I wish he weren't dealing out of your house."

"Come on, Judy, everybody we know deals."

"Sure—a little here or there. But how many people do you know who make trips to Mexico on a regular basis?"

"Maybe three or four from around here. But this isn't Z's life work. This is for now—like one plank in the bridge we're building toward change."

"I hope so," Judy said. "In the letter you talked about fearing you were going off on his trip and forgetting about your own. What's happening?"

"He is all consuming, but I am studying the Tarot and writing my poetry. I don't want to do it without him."

She nodded in sympathy. "It's fucking hard to love somebody. Especially now when we're all trying to be so free—like we're redefining the word love. I have to say I'm impressed with the way he stuck by you through the kidnapping."

"I couldn't have done it alone." I told her the whole story before realizing it was after midnight.

"I need to get Katrina home." I picked her up. She'd fallen asleep hours earlier.

Judy wrapped a blanket around her. "It's a little chilly out there."

Music greeted me as I walked through the kitchen door in the wee hours of the morning. I wondered who was there. As I carried Katrina through the hallway, Z's voice came from the other side of the bathroom door which stood half open.

"That you, Sylvi? Where you been?"

I nudged the door with my foot. "We've been at Judy and Gary's new place. How did you get home from the airport?"

"Took a cab. This bath feels pretty good, baby. Come on in. Let's talk about buying a van."

"A van? I'll tuck Katrina in bed and be right back."

Chapter 12
Busted

McKenzie bought a brand new Chevy van painted the same color as the clear blue Southwestern sky.

On a Sunday just past mid-October, we drove to Ghost Town and picked up Gary and Judy to take a ride in the new van.

"A glorious fall day like this should be spent in the country. Why don't we check in on Lilly and Luther?" Judy slid the back door open and climbed in.

I pulled Katrina up on my lap. "Yeah, it's fun to play with Jonas, Mama. Why doesn't he have any dolls?"

"Maybe he has, but doesn't play with them in the sand box."

"I'll ask him when we get there."

Under Lilly and Luther's cottonwood tree, we sipped iced tea and caught up on news from the valley. Z had brought a hundred tabs of LSD back from California and suggested we trip.

"That would be great," Luther said, "but, since turning on to meditation, we have to bow out."

Lilly added, "But we'll be glad for Katrina to stay here and play if you all want to drive out to Hartman's Lake and trip."

"Okay with me," Z said. "How do you all vote? Shall we drive out to Hartman's?"

We voted a unanimous yes. Z drove across the river and through the farmlands stretching between El Paso and Las Cruces along the Rio Grande River. He turned off the paved road onto a dirt road, following it west a few miles, and stopped. We alighted from the van, crawled under the barbed wire fence, and up an embankment to reach the lake. Not a lake at all, but a place where water pumped from a well collected to irrigate the surrounding cotton crop. A peninsula jutted into the middle of it giving it a kidney shape. Birds sang and chattered in the branches of the globe shaped willow trees, but on our arrival, they fluttered into the sky. From above, the treetops must have looked like a hedgerow that outlined the banks and held the waters captive.

As we soaked in the grandeur, Z fished four blue tabs from his pants pocket and gave us each one. Then he passed around a jug of water.

"Great way to spend a Sunday afternoon." Gary looked heavenward.

Having swallowed down the tabs of LSD, we sat together on the peninsula gazing up at sunlight filtering through the leaves.

"A cathedral ceiling," I mused and silently recalled Pablo viewing the arced waves above him on his surf board as a cathedral ceiling. But the memory of his letter from Vietnam marred my recollection.

Mesmerized by dappled light and a warm breeze skimming the water's surface, we stayed still for a long while. Then, as if on cue, Judy, Gary, and McKenzie stood up. Z moved to the edge of the water where he peeled off his tee shirt and dropped his jeans. For a brief instant, he stood naked on the bank before diving in.

Judy and Gary ambled around to the other side of the lake and into a field of cotton.

As I leaned against a tree trunk, Z called, "Wade in."

I kicked off my sandals, rolled up my jeans, and stuck my toes in the cool water. The acid took hold. Form and color shifted into another dimension while a heightened awareness spread through my mind and body. The sun glinted on the water and burst into rainbow colors. I dug my toes into the gushy mud. Swarms of tiny gnats glistened in the light. Their buzzing became a song intermingled with the wind's lazy breath through the tree branches.

"I'm going for a walk up the dry creek bed," I called to Z, who floated on the other side of the lake. "Join me later if you want."

Time passed slowly in the sandy-bottomed creek. I became a magical fish, with human legs, dancing in a giant river from one flowering bush to the next. Each plant clung to the damp, shaded earth where large rocks jutted up through coarse sand. I evolved from a fish to a native, canoeing to my village. I drew a circle, my pretend teepee. I performed rain dances and dances for the buffalo hunt.

Finally, I sat in the shade of a cliff at a bend in the dried-up creek. Stretching out on the cool sand, I cradled the back of my head in my palms and watched clouds move above me. When I heard footfalls, I lifted my head. An aura of silvery-blue surrounded the tall figure approaching me.

"Hey, baby, you look comfy." Z dropped to his knees beside me. He had dressed. I pushed his wet hair off his forehead.

"Join me." I settled my head back into my palms.

He did the same. "How's it going?"

"Beautiful." I smiled and told him of my adventures. "What about you?"

"Very peaceful." He reached over, cupped my chin in his hand, and kissed me—a long, soft kiss. Our faces blended and bright colors swirled behind my closed eyes. "The sun's low," he said, his lips close to mine. "Maybe we should head back."

"I kind of like it here."

"If it were just us, we could stay." He got to his feet and pulled me up. I felt as if I were rising through Jell-O. "We have to find Judy and Gary and pick up Katrina."

Later, in bed that night, he spoke of the lake water as the womb of eternity. "I swam down to the bottom where plants grew up out of the mud. Small fish swam with me. When I surfaced, the sun hit my face. Long silver strings blew across the sky and around in circles. It was the top of the womb, and I had access to all creation, one with wind, water, and sun."

"I know the feeling," I said. "Oneness."

Through the night, we dozed and woke to make love until daylight crept around the closed blinds.

"Wow. I'm thinking this is the never-ending trip," I said, feeling very much awake and alert.

"Good acid, huh, baby?" Z rubbed his eyes. "But I think I'm beginning to come down. Are you all right to drive to work?" he asked. "I'll fix Katrina's breakfast and walk her to school, if you'll get her dressed."

"Uh, huh," I murmured agreeably. "You know what I think I'll do this morning?"

"What?"

"Quit my job."

At my desk and enjoying a strong cup of coffee when my boss walked into the office, I flashed a broad smile. "Can I talk to you for a minute, Jason?"

"Sure." He looked a little apprehensive. "Anything wrong?"

"You mean like kidnapping my children, or having the flu or going to the doctor for a hangnail?" I teased, feeling free to say anything popping into my head. "As a matter of fact, everything's right."

"Come on in and, if you don't mind, bring me a cup of coffee? My hands are full."

"Love to." I poured two cups, followed him into his office, and pulled a chair in front of his big walnut desk.

"What's on your mind, Sylvi?"

"I've been thinking." I paused. "Since Z's come into my life, things have changed drastically for me. I've been writing more. We've been traveling more."

"I've definitely noticed the latter." He chuckled.

"I guess what I'm trying to say is, I need to quit my job because I'm really not doing it justice."

"You've always done a great job, Sylvi, but your absences have become somewhat of a problem." Rolling his plush leather chair back, he opened the middle drawer of his desk, took out an envelope, reached across, and handed it to me. "I guess we're of like mind this morning."

Probably not. I'm sure you're not coming down off LSD. I looked in the envelope and found a check for five weeks pay.

"Wow, Jason, this is too far out." I laughed.

"I just want to mention you're definitely a one-of-a-kind person. I hope you'll keep in touch."

We chatted a while longer. He asked me to do his astrological chart at some future time. I promised I would as soon as I became proficient.

I drove away from the building—no longer *my* building. I no longer worked there.

I followed my familiar route out of downtown and speeded up. The fall wind blowing through the windows created the sensation of flying. Flying free. It was all I could do not to stop the car, dance at the side of the street, flag down cars, and yell, "Quit your jobs. Don't support the system. Stop the war. Save the earth. Let's all start over."

I couldn't wait to tell Z, but the house sat empty when I arrived. Two options occurred to me. Change clothes. Eat lunch. I did both and got back in the car to pick up Katrina from school. Still, no McKenzie.

Katrina bounced into the passenger seat. "Z told me you'd pick me up."

"Want to get ice cream, sweetie?"

Of course, she said, "Yes." On the way, I drove past the house. Z wasn't there. Over chocolate sundaes, I told Katrina I would be staying home with her from now on.

"Oh, boy. Will you make my Halloween costume?"

"Sure, I will. What do you want to be?"

"A ballerina like the ones we painted on my bedroom wall. I wonder what Kristi wants to be? You could make her a costume, too, Mama."

"Maybe I could. We'll see ." My thoughts were often with Kristi. The memory of her frightened face haunted me, and I longed for an end to our separation. "Let's go see if Z's home," I said.

As I pulled into the driveway, the front of the VW faced the front of the van. Its side door open, parallel to the kitchen door.

"What's happening?" I asked as we got out of the car.

Z stepped out. He carried a large box. One word on the side of the carton caught my eye. AMMUNITION.

"Hi, baby," he called cheerfully as he strode through the kitchen.

Katrina and I followed him toward the den. I paused in the hallway. "Run along to your room and change your clothes, honey bunny." I kissed her cheek.

Z set the box on the floor.

"What's going on? What is this doing in here?" I pointed to the red carton with the large black letters.

"I'll move everything to the closet as soon as I finish bringing it all in." He wrapped his arms around me and gave me a big kiss.

I pulled away, puzzled and irritated. I wanted an explanation to make things right, the way they were when I left in the morning.

"I don't care about putting anything in the closet. What I want to know is why you're buying ammunition?"

"For the guns I bought," he snapped back. A hundred eighty degrees from the warm embrace only seconds before.

"Guns?" The word exploded from my mouth.

"You're mad. I was hoping we could skip this part." He tried to step around me.

"McKenzie." I squared my shoulders. "It has never been my intention to have firearms of any sort in this house. Do you think I only talk about peaceful revolution? You think I don't live it?"

"Whoa, baby, these aren't to fight our revolution with. I respect the way you feel."

"Then what the hell are they for?"

"I'm going to trade them to the farmer in the jungle for weed."

"What?" I couldn't follow his logic, if there was any. "Why not just use the money you're buying guns with to buy weed?"

"Because it's hard for the farmers to get weapons to defend themselves against the *federales*. Sometimes they can bribe the cops. Other times, depending on the regime in power or politics of one sort or another, the cops come in shooting. So the farmers are glad to trade grass for rifles and ammo."

Speechless, I stepped back to let him pass, then sat on the couch in the living room trying to sort out my feelings. I remembered Rob blowing into town and turning me on to weed. I'd felt marijuana was the main ingredient to change an uptight culture driven by social status and material wealth. Getting stoned with Rob had given me a new perspective on my emotionally cluttered existence and a resolve to change where I was at in my life. During that time, I hadn't given much thought to where weed came from, but after Z entered my life, the risk factor seeped into my consciousness. Now, he was making an argument for supplying the farmers with guns. *No way.*

Katrina plopped down beside me on the couch. "Can I go next door to play, Mama?"

"Sure." I gave her a hug. "I'll call you in a little while for supper."

As I ventured into the den, Z set the last box of ammunition in the closet. "Out of sight, out of mind." He closed the door. "How did your day go, baby?"

"I quit my job."

"Bravo."

"Yeah, bravo. We should be celebrating, but you and your fucking guns have ruined my otherwise jubilant day." I jerked open the closet door. "I want them taken back where they came from, not to Mexico. It's bad karma."

"Don't give me the bad karma shit, Sylvi. I don't need it."

"Go to hell." I ran to my room and slammed the door. No longer able to stop the tears, I fell on my bed and cried into my pillow until I slept.

A light knock woke me. Katrina climbed on the bed next to me, her face next to mine. "Is it suppertime yet? My friends went in to eat their supper."

"I'm sorry, sweetie. I lost track of time. Come on. Let's go in the kitchen."

I heard Steppenwolf on the stereo pounding out "Magic Carpet Ride" and stuck my head in the den. "Anybody want to go with me to get groceries to make supper?"

"I'll go." Judy volunteered.

"I didn't know you were here," I said.

"I opened your bedroom door when we got here, but you were sleeping. Are you okay, Sylvi?"

"No, I'm pretty bummed."

As we drove to the grocery store, I told her I'd quit my job then related the afternoon of ammunition and semi-automatic rifles.

"So, you were sleeping to escape what's happening?"

"Probably." I knew sleep was my method of choice to avoid reality.

In the store, we picked up hamburger meat, buns, pickles, and chips, and I told her more about the day.

"What are you going to do, Sylvi?"

"I can't let him do it. He has to take them back. Bad karma."

"What are semi-auto-somethings, Mama?" Katrina asked as she handed me a bag of her favorite potato chips.

Judy and I looked at each other. *How stupid not to realize Katrina was taking in our conversation.* Thankfully, I hadn't referred to them as guns—a word she would have understood.

"Just some kind of equipment Z bought today. It's not important, honey."

I changed the subject. "Are you and Gary settling in at Ghost Town?"

"Sure. We don't have much stuff to worry about. Once the stereo is set up and the philosophy books are on the shelf, we're good to go. If Gary has his music and books, he's at peace with the world."

At the checkout stand, I wrote a check for the groceries.

"Quit your job, but you've still got a bank account?" Judy laughed as we walked out to the parking lot.

"I guess I'm dropping out by degrees. I have to go put my final check in the bank tomorrow, pay off my car, and make the house payment. The van's paid for."

Once at home, I sent Katrina in to count how many people were in the den so I'd know how many burgers to make.

"Little pitchers do have big ears, huh?" Judy began taking things out of the grocery bags.

I grabbed the package of hamburger and turned on the broiler. "Man, this is getting to be too much for me. I have to watch what I say in front of my own kid. Can you imagine what would happen if she started talking to the neighbors about semi-automatic weapons and marijuana?"

"Apparently she and Kristi did talk about weed to their dad otherwise you wouldn't have had to kidnap her. What do you hear about her big sister?"

"Nothing. I sent her birthday things, but haven't been allowed to talk to her. I call from time to time, hoping she'll answer, but it's always Carl, and he hangs up. Katrina and I have sent letters, but I have no idea if she gets them, probably not." I placed the patties on the broiler tray.

"Z seems to think it might take awhile to get her back. He suggested, in the meantime, I stop taking birth control pills, and we'll have a baby sister or brother for Katrina."

"You're putting me on." Judy frowned. "You're not doing it are you?"

"As a matter of fact, yes. Bob and Pat just had a baby. Why not Z and me?"

"Okay, but Bob has a legitimate job."

"Sure, a job they both want him to quit. You're no longer working at the Federal Reserve Bank, Judy. Our world is changing."

"I dig what you're saying. But I have to admit it's a little scary—especially with the guns in the picture."

"Those have got to go. I'll talk to him again tonight."

I put Traci to bed around 8:30. Close to midnight, people began to drift on home except for Syd and Irish, who crashed in the den. Shirtless, barefoot and clad in new bell-bottomed Levis, Z carried dirty dishes from the den to the kitchen. I stood in front of a sink full of hot, soapy water.

"Nice Levi's." I spoke to him for the first time since our earlier argument. *I'll ease into a conversation to convince him to return the guns.*

He set the ice cream bowls on the cabinet and put his hands around my bare middle.

"Nice skin." He pulled me against him, bent his head and kissed the top of my ear. "I bought you and Katrina some things, too."

I stiffened against the persuasive warmth of his hands. "Are they in the closet with the guns?"

"Sylvi, don't be this way. Just let me run my business the way I see fit."

"That would be easy except it affects us all." I turned to face him.

He stared down at me, still holding me close. "Your eyes are definitely turquoise when you're upset."

"My eyes, your Levis, my skin—these are not the things we need to be discussing, and I'm not upset. I'm mad as hell. It's the guns, McKenzie—the fucking guns."

"You want me to say I'll take them back, don't you?" He held me a little less tightly. "I can't do it. I know the road into the jungle. I know the faces at the end of it. It's a different way of life than ours, baby, but what I understand is they need weapons to survive. I can get guns for them, and I'm doing it."

"Don't do it, Z." I stepped sideways, away from him. "I know you think you understand their trip, but I'm telling you guns are made for killing. Whoever pulls the trigger creates their own karma when they take another life. And you're making it possible for them to take a life." My legs went weak, but I couldn't allow myself to lean on him. I steadied myself against the edge of the countertop.

His eyes narrowed. "It's kill or be killed, and I'm creating good karma by doing what I understand to be right. Don't you put out bad vibes to defeat me."

"Fuck you, Z. You don't want to hear me. You're so impressed with the machismo of guns and the whole dealing thing. Whatever happens, you'd better know I'm not being negative. I'm telling you the truth because, God help me, I love you."

I bolted from the kitchen into the bathroom where I squeezed toothpaste on my toothbrush and began brushing with all my might. *I'll make my point again tomorrow. Surely, tomorrow he'll hear me.*

The next day I continued reasoning with him, but instead of hearing me, he enlisted Syd's help to buy more guns. Two days passed, and the tension grew. Midmorning of the third day, no longer able to bear the strain, I decided to get away from the house, the guns, and Z.

"If I'm not back by the time Katrina gets out of school, will you be around to pick her up?"

"Yes." I sensed relief in his voice. I wouldn't be there to nag him for a while. "Getting away from here will do you good, baby. Stay as long as you want, Katrina and I will be fine."

Once out of the house and on the road, I knew it wasn't Judy I wanted to see. She was too much an active part of my now-life, and the present intensity was eating me alive. Jake popped into my head. I pulled up to the first phone booth I came to and deposited a dime.

"Jake? How are you? Do you have time for an old friend?

"You bet I do, Sylvi, want to meet me for lunch at the Lorelei?"

Sitting across the checkered tablecloth from him, I took in the old, familiar surroundings. A twinge of nostalgia tugged at me.

He read my thoughts. "You miss your old life?"

"Sometimes I do, Jake."

"Have you kept in touch with anybody?"

"No, just you."

"How are you and Z doing?"

"We're okay I guess." I lied. "You know Katrina's with us."

"What happened?"

I launched into the tale of the kidnapping.

He responded sympathetically and added, "I'm interviewing a psychologist on today's show. The topic is family break-up. I'll bring some custody issues into it. Thanks for the insight."

"Whatever I can do for talk-radio." I laughed. It felt good.

I relaxed as I devoured my stuffed cabbage. Over his steaming plate of goulash, he caught me up on news of our mutual friends and the local political scene in which he was deeply entrenched.

The atmosphere and conversation took me far away from my own dilemma. "Can we dance during lunch, Jake?"

"I don't see why not. You want to?"

"Put a quarter in the jukebox and play "The Impossible Dream." Let's dance like we used to."

On the dance floor, I closed my eyes. "I may have made a mistake, Jake."

"I knew you had a good reason for calling me. What's on your mind?"

"More like on my heart. I can't tell you the whole story. There are things it's best you have no knowledge of. You remember how easy going my old love, Danny, was?"

"He did give new meaning to the expression laid-back."

"Z is the opposite. His intensity can overwhelm me."

Jake stopped dancing. "He hasn't hurt you or Katrina, has he?"

"No, of course not. He's gentle with us." I led him back to our table. "He's a strong personality, that's all. Maybe I should have married Danny and gone to Europe with him."

"You're not serious."

"No, but sometimes I feel like running away."

"You always have my shoulder to cry on." With his arm around me, we left the Lorelei.

He hugged me as I stopped at his car on the way to my own. Reaching into the passenger seat, he picked up a book. "Here's something to lighten your mood. You can escape into The Hobbit's great adventure. Call me when you're finished and let me know if Dr. Jake's prescription cured your blues."

I spent the rest of the afternoon with Judy. When I returned home and walked into my kitchen, I saw from the mess that Z and

Katrina had eaten. They sat together on the living room couch reading from her fairy tale book. Her wet hair dripped on the shoulders of her pajama top. I detoured by the bathroom, grabbed a towel and joined them.

"Looks like you've had a bath." I rubbed her hair and draped the towel around her.

"I did it by myself." She beamed.

"She wanted to stay up so you'd say prayers with her," Z said, looking up from the story.

"I'm glad you're here, Mama. Z told me he doesn't say prayers." She took my hand and led me toward the hallway.

On our knees beside her bed, she prayed, "Now I lay me down to sleep. I pray the Lord my soul to keep. Keep me well and keep me safe. God bless Mama. Help Z to learn some prayers, and let Kristi come home soon. Amen."

We shared a big hug. I tucked her in and kissed her forehead. "Sweet dreams. I love you." As I left her room, I ran my fingers across the foot of Kristi's bed, turned out the light, and blew a kiss to Katrina. In the hallway, I blew a kiss to Kristi.

At the door to our room, I saw Z in bed. Tossing my clothes on the chair in front of the dresser, I slipped in with him.

Naked beside me, with one hand he cradled the back of his head, the fingers on his other hand held a joint. "I'm taking off at 7:00 in the morning."

"Tomorrow?" I sat up and struggled to get my breath, panic mounting. *How can you drop this information on me like it's nothing? Like you'd say you're going to the store. Nothing I've said to you over the past few days has made any difference. Now I've run out of tomorrows to change your mind. You're leaving in the morning, with the guns, heading for Acapulco.* "It's kind of sudden."

"Not hardly, baby. I've been putting this together for over a week. Are we going to have another discussion about the guns?"

"No. There's nothing left to say." But I had to make one last desperate attempt. "What if I said to you, if you go down there with the guns, don't ever come back to me?"

"Sylvi," he reached for me, "don't put it on that level. I'm not doing this to bum you out. I'm doing what I feel is right."

I drew away from him, understanding we'd reached an impasse. *Maybe I've known it since the afternoon he first brought the guns and ammunition into the house. Still, I've tried to change his mind. In truth, I can't bring myself to put our being together on the line. I'll have to let it all play out.* I reached for him. We pulled each other close.

After dropping Katrina at school, I drove to Judy's place in Ghost Town.

"Seven o'clock this morning, Sylvi? Is he insane?" Judy asked.

"No, he just marches to the beat of a different drummer."

"A cliché understating the obvious, but it sure doesn't address your pain." She poured tea into our cups and set them on the table. I slouched in one of two mismatched chairs.

"I kept it together all the time he loaded the van this morning. Hell, I even fixed breakfast. He kissed me, hopped in the van, and pulled out of the driveway like it was a normal morning."

"When will he be back?"

"A week, I guess, if I'm lucky."

"God, I hate to see you so down like this, Sylvi. If I had any speed I'd lay some on you, but we're dry. We're going to make a run over to Juarez in a while to get some. You want to go?"

"Thanks, but since I'm on this side of town, I'd rather go out to the river, sit in the shade, and escape into the book Jake loaned me."

"Promise me you won't drown yourself."

"Promise. I may try to figure out what keeps me with Z. If you remember, last May before I met him, I was ready to strike out on my own, be a strong and independent woman."

"Scratch the independent, but you're sure as hell a strong woman to go through all this."

That afternoon on my way to pick up Katrina after school, I noticed a blue van coming toward me. The driver waved, and hung a "U." I pulled over and stopped. Excitement swept through me. *He's not going after all. He's back because he thought better of it. Thank you, God.* Z opened my door.

"What's happening?"

"You can't believe the shit I've been through since I left this morning. I'll meet you at the house."

"I have to pick up Katrina from school." I'd never been late.

Katrina and I rushed through the kitchen door, and I shooed her to her room to change clothes.

"What happened?" I asked Z. "I freaked when I saw you. In my head you were driving to Acapulco, but there you were on the road right in front of me, like I was in a dream."

"More like a nightmare, baby." He licked the edge of the rolling paper, and pressed his thumb along it, then twisted both ends. "I got across the bridge this morning—no hassles. About ten miles the other side of Juarez, the van goes out on me."

"What? It's brand new." I lit the joint Z handed me.

"I got it to the side of the road but couldn't restart it. The lights and radio wouldn't turn on, so it had to be electrical."

"What did you do? It's working now." I passed the joint back to him.

"There wasn't much traffic, so I stashed the guns."

"Where for God's sake? You were surrounded by desert."

"Bundled the guns and ammo in the blankets I had in the back and buried them in a mound of sand under a mesquite bush about a quarter mile off the road. Marked the spot so I could find it again." He got up, shuffled through the stack of record albums and put on Led Zeppelin.

"And?"

"The *federales* came along. I told them I needed to get my van back to the States. They got a tow truck and towed me to the border."

"What a mind blower."

"Then I called the God-damned dealer, told him I wanted it fixed today. They sent a tow truck, and I rode with them to their place."

"Is it fixed now?"

"Damned right it is. I looked over their shoulders while they put in a new alternator. I drove home, but you were gone. I thought maybe I'd just head back across the border, pick up the guns and keep on going. But when I ran into you on the road, I decided to hang it up for today. Start fresh tomorrow."

I rubbed his neck. He peeled his tee shirt off. "Feels good, baby." He relaxed. "Tell you what, I'll get a shower then you, and me, and Katrina can go out for a bite to eat."

"Cool with me." I dared not hope he'd change his mind. I knew I wouldn't bring up the subject. *I'll make the best of it and work on sending good vibes, but if today is a sign, wouldn't I be wrong not to point it out?*

I thought about doing a Tarot spread while Z showered. But steeped in turmoil, I doubted my ability to read it.

I awoke to the house enveloped in darkness and stole from bed into the den. There I finished "The Hobbit" before either Z or Katrina woke up. Reading the book kept my own thoughts and fears at bay.

Z touched my hand. "What are you doing up so early?"

"I couldn't sleep."

"Thought I'd find you working on a poem." He smiled and sat next to me.

"My muse took the day off."

"I'm going to get started, baby. The sun will be up in less than an hour, and I want to recover the guns before too many people are on the road."

I smoothed the candy-striped chintz fabric across the kitchen table and pinned the pattern on it. I had promised Katrina I would have her ballerina costume finished by the time I picked her up in the afternoon.

I cut out the pieces and began stitching the top together on my old Singer sewing machine but stopped and gave Jake a call to let him know I'd finished his book.

"I'll be by in a while to pick it up," he said. "We could go out and grab some coffee."

Better get a shower before he gets here.

As I stepped from the bathtub and reached for a towel, I heard a loud knock at the front door. I thought Jake had made record time to arrive so quickly.

With the towel wrapped around me, I opened the door as far as the chain lock allowed, intending to tell him to wait while I threw on some clothes. Hearing a thud, I looked down to see the toe of a boot. I peered through the narrow opening at men in dark suits. The one belonging to the boot held a folded paper.

"I have a search warrant." He handed it to me.

The first thing I noticed was the name McKenzie Raintree typed on it. "He's not here." I gave the paper back to him.

"The warrant is for the property. I'm United States Marshal Wilford. These are my deputies. Open the door."

"I just got out of the shower. You can't come in 'til I get dressed."

"We will break down the door if you don't open it right now."

"Look, I'm in a towel. Let me put some clothes on."

"You can dress after we search your room. In the meantime, you'll have to stay in the living room. Open the door now."

The marshal moved the toe of his boot enough to allow me to release the chain lock. I took in a sharp breath. My hands shook. My heart hammered against my ribs. I stepped away from the doorway, and three men marched through it.

One stood a few feet away while the others searched my bedroom. I held the towel tight around me, wondering where Z was, hoping he was safe, and driving to Acapulco. *How can I get word to him not to come back into the States?* The black-suited deputy stared into space. I listened as the marshal and the other deputy pulled open drawers and slammed them shut. Fifteen minutes had passed when Marshal Wilford came into the living room.

"You can get dressed now, Miss Smith."

"Thank you."

Covers from the bed lay on the floor and the mattress was askew. Underwear hung out of drawers. They'd smashed clothes to one end of the closet, and shoes lay strewn about the floor. It could have been worse. I threw on jeans and a long-sleeved shirt, brushed my hair, and, spotting two matching sandals, slid my feet into them.

The same deputy who had watched me in the living room resumed keeping an eye on me while the others searched. I heard them crawling around in the attic. I wandered into the den, put the Steppenwolf album on the stereo and moved the needle to the cut "Don't Step on the Grass Sam." In the song, the authorities thought grass was terribly wicked. It ended with people being busted.

I picked up a bottle of bright blue tempera paint and a paintbrush from the floor of the den. My black-suited shadow followed me, always at a distance of four or five feet. I painted a message on the inside of the front door so they'd have to read it on their way out.

> To see the ways of Justice
>   in ugliness
> and still love is
>   for those of us
> already in eternity.
>
> Not woe to you,
>   but hope.

In the kitchen, I washed the paintbrush.

"Looks like a peyote button to me," one of the deputies said to the marshal. He lifted it from the shelf above the washing machine and scrutinized it closely.

"I keep it because it brings good fortune to the household," I said.

"Looks like your good luck has run out." He chuckled.

"Fortune can be interpreted many different ways," I offered.

"You look like you'd be smarter than to say a thing like that," he said.

"It's not a matter of being smart," Marshal Wilford said. "She's a flower child, deputy. Aren't you Miss Smith?"

"Maybe so, marshal."

Making small talk with the pigs made me nervous. I went back into the den and restarted "Don't Step on the Grass Sam."

I wanted them to leave. *Jake is going to pick up his book—where is he?* I needed time to think. *Perhaps I can ask Judy to watch Katrina, and I can get someone to drive down to Mexico with me. I can find Z and tell him what is happening.*

The music stopped playing, and I heard their conversation in the hallway.

"Did you tell her she was under arrest?"

"No, not yet. You bag up the trashcan full of stems and seeds in the den closet. It's all we've got, but it's enough."

My God, I've forgotten all about the fucking wastebasket. I've got to find someone to pick up Katrina. Will Carl find out? How can I get word to Z? I wanted to run, but I knew I had to keep it together. Thoughts collided in my head, and I struggled against letting go of the scream stuck in my throat.

Sitting erect on the couch and taking long, deep breaths, I focused on the piano keys. Rob's fingers had skimmed over them playing jazz riffs while he'd talked of a new world. After a few minutes, I gathered my strength, stood, steadied myself, and walked into the hallway.

"Is there something you need to say to me?" I asked.

It startled them.

"As a matter of fact, Miss Smith." The marshal cleared his throat. "You're under arrest."

As one of the deputies read me my rights, I realized I'd never imagined myself being arrested, even with all the talk when Luther was busted. I half listened to the deputy's words and rallied.

"May I call my lawyer? I have to make arrangements for my daughter to be picked up at school."

The marshal hesitated. "Go ahead."

I dialed the number, vaguely aware of the deputies carrying the wastebasket of stems and seeds out of the room. I waited for Don's secretary to answer.

When I told her I was being busted, she put him on the line immediately. "Sylvi, what the hell's going on?"

"The federal marshal is taking me to jail, and Katrina's at school. I think I only have one phone call. Will you call Judy? Call her at

Pat's. She and Gary don't have a phone. Please ask her to pick up Katrina." I gave him Pat's number and the time Katrina got out of school.

"Okay, Sylvi, hang in there. I'll meet you at the jail. We'll get you out on bond."

As I hung up the phone, it rang. I looked at Marshal Wilford.

"Go ahead. Answer it," he instructed.

"Hello." My voice shook.

"Sylvi? It's Judy. I'm at Pat's. Thought I'd give you a quick call. Maybe you can come over?"

"No, I can't. I'm being busted."

"You're putting me on." She laughed.

"No, I'm not. I talked to Don a minute ago and asked him to call you to pick up Katrina from school."

"You're not kidding. Oh, my God, Sylvi."

The marshal motioned for me to wrap it up.

"I've got to get off the phone. Call Don and let him know you're picking her up at the side entrance of her school at 2:30. He's meeting me at the jail. I'll ask him to keep in touch with you."

"Of course we'll pick her up. But please tell me this isn't really happening."

"I have to hang up. I love you all."

The marshal pushed one side of his suit jacket back to reveal a set of handcuffs hanging from his belt. "I don't need to put these on you if you'll come along quietly."

"I'm not the violent type, marshal."

"I can see that, Miss Smith." He motioned me to walk in front of him.

I couldn't tell if any of them noticed the words I'd painted on the door. Would it have made any difference if they had?

The marshal opened the backdoor of the car parked in front. Once I was inside and he slammed it shut, everything in my world stopped. We glided through familiar streets, but looking through the car windows, the neighborhoods took on the surreal quality of a movie.

In the elevator of the county jail, the marshal pushed the five-button. When it stopped, we exited, and walked to a counter. A uniformed cop stood behind it.

Clanging sounds punctuated hostile voices yelling obscenities, making it hard to hear what the officer was saying. I glanced behind me at a row of three cells where men stood cursing and banging their handcuffs against steel bars. The sounds came to me as if traveling through a long tunnel of disbelief.

"Those are the holding cells," the marshal said. "After you're booked, you'll wait in one until you're taken upstairs to the women's floor." He gave me a polite nod and left.

The cop behind the counter pressed my fingers, one by one, against an ink pad, then onto a form. I looked at my inked fingers as though they belonged to someone else. I stood with my toes behind a line. A blinding light flashed. I turned sideways, and it flashed a second time.

After some shuffling of papers, the cop escorted me to an empty holding cell amidst hoots and catcalls from the male prisoners. I sat down on the bench at the back of the cell tried to connect with the reality of what had happened since the knock on my door that morning. I prayed Don would come soon and help make sense of it.

The matron came instead. "Can I get some cuffs over here?"

A cop shuffled across the floor and opened the door.

"Turn around." He snapped the handcuffs in place. The matron took hold of my arm and steered me to the elevator.

"I'm Kate, honey. Don't think I've ever seen you here before."

"I've never been here."

She glanced at me as if to size me up. "We're going up to the ninth floor. I'll give you a sheet and blanket. You'll be in the first tank. Take any vacant bunk."

"Do you know if my lawyer's been here, Kate?"

"Haven't seen any lawyers this afternoon."

"He said he'd meet me at the jail. I've been here over an hour, and I haven't seen him yet."

"Sometimes the wheels of justice grind slow, honey. What are you in for?" She looked at the paper in her hand.

"Weed."

"Weed?" She grinned. "Is your name Sylver Smith for sure? You're not a dancer or a workin' gal are you?"

The elevator door slid open.

"Honest. It's my real name, and I'm busted for weed."

"I see you're a federal prisoner, too."

"Does it make a difference?" I asked.

"Naw." She shook her head. "This is just a place you wait while those wheels of justice turn."

She pulled a sheet and blanket from a closet, led the way to a steel door, and unlocked it. A long hall stretched in front of us, lined on either side with iron bars that reached from floor to ceiling. The door banged closed behind us. The echo jarred my entire body. I wanted out. I rubbed my clammy palms against my jeans. My stomach flip-flopped. Kate opened the cell closest to us, removed my handcuffs, and handed me the sheet and blanket.

"Here's home, honey."

I took a couple of steps inside and jumped at the sound of the metal door slamming. A few women glanced at me from where they lounged on their bunks, five beds on each side of the cell. A long, steel table, with a bench on either side, sat in the middle between the two rows of cots. A vacant bottom bunk caught my eye. I offered a timid, "Hi," to the room at large and made a beeline for the cot.

I tossed the sheet and blanket on the mattress, turned to sit down, and noticed the two toilets and a shower in the front of the tank. The shower had a curtain, but thin air surrounded the toilets. *Maybe I'll be out before I have to go.*

Don arrived. We sat across from each other at a wooden table in a small room off the matron's station. His briefcase stood open beside him.

"I apologize, Sylvi. By the time I got through all the paperwork, it was too late to make the bond hearing this afternoon."

"What does that mean, Don?"

"You'll have to spend the night here. I'll have you out before noon tomorrow. I was afraid this might happen." He reached inside his briefcase. "Remember when you came to see me about kidnapping your daughters? You were extremely open about your lifestyle. I should have advised you to be more careful."

"You did, Don. Where is Katrina? Is she all right?"

"I only have a little information. Someone else picked her up. She was gone when Gary and Judy got there."

"Oh, no." I dropped my head into my hands. Tears fell against my open palms. "How could I have let her down? I was making her Halloween costume and told her I'd have it finished by this afternoon. She must be so scared. Who picked her up?"

Don shifted in his chair, uncomfortable with my distress. "I think it was some of Carl's people, perhaps his parents. At least she would know them. I'll have more information by tomorrow," he said and hesitated. "McKenzie's here in jail, too."

"What?"

"He was busted at Customs with guns, which is why they searched your house. What the hell is going on, Sylvi?"

"I wish I knew." I reached for a tissue to blot the tears running freely from my eyes. His words stuck in my head. I couldn't think.

"I'm sorry I don't have any good news. You've got to pull yourself together and tell me what you know about this. I assume you want me to represent you."

"Of course, and Z, too."

In a desperate effort to present coherent facts to Don, I took a deep breath and tried to organize the events of the last few weeks in my mind. Then I let them spill out, stopping only to answer specific questions he would ask intermittently.

"That's it, Don. There's no more to tell."

He scribbled additional notes on the long yellow pad in front of him before looking up.

"Man, Sylvi, you couldn't have hooked up with somebody a little less …" He searched for words.

"Different?" I offered.

"That's putting it mildly." He looked over his notes. "We have to discuss the cost of bond and my retainer. What kind of cash can you get your hands on?"

"I've got three hundred dollars in the bank right now. And I think Z's got five hundred on him."

"It's enough to cover bond," Don said. "Although I'll warn you, it's going to be tough getting him out."

"Why?"

"He's not local. He doesn't have a job. The court will have no reason to believe he's not a flight risk."

"The whole idea of bond pisses me off," I snapped. "Aren't we all innocent until proven guilty? Why should we be locked up before guilt is proven?"

"A good question in theory, Sylvi, but in the reality of our justice system, bond is valid."

"Thanks for clarifying. What real chance is there for justice to be meted out in our system?"

"I understand you're having a real problem with all this, but we don't have time for a meaningful debate this afternoon."

"I realize that," I said through clinched teeth. I tried to relax my jaw. "What about your retainer?"

"If bond takes all your cash, what kind of assets do you have?"

"My house. Remember? You handled the quitclaim deed from Carl when we were divorced. There's some equity in it."

"I'll have papers for you to sign tomorrow before the bond hearing. You can sign the house over to me. Then when this is over we can settle."

"Okay." Thoughts tripped over themselves inside my head. *Where will we live? Will I get Katrina back? Will we go to federal prison? How can I get Z out on bond?*

"I've got to wrap this up, Sylvi, and get back to the office. Any questions?"

"Will we go to prison?"

"I can't answer right now. My best guess is, you won't. But I don't have enough information on McKenzie's case to even make an educated guess."

I didn't ask the other questions. Exhaustion settled over me as I watched him put his papers in the briefcase.

"I'm sorry I couldn't get you out today, Sylvi. Try to keep your spirits up. I'm almost certain Katrina is with Carl's parents. Get some sleep. I'll be up here around nine in the morning."

Kate came in as Don left. "I'm glad your lawyer showed up, honey. Sometimes they say they will, but they don't." She opened the steel door to the tanks.

"Thanks, Kate. I wish he'd come in time to make bond."

"Well, this ain't the Hilton, but you'll make it 'til morning. Dinner will be out soon. I'm pulling a double shift, so I'm hoping for a quiet night."

She unlocked the cell door.

"Me, too." The key clicked in the lock.

Nobody paid any attention to me as I used the toilet then washed my face and hands in the sink next to it.

Dinner came on metal trays handed through a slot in the cell door. We lined up to receive them one-by-one then carried them to the long table. I was the last to sit down. Some pouted, others joked about the feast before us—three pieces of stale bologna, two thick slices of white bread, and a cup of weak coffee.

"What are you in for?" The woman next to me pushed her dark curls back from her face with one hand and put the bologna on a piece of bread with the other.

"Weed. How about you?"

"They say I stabbed a woman living next door to me. It's a mistake, but I have a lousy lawyer. I'll probably rot in here."

"You'd deserve it, too," a small round-cheeked black woman hooted from the other end of the table.

"Get out of my face, bitch, and go turn your tricks. Leave the rest of us decent people alone," my neighbor shouted. Then, lowering her voice, she turned to me. "She's a trouble maker. Pay her no mind. My name's Florence. What's yours?"

"Sylvi."

"This is my friend, Sylvi, everybody. She's in for weed." Florence took a bite of her sandwich.

No one seemed overjoyed at my introduction, but several nodded at me as they chewed. Then conversations started between groups of two or three all along both sides of the table. I relaxed a bit and put my sandwich together, hoping the thick bread would help the bologna not to taste as stale as it smelled.

I studied the faces and caught bits of what was being said. Florence told me to call her Flo and elaborated on the fight with her neighbor.

"It was self-defense," she concluded. "What was I supposed to do, stand there and let her jump me? She's a crazy one, anyway."

I responded sympathetically. I felt sympathetic toward each one of them, but helpless. I'd never experienced a feeling like it, having no power to change anything for myself or anybody else.

After lights out, I lay back on my bunk and breathed in the darkness, hoping it would soothe my anxious mind. But questions rolled over me like giant waves in a black sea. *Where is Katrina? Where is Z? When morning comes and Don bails me out, how will I get Z out on bond?* Sleep overtook me, and dreams, like tormenting marauders, swept through my soul.

Don and I sat across the wooden table from each other for the second time. It was 9:30 in the morning, and we had to hurry. The bond hearing was at 10:00.

"What have you found out, Don?"

"Katrina's with Carl's parents here in El Paso. A private detective picked her up from school yesterday. He had a court order. I contacted them, and they're refusing to return her to you."

"The school had no right to release her to a private eye. What kind of court order could he have had? My poor baby. They can't refuse to give her back. I have custody in Texas."

"It would be waived in light of the charges you're facing. And I don't have all the details on the private eye nor the court order yet."

"What exactly am I being charged with?"

"Failure to pay taxes on an illegal substance. The same thing Timothy Leary was charged with a while back, and he's appealing to the Supreme Court. That's another story we don't have time to go into right now."

"What about Z?"

"He's being charged with importing guns and ammunition with the intent to overthrow the United States' government."

"Importing?"

"Yes. He was stopped at Customs coming back into the States with the guns."

"Coming back? He was supposed to retrieve the guns from

where he buried them and be on his way to Acapulco. What could have made him come back again?"

"Beats me, Sylvi. I'll see him after we get the bond hearing behind us. But right now, let's get this house thing taken care of or we'll be late."

I signed the papers deeding my house to him in exchange for his legal services. He assured me I could stay in the house and make payment to him each month. I nodded, not even thinking twice about what I was doing. It simply had to be done. Don had contacted a bondsman, and everything was in order. We were third or fourth to be called before the judge. It took no more than ten minutes to complete. We trekked back to the fifth floor of the jail, presented them the papers, and picked up my few personal belongings.

"I'll go by my bank and get the cash for you, Don, meet you at your office."

"Okay. I'll see McKenzie now and see you in an hour. And, Sylvi, do not contact Carl or his parents. I'll follow up on things as soon as I get back to the office. Promise me."

Reluctantly, I gave him my word.

Once on the sidewalk outside the jail, I gazed up ten stories of blond brick and wondered if Z could be looking out one of the windows. I held his face in my mind, sent him my love, and prayed for his safety.

The sun, almost directly overhead, flooded the canyons between the tall, city buildings. Its warmth encouraged my heart as I walked to the bank. My final car payment had cleared, and there were no outstanding checks. I closed my account. The teller handed me the balance in cash.

The symbolism of closing a chapter of my life did not escape me. What kind of courage, I wondered, would I have to muster in order to begin the next chapter?

Chapter 13
Leaving Home

I met Don at his office following his visit with Z. "Jeez, Sylvi, McKenzie is one hostile man. Is he always so angry?"

"Not always. Jail is hard on him."

Don then told me why McKenzie was arrested coming into the U. S. "Z went to pick up the guns where he'd buried them in Mexico, found two missing, and decided to hang it up. He put the remaining guns and ammunition in the back of the van, threw a blanket over them, and headed back to the border. Customs searched the van and busted him. That's when the feds got a search warrant for your house." Don leaned back in his leather chair. "They're going to throw him in solitary if he doesn't calm down. He's blaming himself for you getting busted and Katrina taken. In my book, it is his fault."

"I hope you didn't say that to him."

"Easy, Sylvi. I didn't say it, I just thought it. I was trying to be the soul of diplomacy, but he wouldn't stay in his chair, kept jumping up ranting and raving about the fucking pigs and his rights. Two guards took him back to the tank before we could finish talking."

"I've got to bail him out before he loses it completely."

"It will take a miracle. If he can't quiet down, he doesn't have a prayer."

"Don't shrug your shoulders like you don't care, Don. I need to get clean clothes to him and let him know I'm working on his bond—give him hope."

"I'm not going up there again until he gets himself under control. They won't let you see him, Sylvi, since you've just been released."

"I know. I'm going to get my friend Jake to help me. Z knows him. Maybe Jake can reason with him."

Gary and Judy picked me up in front of Don's office building. Our conversation retraced the events of the last twenty-four hours—part of my nightmare over, with more to come.

Judy helped me clean up the mess the marshals had left. Gary kept the music going, petted Daiquiri, and took out bags of trash. We had the house together by late afternoon. Over sandwiches, we talked about getting Z out on bond. Since he had been hostile toward Don, I mentioned enlisting Jake's aid to communicate with him.

"Good idea, Sylvi. I hate to admit it, but both of us are too paranoid to go into the jail." Gary put his hand on mine. "Forgive us?"

"Nothing to forgive. This is a bad time for us all."

I called Jake once Judy and Gary left. He showed up late in the evening. As weary as I was, I ran down the story of the bust. We sat at the kitchen table. He drank a beer, and I had coffee. I knew I was telling him more than he wanted to know, but it was only fair to be honest with him.

"You know, Sylvi, something told me not to knock on your door when I saw that official looking car out front."

"Sorry I couldn't let you know what was happening. I'm glad you didn't get involved in the mess." His book, "The Hobbit," still lay on the table. I handed it to him.

He stuck it in his jacket pocket and shook his head. "Damn, how could you let this happen? When Z bought the guns, why didn't you kick him out?"

"Kick him out? Like our love for each other means nothing? I tried to persuade him to return the guns, Jake. I asked him what he'd do if I told him not to come back to me, if he took the guns to Mexico."

"What did he say?"

"He asked me not to put it on that level. He said, as much as he loved me, he was totally committed to getting the guns to the farmers in the jungle."

"And you just let it go?"

"I had to. Loving someone doesn't mean controlling them."

"Don't you see what's happening?" Jake leaned forward in his chair intending to drive his point home. "You've lost Katrina and Kristi. Do you realize what you're giving up for McKenzie? Walk away from him now, Sylvi, before it's too late."

"I understand what you're saying, but we'll get the kids back. I know we will. I can't walk away. It's more than loving him, we're connected. We're forever."

Jake looked away. Was he waiting, like a parent, for the response of a wayward child, waiting for me to admit I was foolish and irresponsible? I could not renounce my love for Z, nor could I apologize for it.

The silence in the kitchen intensified. Attempting to relieve the tension, I rose to get more coffee. The liquid pouring into my cup broke the stillness.

"Your passions will consume you, Sylvi." His prophecy disturbed me, but I told myself he was wrong. "I'll go see McKenzie. What is it you want me to do?"

"Thank you, Jake. Go to the jail in the morning. Leave Z this bag of clean clothes and talk to him." I pointed to the paper sack on the chair next to him. "He'll listen to you. Right now, he's out of control and refuses to talk to our lawyer. Make him understand he has to calm down, or no one will go his bail. I'm putting my all into it and will have him home as soon as I can. I swear." I studied Jake's face.

"Goddamn, Sylvi. You and I have been through a lot together, but I never thought I'd be visiting the El Paso County Jail to talk to your old man. I do have one condition."

"What?"

"I want your assurance he's not going to attempt to overthrow the government."

"Of course, he's not. The guns were for the farmers in Mexico. Z may be radical, but he's not connected with the communist party or any revolutionary groups. The guns were not to overthrow our illustrious government."

"In spite of the fact I disapprove of your involvement in this, I hold our friendship in high regard. I'll try to help any way I can."

I assured him I respected his position. "If I had anyone else to turn to, I wouldn't involve you."

"It's okay, Sylvi. I can't turn my back on you."

After Jake left, Daiquiri and I sat together on the couch. As was her habit, she stretched from my lap to put her paws around my neck. She licked my ear and my chin. "I missed you, too, Daiq. Jail is not a nice place. Kitties are not allowed there." She jumped down and meandered over to her food dish in the kitchen.

I ran a hot bath into which I poured a generous amount of perfumed oil and bubbles, lit a candle, and peeled off my clothes. I'd been in them since the previous morning. With my body submerged in warm, fragrant water, the tension slipped away through my toes, fingertips, and breath to waft upwards in the slender wisp of smoke rising from the candle.

Z will be out soon. We'll never have to go back to that concrete and steel cage.

In my bedroom, I sat in the middle of my bed and laid out the Tarot cards to discover what I'd be up against in trying to get him out on bond. As I turned them over one by one, the cards revealed an initial struggle, followed by persistence, then success.

I waited for Jake in the parking garage across the street from the County Jail. An hour had passed before I caught sight of him in his dark suit and red tie emerging from the entrance of the jail. He wasn't carrying the bag of clothes I'd given him for Z. My high-heeled shoes clattered against the concrete as I ran toward him.

"Did you see him? What did he say? How did he look?"

"Slow down, Sylvi. I talked to him through a rectangular glass with a kind of microphone thing in the solid wall of the tank. I could only see his face."

"Tell me on the way to the bondsman's office." I hooked my arm through his and steered him to the left.

"I told him everything you told me to. I stressed how determined you were to get him out on bond, how much you loved him."

"What did he say?"

"He said he loved you and was sorry for getting you into this mess. He promised to stay quiet and wait for the bond hearing, even agreed to talk to Don."

"Thank you, Jake. Did he say anything else?"

"He said he appreciated my coming then blew my mind. He teared-up, said you meant everything to him. But he thought you'd be better off without him."

"Did you agree?" I asked.

"No. I did tell him if he wanted to make you happy, he'd better shut the fuck up and let you bail him out."

"What did he say to that?"

"He just nodded, and thanked me again for coming."

We stopped in front of the door to Ben Shaddad's Bail Bonds.

Ben was not in because it was Saturday. His associate heard me out but blew me off. He explained how he felt Z would be a flight risk. I politely insisted McKenzie would get a job and stay in the area because we were together. Jake, in a moment of generosity, vouched for him. But his associate was having none of it. I asked for an appointment to see Mr. Shaddad. He wrote me into the book on the front desk.

"One o'clock on Monday," he said.

From there we walked to Don's office. I introduced him to Jake, and asked about Katrina.

"Her dad picked her up from the grandparents and took her to Phoenix yesterday. He's retained a lawyer who's already been in touch with me. There will be a custody hearing. I'll let you know the date."

"He's such a bastard."

"Under the circumstances," Don said, "I expected it. I should also mention I don't think you have a prayer."

"Carl's an alcoholic." My temper flared. "What right does he have?"

"Get a grip, Sylvi. He's got the rights of the natural father. And since you've been busted, you're pretty much screwed."

"I'll still fight it." Tears spilled down my face. Jake handed me his handkerchief.

"My visit with McKenzie went well," Jake said, and filled Don in on the details.

"Thanks for laying the groundwork. I'll follow up with him this afternoon."

"Be sure you tell him I'll have him out in a few days."

"I will, Sylvi," Don said. "In the meantime, you take it easy. I'll call you this afternoon and let you know how things are going."

Playground merry-go-round
spins slow at first
then faster.
Laughter joins the blur
of trees whizzing by.

Why didn't I notice
the platform leaving the ground?
I struggle to hold on.
How do I land this metal circle?

It shudders now under my feet,
shaking out of control,
threatening disintegration.
Do I continue laughing,
close my eyes,
commit to the ride?

Laughter becomes one long scream.
I hang on with one hand,
reach out with the other.
It is clasped by another.
Voice in my ear tells me,
find balance.

As I wrote the images popping into my head, I wondered if it was a poem or a bad dream. I laid my pen and paper aside. No one came by after Jake brought me home. Katrina gone, Z in jail, no call from Don. Dark night wrapped around my house and sealed me inside. Exhaustion cloaked my mind and body in heavy, gray depression.

"Find my balance?"

Daiquiri curled beside me on my bed. I reached in the drawer for the Tarot cards, removed the lavender cloth, shuffled them, and placed them in a stack in front of me. I drew one, face down, from the middle of the deck. "How shall I find my balance?" I asked.

I turned the Justice card over. *There is no justice, how can I find balance in it when it does not exist?* I cleared my mind and again contemplated the card until new meaning began to form in my head. *Courage, patience, and gentle persuasion might equal balance. Can I dredge up those qualities from somewhere deep inside my tired body? Can I resurrect them through my great desire to recover my children, and get the man I love out of jail?* I turned out the light and laid my head on the pillow thinking I would leave those questions with the Creator. I possessed no more energy of my own.

A sharp knock jarred me awake.

"Who is it?" I struggled to sit up.

"Just us." Syd and Aiden stood in the door of my bedroom.

"Damn. Where'd ya'll come from?" I rubbed my eyes. It was daylight. "I must have fallen asleep in my clothes."

Syd grinned beneath his red mustache. "We came through the front door."

"What's happening with Z?" Aiden asked.

"I'm still trying to get him out." I got to my feet. "Why don't you two go make some coffee while I hit the shower?"

"Cool. We came to take you to breakfast if you're up for it," Syd offered.

"I am." I gathered my robe from the closet and headed for the tub.

Before we left the house, Judy called to say she would go with me to see Shaddad on Monday. The gray depression from the night before slipped away in the blessed light of friendship, breakfast, and a new day.

There's something sacred in the gathering of women, a connection that happens nowhere else. It was so with Judy, Pat and me on the Monday before Election Day 1968. The Monday Judy would accompany me to the bondsman's office.

Homemade vegetable soup simmered in a big iron pot on the stove in Pat's kitchen. Its rich aroma enveloped us as we filled our bowls. We tore off pieces from a loaf of French bread on the countertop then sat down at the round oak table.

"Thank God you're here today, Sylvi, and not rotting in jail." Pat took my hand as she spoke. "Also, I'm thankful my sweet baby daughter chose this time to take a nap."

Judy reached for my other hand. "I'm glad to be holding your hand instead of looking at you through some little window in jail. I'm sorry Z is still there. I promise we'll do what we can to help you get him out."

"How about a jail break?" I quipped. "It might be easier than convincing Shaddad to go his bond."

We laughed. It felt good and released nervous tension I'd struggled with since Z first brought guns in the house a few weeks earlier.

"Thanks for being here." I squeezed both their hands. "I feel life returning to my frazzled psyche. What do you hear from Lilly and Luther?"

"I talked to her yesterday," Pat said. "They're in limbo with charges pending and no court date set. They're trying to put together a small show at a gallery in Las Cruces. Lilly has a dozen paintings, and Luther has done four sculptures. Money is tight. I think the biggest drag is not being able to come and go freely with the bust hanging over their heads."

"I can relate, Pat. I've never felt anything like this. My life completely stopped by something over which I have no control. It's a major bummer."

Judy began clearing our bowls off the table.

"I hear Merry Cloud." Pat went into her room and came back carrying her infant daughter bundled in a soft, cotton blanket.

"Let me hold her a minute." I cradled her in one arm and offered her my little finger to clutch in her tiny hand. "Look at those eyes bright with the future of our world. She's hardly a month old, Pat, but her eyes hold infinity. I wish we possessed her wisdom."

"We did once." Pat kissed her cheek.

"We've got to get going, Sylvi," Judy called from the kitchen.

I gave precious Merry Cloud back to Pat. Judy nudged me toward the door.

"My gut tells me he'll be out before Friday," Pat called from the front porch. She lifted Merry Cloud's hand and waved as we drove off to meet Ben Shaddad. Don met us there.

The Monday afternoon meeting bummed me out. Despite Don's logical reasoning and my endless assurances, the bondsman remained steadfast in his refusal to go bond for McKenzie. Judy reminded me the struggle would not be in vain, there would be victory. And, if Pat's intuition was right, it would come before Friday.

"Hang tough, Sylvi," she told me after we said good-bye to Don and walked back to my car. "This is only the first round."

Tuesday dawned and the polls opened at seven in the morning. Although I knew it was futile, I wrote in Eugene McCarthy, completed the rest of the ballot, and went on my way. The vibes throughout the day were grim, as though the wind carried a quiet message of despair on its cold wings.

"It doesn't matter about the elections, Sylvi," Judy cautioned me when I picked her up to head downtown. "Don't let bad vibes make you falter. The task at hand demands your full attention."

"You're right."

Our plan was to visit Shaddad everyday—twice a day if necessary. I had to stay totally focused. Even so, Ben did not relent on Tuesday.

I called Jake in the evening. After much persuasion on my part, he agreed to meet me at the bondsman's office the next day.

Wednesday morning's paper carried the news of Nixon's victory. Instead of despairing, I marched resolutely forward and met Jake at Shaddad's office around mid-morning. Jake explained to Ben the charges against Z were false, and went so far as to say he would hire Z at the radio station. I knew he was bluffing, but he sounded convincing. I could see Ben Shaddad's resolute refusal begin to crumble, kindling a small fire of hope in my heart.

After leaving the bail bonds office, I thanked Jake for his help, kissed his cheek, and told him I'd keep him posted. Then I marched myself to Don's office.

"Sylvi, good to see you." He greeted me in the outer office with his briefcase in hand. "I'm on my way to the courthouse. Can we talk later?"

"I'll walk along and talk to you now, if you don't mind."

He didn't, so as we kept up a brisk pace, I told him I thought Shaddad was about to back down. I asked him if he could possibly squeeze in a few minutes in the afternoon to go with me and really press hard to get Z out on bond.

"Jake came close to convincing him this morning, Don. I'm sure if we follow up this afternoon, we'll break him."

"Okay, Sylvi. Meet me at my office around one-thirty. We'll go see the man."

Don and I closed Shaddad's door behind us. "Thank you, God," I whispered. Aloud I thanked Don for his tireless efforts and asked,

"Now he's agreed, what's the next step to get Z released?"

"The paperwork and the appearance before the judge at the bond hearing in the morning."

"What time?"

"Meet me at the court, nine tomorrow."

"Thank you so much, Don. One more favor?"

"What is it?"

"Will you see McKenzie this afternoon and tell him?"

"Sure, it will be after five, but I'll let him know."

"Thanks again, Don." I ran to my car and immediately drove to Pat's to fill her in on the fulfillment of her prophecy. Then on to Judy's and Gary's place. We passed around a joint and rejoiced.

It surprised me when my head hit the pillow that I did not fall immediately to sleep. Instead, I re-examined the events of the last week. I didn't know how Z's week had gone. Was he aware that the feds had not only seized the guns and ammunition but the van, as well? Don had made it clear that we'd never get the van back. Would Z have reconsidered his position on supplying the farmers with weapons? Could he see his obsession about the guns had brought all this down on us? What if he didn't?

Free on bond, Z looked pale, thinner than when I'd last seen him. I told him the details involved in getting him out. He praised my persistence in one breath. In the next breath, he cursed the system making us jump through hoops. He railed about the process of dehumanization behind steel bars. "Like cattle in a pen. You get your blanket, a bunk, and a tray of sorry-assed food shoved at you through a slot. There were men in there who didn't even know if they had a lawyer or not."

He addressed the gun issue by saying how sorry he was to have involved me.

"You mean you would not take the guns down to Mexico if you had it to do over again?"

"What I mean is, it was my trip to get them down to the farmers. I shouldn't have come back and spent the night with you after I got the generator fixed. If I'd headed right back to Mexico, picked up the rifles and ammo and kept on going, we wouldn't be busted now."

So much for any epiphany about the karma attached to the guns. I wanted to ask him why he didn't see the obvious? But he'd been through enough.

He resumed condemning the system for its injustices but ran out of steam by the time we pulled into the driveway.

My head rested on his bare, outstretched arm as we shared the joint Gary and Judy had given me the day before. Although I cherished the satisfaction of the moment, I knew I had one more thing to tell Z. But I feared it would negatively affect his client-attorney relationship with Don.

I took the last toke on the joint, and reached across Z to drop it in the ashtray on the nightstand.

"God, you feel good, baby." He ran his hand slowly from my thigh up to the back of my neck and kissed me.

I struggled against the passion rising in me. I had to tell him I'd signed the house over to Don in exchange for his representing us—but decided to do it later.

Later came after we showered and sat down to a mid-afternoon breakfast in the kitchen.

"Man, I've got to get some cash in our pockets. It took most everything we had to go bond," Z said.

Mustering my courage, I forged ahead. "I need to tell you about the retainer for the attorney."

"Don? What about it?"

"There was no money to cover his retainer, so I signed the house over to him." I said it fast before I lost my nerve. "If we can pay him outright, he'll put the house back in my name. Otherwise, we can settle after he sells it. In either case, we can live here in the meantime, and pay him rent in the amount of the house payment." I took in a breath.

His eyes narrowed slightly and a corner of his mouth twitched. "Fucking lawyers. Fucking legal system all the way around. They've got us by the short hairs, don't they?" He scooted his chair back from the table, got up, and stared out the kitchen window with his back to me. "He had no right to take the house. We're not staying here, baby. I'll be damned if we'll pay the bastard rent. We'll find a place in the lower valley. Come on."

"Right now?" I cleared the table, dumping plates and cups into the sink.

"Yeah, right now." He ran to the bedroom, got his wallet, grabbed our jackets, and we dashed to the car.

"When are you getting Katrina back?" he asked as we drove out of the neighborhood.

"How much did Jake tell you about that?"

"Some of Carl's family picked her up from school. I thought you might have her back by now."

"No, they sent her to Carl in Phoenix. Don says there will be a child custody hearing. He'll let me know as soon as he finds out the date."

Z's jaw clamped tight, his knuckles whitened as he gripped the wheel. "How could I have let this come down on us, Sylvi?"

I had no answer.

"I have to make it up to you, baby."

"Quit blaming yourself. I understand where you're coming from. It's different from where I'm at." I looked away from him and watched houses and shopping centers whiz by as we sped down the newly built freeway. "Z, I believe your choice to bring guns into the picture created bad karma. You feel you were right in trying to get arms down to the farmers, and your only regret is you were busted in the process."

"Look," he interrupted. "I take the responsibility. I'm sorry."

"I don't think you get it, Z. I don't blame you for the bust. I wish you could see the karma guns and violence create, but I can't make you see. Let's drop it."

We'd covered twenty miles on the freeway, and exited east of El Paso at the Clint off-ramp before we resumed our conversation.

"Why the lower valley?" I asked.

"Because all the heads live in the upper valley, so there's a lot of undercover cops hanging out there. Maybe we won't be harassed in the lower valley."

The narrow blacktop wound through cotton fields. Coming around a bend, we spotted a rent sign in front of a place thirty feet off the road and stopped to have a look.

The empty house, built of adobe and coated with white plaster had a barn-like garage attached to the back. Behind the garage, a long building of weathered wood stretched twenty-five feet. We stepped into its one room through an open doorway. After our eyes adjusted to the diminished light, we could see a squat woodstove at the back and six iron cots spaced randomly on the rough wood floor.

"This must be *bracero* quarters."

"The program where Mexican labor came across to pick cotton then go back when the harvest was over?" Z asked.

"Yeah, but it's been discontinued—don't remember when."

"Doesn't look like they were provided with very luxurious accommodations." Z stepped outside.

I lingered in the doorway. "A wood stove to cook a pot of beans on and a place to sleep after a day of back-breaking labor. Seems harsh, I know. But it was a way of life for years around here. People, like me, who lived in the city never thought too much about it, but when you step into the ghost of it like this, it's eerie." I shivered in the mid-afternoon sunshine.

"I'd call it the ghost of oppression." He put his arms around me.

His embrace and the sun quieted me as we stood surveying the field surrounding the sides and back of the house. Some wads of cotton had escaped the hungry mouth of the giant harvesting machines and spilled out of bolls hanging from dry, brown sticks.

"What do you think, baby, fifty acres?" Z asked. He shaded his eyes against the western light. "Let's find a pay phone and see how much they want to rent the house."

I tagged after him on our way to the car and jotted the phone number from the sign on a scrap of paper.

We drove into the next village, San Elizario, which consisted of a grocery, hardware and feed store. A Catholic Church built of stone dominated the main street. Great cottonwood trees, bare of leaves, lined the few streets. We found a phone at a gas station. Z dialed the number and talked for a few minutes then motioned for me to get something to write directions to the owner's house.

By the end of the day, we'd parted with fifty dollars from the little money we had left. It paid our rent for the month of November.

Although bummed by the news of our move to the opposite side of town from them, Judy stepped up to the task of helping me pack. "Are you moving your furniture and everything?"

"I don't know. I'm in limbo." I picked up a photo album from the bottom shelf of the nightstand and sat down on the bed.

She joined me.

I pointed to a picture on the third page of the album. "There's miserable Carl playing with the kids at the park. It's probably the one and only time he did. Now he's going to take me to court for custody."

"Do you know when?"

"Not yet. I have to call Don to find out."

Looking up from the album, I met Judy's eyes. They said more than our words, and I began to cry. She moved the photos off my lap and put her arm around me.

"I'm afraid to leave here, Judy. I mean this house. It's like jumping off a cliff. I know Z will make everything all right, but I'm losing my kids, my house. I quit my job a few weeks ago, and I don't know what will happen to us."

"It's okay to be afraid. Okay to cry."

I accepted her permission and ran on about the anger I felt toward Carl. About how much I missed my kids and what they'd been told. What must they be feeling? I didn't know if my hysteria would take me over the edge or if I could return to any degree of sanity. I unloaded about the crushing jail experience and my exhaustion from pouring every ounce of energy I had into getting Z out of jail. "Now, Judy, all of my tomorrows are uncertain."

There was a knock on the bedroom door and Z came in. His face registered surprise at seeing me in distress.

"Can I talk to Sylvi alone, Judy?"

"Sure," she turned to me. "Are you going to be okay?"

"Yes. No. Both." I took a tissue from the box, wiped my face, and blew my nose.

McKenzie did not sit down. Instead, he stood halfway between the door and me.

"You know what, Sylvi? You're going to have to pull yourself together. We don't have time for this shit."

"What?" I looked at him in disbelief, unable to stop the sobs shaking my body.

"I said, we don't have time for this."

I leaned back on the bed and turned onto my stomach, trying to comfort myself and stop my anxiety.

"I can't help it." I choked on my words.

"Sylvi, I can't change what's happened. I don't know what you want me to do. All I know is to keep on truckin'. As much as I want to take back the last ten days and make them different, I can't." He remained in the middle of the room. "I can't change it, and I can't take your crying. You're stronger than this, baby."

"Maybe I'll be stronger tomorrow, Z. Right now I'm just fucking wiped out. I'm not blaming you for anything. If you can't comfort me, just get out."

He walked toward the door. "Look, it's like I said, we don't have time for this shit." He closed the door and left me alone in my sorrow.

"Son-of-a-bitch." I buried my face in my pillow.

Fatigue overtook me, and sleep came.

Sometime later I became vaguely aware of being lifted. Z pulled down the covers. He helped me off with my clothes. I could not come fully awake, but I remember he crawled into bed, and kissed my cheek.

"I'm sorry," he whispered.

At least, that's what I think I heard. Maybe I only dreamed it.

I awoke early, got up, threw on my robe, and put on a pot of coffee before sitting down on the couch in the living room. I pulled the drapes open, turned my face to the east, and recalled the morning I walked home as the sun rose from behind the Guadalupe Mountains. It was a little less than a year ago, the day Rob and I drank the peyote tea.

Outside the window, the eastern glow swathed the sky in sheets of golden coral, taking on a radiance of holy significance. The beginning of a new day. This same sun shined on Katrina and Kristi. I embraced them with my thoughts and sent my spirit to kiss them.

I know the sunrise before the peyote trip has forever changed my life. Now I'm moving away from this address to embark on a new road.

Do not look for me here.
I'll be dancing on the far horizon.
Opening my mouth every morning
to feed my spirit
with wild bird songs,
feast on fiery sun and crystal wind.

Fears will flee away
as Love's strong arms
hold me steady.
Love will open my eyes to visions
Love will give me wisdom
for this new time and place.

I wrote down the lines to help me with a new perspective, help me find the strength that failed me the night before. The sunrise always imparted courage.

Z emerged from the hallway, paused and looked my way before going into the kitchen. His flannel shirt hung open above his jeans.

"May I get you some coffee, baby?" he asked.

"Please."

He set the hot, brimming cups on the coffee table and picked up my poem. He read it aloud.

"Yes," he said. "I promise we will dance on far horizons."

I didn't give a damn and said nothing. The silence seemed to weigh heavy on him.

"About last night, Sylvi. I didn't mean to hurt you. I don't know why I can't handle your tears."

"I only wanted you to hold me."

"Like this?" He put his arms around me.

"Yeah. Is it so hard?" I pressed closer to him.

"It's hard when I know it's my fault you're crying, and I don't know how to fix it."

"It's not about your guilt."

"Then, what?"

I explained my doubts and fears as I'd blurted them out to Judy, only I remained calm in the morning's telling.

"I guess I hadn't thought of it like that, baby. All I can think about is I need to get us moved then make a run to Mexico for some weed. I've got to turn some cash around or we'll be flat broke."

I pulled away from our embrace. "Yesterday morning you were still in jail. By last night, you were ready to press on, move forward. I suppose it's impossible for you to see I'm still reeling from the bust."

We drank our coffee in silence.

"I'm going to take you over to Judy's, baby, give you a little more time. I'll get things going here, connect with Aiden, and see if he knows anybody with a pickup.

Early the next morning my neighbors who had noticed Z and Aiden loading the stereo and boxes onto the borrowed pickup, stopped by to ask if anything was for sale.

"We'll take whatever you don't want to keep, depending on the price, of course," my neighbor offered as I invited him and his wife in.

Starting in the living room, I walked through the house with them. "The couch, two chairs and the coffee table," I said as though reading off an inventory list.

"What about the piano?" the wife asked.

"Let's come back to it." I went into the den. "We're keeping one piece of the sectional. Everything else can go."

They stood for a moment looking at the revolutionary murals on the walls and ceiling and the stone altar in one corner.

"Someone's done a lot of painting in there," she commented, following me into the hall.

"Yes, it was something of a community project." I gave a little laugh. It must have surprised them. They'd lived down the street from me for six years and never knew I was a crazy person. "Here in the bedroom we're selling the dresser, chest, bedside table, and bed frame. We'll keep the box springs and mattress."

I wanted to get it over with. I didn't place importance on material possessions. In the girls' room, the matching twin beds and big double chest of drawers gave me pause. My dad had built those and painted them a peachy pink for my sister and me then passed them on to me for Kristi and Katrina. *Does selling them mean I'm admitting I will lose my daughters when the custody hearing happens? No, superstitious nonsense.*

"Everything in this room," I announced from the doorway of the girls' bedroom.

In the last room at the back of the house, Estelle's room, I stopped, overwhelmed at what I was doing. But I forged ahead.

"Take this twin bed, chest, and everything in the closets." I opened the doors of two walk-in closets at either end of the room.

"Even the cans of paint?" he asked.

"Sure, I don't think we'll need them."

"What about the kitchen?" the wife asked.

"I almost forgot." I led the way to the front of the house.

"Stove, refrigerator, washing machine?" She ran her hand along the top of the stove, the one on which I learned to cook when I lived in my parents' house. I loved the griddle set in between the two sets of burners. I'd created a thousand pancakes on it.

"Yes, take those and the stove. We'll keep the dinette and chairs."

"Okay." She smiled. "And the piano?"

As she asked the question, Z came in from outside. "Might as well, don't you think so, baby? What are we going to do with it?"

I hesitated. I could play it. I'd taken eight years of lessons but did not play well. I'd used it in high school when I took voice lessons. Once I left for college, my parents gave it to my older sister. She passed it on to me when her husband bought her a baby grand. I remembered Rob playing jazz riffs on my piano the day we dropped peyote. *Z is right. It is too heavy to cart around.*

"Take the piano."

They offered us two hundred dollars for the lot. I bargained for three, and we settled on two hundred, seventy five.

I spent the remainder of the day packing. Going through Kristi and Katrina's clothes plunged me into depression. I gave up and put them into give-away bags. *By the time they come home, they'll be wearing larger sizes.*

I cleaned out closets, and sorted through the accumulated debris of my life. *Six years ago, Carl and I bought this house. Then came those violent times surrounding the divorce, his drunken rages. No, I'll never marry again. It is right, the way Z and I are—traveling the road of life together. This road, right now, is a damned rough one.*

The next day, a chilling breeze blew through the house as Z helped my neighbors move what they'd bought. With that task complete, Z, Irish, and Syd loaded up what was left of our belongings and headed for San Elizario.

Alone, Daiquiri and I sat down in the middle of the empty living room. I cried. It was safe to cry with Z gone. I could recover before he returned. I did not mourn the loss of the furnishings. Rather, I mourned the loss of the innocence I'd regained when Rob and I smoked my first joint and later when we tripped on peyote. The bust took the innocence away. Still, I knew there was purpose in pursuing this kind of life. Before the bust, I'd read a magazine article that referred to people like us as a subculture or the counter-culture.

Rather than feel intimidated, I'd experienced a surge of self-worth. *Our movement will save the country from this hideous war. We will light the way for people to evolve spiritually into a loving, caring society where material wealth has no value.*

But with the arrest came the harsh reality that the law, and those who enforced it, didn't care whether we evolved into a loving, caring society. It was their job to defend the status quo no matter how wrong it was. So with innocence gone, a new dimension revealed itself to me—the task of making it all happen while knowing what the cost would be. I walked, as though I might tumble from a tightrope, into the den. I sat down next to the stone altar, lit a candle, and let the pain of my old, familiar life go up with the smoke, allowing the birth of a new life. No longer only a lovely philosophy, I experienced its integration into my being and was both thrilled and terrified, knowing I would follow the new road out of this front door and into the next. The road would directly involve my children, the man I loved, and me. Indirectly, it would affect the evolution of our collective consciousness. I stared into the candle flame and searched the cavern of my psyche for a small shred of courage. Without the burden of material possessions, my spirit lightened, but my heart trembled. I was leaving the familiar for the unfamiliar.

The move completed, we drove that evening to the farmhouse. Daiquiri rode on my lap. She didn't look happy about the changes and sulked in a corner of the bedroom.

I finished organizing things by early afternoon of the following day and drove to a laundromat. I called Don from the pay phone to tell him we'd moved.

"We don't have a phone. I thought I'd check in and give you our post office box in San Elizario."

"Damn, Sylvi, you know you didn't have to leave your house. Why did you move way out there in Timbuktu?"

"Z wanted to, and I'm okay with it. When is the child custody hearing?"

"The day after Thanksgiving. Be at my office around nine o'clock. Court starts at ten. Less than three weeks away, Sylvi. Call me before then."

"I'll check in once a week," I promised.

"Why don't you just get a phone?"

"If there's no phone, Don, there's no phone to tap is there?"

"I get it. Stay in touch."

I gave him the post office box number, and we said goodbye.

When I got home, I found Z throwing clothes in a suitcase.

"What are you doing?" I set the laundry baskets on the floor.

"The friend of Aiden's who loaned us the pickup fronted me a couple hundred, and I got a little more lined up with people Syd knows. Combined with what we have from selling the things at the house, it adds up to what I started down there with when I was busted. I'll leave you some money, take the rest, make a trip, and score enough weed to get us on our feet."

"You're putting me on, Z. You can't go to Mexico when you're out on bond."

"I told you the day I got out of jail I had to get some cash in our pockets. You'll be okay, baby. Since we're out here in the middle of nowhere, I want to know you're safe while I'm gone. Here, take this 22 pistol."

"My God, Z. You are out of your fucking mind. You know how I feel about guns."

"It's just a little 22, Sylvi. Here, I'll show you how to use it."

"You don't hear well, or what?"

"I don't have time to argue, so watch."

He instructed me how to load and cock it.

"Okay." I listened, knowing I'd never use the gun. "Why are you in such a hurry?"

"I'm driving to Aiden's. He's taking me to a rent a car. I want to get to Acapulco and back while my visa is still good. Aiden will return the VW to you in the morning. I'll be back in a week."

One long kiss and he was gone. I put the gun under my pillow on our bed, a symbolic burial.

Over the next few days, I settled in. We had no refrigerator, but I kept cheese and eggs in a box on the screened-in porch. It was cold enough to keep most things from spoiling. I had no stove, but I did have an electric skillet and the coffee pot. I got by quite well.

Daiquiri and I explored the cotton fields around us. I awoke early each morning to gather strength from the sunrise. Some days I drove the thirty miles to see Judy and Gary. Other days I read, wrote, and listened to music. I found a sturdy wooden crate and sat on it at the west side of the house. In the evenings, I watched the sun slide behind the horizon where it splashed red and gold across the vast western sky. There I put my days away and gathered in the peace twilight brought.

When a week and a day passed, and Z had not returned, the sunset brought me no peace. Troubling clouds blocked the last light of day. Unsettled, I went inside. Taking my Tarot cards from their wooden box, I unwrapped the lavender cloth, and sat down to do a spread. Daiquiri stretched out on the cloth and rested her head on the box.

"What question should I pose, Daiq?" I studied her gold eyes. She closed them. "You're absolutely right. I should ask what's on my heart." I shuffled the cards.

"What circumstances surround Z at present, and is he safe?" I spoke the words aloud, laid out seven cards. The spread revealed chaos, disorganized effort and delay in completing a task. When I turned the last card up, it was not conclusive about Z's safety.

I decided to use Daiquiri as a medium through which to ask for a clearer outcome of the situation. I moved to the couch, sat quietly, inhaling, and exhaling deliberately to induce a meditative state. I closed my eyes and heard traffic sounds intermingled with incoherent voices. They sounded uptight and argumentative. I remained quiet, hoping for more. Nothing came.

I tied the cards in the cloth and put them back in their box. Daiquiri and I went to bed where I turned on my side and closed my eyes. She curled up at the small of my back. I listened to her purr and tried to quiet my mind. It was then I heard faint footsteps. Something touched my foot, like fingertips pressing against the ball and sliding down to the heel. I tried to open my eyes and say, "Z." Unable to do either, I lay frozen, pinned to the bed. Then I felt hands, on either side of my face, lift me to a sitting position. Time stopped. Desperate to see and speak, I mentally struggled against my paralysis.

Without warning, the hands released me. My eyes flew open. "Z?"

No response—nothing in the dark room except a shaft of pale moonlight coming through a window. Sitting up in bed with Daiquiri on my lap, I peered into every corner. Electricity charged the air. Daiq and I walked throughout the house looking for any sign of someone or some other being. Cold shivers and emptiness overwhelmed me, drove me back to bed where I burrowed under the covers with Daiquiri. Warmth and peace settled over us.

"Do you think I could call the presence back?"

Daiquiri purred her answer.

"No, I thought not. I wonder what it was? A spirit? What would it have come for?"

Daiq shifted her position.

"Perhaps, if I'd stayed calm, I could have invited it to stay."

Could we have conversed, or would it have been vibrations, or an aura radiating spiritual understanding?

Somewhere in the midst of my contemplation, I drifted off to sleep.

Cold winter morning light sliced through the bedroom shadows. My eyes swept the still, empty room. My mind sorted through the events of the night until a surge of energy prompted me to throw off the covers.

I donned jeans, shirt, shoes, and grabbed my jacket from the closet. After stopping on the back porch to feed Daiquiri, I stepped out into the dry, breezy cold of the morning. Clouds on the horizon battled the sun for supremacy. Frost glistened on the fallow cotton fields.

I walked with Daiquiri through the furrows, hoping I might encounter whatever had visited me the previous night. Nothing appeared.

Close to noon, I knew I needed to tell someone about my experience. I hopped in the VW and headed for Judy's. Halfway there I remembered she and Gary had gone to Mexico, but Bud, Gary's musician friend, would be staying at their place.

I rapped lightly on the front door. "Hey, Bud, it's Sylvi. Are you in there, man?"

"Come on in. It's open."

I pushed the door inward, and quickly shut it behind me.

"You're ankle deep in weed, Bud." I exaggerated. "What are you doing?"

"Cleaning this kilo." He glanced down at the floor from his perch on a stool at the table. "Don't worry. I'll sweep up when I'm through." He waved a hand toward another stool. "Sit, roll a joint, and make yourself at home."

I laughed. Seeds and leaves dotted his curly black hair, rested in his lap, and on the tops of his hairy toes. He diligently pressed the grass through a large strainer into a bowl.

I rolled a joint and took a hit.

"Michoacan green. Nice, huh?" His eyes twinkled.

"Yeah, nice." I offered him the joint.

"You go ahead, Sylvi. I'm so fucking stoned I'm afraid if I get up I'll disappear. This," he patted the stool, "is my anchor as I drift in the sea of green." He sang a few bars of the Beatles' "Yellow Submarine." I joined in, and we cracked up laughing.

"Seriously, I've got something to tell you," I said and launched into my tale of the previous night. As I talked, he quit cleaning the weed. His dark eyes grew wide. He began stroking the stubble on his chin.

"What do you think?" I ask him.

"Wow. I think I would have been scared shitless."

"At first, I was shaken. But after I got up and looked, it became apparent. It had to be spirit. It wasn't like an intruder who would kill me or anything like that."

"How do you know?"

"I could feel it here." I put my hand over my heart. "It was a benevolent presence. I think if I'd received it more graciously, it would have stayed a while and imparted some spiritual truth."

"You think that was the purpose of the visit?"

"What else, Bud? Why would some kind of spiritual being come calling?"

"What if you're wrong? It could have been evil." Bud dislodged himself from the stool and tiptoed to the front window. Pulling back the curtains a little, he looked out then returned to his stool. "What if it followed you?"

"It didn't follow me."

"Look at it this way, Sylvi. You must have stirred up a lot of activity in the spirit world when you used Daiquiri as a medium to pick up info on Z. Maybe it was some confused soul passing through looking for someone else."

"You could be right, but it touched a chord in me. I have to go with my intuition."

The following evening I sat in my usual spot watching the sunset where the mountains dipped to meet downtown El Paso. A car pulled into the driveway and stopped a few feet from me. "Who the hell?" I squinted to make out the face of the driver.

"Hey, baby, what's happening?" Z stepped from a late model, white Chevy.

"My God, it's you. It's really you." I jumped up knocking over the crate.

"Were you expecting someone else?" He gathered me in his arms.

A cold evening wind blew from the bare, cotton field. Both relief and excitement coursed through me as I leaned into his kiss. "Thank God, you're safe. I was beginning to worry. Are you okay? Why are you so late?"

"I'm only a couple days later than I expected. I got hung up because Miguel needed to borrow my wheels. It worked out. He laid some extra weed on me for my trouble." He slung an arm over my shoulder. "Help me unload this stuff, baby. I need to get the car turned in."

I ran to open the two barn-like doors of the garage and closed them after he pulled in.

We lifted the backseat from the car, and carried it through the door leading into the extra bedroom as I began relating my tale of the spirit who visited me. He listened impatiently as he finished stacking the packages of weed.

"So you think we have a ghost?" His skepticism showed.

"I wouldn't call it a ghost. But I know for sure it came from the spirit world."

"I left you the gun, baby, in case some one came in. You never know what can happen when you're all alone out here."

"It was not some one. It was a spirit, Z. Maybe I stirred up a lot of psychic energy using Daiquiri as a medium. I wouldn't have done it, but it was killing me not knowing if you were okay."

"You don't have to worry. I take care of myself. But this thing about a stranger in the house bothers me. You're probably lucky to be alive." He splashed water on his face at the bathroom sink.

"Why can't you believe me? It was not a human. I was not in danger."

"I believe what I can see, feel and touch. Right now, baby, I need to get this weed stashed. Got any paper bags?"

I trotted off to the kitchen to find sacks.

"Where'd you put the gun?" he called after me.

"Under my pillow."

I gathered a dozen or so folded bags and carried them back to the bedroom to find Z throwing the pillows on the floor and stripping covers off the bed.

"What are you doing?"

"Looking for the fucking gun." He pulled the bed away from the wall. "It sure as hell is not under your pillow. Maybe you put it somewhere else?"

"No, I didn't. I buried it under my pillow." I sat down on the bed hardly believing what I was thinking. "Don't you see, McKenzie? When the spirit lifted my head off the pillow, it must have taken the gun from under it. Maybe to keep something awful from coming down on us. I know it was a benevolent being."

"You're crazy, Sylvi. There's nothing wrong with keeping a gun for self-defense." He took my hand and pulled me up from where I sat then lifted the mattress to look under it.

"Was anybody here while I was gone?" he asked.

"Lilly drove out once, but she didn't stay long."

"She probably took it."

"She didn't even know it was here. Why would you say that?"

"I was by their place a day or two before I left. She was all over my case about the guns, said I got you busted."

"Doesn't sound like Lilly."

"She took it."

"No, she didn't. The spirit took the gun when it lifted my head off the pillow."

"Okay, baby, whatever. But if the gun can disappear, what do you think is going to happen to any weed I stash here?"

"Stop it, McKenzie. Spirit doesn't care about your weed. Until you started looking for it, I never connected the ghost, as you call it, with the gun, but now it's perfectly clear. Why can't you see it? The 22 being gone is for our own protection."

Z stopped searching and looked at me. I hoped he grasped the significance of what I was telling him.

"You know what, baby?"

"What?"

"I drove a hell of a long way today. I wanted us to return the rental car and grab dinner. I wanted to come home, have a nice hot bath then make love for a while. I probably thought about it most of the way home."

"Let's do it then."

"We can't. If someone stole the gun from the house, what's to stop them from stealing the weed? I can't stash it here. I have to do something else with it."

So much for him grasping the significance. "Look, love, bag up the weed, stash it in those metal cabinets in the garage, put a chain through the handles, and lock it." I handed him the grocery sacks.

"With what?" he asked.

"The heavy-duty lock in the kitchen drawer." I left him standing in the bedroom while I found the lock. "You take care of your Acapulco gold. I'll straighten up in here."

He took the bags. "Okay," he looked over his shoulder at me. "I'll be in shortly. Will you follow me to the car rental place?"

"Of course." I shoved the bed back into place. I wanted him to have been as enthralled with the whole spirit visitation as I'd been. Why wasn't he able to trust what I told him? Why did he jump to other conclusions? I guessed for the same reason he believed in violent revolution. We were on a seesaw, and I wanted to get off.

Somehow, our love glued our humpty-dumpty relationship together in time for Thanksgiving. There was more to eat than I'd seen in a while. Judy, Gary, Syd, Irish, and Aiden came to our place and brought food for dinner. Judy and I arranged bowls and platters on the small table in the kitchen and laughed as we inhaled the aromas from the food, weed, and incense. Thankfulness for this gathering of friends washed through me. One cloud marred my celebratory mood—the child custody hearing the next day.

We filled our plates in the kitchen and, since we had little furniture, sat in a circle on the smooth, hardwood floor of the dining room.

By the time I joined the circle, Irish was telling us about an issue of the *Berkeley Barb* circulating among the heads on the military base. "Eldridge Cleaver was lecturing on Black History at Berkeley and after three weeks, good old Governor Reagan shut it down."

"How come?" Judy asked.

"According to the paper, Reagan thinks if a Black Panther teaches a course at a university, our young men and women will go home and slit their parent's throats or some shit like that."

"I don't imagine the campus is taking it too well." Z set his plate down to go change the record on the stereo.

"Not well at all," Irish said. "Over three thousand students demonstrated."

"Protested on campus?" Gary asked.

"Yeah." Irish nodded. "A few weeks ago students occupied some of the buildings, like Columbia last spring, remember? But in Berkeley, the cops descended on them, made arrests, and pounded on people until they broke it up."

Aiden brought up Camus' book "The Plague." Said he'd read it for a class in school. A rowdy discussion ensued with each one in the circle offering their opinion of what the plague represented.

"The book was damned depressing." Gary concluded.

Aiden hushed everyone. "All of you have a different concept of the plague. Basically, it is *injustice.* The point I'm trying to make is not what the plague is. My point is that in fighting against it, we change into something other than what we intended and are emptied of the passion and purity of purpose that drew us into the fight. We then see our emptiness as inevitable. And if inevitable, are we able to continue our struggle when life, as the doctor felt, became meaningless?"

"Hell, yes," Irish shot back. "I don't think life or our battle against this unjust system will become meaningless. I see it as our chance to change what's wrong, don't you?"

"Aiden's trying to imply the movement will become ineffective, defeated, burnt out." Z got to his feet and collected our empty plates. "Didn't stop Che. I say it won't stop us either."

He disappeared into the kitchen and returned with the pineapple upside down cake I'd made in the electric skillet. He set it in the middle of the circle. I cut the cake while Judy poured coffee.

After dessert, Judy announced she and Gary had to make an appearance at her family's gathering, and they left. Irish, Syd and Aiden helped us clean up then we followed them outside as they prepared to leave.

"You think we'll burn out like Camus' doctor, Sylvi?" Irish asked before he closed the car door.

"No. I intend to persevere without disillusion."

The day after Thanksgiving, Don held the courtroom door open for Z and me.

"My kids aren't here, are they?" I asked.

"No." Don led us to a table up front. We were the first ones there.

"Will Carl sit at the table across from us?" I asked.

"Carl and his lawyer. We're early because I wanted you to get comfortable before the others arrive." He opened his briefcase, took out a couple of files, and laid them on the dark wood table. "As I mentioned in my office, this will be a closed hearing, so anyone testifying will not be allowed in the courtroom until time for their testimony."

"What about McKenzie? Can he stay?"

"It's probably best if you wait in the hallway, Z. What goes on in here could make you extremely angry."

"If you think so."

"I have to warn you. You'll be in the hallway with family members who are waiting to testify. They'll stay there until summoned to come in and take the stand. When they finish with their testimony, they'll return to the hallway."

"I'll keep my distance."

Don turned to me. "This is likely to get rough. If it gets to be too much for you, Sylvi, tell me, and I'll ask for a recess."

"I'm okay." I said it without heart, wishing I had some speed to give me the clarity I needed to counteract the accusations that would surely come.

"I mean it, Sylvi, let me know if you're about to be overwhelmed."

"I will." I honestly thought I would.

The door opened at the back of the room. Carl and his lawyer strolled in and sat down. Carl glanced with contempt at me, then

Don, and Z. McKenzie met Carl's eyes. Don fidgeted with the folders on the table. I smiled.

"It's probably best if you wait in the hall now," Don said.

Z put his arms around me. "I love you."

We released each other, and I watched him walk away. I thought about him pressing his slacks earlier, both of us trying to appear as normal as possible. He looked back at me, and nodded before exiting.

Across from us, Carl and his lawyer conversed in low tones. The door opened at the back. My sister, Carl's mother, and his wife, Jazelle, came into the courtroom. They sat together as though unified against me.

"All rise," barked the bailiff, after which opening formalities kicked off the proceedings.

The judge droned out the matter at hand. I tried to listen, but his voice sounded far away.

"Do you swear to tell the truth, the whole truth, and nothing but the truth, so help you God?"

"I do."

Sitting down in the witness chair, I wished my long sleeved mini-dress had a few more inches to its hem. At least, instead of fishnet, I'd found regular pantyhose to wear.

I waited while Carl's lawyer gathered himself. His nonchalant attitude unnerved me.

"Sylver Smith, do you reside at 102 McConnell, El Paso, Texas?"

"I did."

"Where do you now reside?"

I answered his question.

"Did you move there subsequent to being arrested by a federal marshal October 31, 1968?"

"Yes."

"Did you also plead guilty to failure to pay taxes on an illegal substance, marijuana?"

"I did."

He then asked me specific questions about the arrest and the whereabouts of my children. All of which I answered without elaboration.

"You are presently living with a man named McKenzie Raintree who is not your husband. Is that correct?"

"Not correct. He is my husband."

"How can that be? There is no public record of a marriage between the two of you."

"It is possible because we have declared ourselves a union under God." I spoke distinctly, growing bolder as he self-righteously delivered his petty questions.

Carl's attorney announced he had nothing further at present. He must have felt he'd established the facts. Not only had I been busted, I also lived in sin.

The court clerk called my mother to the stand. She looked gaunt, dressed in a tailored black suit. I remembered the last time I'd seen her was the weekend before we took Kristi and Katrina to Phoenix, the end of May.

She stated that things the girls told Carl raised his suspicions about what was going on at my house. He telephoned her and my dad, and they hired a private detective to watch me. She testified as to the content of the detective's report. I'd been investigated since mid-June. Neighbors told the private eye they'd seen men going in and out of my house at all hours of the day and night. They had also observed one of these men holding his arm as though he'd been using a hypodermic needle. The clincher came when she testified she had smelled marijuana smoke when she had come by my house a year and a half earlier. In her opinion, my daughters were not safe with me.

By degrees, throughout her testimony, I became more outraged than hurt. *How can she testify to such atrocious assumptions? There are people going to and from my house, both male and female. No one I know shoots up anything. A year and a half ago I didn't know what marijuana smoke smelled like. Kristi and Katrina are definitely not safe with their alcoholic father.*

"How are you doing?" Don whispered.

"Put me back on the stand," I demanded. "She can't make those accusations and get by with it."

"Calm down, Sylvi. You'll get your chance, but are you sure you want it? They're going to crucify you. Maybe I should ask for a recess."

"No. Let's get this over with. They may win, but I'll fight to the bitter finish." I pounded my fist on the table. "Goddamn them," I said aloud.

The judge pounded his gavel. "Please control your client."

Carl flashed a smug smile.

Don did return me to the stand where I explained my relationship with my daughters and how important their well-being was to me.

Then in cross-examination, Carl's lawyer asked the ultimately damning questions.

"What does Mr. Raintree, your so-called husband, do for a living?"

"He's an artist."

"Isn't it true he smuggles marijuana from Mexico into the United States?"

"I object." Don stood.

The judge looked over the top of his glasses. "Please rephrase your question."

"Isn't it true Mr. Raintree is facing charges of importing guns and ammunition with the intent to overthrow the United States Government?"

"Those are the federal charges against him, but he's not guilty of those charges."

"Very well, Miss Smith. Or should I refer to you as Mrs. Raintree?" He mocked.

"Whatever you prefer." I tilted my chin up and met his disdain with dignity.

"As a matter of fact," he cleared his throat, "you are both unemployed, are you not? How do you expect to support your children?"

"Just because I'm not working right now doesn't mean I won't get a job in the near future. My husband, as I said before, is an artist. We'll be more than able to support Katrina and Kristi."

"Not likely when you and McKenzie Raintree are facing the charges I've already mentioned. Who would hire you, Miss Smith?"

I couldn't answer.

"That's all." Carl's lawyer sat down.

Don began questioning me, giving me plenty of latitude to refute my mother's testimony. As I spoke, I could see my sister's face go utterly blank. Next to her, Carl's mother and Jazelle looked triumphant. Don moved into my line of vision.

"Would you say your house is not the wicked place your mother described?"

"It is not. My mother is obviously paraphrasing from the detective's report. Neither she nor my father have bothered to ask me what the girls were talking about. Instead, they hired someone to look into it for them. And whoever this person is, has talked to neighbors who have negatively interpreted events at my house." I paused. Don nodded for me to continue.

"I have several friends who come and go. They are both men and women, not just men, as my mother said. And I definitely do not know anyone who uses a hypodermic needle for any purpose."

"Your mother testified, in her opinion, the children are not safe with you. Can you comment?"

"I know they are safe with me. I've cared for them all their lives. I know when they're happy or sad. We talk together, play together.

The evening of Katrina's birthday last June, I called her in Phoenix only to discover her father was insisting she eat her cold breakfast for dinner. It seems she hadn't cleaned her plate at breakfast. Therefore, he placed the same plate in front of her at noon and again at dinner. It was her birthday, and she couldn't even have a decent meal and certainly no cake and ice cream."

"Did you ask her father about it?"

"Yes. I pled her case. He told me they had rules in their house, and all the children had to abide by them."

"Do you feel your children are not safe with their father?"

"I don't believe their emotional needs are met, or even addressed. I do not believe they are safe with him. He's an alcoholic. His only loyalty is to his addiction, not to his children."

"Thank you, Sylvi."

Carl took the stand. His lawyer questioned him in such a way as to make him look like a most decent sort of person, and Carl lied about everything when Don questioned him. No, he was not an alcoholic. No, the birthday incident was not true. Yes, he cared deeply about the welfare of his children. He couldn't understand how I had become so morally bankrupt.

I felt nauseated. I kept trying to catch his eye to let him know I knew he was lying. He wouldn't look at me.

A few minutes after Carl stepped down, the judge announced he had made a decision.

"Whatever happens, Sylvi, keep your cool," Don whispered.

I sat rigid in my chair, gripping the edge of the table.

"I grant complete custody of Kristi Ann and Katrina Jane Stevens to their father Carl Stevens. I grant no visitation to their mother, Sylver Smith, at this time."

I rose from my chair, and heard my voice. "You haven't been listening to anything I've said, have you?" I spoke directly to the judge.

He banged his gavel and glared at me.

"Sit down." Don pulled my sleeve.

"I won't sit down. I won't be quiet," I yelled, and grabbed my coat from the back of the chair. It crashed to the floor. "This is not justice." I ran to the door. "I'll have no part of it, you ignorant bastard," I shouted over the banging of the gavel.

Z rushed forward to intercept me as I stormed into the hallway where my mother and father sat on a bench. I pointed a finger in her face and screamed, "Are you happy now? You've made me look like a whore and God knows what else. Why didn't you ever talk to me? What's the matter with you? I lost them, Mom. I lost my kids."

My father stood and faced me. I looked him in the eye.

"Don't talk that way to your mo. . ."

I didn't let him finish. "What are you going to do, Daddy, now that you've let her castrate you?" I hissed through clenched teeth.

Z took hold of my arm and pulled me toward the stairs.

"What the hell are you going to do?" I yelled over my shoulder. Beyond my father, I saw the bailiff burst into the hall.

"Let it go, Sylvi. Let's get out of here." Z supported me as we fled down two flights of stairs.

In the lobby, he helped me into my coat before we raced onto the sidewalk. A block from the courthouse, we slowed down.

"Sylvi, I'm so sorry, baby. What happened in there? I've never seen you like this."

"I've never been like this."

I stopped, flung my arms around him and cried. He held me steady.

I became aware of people stepping around us on the sidewalk. I heard traffic sounds on the busy street. I noticed the winter sun hidden behind tall city buildings casting long shadows where we stood.

"I didn't mean to come unglued" I shook with sobs.

"It's okay, baby." He hugged me. "Hang on to me."

"Let's get to the car, Z." I wiped my face with the back of my hand and took a tentative step forward. "I can make it if you hold my hand tight."

He maneuvered the VW through late afternoon traffic, while I filled him in on the courtroom drama.

"I expected the bailiff to be right behind you when you burst into the hall," he said.

"I don't know what delayed him. I'm grateful you got me out of there before they locked me up. All I need is contempt charges on top of everything else."

"I knew it was going to get all fucked up when I saw your mother go in the courtroom. All the time I stood in the hallway across from your mom and dad, neither one of them spoke to the other. Of course, they sure as hell didn't say anything to me."

"They're not great communicators, are they? I just can't believe all this shit's come down. How could I let it happen?" I rested my head against Z as he drove.

He tried to reassure me. "This isn't the end of it. We will get your kids back. It's not your fault, baby. What blows my mind is the private detective. We knew they'd tapped our phone, and I figured a narc was watching us. But, I swear to God, I never thought it was a private eye your parents had hired."

"It's like a bad acid trip."

Early evening when we pulled into Ghost Town, I wished on the first star I saw in the twilight sky. I wished the kisses I blew would light on Katrina and Kristi's cheeks, wherever they might be. Z knocked on the door.

"Thank God," Judy greeted us. "I was beginning to worry. What happened?"

"You tell them, Z. I can't say the words right now."

"The court gave custody to Carl."

"They what?" Gary came through the bedroom door into the front room. Judy slipped an arm around me and steered me into the other room. We sat down on the India-print bedspread covering their mattress on the floor.

"Sylvi, I'm so sorry."

November ended. Z left for Mexico, and I stayed in San Elizario. Alone once more. He had been gone less than a week when the flu flattened me. It began with a high fever followed by violent coughing spells. At first, I brewed a little tea to sip. After a day or so, I could only manage to fill a glass with water then sit in the kitchen for a moment to gather enough strength to return to bed. Then I would lose consciousness for hours only to wake in a sweat and wracked with coughing. I gave up trying to keep Daiquiri fed on a daily basis and put the open bag of cat food on the floor.

Looking forward to Z's return, I kept track of days by marking the calendar. The day I marked my birthday, I remember getting a glass of water and carrying it to the couch. I collapsed there, thinking I would die on the day I should be celebrating my birth. My lungs ached, sweat dripped from me.

"Baby, you're burning up."

I opened my eyes, but succumbed to a coughing fit and couldn't recover to reply. Z lifted me from the couch and carried me to the car.

"We'll get you to the clinic, baby. You'll be all right."

During the next ten days, while I recovered from the Hong Kong flu, I used some scraps of material and made big, rag dolls for Kristi and Katrina. I embroidered the dolls' faces and made long fat braids of yarn. One had pink hair and the other blue. I finished them a few days prior to Christmas, put them in a box, wrapped it, and addressed it. Z mailed it to Phoenix before he left for California.

My heart and soul went with their package. I prayed Carl would allow them to have it.

Chapter 14
Leaving

I walked out of the heavy wooden door into the front yard. A cobweb stretched from the bare grapevine to the frozen brown grass—a mandala of silver threads swaying in the frosty morning breeze. Christmas morning, one without excited children ripping open their gifts.

I sat on a bench between the front stoop and the bare grapevine, hugged my knees against my chest, and watched my breath clouds disappear into the bright, blue morning. Chattering sparrows darted and swooped from the naked trees in the yard to alight on the leafless elm at the edge of the cotton field. As they searched for food to nourish their bodies, I sought nourishment for my spirit.

In the last two months, I'd gained and lost so much. The difficulty lay in the distribution of good and bad on life's balance scale—if indeed, there is such a method for sorting through one's life. I faced the brilliant sun hanging above the eastern edge of the world. It warmed me despite the heavy frost on the dried grass at my feet. Absorbing its healing rays, I wrote:

> There is only one mathematical truth:
> Today I am the sum of all my yesterdays.
> Peyote tea and children playing,

the wonder of innocence crumbled in pain,
a psyche washed in tears.

I don't remember making decisions.
I only remember the energy flowing
like a river smiling in deep turquoise pools,
racing in laughter, dancing in sunlight
until it fell, crashing,
not sure it could or would continue its course.

I tucked my writing in my pocket and emptied my thoughts into the center of the mandala web.

"Hey, baby, what are you doing out here in the cold?" Z sat down next to me.

"Where'd you come from? I didn't hear the door." I scooted closer to him.

"I'm not surprised. You looked lost in a trance. Come back inside so we can open presents." His hand slid into mine as he led the way.

Z poured coffee while I lingered at the Christmas tree silently sending love to my daughters—my children's love absent and Z's love present. Another sort of balance I could ponder on some other cold winter morning.

Cold winter mornings piled one upon another. Some days brought a light snow while others, bleak and dry, chilled me to the bone. During the week between Christmas and New Years, we visited with friends, gathering either at our place, or at Bob and Pat's, Judy and Gary's, or Luther and Lilly's. Paranoia, an odorless vapor, twisted its snake-like poison throughout the community. Before this time, love and trust had bound us together, but at the end of 1968, a subtle fear of betrayal permeated the scene. A crumbling innocence.

Still, the busted and un-busted gathered, hoping for better tomorrows, sharing our spiritual journeys, discussing our individual karma and the karma of a nation about to be led by Richard Nixon. We compared notes on advice given us by our lawyers and speculated on what to do about our pending cases.

I did not consider smoking weed a crime. We were not criminals. Had we murdered or caused bodily harm to someone, committed robbery, arson, or forgery I would feel our arrests and convictions might be justified, but none of us had done those things. To think of doing jail time because of weed didn't make sense to me, yet the possibility loomed before us, a great, unseen specter.

New Year's Eve we drove to Ghost Town and found Gary jamming with a few musician friends. After an hour, all of us moved on to a party in full swing near the college. In a while, the partiers doubled in number. Several brought booze, and it got loud and rowdy. Midnight had passed when a rumor circulated that the neighbors had called the police. I warned Judy while looking for Z—found him drinking the last drop from a wine bottle.

"Someone called the cops, Z. We've got to split"

He dropped the empty bottle on the lawn. "Fuck the pigs."

I'd never seen him drunk and didn't know how to handle the situation. I did know we had to get out of there. "Look, Z, it's one o'clock in the morning. We've got a thirty-mile drive. Let's get going."

"Fuck one in the morning. Fuck the cops. I don't have to go anywhere."

"I'm leaving. You can stay here, but don't look for me to bail you out. That won't happen again." I ran across the lawn to the car. As I reached it, he came up behind me.

"Get in, baby. We're going home together."

It scared me to think he was stoned, drunk, belligerent, and getting behind the wheel. But we had to get the hell away before the police arrived. I jumped in the passenger seat and fastened the lap belt. He started the engine and revved it like a maniac. I gripped the chicken-bar on the dash. He pulled into the street and drove for a block when we heard sirens. Looking behind us, I saw the cops getting out of their cars where we'd been partying moments earlier.

"I hope our friends made it out." I said.

"I hate running from the cops. I'd just as soon shoot them." He turned a corner and headed for the freeway. "Bastards. They've got no right. Fucking puppets of the government, bought-off sons-of-bitches."

As we covered the miles, he ranted variations of this theme. The speedometer needle went back and forth between eighty and ninety as his voice filled the car. I neither encouraged nor refuted what he said. Either would make things worse. I prayed for us to make it home in one piece, thankful for the almost deserted freeway.

He veered toward the off ramp at the Ysleta exit then cut the wheel sharply back onto the freeway. I felt the tires lift off the road. My left shoulder smacked against Z.

"We're going over." I tightened my hold on the chicken-bar.

The night whirled around us before the thud of our landing upside down threw my upper body forward. The top of the car spun against asphalt, screamed in my ears.

"We're okay, baby." I heard Z shouting. "Don't panic."

When the spinning stopped, the headlights shone on the guardrail separating the eastbound lanes from the westbound. *Will the car crumple—burst into flame?* I hung by the seatbelt, suspended in a silent cocoon of terror unable to speak.

"Don't move, baby. Stay here." Z opened his door.

I found my voice. "Goddamn you. What the hell are you doing?"

From out of nowhere, two pickup trucks appeared on the other side of the freeway and stopped at the same time Z freed himself.

"Help me get it back on its wheels," he yelled at the three men emerging from their vehicles.

They hopped the guardrail and took hold of the VW.

"Hang on, baby," Z shouted. They gripped the VW and started rocking it.

My wreck of a year and a half ago paraded in living color across my consciousness. It had taken twenty-four stitches to sew up my forehead, a cast on my left arm, and my jaw wired shut. I could still see the horror on Kristi and Katrina's faces when they saw me bloodied and torn, and I remembered how precious life suddenly became when the doctors sewing up my head said the accident should have killed me.

Hanging by the seat belt, I prayed as they rocked the car. A jolt slammed me against my seat, upright. Once it rested on all four tires, I rolled down my window and heard Z resume cursing the government, the police, and the powers-that-be.

"You probably buy into all that bullshit," he called after the three strangers as they ran back to their trucks.

Horrified that he was not expressing one iota of appreciation to the good Samaritans who rescued us, I cupped my hands around my mouth and shouted, "Thank you all. We appreciate your help. Thank you."

They waved and drove off while Z continued ranting. "It's going to take more than a little accident to get us, baby. We have a revolution to fight." He started the car.

"Fuck you and your revolution." I grabbed the chicken-bar.

"You can let go of that bar, baby. I only flipped the car to prove a point. We're not going to die in a simple wreck."

"I totaled my Dodge last year," I said through clenched teeth. "I could have been killed. At least, it was real. I didn't create it on purpose to prove a point." My voice shook. "So shut the fuck up and get us home."

He drove the next few miles in silence, slowed to exit at the Clint off ramp, and maneuvered the farm roads until he came to a stop in our driveway. We went in the house and to bed without exchanging another word.

I awoke mid-morning with the terrors of last night's accident converging in a rush of questions. *Had Z done it on purpose, flipped the VW to prove a point? Or was he drunk and functioning in a blacked-out condition? God knows, I know about blackouts.*

I encountered Z getting out of the bath. We did not speak. Refilling the tub, I reclined in the water and melted into its warmth. With eyes closed, I became aware of my breath coming into my body then going out. Thoughts from the night before disappeared until I pulled the plug, stepped onto the floor, and draped a towel around me.

Sitting on the edge of the bed, Z pulled on his moccasins and looked up as I entered.

"Why did you flip the car last night? You could have killed us. You were drunk, stoned, and raving like a maniac. Why?"

"Sure, I was drunk, but you need to understand I knew exactly what I was doing."

"Understand what? We're invincible?" I pulled on my jeans and pushed my arms and head into a sweater. He pulled it down and adjusted it around my hips—stood too close. I stepped away.

"Of course, we're not invincible, Sylvi. But it will take more than a car wreck to kill us. We have things to do. I don't want you to be afraid."

"Tell me what you felt when the wheels left the road last night." I faced him.

"Shook me for a second, but I knew we'd be okay."

"So you didn't really do it on purpose?" I registered surprise. "You said last night you were proving a point."

"I was drunk, no telling what I said." He fiddled with adjusting the bottoms of his jeans over the tops of his moccasins. "Look, baby, when I realized I was about to take the wrong exit, I whipped the wheel to the left but didn't lose control. I knew what was happening and focused on getting us out of it. Look at us. We're not hurt, not even a scratch."

"Goddamn you, Z. It's like everything you do pushes beyond the norm. I love you for it. I hate you for it."

"Yeah, baby, I know. Most people just walk away from me, but not you."

"Are you trying to drive me away?"

"No, I don't want you to go—not ever." He crossed the bedroom and reached for my hand.

I had no words.

"Let's go outside and get some fresh air," he said.

Outside we stood in the middle of the driveway. I lifted my face to the sun and closed my eyes.

"Hi, neighbors," a male voice called from across the road in front of a small, adobe shack.

"I didn't know anyone lived there." I opened my eyes.

A man wearing a black cowboy hat, and a woman with long blonde hair tied at the back in a red scarf crossed to our side of the road. The man, slightly shorter than Z, extended his hand and introduced himself and his wife.

"We just moved in a few days ago," he said.

"I'm Sylvi," I offered. "This is Z."

"McKenzie," Z affirmed. "What brings you two to San Elizario?"

She smiled. "We're Vista Volunteers."

"We work with the people around here," he said. "You know, on projects. It's a pretty depressed area."

"What kind of projects?" Z asked.

"Training them in skills so they can get jobs. It's tough because they're definitely a lazy bunch."

"They've been kept down a long time." Z defended them. "Tigua Indians. The original people here, you know. It's not easy for them to make a living."

"Tigua Indians, my ass," the man said. "They're nothing special—just Mexicans, like everybody else."

"Just Mexicans?" His prejudice shocked me.

"Man, how are you going to help these people if you don't know who they are?" Z came right to the point.

"I think I know who they are." He kicked a rock aside with the toe of his boot. His scraggly beard moved up and down as he worked his jaw.

She cast him an anxious look, but said nothing.

"The way I see it." Z nailed the Vista Volunteer with a look-to-kill, "you people blow in here from God knows where not to help the locals, but to somehow put them in their place. Let them know the white man reigns supreme. Isn't that the way it shakes out?"

"Look, man, we're just trying to be neighborly. Why are you attacking us?"

"I wouldn't call this an attack, but I'll tell you straight. I don't like so-called do-gooders like you. You've been here a few days, labeled folks, and feel real good about yourself, don't you? In my book, you're part of the problem. You're no solution. You'll never have any success here because you have no respect for the people you're supposed to be helping."

"Come on." He grabbed his wife's arm and headed back to their place.

I watched them go. "Weren't you a little blunt?" I asked as we turned and strolled toward the fields behind us.

"I've got no time to be neighborly with people who are paid to watch us."

"Are you putting me on?"

"No. They may be Vista Volunteers, baby, but they're on somebody else's payroll, too."

"I guess I didn't think we were big enough game to warrant being watched." I shook my head. "The feds must think you imported those guns and really intend to overthrow the U. S. Government."

"I do intend to be a part of putting an end to this sorry, self-serving system. We will overthrow it and give the power back to the people where it belongs. The feds should consider me a threat but not you, baby. You're a peaceful soul. I'm sorry I got you mixed up in all this shit."

"The last time I checked, Z, I'm responsible for my own actions. It's not like you're twisting my arm.

The sound of a car in the driveway interrupted us. Z ran from the field to see who it was.

In a moment, Syd drove his old green Ford behind the house between the *bracero* quarters and the incinerator pit, parked and, joined me in the cotton field.

"Happy 1969, Sylvi." He hugged me. "How's it going out here in the country?"

"Everything's cool, man." I kissed his cheek.

"Sylvi's being generous." Z walked up behind us. "I flipped the car last night. And we've got Vista Volunteer narcs for neighbors."

"No shit." Syd glanced quizzically at me.

Not wanting to revisit the subject of the accident, I said nothing.

We brushed dead cotton plants aside and sat down on two of the rows, Z and I facing Syd. Z told him about the car wreck.

"That's some tale." Syd looked at me as if waiting for confirmation.

"It is," I said. "Personally, I'd rather not comment."

"So what about your narc neighbors?" Syd asked.

"See the little adobe shack across the road?" I motioned with my thumb.

He nodded

"An hour ago we met the couple who lives there. They're Vista Volunteers, but I think somebody's paying them to watch us." Z recounted our conversation with them.

"So that's why you had me park back here," Syd said. "You think they're on the fed's payroll for real? Maybe you're too paranoid."

"Maybe I'm not paranoid enough." Z laughed.

"I'm personally trying to evolve beyond paranoia," I said.

"She thinks mankind should be evolved to a higher plane. Like, we shouldn't have to worry about narcs, or prisons, or war," Z said.

"It would make life a lot easier." Syd smiled.

"Not necessarily." I stood and brushed the dirt and cotton twigs off the back of my legs and the tail of my jacket. "It would mean we'd share a greater responsibility for each other. I'm not talking about utopia. I'm talking about a culture of peace. Hard work, but the end result would be beautiful, if only we can embrace it."

"How do you figure we're going to get there?" Syd asked.

"By starting with today." I paused, watching a cloud sail along the horizon. "Why would you say you don't like our neighbors, Z?"

"For one thing, they're spying on us. For another, they have no respect for the people they're supposed to be helping."

"You'd call them narcs for watching us? And you'd call them bigots for demeaning the people they've volunteered to serve?"

"Yeah, I would."

"So you've tagged them in the same way they've labeled the locals. The names we call each other only pronounce our differences and threaten each one's way of life. Labeling is a big problem to overcome in order to evolve." I stuck my hands in the warm pockets of my jacket and searched for the right words to explain my philosophy. "Labels like capitalist, communist, royalty, common folk, middle class. Or Hebrew, Christian, Buddhist, Muslim. Or hypocrite, narc, bigot. The list goes on forever."

"I dig what you're saying, Sylvi." Syd tugged at one end of his mustache. "But it's not that you and Z just perceive the Vista people as a threat. They really are."

"That's part of the evolution process. It's like this. Can we forgive them? Can we accept them where they're at? If we can, then we've helped them as well as ourselves attain a higher plane."

"Heavy duty." Syd got to his feet, shivered and zipped up his jacket. "They can help send you to jail. How can you overlook that?"

"We don't overlook it, Syd. We follow our own actions as far as we can understand them."

"What the fuck does that mean?" Z asked.

"By understanding if I repay mistrust with mistrust then I am continuing the cycle. By befriending them, I can stop the cycle. I know where they're coming from, but I don't expect anything from them. Follow? Without my judging them, they're left free and are, therefore, more evolved than when I met them."

"That's okay for you, baby. But it doesn't work for me."

"I can see the wisdom in your words, Sylvi." Syd shielded his eyes from the sun. "I don't think I'm there yet. It probably won't happen in my lifetime."

"Maybe not, but if we recognize and respect each other as children of the Creator, we would lovingly care for each other, wouldn't we?"

"It's more like people trample each other to come out on top." Syd bent to pick up the brown skeleton of a cotton plant.

"We have to change, to be more concerned with healing the earth and her people from the trampling we've all endured for far too long," I insisted.

"True, baby. But I'm not sure how to heal it. I do know how to fix it. We need to advance politically, take up arms, and bring on the change."

"Spiritual growth has to precede the political."

"Perhaps the political has to create a climate where the spiritual can grow." Syd suggested a compromise.

"You've listened to Z too long, Syd. What can bloodshed possibly have to do with peaceful spirits, with loving, and nurturing?"

We'd reached an impasse.

After the New Year, people scattered. Gary and Judy traveled to San Miguel de Allende in Mexico. Lilly, Luther and their young son went to Santa Fe to visit friends on a commune.

Z and I stayed. He took a job with a construction crew. Daiquiri and I took long walks in the cotton fields. I availed myself of every opportunity to befriend our Vista Volunteer neighbors, hoping to weave better karmic fabric for us all.

During a late afternoon foray into the field west of our house, Daiquiri halted and when I coaxed her, refused to budge. Looking ahead, along the furrow where we walked, I saw a large brown bird flopping about, unable to fly. At the same moment, I heard our VW in the driveway. Daiquiri raced ahead of me toward the house.

Before I had him in sight, I yelled, "Z, come quick." He intercepted me at the edge of the field. Out of breath, I pointed down the row, caught his hand, and pulled him along. "A huge bird, Z, it's hurt."

"A hawk," he said, as we got closer. "Circle round to the other side. If I can stay clear of the talons and get hold of the legs, maybe we can help."

Maneuvering around this magnificent creature, I fixed my eyes on hers, bright in her fine head and chiseled face. Recalling the spirit hawks from my dream-state after the wreck and during my peyote trips, I recognized her great feminine strength.

We rescued the great bird and placed her in a vacant chicken coup in the backyard. I brought a pan of water from the house while Daiquiri surveyed our efforts with disdain. Every day as Z drove home from his temporary construction job, he shoveled road-kill for the hawk to eat. As the beautiful bird grew stronger, Z left the door to the coup open a little more each day, and our patient would hop out a bit, try her wings, and go back inside. Some weeks passed between the time of the hawk's arrival and the day she flew away.

The hawk left us early the morning of February 1, a Saturday. Mid-morning I made a routine trip to the laundromat in Ysleta and called Don from the pay phone.

"Your sentencing date is February 5, Sylvi, in the afternoon. But you both need to be at my office early that morning because McKenzie will be formally arraigned at ten o'clock."

My stomach flip-flopped. *This is real and happening in a mere four days.*

"What's your take on this?" I asked Don, hoping he would assure me all was well.

"It's only an arraignment to formally charge Z Since you were arraigned previously and pled guilty, your sentencing should go all right."

"What does 'all right' mean?"

"They won't cut you loose completely, Sylvi. I'm hoping for probation."

"What if I don't get it?"

"More than likely they'll give you six months to actually serve."

"Six months? And what's going to happen to Z?"

"His intent to overthrow the government is more serious."

"But you know that charge is bogus. You know those guns were meant to go to Mexico."

"I know it, Sylvi, and we'll have time to build his case."

"Will I serve time, Don?" It took all my strength to ask the question.

"I won't bullshit you. You very well could. Maybe six months, maybe a year."

Panic gripped me. "I'm at the laundry, Don, and I have to get my clothes out of the dryer."

"Okay, Sylvi. You and Z be in my office at eight, the morning of the fifth. We'll have a little time to talk before we go to court."

I breathed deep, tried to calm myself. "We'll see you then. Bye." I hung up but did not let go of the receiver. I could not stand without hanging on to something. For the first time, I faced the reality of prison and wept as I gathered our clothes into my laundry baskets. By the time I left the parking lot, sobs shook my entire body. I gripped the steering wheel with one hand and the gearshift with the other in an attempt to steady myself.

My mind had no such anchors, however, and conjured every possible scenario. *I will never again see my children. Nor will I see Z. I will freak out, be thrown in solitary confinement, lose my sanity.* I could see no life beyond prison.

I skidded to a stop and ran toward the house. "McKenzie!"

He burst through the back door. "What is it?" He drew me close, and I buried my face against his chest.

"I called Don. Your arraignment is the morning of the fifth, and my sentencing is the same afternoon. He thinks I might do six months, maybe a year." My voice broke.

"Calm down, baby. You're not going to jail. Come in the house. Tell me what he said."

After relating the conversation from the laundromat, I fell quiet, deep distress clouding my soul. Z paced the length of the dining and living rooms and after some minutes, sat down next to me on the couch.

"We're going to Mexico," he announced.

I nodded, unable to audibly agree or disagree. I thought about the latter, but did not trust my judgment. Too vulnerable to make the decision, I thanked God McKenzie could.

"Sort out what you want to take. I'll pull the car into the garage and start loading the stereo and record albums. We should leave in the next two hours." He stood. Then noticing I hadn't moved, sat down again and put his arms around me. "I promise you we'll make it."

"What about Kristi and Katrina? How will I get them back if we're in Mexico?"

"Once we get it together in Acapulco, we'll get forged I.D. and papers so we can travel between the States and Mexico without any hassles. By that time, Carl will think we've disappeared, no longer a threat. Then we'll grab the kids. He won't have a clue."

"Can we get good I.D.?"

"Miguel knows the right people, baby. Everything's going to work out. Come on, let's get packed."

Standing, we melted into a kiss. It gave me the courage I needed.

The garage doors creaked open, Z pulled the car inside, and I closed the doors after him. I gathered a few towels and sheets and piled them on the bed. Z made trips to and from the garage as I sorted, folded, stacked, and packed. Once I had the essentials together, including my vintage Singer sewing machine in its wooden carrying case, I sat down on the foot of the bed. There I began looking through a box of things I'd brought from the old house.

I had no recollection of packing it. Judy must have done it. *My God, this is the corsage from my senior prom. Has it been only eleven years ago that Bob and I began our courtship, married the year after, and divorced two years later? All a dream now, but here's the dried orchid, tangible evidence.*

I tossed the corsage on the floor and placed a few other mementos from the box next to it, programs, letters, silly things. A pile of trash. I placed a brown accordion file full of my old poetry and essays on the bed to take with us. *I'll go through it in Acapulco.*

Four high school annuals lay in the box on top of some stuffed animals. I ran my fingers over the brown leather-like plastic cover with the raised number—1957—my senior year. Flipping through, I glanced at the comments and autographs, friends' names scrawled on group pictures of the modern dance club, a cappella choir, the writing club, and ROTC sponsors. *My God, how could I have participated in ROTC? I just didn't know any better.* Everything in high school had to do with achievement or popularity. Utterly unaware in those days, I had no concept of the military-industrial complex and its invasion into the public schools. *The National Honor Society photo—that's me in the second row—made my mother happy. I wonder where my classmates are now and how many of them are jumping bond, going off to Mexico?* I dropped the annual back in the box. *I don't have time for this.*

I picked up all four books and put them on the floor in the pile to go out to the trash pit. *I'll burn everything. My past will go up in flame. From here on, it will only exist internally.*

Reaching for the box of photos, I sorted through them. Tears came—pictures of my old friend Maria and me wearing our bathing suits in a big snowstorm. The snowman we built. The snowball fight with friends in McKelligan Canyon. Black and white snapshots of Carl's arm around my shoulders as I cradled tiny, newborn Kristi. Carl was the most unpleasant memory of my life. There was no time to cut him out, so I gathered the photos of Katrina and Kristi and put them into the open suitcase—*all I have of the girls until they once more live with me.*

Z passed by a few times going to and from the car. We'd been absorbed in our tasks and had not spoken. He noticed me wiping my eyes on my shirtsleeve.

"Can you do this, Sylvi?" He set the stereo speaker he carried down on the floor and sat beside me.

"Yes." I reassured myself as well as him. "I have to get rid of any evidence of my past life. Maybe I'm paranoid, maybe crazy, or hysterical or something."

"No, you're not, baby. Things will be okay, but you're right to trash this stuff. Why leave it laying around for the feds. The less they know about you, the better." He gave me a quick hug, picked up the speaker, and headed for the garage.

He'd long ago rid himself of his excess baggage. When I met him for the first time, I noticed he traveled light. Even when we went to San Francisco to pick up the rest of his things, there was hardly a duffel bag full.

I didn't look any further into the box. I picked up the trash from the floor, returned it to the carton, dragged it out of the house, and dumped it into the pit behind the *bracero* quarters. I ran to the garage, grabbed a gasoline can, and a box of matches. Back at the pit, I dowsed the box and its contents, then struck a match and threw it in fast—before I changed my mind.

From the edge of the pit, I watched the corsage ribbon curl and flames lap the corners of the photos. I felt lives, memories, joys, and sorrows pulled from my flesh. The heat warmed my face as the fire seared my soul.

I stood in a spot of warmth on a cold day. Time stopped. I balanced on the threshold of a doorway suspended in my painful present moment, able to look both backward and forward.

I refuse to look back. It drags me down with the "why did I's" and the "what if's." I can't go back there. Just like McConnell Street— can't go back. But what about the peaceful revolution—the conscious evolution? How can I be part of it when I'm running for my life? I can choose to stay here and let Z go—I can go to jail—no, I can't.

Whatever road I follow, at this point, will be filled with obstacles. I know there is no perfect path I can trod that will be marked with direction signs—all pointing me the right ways to go. Mexico is the only place now, and it is a dangerous place. When Z and I were there last September,

I witnessed breathtaking beauty on the one hand and sure death on the other. But Z knows how to live there.

If I thought leaving McConnell Street was frightening, Mexico is terrifying. Life hangs in the balance there every day. Is Mexico less of a risk than prison in the U. S.? How many choices do I have? Now, today, right this minute?

"Sylvi? Where are you? Grab Daiquiri—time to hit the road."

While the nation continued grappling with the inhumanity of a bloody war and the insanity of the status quo, we left it to travel our own uncertain path into Mexico. A long, dark road to Acapulco and back. Another story for another day.

Acknowledgments

This being my first novel, I think of all the people who, in one way or another took this journey with me. Without their encouragement, expertise, and friendship, I'm not sure my work would have come to fruition.

My dear friend of many years, Judy, called me on the first morning of 1988, and reminded me that two decades had passed since "the old days." She nudged me to write seriously about those days. As a result, I gathered scattered notes and began a task both demanding and therapeutic. The writing, by necessity, was interrupted with rearing my children (a privilege I cherish) and holding down a job to provide for us. But, a little at a time, my perseverance brought forth this work and the sequel that will follow. Thank you, Judy.

During my sojourn in Southern California, I joined a critique class taught by Kaye Klem, whose instruction I will always value. From her class, an independent group evolved in Fullerton. I extend deep appreciation to Jan, Hal, Ryan, JoAnn, Eileen, Bob, and Vivian for their devotion to the craft of writing and, most of all, for their cherished friendship. Without their encouragement, I could not have continued.

My working environment brought me into contact with four people who helped me through a rough ten years. Thank you, George, for your friendship. Never ending love to Laura and Mary

Lou, you are like family to me. And, thanks to Dale for keeping the music going.

Barbara, who founded Living Ubuntu, befriended me, and helped me find my way to an open and compassionate heart. And Anshul, who cofounded Living Ubuntu, guided me through many technical difficulties. I love you both and treasure our adventures along the way.

Back home in Texas, I discovered a group called Texas Mountain Trail Writers. I thank you all for sharing your lives and talents with me these last several years. A ton of love and appreciation goes to my Alpine critique group: Elaine, Jackie, Ron, and Reba, who all helped me put this task to bed. Many thanks to Marion, computer guru and friend.

I thank my children for the love we've shared over the years—Kelli, Traci, Alex, Becca and Josh—without your love and challenges, life would have been dull. Thanks, too, to my sister, Lou and her family. I love you all.

Last, but definitely not least, I thank Greg for making this story possible.

CPSIA information can be obtained at www.ICGtesting.com
Printed in the USA
LVOW132007280513

335630LV00001B/3/P